ALEX REEVE lives in Oxfordshire and is a university lecturer. *The Butcher of Berner Street* is the third in the Leo Stanhope series, following on from *The House on Half Moon Street* and *The Anarchists' Club*. The acclaimed series has been shortlisted twice for the CWA Sapere Books Historical Dagger, with *The House on Half Moon Street* also shortlisted for the Polari First Book Prize and the RSL Christopher Bland Prize.

THE
BUTCHER
OF BERNER
STREET

ALEX REEVE

RAVEN BOOKS
LONDON · OXFORD · NEW YORK · NEW DELHI · SYDNEY

RAVEN BOOKS
Bloomsbury Publishing Plc
50 Bedford Square, London, WC1B 3DP, UK
29 Earlsfort Terrace, Dublin 2, Ireland

BLOOMSBURY, RAVEN BOOKS and the Raven Books logo
are trademarks of Bloomsbury Publishing Plc

First published in Great Britain 2020
This edition published 2021

A catalogue record for this book is available from the British Library

ISBN: HB: 978-1-5266-1271-7; TPB: 978-1-5266-1270-0; PB: 978-1-5266-1274-8;
EBOOK: 978-1-5266-1272-4; EPDF: 978-1-5266-5154-9

2 4 6 8 10 9 7 5 3 1

Typeset by Integra Software Services Pvt. Ltd.
Printed and bound in Great Britain by CPI Group (UK) Ltd, Croydon CR0 4YY

To find out more about our authors and books visit
www.bloomsbury.com and sign up for our newsletters

For Rob and Rachael

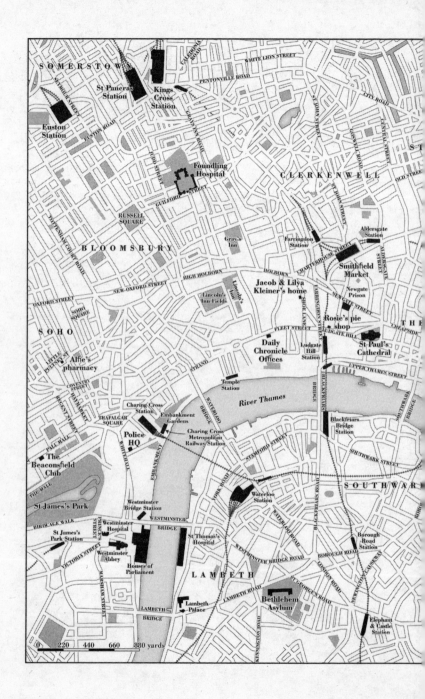

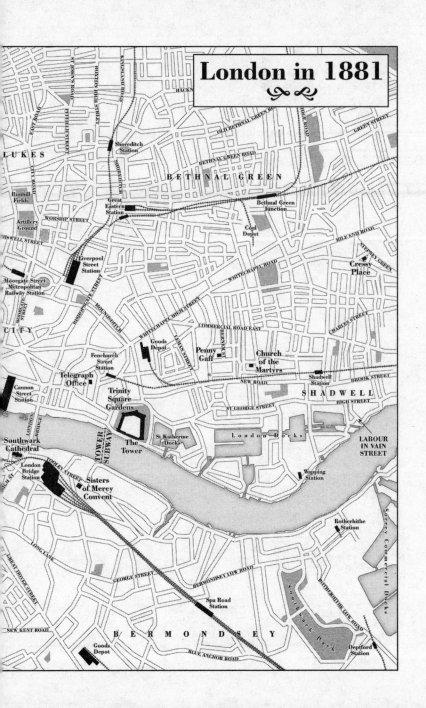

London in 1881

THE TWO WOMEN CLIMBED into the ring and faced each
other as if they were about to dance. Both were wearing
long-sleeved buttonless vests, but while one had chosen a
long skirt, the other was sporting a pair of linen drawers
belted at the waist. The bell rang and they grappled for
four, perhaps five seconds, until the one wearing the
drawers, who was a fearsome specimen indeed, with hands
like chuck steaks and features that seemed too large for her
face, wrenched the other sideways, sending her off-balance.
From that point on, the bout's conclusion was inevitable.
The soon-to-be victor shook the soon-to-be loser as if she
was emptying a sack of flour, before slamming her down
and forcing an arm across her throat, causing the poor
woman to go pink and slap the floor in surrender, raising
a mist of chalk dust.

The winner leapt to her feet, arms aloft, and accepted
the scattered, cursory applause of the crowd.

'I beat her!' she declared in an accent as thick as her
forearms. 'I beat everyone! I win always!' The purple bow
she was using to tie back her hair bounced up and down
as she jumped.

The referee sprang on to the stage, stepping over the prone figure of the defeated.

'The Hungarian Lady Vostek is our champion!' he bellowed. 'All the way from Budapest!'

I exchanged a look with Constable Pallett, who was standing near the back of the hall, his height giving him a view over the flat caps and occasional bowler. I had suggested to him that he should try to merge into the throng, drinking ale and laying bets as if his week's rent depended on it, but he was as inconspicuous as a lighthouse. He might as well have been wearing his police uniform.

The few who had bothered to gamble on the Hungarian Lady Vostek at terrible odds of one-to-ten on collected their meagre winnings while the rest waited for the real match. The ladies' bout was little more than a novelty, a diversion, and many of the spectators had missed the excitement completely, taking the opportunity to visit the bar.

But the referee had not finished. He was a handsome fellow with a build that might have made him a wrestler himself, though his pristine face had surely never been pummelled by an elbow or squeezed between a pair of mighty thighs. He drew in his breath and swept an arm across the crowd.

'It's time, ladies and gentlemen,' he proclaimed inaccurately, for there were only men watching as far as I could see. 'Time to see which among *you* will dare to fight the Hungarian Lady Vostek. She's taken on all comers for the last six weeks, men and women alike, and she remains unbeaten. Will you be the one? Fame awaits, ladies and gentlemen. Which of you will risk your good health and reputation to battle … *a lady*?'

He jabbed an accusing finger at us, and we all looked at each other, wondering whether anyone would be foolish enough to accept such a challenge. There was some good-humoured shoving as a couple of chaps attempted to volunteer their friends, but otherwise the response appeared primarily to be embarrassment.

'Why don't *you* do it, Mr Drake?' shouted someone from the back.

The referee, Drake, grinned and stood back from the Hungarian Lady Vostek, assessing her top to toe. 'I don't think I'm the man for such a task. Anyway, it's my gaff, my rules.' He rooted around in his pocket. 'But perhaps an incentive. Will anyone take her on for a quid?'

This seemed a far more attractive proposition, and I could see a few men giving the idea some thought, their eyes flicking between the Hungarian and the pound note now being waved in our faces.

'As a fee?' demanded someone at the front.

Drake rustled the note between his fingers. 'As a prize, my friend. If you win.'

The fellow turned to the crowd with comical incredulity. 'If?'

They hooted with laughter.

I stood on tiptoe to see the prospective challenger, a local man from his accent, probably a navvy on the railways. He took off his jacket, revealing rolled-up shirt sleeves and a knitted waistcoat straining at its buttons, and placed his glass of ale on a table. The crowd whooped and cheered as he clambered on to the stage and into the ring.

Now, everyone was watching.

He set himself as if about to engage his opponent, but then stopped and took her hand, placing a courtly kiss on the back of it.

'Your ladyship.'

The crowd hooted even more loudly, waving their glasses, some slapping each other on the back.

The Hungarian Lady Vostek snatched her hand away, scowling, and Drake rang the bell. The bookmakers quickly began chalking odds on to their boards, strongly favouring the challenger. So few bets did the lady receive, the one nearest to me was offering seven-to-one against and still finding no takers. I sidled over to him.

'Sixpence on the lady.'

He took my coin and gave me a chit without taking his eyes off the fighters.

The navvy smoothed his hair and started cavorting around the stage, making as if to grapple with her and then standing back, leering all the while. She shadowed him, her face grim and her feet set well apart. They were about the same height, but he was weightier and less athletic, more interested in exchanging lewd jokes with his friends than paying attention to his adversary. Eventually, he capered too close and she clouted him with the heel of her hand. I heard a crack and was unsure whether it was his chin or her wrist which had caused it. He reeled backwards, and she shuffled towards him, taking one flailing punch just below her eye and ducking under another. She twisted and elbowed him twice in the stomach, followed by a downward kick that tore a gash in his trouser leg from his patella to his shin. He went down like a rotten tree.

From there, the poor fellow didn't stand a chance. She dropped to a crouch and sank her knee into his stomach. The crowd leaned forward eagerly, making a communal low of disappointment when they realised he wasn't disembowelled, but was rolling to and fro on his back, cupping his manhood in his hands. They shrank back, wincing with an empathy they hadn't hitherto appeared to possess.

The Hungarian Lady Vostek raised her arms above her head and roared. The crowd, even those who had backed her opponent, cheered and waved their chits. A couple of men removed their hats and proffered exaggerated bows.

Drake handed her a robe to cover the drawers and shirt she was extravagantly occupying, and held up her hand.

'Victory to the Hungarian Lady Vostek! Maybe next time she should fight *two* men!'

She shot him a glance which would have panicked a less confident individual, but he grinned and winked at her, even taking the liberty of slapping her behind as she left the stage.

The cigar smoke in the room was getting thicker, catching in my throat and stinging my eyes. I peered through it at the constable, who checked his pocket watch and held up ten fingers. He'd only promised to stay until ten o'clock as he had a new wife at home and was doing me a favour attending at all. Berner Street was far to the east of his usual patch, slotted among the slums between Commercial Road and Cable Street, and this penny gaff had not been easy to find. The sign propped up outside was still advertising a production of *Othello*, the place having made a natural progression from Shakespeare to wrestling, affording the audience a more sporting outcome and fewer speeches.

I collected my winnings from the ratty-looking book-maker, who was counting his money and smirking. He might have found himself in difficulties with his less glee-ful punters had Pallett not stepped forward, speaking to the fellow from the side of his mouth, making him more noticeable than ever. Saving smug bookmakers from a beat-ing was all very well, but not what we had come here to do.

We had come to prevent a murder.

Even so, I was more than ever convinced we were wast-ing our time. The letter I'd received that morning had been circumspect to say the least. When I'd shown it to Harry Whitford, my colleague at the *Daily Chronicle*, he scoffed and went back to his conversation with Miss Chive, who was taking a break from her typewriting duties to giggle and touch his shoulder, occasionally expressing the opin-ion that he was a proper rogue and no mistake.

And yet, there remained the possibility that it was true, and someone at this event was about to be killed.

I slipped the letter out of my pocket and held it close like a betting chit.

Dear Mr Stanhope.
I am writing to confide in you a matter of the highest ur-gency. Though we have not met, I have read your newspa-per articles and applaud you for their extraordinary clarity and erudition. Indeed, I believe you to be …

I was briefly distracted by the memory of Harry's response to this claim, which was to state that the author was clearly mad or, alternatively, a close relative of mine. He said all this with a smirk, and read the passage aloud to Miss Chive, his tone at first sardonic and then disbelieving as the letter's meaning became clear.

> … a man of unusual curiosity and rigour, who has on occasion solved crimes unfathomable to the police. I therefore place this burden upon you, as Zeus once did to Atlas, with faith that you will have the strength to endure it.
>
> The penny gaff on Berner Street in Whitechapel is an excellent establishment with honest sport and tasty food and ale at modest prices. It is generally agreed by all the good people of the neighbourhood to be in every way beyond reproach. Yet this most well-reputed venue will, this evening, become the scene of a tragic death. And not merely a death but a cold-hearted murder.
>
> I can say no more. I beg you to attend.
>
> With my kindest regards.

There was no signature. And no murder either, at least not yet.

The stage was empty in anticipation of the next match, and the room had become hot, lacking proper ventilation and packed so intimately I had long since given up apologising for treading on other men's heels. Earlier that evening, a fellow had leaned on my shoulder to bawl at a wrestler whom he judged to be insufficiently combative, spraying my ear with spittle. He had no right to be so demanding as he was skinny and something of a dandy, wearing a blue velvet jacket, matching waistcoat and a satin opera hat which made him considerably unpopular with those standing behind. To avoid further intimacy, I had adopted a pillar to lean against, but despite myself, by the second or third bout, a reckless good humour had over-come me, and the dandy and I were opining together on the relative merits of reach and strength as if we were old friends. Perhaps it was the alcohol. I might actually have enjoyed myself had my mission not taken precedence.

The fight at the top of the bill was a challenger, Dublin Dick Dooley, taking on the local man, Electric Jimmy McMahon, who was the Whitechapel champion and enjoyed a good deal of local support. McMahon was carried through the crowd on the shoulders of two lads, leaning down to shake the hand of everyone he passed. When the bell rang, the two men embraced each other in a statuesque fashion, seeming at first so equally matched that neither could shift the other no matter how hard they stressed and strained. But, after half a minute or so, Dooley began listing to the right like a badly laden cargo-boat and, finally, having no choice, he collapsed to the floor. McMahon fell upon him and energeti-cally pounded his kidneys until the Irishman cried out, 'Enough! I give up!'

Mr Drake leapt on to the stage once again and held up the winner's hand. 'Electric Jim McMahon! Still undefeated!'

At that second, the lights went out. We were thrust into almost complete blackness. There was a general muttering in the room but no great panic. This was the East End of London, not Westminster. The gas went off all the time.

I put out a hand for the pillar to orientate myself, feeling reassured by its solidity. As my eyes grew accustomed to the dimness, I could see figures on the stage, and then the spark and glow of a match flame. A lamp was lit, and a slow gasp rippled backwards through the crowd.

Above the stage, a rope had been slung over a beam and made into a noose. Hanging from it by his neck was the referee, Drake, as limp as a puppet, swinging gently from side to side.

———

Pallett was the first to react and I followed in his wake. We jumped up on to the stage and he lifted Drake's legs, trying to relieve the pressure on the man's neck, in case he was still capable of breath. I ran to the cleat where the rope was tied off and frantically tried to free it, but it was jammed tight.

'Help me!' I shouted to the dandy, who had joined me on the stage, but to my horror, he started laughing.

'Leave off,' he said. 'You'll do 'im an injury.'

I saw a movement in Drake's body: a wriggle and shake. His hands reached up and he gripped the rope. The muscles in his arms tautened and he started to rise, slackening the noose, leaving a red weal on the skin of his neck.

He took a breath.

'That's better,' he croaked, and pulled his mouth into a fierce grin.

He jerked his head backwards out of the noose and landed on the stage as neatly as a dancer. The audience broke out into wild applause.

He bowed deeply. 'Thank you. That's all we have time for tonight, my friends! I hope you've enjoyed your evening and we look forward to seeing you all again soon.'

With that, he dropped nimbly off the stage and went out through a low door to the back of the gaff.

Some among the crowd were chortling and pointing at us, enjoying our discomfort. Others were already settling up with their bookmakers.

'My goodness!' I exclaimed to Pallett. 'What right do they have to laugh? At least we *tried* to do the right thing.'

The constable was more sanguine. 'I think they've seen the trick before, sir.'

'Oh.' And now I felt foolish twice over, once for being humiliated and once for not realising that everyone else was in on the joke.

Pallett checked his pocket watch again and glanced towards the door. 'Never mind. It's no bad thing to be blessed with a kind nature.' He tipped his hat. 'I'll be on my way now, sir. You might do well to come with me. These streets aren't safe for a gentleman.'

I was touched at the nomenclature, but he was mistaken. No gentleman would've walked here rather than taken a cab, nor had to count out five halfpennies for our ales, nor, if the truth were told, have chosen to visit this penny gaff in the first place. What he really meant was that I was better spoken than the average man and had been kind enough to knot his Ascot tie for him on his wedding day.

'I'll stay, thank you. I want a word with Mr Drake.'

Ten minutes later, the last punter had shoved his winnings into his pocket and scurried out with cap pulled low, no doubt wary of men who'd had a less rewarding evening and might seek to recoup their losses.

Finally, Drake appeared again, now in more regular attire than the white jacket he had been wearing, and began unhooking the rope, humming under his breath. From that and his jaunty manner, I had the feeling he considered the evening a success.

'What the hell were you doing?' I demanded from across the room.

He chuckled, not even looking up. 'My party piece. It's been a while and I have to admit it hurts more than it used to.' He cleared his throat productively. 'I was a strongman, see? Exhibitions and such. People love a good hanging.'

He put out a hand for me to shake, but didn't bother walking to where I was standing. He expected me to come to him. When I did, he pumped my hand so hard I thought my elbow would dislocate.

'Oh, don't look like that. You've got to allow performers their tricks. Come on, it was a bit of fun, don't you think? Your face was a picture.'

'I presume the letter I received was written by you.'

He slapped my shoulder. 'A bit of publicity, see? None of you lot from the newspapers ever come out to the East End, so I thought I'd do something to persuade you. You're the only one who showed up, Mr ...?'

'Stanhope. The *Daily Chronicle.*'

His eyes flicked to my left cheek which could, in certain lights, appear burnished and pink where it had been scorched by a fire the previous year. I had become used to people's glances and frowns, as if they were unsure whether I was disfigured naturally or by calamity. His face, by contrast, bore no blemish at all that I could see. Where his chin was supposed to be clean-shaven, it was, perfectly so, and where it was supposed to be bearded, dark hair sprouted with eager fullness.

'Yes, I've heard of you. You solved some murders in the past, so I thought you'd be game.' He smiled broadly, showing me his teeth. 'Oswald Drake. I'm sorry for the false pretences, but I'm glad you're here. I hope you'll write charitably in your newspaper about my little venture.'

'I don't like being deceived.'

'I prefer to say "entertained", Mr Stanhope, but you're the man with the vocabulary, not me. I'd be willing to put something your way for the right words in the right order, if you know what I mean. Words like "honest establishment" and "sporting contest" are the sort I have in mind. And "well-priced ale" wouldn't go amiss, neither.'

He had a peculiar charisma, this man, like the lead dog in a pack of strays. I didn't trust him, but at least he was honest about his dishonesty, which was more than some could say.

'Is this your place?'

He nodded, still coiling the rope. 'Not bad, eh? Not long ago I was doing my act for a few shillings a week, and now all this. Goes to show what a man can achieve with a little ambition and some wise investors.' He indicated the room. 'Before me, this gaff was half empty most of the time, or worse. Folks don't want actors spouting about things they know nothing about, they want a couple of blokes punching each other and the chance to win a few bob. Human nature.'

'And women fighting too?'

He gave me a wink. 'Pioneer, ain't I? Folks like to see some variety, and maybe a lady's dugs too, on occasion. You'd be surprised how easily their clothes come apart.' He chuckled. 'Though Miss Vostek's fights don't last long as a rule, and I can't imagine anyone wanting to see *her* dugs.'

I gathered my coat more closely around my chest.

The door opened and the dandy I'd been speaking to earlier walked in. Drake gestured towards me.

'This is Mr Stanhope from the *Chronicle*.'

I put out my hand for the dandy to shake, but he didn't take it. His right sleeve was empty below the elbow. 'I guessed you was one of the press. You don't seem like the wrestling type.' He searched my face. 'We're honoured, I'm sure.'

They exchanged a glance, and I got the sense they were close; cousins, I thought, or boyhood friends. Perhaps even brothers, though they looked nothing alike.

Drake hung up the rope on a hook and thrust his hands into his pockets. 'Why don't you come and have a look round, Mr Stanhope. I'm a believer in doing what we can for the neighbourhood, and you might learn something interesting.' He indicated the door through to the back, and I hesitated, feeling a shiver run through me. I knew nothing about these men.

He clapped me on my upper arm. 'Come along. Doesn't everyone want to know what goes on behind the scenes?'

I steeled myself and followed him, ducking under the low lintel. The dandy, who still hadn't given me his name, trailed behind, his shoes ringing on the hardwood floor.

At the back of the hall was a dismal yard full of crates and boxes, and beyond that a substantial shiplap hut erected alongside the road running perpendicular to Berner Street. I could hear footsteps on the pavement just a few feet away behind the wall, quickly drowned by the roar of a train in the distance. I shivered in the drizzle. Would all men be afraid at such a moment, I wondered, or was I especially craven?

Drake fiddled with the handle to the hut, eventually throwing the door open. We basked in the thin light from inside.

He seemed to sense my dread and raised his eyebrows. I knew that look; my brother had the same one. Everything was a sport, a contest, with the victor's hand raised aloft, and the loser slapping the stage in surrender. It was all good-natured fun, as long as he was winning.

'After you, Mr Stanhope.'

Curtains had been hung from the ceiling, dividing the hut into rooms, and lamps were spitting and flickering in the draught. The top-of-the-bill fighters, Dooley and McMahon, had changed into their normal clothes and were playing Black Peter for tots of gin, throwing the cards down at fearsome speed. They stood up as we entered, though not for my sake. Their deference was for Drake and he took it as his due, indicating they should carry on, much as a colonel favours his battle-hardened troops.

A curtain was pushed aside and the Hungarian Lady Vostek emerged, dressed in the most garish garb: a bright yellow dress, fitted jacket and blue bonnet. She seemed to have no clue what combination of colours would be pleasing to the eye, which together with her lavish features and the bruise blooming on her cheek, lent her a clownish air.

Drake held out his arms as though about to embrace her. 'Ah, here she is! Irina Vostek, our lady champion. She fights every Tuesday, men and women alike, makes no difference to her.'

She leaned away from him. 'No putting hand on my arse next time,' she instructed, cutting the air between them with a sharp gesture. 'No hand. No arse. Agreed?'

He ignored her demand, which I thought considerably rash. 'She's from Budapest, aren't you, Irina?'

'No!' She shook her head vigorously. 'Always you say Budapest! *Budapest, Budapest.* Is not true. I am from Szeged.'

The dandy laughed, stuttering into silence as she threw him a look.

'Well, no one's ever heard of … that place,' Drake mumbled, scratching his ear. 'It's impossible to remember.'

He pushed aside the third curtain, where another wrestler was washing blood from his face with a flannel. I recognised him as a loser in one of the earlier bouts. He sat up straight as we entered, and Drake examined his injury, pinching the broken skin above the man's left eyebrow to close the wound. Without careful attention it would fester. The poor fellow winced, clenching his fists, but he withstood it.

Drake rinsed his hands in the bowl. 'You need stitching,' he said to him. 'Coffey here will get it done.'

The wrestler appeared disconcerted at the idea of a one-handed man suturing his face, but he didn't dare object.

'Let me help,' I said. 'I have some experience at stitching. I was an assistant to a surgeon.'

I didn't mention that all but one of my patients had been corpses, sewn up like old sacks after their post-mortems. Nor that the single exception was a cat.

The wrestler looked relieved, the fool, and I sat with him while the dandy, Mr Coffey, dipped the needle and thread in alcohol.

'What's your name?' I asked the wrestler.

'Trafford, sir.'

He was a local lad, from his accent, and a stolid individual, with a drinker's complexion and creeping baldness, though he was no more than twenty years old.

Coffey reached into his pocket for a flask. 'This'll ease the pain a little, Bert. Wouldn't want you weeping on the floor like a little girl, would we?'

I took the flask from him and sniffed, recognising the sickly smell of laudanum. 'I wouldn't,' I advised Trafford, remembering my own past addiction to a similar substance. 'It'll give you powerful nightmares.'

I could feel my heart pattering in my chest. It had been two years since I'd last sunk into that black water, salving my grief, and yet the scent of it could still awaken the craving, almost overwhelming me.

I compressed the wound as Coffey wielded the needle, and afterwards put my finger on the knot as he pulled the thread tight. Trafford was stoic, gritting his teeth but not flinching.

I stood back to admire our work. 'Don't worry, you haven't lost your good looks.'

My humour was wasted on him.

He swallowed hard and shook my hand. 'Thank you, sir.'

Coffey whisked out a dented gold pocket watch on a chain.

'It's almost eleven,' he said.

'Of course.' Drake was all business once again. 'One last thing. Come with me, Mr Stanhope.'

He led me back across the yard to the back door of the gaff and through the hall, which was still covered with the detritus of the evening: broken bottles, empty bags, discarded chits and glistening drivels of spit. I followed him outside to the pavement and was surprised to see a queue of fifteen or twenty children lined up along the street. They were clothed in rags and many were barefoot, some no higher than my hip and others almost adults. All had sharp eyes, darting from each other to Drake, resting quickly on me and then flicking away. They knew I was no threat.

Drake put his hand on my shoulder and pulled me close to him. He smelled of sweat and talcum, and I tried not to shudder at the sudden intimacy. 'I like to share my good fortune.' He beckoned to the first lad. 'Lead 'em in, Lewis.'

The lad, heavyset, with the first brush of beard on his chin, accepted a farthing from Drake and nodded his thanks, passing into the hall. Each child followed him, one at a time, and each received a farthing, pressed into their palm. Their fingers closed over the coin as if their lives depended on it. Perhaps they did. Some were carrying bundles of clothing tied with string and others sacks or rolled blankets on their backs. Last in line was a moon-faced girl who met Drake's eye and, as she passed inside, performed a neat little curtsy that seemed almost sarcastic.

'Where are they from?' I asked, thinking of two orphans I knew well, whose fate might not have been so different, had I not found them. I was looking forward to seeing them again on Sunday afternoon.

'Nowhere.' Drake waved a blithe hand towards the city. 'Leastwise, nowhere that matters. We give 'em what little we can; a place out of the rain to lay their heads, a bite to eat if we have it. All we ask in return is that they clean up the place after the punters have left. Small favour to ask in exchange for such charity, see?' He held up his hands to indicate his empire. 'This is what we are; decent sport for the paying public and a little aid for those who'd otherwise starve. Surely we're worth a few kind words in your *Chronicle*?'

I didn't like to tell him that my articles were mostly about science, appearing on page eleven or twelve at best, and often getting cut altogether when a more amusing story came along: a policeman getting his foot caught in a drain or a dog barking the national anthem. I'd only taken up this enquiry because the letter had been addressed to me personally and Harry had refused to come, saying it was most likely a prank and adding, with a wink at Miss Chive, that he already had plans for the evening.

Without the promised crime, there was no article worth writing.

I bade Drake farewell and trudged away along the pavement, my coat collar raised against the chill. All was silence but for the clank of the bolt as the door to the gaff was locked from inside.

Two days later, I went to see Rosie. Her conversation was generally good, and her pies were always outstanding, especially if they were free of charge. Granted, she would be unwilling to donate a fresh one, which I imagined bubbling and steaming as she spaded them out of the oven, but even one of yesterday's was better than any other food one might purchase in London.

The distance from my newspaper office on Fleet Street to Rosie's pie shop was only a few hundred yards and I took it at a saunter, enjoying the spring sunshine and hoping Rosie's trade had not been so brisk that she'd completely sold out. I arrived just as St Paul's was dully announcing one o'clock.

Her assistant, a leather-skinned woman named Anne, or possibly Angela, I could never remember, informed me that they had but a single pie left over from yesterday.

'Chicken and cherry,' she grunted, wiping her hands down her apron. 'Cold.'

There was only one other customer, but still the little shop seemed crowded. He was leaning his ink-stained forearms on the counter, explaining the workings of a printing press to Rosie, and seemed displeased by my arrival. It must be the weather, I thought. Everyone thinks it's mating season.

Of course, he didn't know that Rosie, as a young widow, brilliant cook and owner of her own business, was accustomed to suitors, and treated them much as a hill treats a wind that wails and sighs but never so much as shifts a pebble on its upper slopes. After a couple of minutes, she threw me a look and I half smiled back.

I admired the printer's perseverance and was curious to discover whether his explanation of the mechanics of cylinders under pressure – and this to a woman who operated a mangle twice a week – would yield an encouraging simper. It did not. Nevertheless, I remained attentive despite the tedium, wary in case his disappointment led him towards a more robust approach.

When he finally gave up and pushed past me into the street, Rosie turned to her assistant. 'Would you mind taking over for a few minutes, Alice? I believe Mr Stanhope is in need of my advice.'

Of course: Alice! I made a conscious effort to commit her name to memory. After all, I had known the woman, albeit only slightly, for more than two years. I couldn't call her "Excuse me" for ever.

Alice – *Alice, Alice, Alice* – nodded, her arms folded and her mouth set in a flat, hard line like a schoolteacher disappointed, but not surprised, by her pupils' disregard for the rules of polite behaviour.

Rosie pulled on her coat and grabbed her umbrella, and we set off to make a circumnavigation of St Paul's, as was our habit. When we reached the cathedral, I glanced up at the statue of the long-dead queen spoiling the entrance, what was left of her. She was defaced in every sense, missing a nose, jaw and most of her crown. On her plinth someone had scraped the words:

> Mad Brandy Nan
> Soft In The Head
> Thought She Was A Man
> All Her Children Dead

Rosie had little interest in such things and was more entertained by my recent humiliation. 'You honestly thought it was real?'

She could hardly keep the glee from her face.

'Anyone would've been taken in by that letter.' I ignored the fact that Drake had sent similar ones to several newspapers and I was the only journalist who'd turned up. 'It was unsigned. I had no way to tell it was from the supposed victim.'

'Do you still have it?'

I showed it to her, and she read as we strolled, her expression obscured by the brim of her hat. When she reached the end, she tapped her umbrella on the ground, a sure sign of irritation.

'Who's Zeus?'

'A Greek god. He placed the heavens upon the shoulders of Atlas, a Titan warrior.'

She pulled a face. 'Then you should've known it was from a man, at least.'

'What makes you say that?'

She raised her eyebrows in a manner I knew preceded some sort of a tease. 'Only a man would think it was another man who holds up the heavens.'

At that moment, we heard a voice behind us. 'Leo!'

We turned in unison, and to my surprise, Harry Whitford, my colleague at the *Chronicle*, was hurrying towards us, his coat flapping behind him and his hand clamped on to his brown felt hat.

He arrived, puffing, and had to bend down, his hands on his knees, to recover his breath. For a fellow of barely twenty-one, slim and apparently healthy, he was woefully lacking in youthful vigour. He believed in living well, did Harry, and rarely stinted on ale, cigars and, I had no doubt, other diversions readily available in the bars and back rooms of Soho.

He introduced himself to Rosie between gasps. 'You must be Mrs Flowers.'

She acknowledged that she was while I waited for him to finish his puffing.

'How did you know where we were?'

'The woman in Mrs Flowers's shop told me. Alice, is it? She was very helpful.' He held up his hand, and I stepped backwards, thinking he was going to puke, but he regained control of his stomach. 'Sorry. I was out celebrating last night. I'm not yet ten out of ten. A six at best.' He belched and clutched at his chest. 'Possibly a five.'

'What were you celebrating?'

'Eh?'

He seemed confused by the question, so I changed the subject back to the more pertinent one.

'What do you want, Harry?'

'Right, yes, of course. There's been a death at that penny gaff you were at last Tuesday evening.'

'What?' I exchanged a surprised look with Rosie. 'Who?'

'Does the name Drake mean anything to you?'

'Yes, he's the owner of the place. Is it him?'

Harry nodded cheerfully. 'Hanged. Dead as a doornail, apparently. We got a telegram. I mean, it was addressed to you, but you weren't in the office.' He beamed at Rosie. 'Your pies are quite something, Mrs Flowers. I've been meaning to try one.' He thumbed in my direction. 'Stanhope brings them back from time to time and they smell divine, but he never shares them. Mean-spirited, if you want my opinion. I shall have to come to your shop and choose one for myself.'

Rosie replied that he would be very welcome, going on to explain with an uncharacteristically warm smile that her pies were baked fresh every day, not like some places, and were a steal at ninepence apiece.

Again, I had rather firmly to redirect the conversation.

'Was Mr Drake murdered?'

Harry grinned. 'Of course. A vicious crime in the East End, maybe a link to gang warfare, none of us are safe in our beds, you know the sort of thing. Practically writes itself.'

'Are you sure he's actually dead? He has a trick of hanging himself by the neck that he uses to take advantage of people's decency for the amusement of himself and his customers. He might have faked his own death so he can be miraculously resurrected. The world would come flocking to his door, no doubt, with wallets at the ready.'

'Truly?' Harry looked impressed. 'I must confess I love all those entertainments, bending iron and lifting weights and so forth. I wish I could come with you, but Father said he wants you to write it.'

Harry's father, J. T. Whitford, had been newly promoted to the position of Assistant Editor at the *Chronicle*. He tolerated his son's occasional lateness and less occasional insobriety with a patience bordering on despair. But Harry was possessed of some finer qualities too: he wrote succinct prose and had a knack for unearthing a good story.

'I see. Did he say that you should come as well?'

Harry leaned in to whisper to me without Rosie hearing. 'The thing is, Miss Chive knocks off at six and her landlady comes home at seven, and I'd rather we didn't run into her again, after last time.' He rubbed his upper arm, pained by the memory. 'You know how it is. I'm sure you can handle this without me.'

He waved us goodbye and I was surprised to see Rosie raising a hand in response, and afterwards remaining silent as we hurried back to her shop.

When we got there, she exchanged a brief word with Alice and turned to face me.

'I'm coming with you, Leo. You plainly don't know what's what without me.'

There was no arguing with her, and in truth I was grateful for her company.

———

When I explained to the cabbie where we wanted to go, he groused that I had no business escorting a lady into an area like that. Only after Rosie protested that she was willing, indeed eager, to take the risk did he agree to carry us the full distance, all the while complaining that we would certainly be slain, and his horse cut up for meat. He seemed mostly concerned for the horse.

We followed an omnibus along Commercial Road, stopping every couple of hundred yards for ladies to hop on and off with their baskets, bustling into the shops on either side. The awnings that lined the street were as colourful as any in the city, advertising magazines, medicines and tobacco, but as soon as we turned off the main thoroughfare, the prosperous atmosphere faded, and those few people we could see were barefoot children or idle men watching us through clouds of bacca smoke, their clothes as grey as the buildings and factory fumes.

From the road, the gaff resembled a large shop with bay windows. I was perturbed to see that a small crowd had gathered outside, jostling to peer between the posters covering the windows. This was going to be hard enough without an audience, especially one which might take offence at the presence of a newspaper man.

Over everyone's heads, I was surprised to see Pallett in his constable's uniform, blocking the doorway and keeping everyone out. We were far from his normal domain.

I pushed through the crowd, keeping Rosie close behind me. One of the fellows was telling another that he'd seen the corpse personally and there'd been a terrible mistake: it wasn't Oswald Drake at all, but a different man, far less handsome and altogether smaller in stature who'd been dressed to resemble Mr Drake to mislead the police, who, in his opinion, were prone to jump to conclusions, not having much familiarity with the notables of Whitechapel.

I wondered if he was correct or if he was just wishing it to be true, unable to conceive that a man of Mr Drake's standing could possibly be dead.

'You can go through, sir,' said Pallett. He tipped his helmet to Rosie. 'Good afternoon, Mrs Flowers. How are you?'

She gave him a rare smile. 'I've asked you before to call me Rosie. And I'm quite well, thank you, Norman.'

I admit, I had forgotten that Pallett had a Christian name, though if I'd remembered, I might have guessed at Norman. He was exactly like a Norman.

'And how is Cecilia?' I asked him.

Cecilia was the poor sap who'd given up the name Rasmussen to become Mrs Pallett. She'd been a nurse at the hospital where I'd previously worked.

'She's very well *indeed*, sir,' beamed Pallett, and seemed about to expand on the theme when he stopped himself, seeming to realise this wasn't the moment for personal revelations. I could guess what he'd been about to announce; there would shortly be an infant Pallett in the world who, within a very few years, would no doubt be keeping his or her schoolmates in line and hauling miscreants off to the headmaster to answer for their transgressions. Good for you, Norman, I thought. He was born to be a father.

Inside the gaff, a young woman was seated in the centre of the hall on a wooden chair. Her face was white as chalk, as if she was unable to weep for shock. In her arms, a baby was fast asleep.

The dandy, Mr Coffey, was sitting on the stage, his head in his hand.

Beside him was the body.

There was no doubt it was Drake. He'd been laid out on his back, eyes closed, arms placed along his sides. The skin of his neck had been lacerated, staining the collar of his shirt red. Above him, a rope was dangling, moving slightly in the breeze, the end curled and twisted.

'Mother of God,' whispered Rosie, and crossed herself in the Catholic manner. I wondered whether I should have left her behind, but supposed she was tough enough to look upon a corpse without fainting. After all, she had killed two people, attempted to kill another and strongly advocated leaving a fourth to die. None of these acts were the result of ill intent, but they would surely harden one's constitution.

'Ah, Stanhope,' said a familiar voice. 'I'm glad you've turned up, though I'm sure I won't be so for long.'

Detective Sergeant Ripley slouched towards us with his hands in his pockets. As ever, he spoke slowly, one eye half closed, his jacket covered with crumbs and smeared with what I thought at first was butter, but might have been egg. I knew not to be fooled by his appearance though; he had a mind as sharp as any in London.

He removed his hat and scratched his head. 'Constable Pallett tells me you were here a couple of days ago. You got a tip there'd be a crime.'

'Yes. A letter. But it turned out to be a deception. Mr Drake wanted publicity, nothing more.'

He scratched his ear. 'Pallett said you were rather upset and chose to remain here and take up the issue with the deceased.'

I frowned, getting his meaning. 'You think I killed him? Out of *embarrassment?*'

'Why not? Men have killed for less.'

I could tell he was testing me, looking for a reaction. I was determined not to give him one.

Rosie wasn't so reticent. 'That's ridiculous. How would a man of Mr Stanhope's slender build force Mr Drake, who must weigh two hundred pounds if he's an ounce, into a noose? Did he ask him nicely, do you suppose? Please place your neck into here and be kind enough to pull on the rope while I cleat it off. Is that how it was?'

Ripley rubbed his fingers together and pulled a cigarette box from his pocket. 'I didn't say he worked alone.'

She rolled her eyes. 'You can't mean *me*?'

He had the decency to look abashed. 'Of course not, Mrs Flowers. You're a respectable lady and he's lucky to name you a friend. But he has other acquaintances with more greed and fewer scruples.' He squinted at me, one of his eyes almost shut. 'What happened to your face? Looks like you've had a misfortune since we last met. Did some-one burn you?'

I chose not to answer him, instead pinching the skin between my thumb and forefinger, letting the pain wash away my agitation.

'May I take a closer look at the body?'

I had examined dozens of corpses, whole and partial, young and old, intact and spilled across the slab like tripe. But I had never grown completely *comfortable* with such proximity. Death should always be awful, a hole in the world where a unique and irreplaceable person used to be. No one should ever grow comfortable with that.

Ripley waved a hand. 'You can look, but don't move him before the surgeon gets here.'

I knelt beside Drake and felt the skin on his forehead with the back of my hand, almost a caress. He was as cold as the room, so must have died some hours ago. I gently bent his wrist and fingers and felt a stiffening, a resistance. Rigor mortis was on its way.

'Most likely he died very early this morning.'

'You mean he was *murdered*, Stanhope.'

I shook my head, still looking at Drake's face. Some corpses sagged as their muscles lost tension, gravity tugging at their flesh. But Drake looked much as he had in life, with high cheekbones and a strong, broad jaw. Aside from the paleness of his skin, one could believe those eyes would open and he would burst out laughing and tell us it was all a joke.

'What happened to you?' I whispered to him.

'Pardon, Stanhope? Speak up, will you? I worked at the plant as a kid and can hardly hear a damn thing any more.' Ripley took a pull on his cigarette. 'Though it's a blessing on occasion.'

'I said, it's most likely this was an accident. My guess is he decided to have another go at hanging himself and something went wrong.'

The palms of Drake's hands were rough – he was a working man – but there were no lesions or signs that he'd desperately clawed at the rope. He hadn't wrestled with death. I remembered how easily he'd hoisted himself up, his arms like dock cranes, and how gracefully he'd alighted back on the stage. Why hadn't he been able to free himself this time?

'Who found him?'

'His wife.' Ripley nodded towards the woman in the chair.

She was gently rocking her baby, and might have been singing to it too, though I couldn't hear her voice above the racket from outside. Knuckles were rapping on the windows, and I could see a man's silhouette as he cupped his hands against the glass and tried to peer between the advertisements. But the widow had eyes only for her baby. For all the notice she took of us, she might have been enjoying a breather on a park bench after a pleasant walk.

Rosie pursed her lips. 'Poor thing. Too young to be a widow.'

I glanced at her, but she mulishly refused to meet my eye. She'd been widowed at just twenty-five, and not a day went past when she wasn't glad of it.

'She'll inherit all this, more than likely,' Ripley muttered. 'She's sitting pretty.' He cracked his knuckles. 'Right, now, down to business. I've told you what I know, it's time for you to return the favour. Hand over that letter.'

I found his tone galling. Like all policemen, he believed his own needs and demands were paramount and the rest of us should simply do as he instructed.

'Why? It's not relevant.'

He took another deep draw on his cigarette and blew a smoke ring, which hovered and faded between us.

'I've been told I have to tolerate you newspapermen, though Lord knows why. It's not as though you ever print anything close to the truth. But all the same, if you don't hand over that letter, I'll arrest you and put you in a cell overnight. If I remember correctly, you didn't like that too well last time.'

I dug the letter out of my pocket and handed it to him, trying to keep the resentment from my face. He thought me pampered, afraid of a little hardship, but he was wrong. I'd slept on scores of steps, pavements and the stone floors of strangers' basements, listening to the rats scratching in the walls, unable to move in case someone heard me. I just couldn't risk spending a night in jail with other men and a pail in the corner to piss in. And I couldn't withstand a search. I would be discovered for certain.

Rosie cleared her throat and looked up at the rope. 'How was it tied?' she asked. 'Was it a slip knot or a bowline?'

The detective frowned at her. 'If I'm honest, Mrs Flowers, I can't see how your expertise in rolling pastry qualifies you to ask questions about a hanging.'

She didn't blanch. She didn't even feel the need to sharpen the edges of her voice. 'Detective Sergeant Ripley, you come to my shop once in a while and I sell you a pie, not worrying about the odd farthing or two you might be short. And the same for Mrs Ripley, who's a good-hearted lady and often inclined to stay for a chat about this and that.'

Ripley started to answer, but she hadn't finished.

'So, if I want to ask a sensible question about a knot, you'd do well to answer it, or you'll be paying full price for my pies and your wife will be hearing a great many more of my opinions on a wide range of topics.' She paused for a moment, but he was too startled to respond. 'A slip knot would strangle a man, would it not, by tightening at his throat? And if Mr Drake was practised at his act, as we believe, then he would know that. He'd tie a knot that wouldn't slip, like a bowline, enabling him to extricate himself when the time came.'

'I suppose so.' Ripley sounded like a boy caught with his hand in the biscuit tin. 'The knot was undone when we arrived.' He indicated Coffey, still sitting on the edge of the stage in his foppish clothes. 'His mate and one of the wrestlers had already taken Drake down. They said they couldn't bear to see him dangling like that.'

I looked down at the body and wondered what went through a man's mind in those final moments. Probably nothing. Was it not strange? Through all of life, the body is servant to the mind, but in that extremity the body takes charge, thrashing to keep itself alive, no matter that the mind has accepted death. On its last journey, the mind is nothing but a passenger.

I touched Drake's jawline and the coarseness of his beard, running my fingers down to his throat where the skin had been ripped by the rope. If we'd been alone, I would have talked to him again. I wouldn't have expected an answer – I wasn't mad – but it gladdened me to think that a soul might be comforted by a kind voice as it drifted towards the afterlife.

I turned Drake's head gently. At the base of his neck, a hole had been made in his flesh, no bigger than the pupil of an eye. A smear of blood proved it was recent.

'I was wrong,' I said, looking up at Ripley. 'This wasn't an accident.'

3

RIPLEY KNELT BESIDE ME and peered at Drake's neck. 'Did that pinprick kill him? It must've nicked his artery, the one where you die if it's cut. The carrot one.'

I didn't know why, even after all these years, I was still surprised by the paltry level of knowledge the average policeman held concerning the body. They learned a single fact, be it about the arterial system or the effects of arsenic, and spouted it religiously – and usually erroneously – at every murder scene they attended.

'The *carotid* arteries, and it would take a remarkably accurate insertion to hit one of them. It certainly wouldn't be a reliable method for murder.'

'Then what?'

'A hypodermic needle, I suspect.'

'Poison, then? Bad way to go.'

'Not necessarily. At least it's painless.'

In my time, I'd considered all the methods by which one might die: slicing open my wrists; crushing my body under train wheels; falling from a balcony; drowning myself in the river near my childhood home, the bag of rocks I'd cinched around my waist tugging me down to the darkness and the weed. But surely the worst of all choices was dancing on the end of a rope, writhing and kicking for a breath that would never come. Any poison would be preferable to that.

I dug my thumbnail into my wrist.

'It was a large needle,' I said. 'He bled where it was inserted.'

Ripley stared down at the stage, which was stained with black and brown blotches. 'The perfect spot for a murder, isn't it?' He wiped a finger across the wooden floorboards, but the stains were old and long-since dried. 'A place where men fight. No way to tell whose blood is whose.'

'And women.'

He peered at me through his half-closed eye. 'What?'

'Not just men, they have women's bouts here, too.'

He rubbed his chin, not believing me, until he saw I was serious. 'Jesus. This blasted city. Not enough to be lousy with murderers and thieves, we have to watch women fighting for sport as well.'

'Why would any woman agree to such a thing?' asked Rosie, her voice rising incredulously. 'Why follow men into such foolishness?'

I was amused that Rosie and Ripley were on the same side in this. 'The women wrestlers were quite spirited. Two of them fought each other and then one of them took on a man from the audience. She beat him soundly too. It was all over in seconds.' In my mind's eye, I could picture Miss Vostek's broad smile as she celebrated victory, and Drake's hand slapping her backside. 'She didn't seem to like Mr Drake very much.'

Ripley looked sceptical. 'She beat a *man*? How?' He drew his own conclusion without waiting for me to answer. 'Ah, of course. A plant. When I was a kid, there were contests in the pub up our street. They'd stick a big man up against some scrawny milksop and watch the bets come in, and then the big 'un would keel over at the first punch. Easy money.'

I pictured the man Miss Vostek had defeated, curled up and squeaking like a baby squirrel.

'I honestly don't think it was part of a ploy.'

Ripley was still examining the wound on Drake's neck. 'If you're right, then someone's tried to hide how he was killed. Made it look like one thing when it was another. That takes some planning, I'd say, and knowledge of chemicals and the like.'

His glance fell on Drake's widow, but my attention was elsewhere: on Mr Coffey, who was sitting on the stage, his opera hat in his hand, tears falling into his bright blue waistcoat. He looked piteous, but I'd learned to distrust such displays of emotion. Killers were always liars, and the fellow had some expertise in medical science. He'd offered the wrestler, Trafford, laudanum, and his stitches had been neat and evenly spaced.

I caught Ripley's eye and nodded towards the dandy. Ripley frowned, looking at the fellow's empty sleeve, clearly doubting he had the physical capability for murder by hanging. Still, the detective climbed to his feet and tossed his cigarette on to the floor, where it glowed, a thin curl of smoke rising and dissipating in the draught.

'You got any experience with medicines, young man?'

Coffey started like a hare and made a wild dash for the door, his tailcoat flapping behind him, but he had reckoned without Pallett. The young constable reached out a giant arm and shoved the dandy back towards us. Coffey tottered and fell on to his behind, and Pallett stooped to grab him, but for once his bulk was a disadvantage. Coffey twisted and scuttled away on all fours or rather, missing a hand as he was, on all threes. Pallett set off after him like a farmer trying to catch a chicken, unwisely leaving the door unguarded.

Immediately, men started pouring in, twenty or more, spreading out across the room and eyeing the body. Within a few seconds the place was chaos. Two of them jumped on to the stage and shoved me out of the way, pulling at Drake's clothes and rolling up his eyelid in the hope that a still-living man might be staring back at them.

'Stop that,' I demanded. 'You'll disturb evidence.'

The larger of the two men, a docker by the look of him, whirled round. 'Evidence of what?' he growled.

I backed away, feeling my heels rocking as I reached the edge of the stage. 'Mr Drake was murdered.'

He looked up at the rope and down at the corpse, and then at me. 'It ain't possible. No one could do that to Oswald Drake. No army, even. Who are you, anyway?'

Things might have gone badly had not Rosie stepped to my side. 'We don't know what happened,' she declared, lifting her chin. 'We had some questions for that gentleman over there, but he was reluctant to answer them.'

The fellow looked at where she was pointing. Coffey's blue velvet jacket was easy to track. He was attempting to get out through the door even as everyone else was trying to get in, finding himself repeatedly buffeted to one side, eventually clinging to the door jamb like an infant to its mother's skirts.

The docker jumped down and waded through the crowd. He grabbed Coffey by the hair and dragged him back to the foot of the stage. Coffey tried to pull away, going so far as to hit his captor on the nose with his stump, but the fellow barely flinched.

Ripley, who hadn't moved or spoken during the excitement, lit another cigarette. 'You haven't answered my question, son.' He sounded almost casual, but I could tell that his attention was fixed, like a cat feigning disinterest in a mouse before pouncing.

'It weren't me,' Coffey bleated, sagging at the knees. His trousers were covered with sand from the floor, making him look more ridiculous than ever. 'I know a bit of stitching, that's all. I mend the fighters when they've been cut and keep a gill or two of laudanum on hand to dose 'em. But I never did this. How could I?' He held up his empty sleeve and stared from side to side at his east London neighbours, who were gathering round to watch.

Ripley eyed the man's velvet jacket and silk cravat with distaste. 'Maybe you had help.'

Coffey shrugged off the docker and approached Drake's widow, placing his hand on her shoulder. She didn't look up. 'Tell 'em, Elsie. Tell 'em I'd never do anything to Oswald. Never. We were best pals since we were nippers. Born and raised on Spicer Street. I wear these pretty clothes, but I'm much as you are underneath. But what about *him*, eh?' To my surprise he pointed a shaking finger at me. A glint of hope was shining in his eyes, as if the mouse had found a gap in the wall. 'We don't know him, do we? He came in the other day asking questions, talking about crimes that might or might not have been committed.' He raised his voice to address the whole room. 'He knows how to do surgering and mixing medicines too. He told us he'd been an assistant to a surgeon, and it was true. He aided me with the tying off. If you want my opinion, it was him who did for Oswald.'

Having said his piece, Coffey edged away towards the door, his expression solemn and his hat held reverently to his chest.

The docker glared at me, clenching and unclenching his fists. 'You never told us your name.' His voice was like a cartwheel rumbling over wooden paving.

I went red in the face. I couldn't help it.

'Stanhope.' My own voice was high-pitched and queru-lous, like a perambulator wheel missing some grease. 'I'm a journalist with the *Daily Chronicle*.'

He nodded, not in agreement or geniality, but in confir-mation of his previous supposition. 'You don't belong here, Mr Stanhope.'

Of course I don't, I thought. I don't belong anywhere.

'Why would I wish harm on anyone? I've only been in this place once before.'

'Ay, well, that's the question, ain't it?' The brute took a step in my direction.

Ripley inhaled his cigarette and blew smoke out through his nose. 'Best not, my friend. Mr Stanhope here is a galling fellow to say the least and might be improved by a good hiding, but not at your hands. Folk who decide they're better than the police at dealing justice always come to regret it.'

The fellow paused, but the group behind him, ten or more men, had started to surge forward, jostling him along with them. They were breathing heavily, and I recognised the look in their eyes, that wolfish hunger, tensed for the lunge. One glance, one word, one twitch of my feet and they would be on me.

'We should leave,' I hissed at Rosie, thumbing towards the back door into the yard. I was on the brink of running. The balls of my feet were aching for it.

She nodded and took a tiny step backwards.

Pallett was attempting to swim through the crowd, but more men had come in and the space around the stage was tightly packed. He was grimacing as he looked up and caught my eye. He wouldn't make it to us in time.

'Stop that!' The wrestler, Trafford, pushed between the men and stood beside us. He wasn't a tall man, but he was bulky, his jacket straining at the seam. 'You lot move away.'

'Clear off, Bert,' growled the docker. 'We just have some questions for 'im, that's all.'

Trafford shook his head and cracked his knuckles. He was brave, but he was alone. I knew I should be standing shoulder to shoulder with him, so we could go down fighting together. But I was starting to shake. The best outcome I could foresee was being questioned with menaces, and the worst was the ultimate horror: discovery, exposure and whatever came next. Crowds who believed themselves to have been fooled tended to seek the most obvious means of retribution.

Things would have gone ill had another man not entered the room, slamming the door with a thunderous crash. All heads turned.

'What's going on? Let me through.'

His voice was calm and unhurried, but it cut through the hubbub like an oar through water. The effect was remarkable.

The three men at the front exchanged looks and stepped aside, and the crowd behind them sagged like bellows deflating.

'What on earth are you doing? Let me through, I say.'

He was wearing the long black garb and collar of a clergyman, and from the authority of his manner I would have thought him a bishop, or at least a vicar. But he was much too young, my age or even younger; a curate at most.

Ripley climbed down from the stage. 'That bloke with the fancy rags has scarpered. And him a childhood friend of the deceased, too. This godforsaken city.'

The young clergyman studied Ripley, his hat in his hand. 'Godforsaken, sir? Nothing is ever that.'

The two men couldn't have been more different: Ripley, forty years of age or thereabouts, sallow-skinned, the remains of his breakfast smeared down his jacket; and this young man, spotless and clear-eyed, fair hair trimmed neatly, his stance as upright as a candlestick.

'Iain Sutherland from the Church of the Martyrs.'

Not a curate, after all. He was a Roman Catholic.

'This is your parish, is it?' asked Ripley.

'I'm the deacon here, yes.'

The young man put out a hand for Ripley and me to shake in turn, and I felt Rosie shift irritably beside me. She did so hate to be ignored.

Ripley scratched the stubble on his chin. 'These hooligans have a fondness for the deceased, it seems, and are inclined to take matters into their own hands. This place is like a tinderbox.'

'Oswald Drake was a prominent man.' Sutherland spoke with the manner of one declaring a truth the rest of us had only guessed at. 'He lived a high life, it's true, but everyone respected him. It's very sad that he's dead. This establishment has the potential to be a real success.'

I noted he hadn't yet looked at the corpse. Instead, his eyes were flicking between us, Drake's widow and the crowd of men, who had taken a few steps back and were watching the exchange with the sheepish expressions of schoolchildren whose teacher has unexpectedly returned. Their moment of insurrection had been lost and there was no recapturing it.

Ripley opened his cigarette case and offered one to each of us. Sutherland refused with a brisk shake of the head, but I took one. Ripley lit his own and mine, and the smoke filled my head like soft sleep after a long day.

'Strange times,' he said. 'Criminals running amok. Back home, we'd have gathered up these lads and beaten the piss out of 'em, just to show 'em who's boss.'

I tried to remember where Ripley was from. Somewhere in the north, I was sure; Doncaster or Sheffield. My sister would have been able to tell in an instant, her parlour trick being to detect a person's place of birth from their accent with remarkable accuracy, an inane facility that at once demonstrated both her vast intellect and her squandering of it.

He nodded towards the corpse. 'Seems Drake might've been poisoned and strung up to look like he was hanged. Know anyone who'd be inclined to do a thing like that?'

'Of course not.'

I sensed that Sutherland disliked being asked questions. Like all of his vocation, he enjoyed the eminence conferred on him by his vestments and was discomfited by Ripley's casual insolence. I wondered how much of the young deacon's composure was real, a part of him as a man, and how much was mere performance. I'd seen my father behave with patience worthy of St Francis when among his congregation on a Sunday morning, and in the afternoon yell and bang his fist at the tiniest thing, a spillage of his tea in the saucer or a missing penny he could swear had been on his desk. He didn't understand that his volatile temper was what had made my hand tremble and also why I'd needed the penny, saving up for my escape.

Sutherland glanced back at Drake's widow. Her face was lowered, dark hair hanging down and hands clasped daintily around her child.

'You'll have to excuse me,' he said.

He approached the widow and took her hand. She seemed consoled by the gesture.

I felt a presence at my side and must confess that I jumped, still flustered from the earlier confrontation. But it was Trafford, the wrestler. He seemed shy of Ripley, half turning his back on the policeman and speaking quietly in my ear.

'Who do you think did for Mr Drake, sir?'

'I don't know. But I must thank you, Mr Trafford. You saved us. I'm sorry I didn't stand with you.'

'It's not necessary, sir. You're not built for such things, being a gentleman. I've been fighting since I was a kid. Mr Drake used to tell me I most likely punched the midwife on my way out the womb.'

His talk of kids made me think of something. I looked around the hall. 'The children who sleep in here. Where do they go during the day?'

He shrugged, still not meeting my eye. 'Could be anywhere, sir. They roam about the city. If they sees a gentleman with heavy pockets or a loose buckle on his briefcase they might follow 'im all the way to Westminster.'

Ripley overheard our conversation and narrowed his eyes at Trafford. 'You mean Mr Drake was training them for thievery?'

It was hardly a surprise but still disappointing. I'd thought Drake was doing the children a kindness, but perhaps he was simply harbouring quick-fingered urchins to make himself a profit.

Trafford shook his head vigorously. 'Weren't them who did this, sir. They loved Mr Drake like he was their father.'

'How can you be sure?' asked Ripley.

Trafford spoke to his own feet. 'I was one of 'em once, sir. If it weren't for 'im, I'd've ended up in the clink or worse. He made me lead an honest life. He said it was the only way, if I wanted to make a name for meself in the ring.'

Looking at the man's open, earnest face it was impossible to disbelieve him, and yet his trusting nature would make him easy to fool. We couldn't be certain Drake hadn't been a modern-day Fagin, sending children out to pick the pockets of the wealthy and careless.

Pallett joined us, rather in the manner a tall ship joins the dock. 'The local coppers are here,' he announced.

Sure enough, two young constables in ill-fitting uniforms had entered, carrying a stretcher between them. 'We'll be off in a few minutes,' Pallett added. 'Why don't you and Mrs Flowers wait for us in the carriage? We'll take you back.'

Something was nagging at me. 'Why are you and Ripley even here? This isn't your neighbourhood.'

He raised his eyebrows. 'Word was sent to us by Mr Whitford at your newspaper, sir. The elder Mr Whitford, I mean.' Pallett seemed to know everybody. 'A telegram was received alerting him to these events. He considered it a police matter and here we are.' He brushed his hands down his jacket as if trying to remove the dust of east London. 'There's nothing else to be done now, at least for him.'

He nodded towards the body. The two local constables were preparing to pick it up, one at the feet and the other trying to get purchase under the armpits.

Ripley had his notebook in his hand. 'Right. You mentioned a woman wrestler who disliked Drake. Where is she? What's her address?'

I scanned the room, but there was no sign of Irina Vostek. Most of the other wrestlers were huddling in a group near the door, but she was nowhere to be seen.

It was Trafford who answered him. 'I don't think she ever said, sir. She just turned up a few weeks ago and asked if she could have a go. She was such a specimen, Mr Drake put her on the bill. But she kept herself to herself, never spoke to any of us much.' He indicated the widow, now walking aimlessly around the room soothing her baby. 'Aside from having a soft spot for Mr and Mrs Drake's little boy.'

'So, in other words,' I said, glancing in Ripley's direction. 'We don't know where Miss Vostek lives or how to find her.'

4

THE BLACK MARIA DROPPED us outside the pie shop. The driver offered to take me further, as far as the police head-quarters on Whitehall, but I wanted to speak to Rosie out of the earshot of prying policemen. We stood together on the pavement, which was cold and almost deserted in the twilight, the only sounds coming from a robin above our heads adding a tune to the thrum of the printworks in the alley.

'I spoke to the widow,' Rosie said, fiddling with her gloves. 'Only briefly. She's very young. She seems devoted to her husband and I doubt she could poison anyone.'

'Hmm.'

'What is it?' She looked up at me quizzically, attuned to the many timbres of my doubts.

'Why did the killer poison him *and* hang him? One or the other would kill him, so why risk doing both?'

She thought for a moment. 'Maybe he specifically wanted Mr Drake displayed that way. And can you imagine the problems trying to hang a living, breathing man? A man like that? Quite a battle, I'd imagine.' She shuddered at the thought of it. 'Overpowering him, putting a noose over his head. You'd as likely be the one killed as doing the killing. So, he poisoned him first to make it easier.'

'Or *she* did.'

'Do you really think it could be the Hungarian woman?'

'Perhaps. You didn't see her. She's very strong, and she seems a bit of a mystery, wouldn't you say?'

Rosie gave a deep sigh. If she'd been male, she would've put her hands in her pockets. 'That doesn't mean anything. A woman in a masculine profession, she might have any number of reasons not to make friends. And even already dead, a full-grown man would be quite a burden.'

She had a point. I'd been required to lift corpses on occasion when I was assisting Mr Hurst, the surgeon at the Westminster Hospital. A dead man was an awkward load even for two people, all floppy arms and lolling head. I'd been forced to grasp them in all sorts of ways and places, my face pressed up against their belly or backside, heaving and sweating to move them from a stretcher to the slab, or even pick them up them from the floor if a porter had been too impatient to wait.

'I'm not even sure he was poisoned exactly, at least not fatally.'

It had been bothering me since we left the gaff. I'd been turning over the scene in my mind, trying to make sense of it, imagining Drake sitting in his hut, perhaps working on the schedule for the coming week, unaware of his impending murder. A footstep sounds behind him and he feels a sharp pain in his neck. He turns and makes a grab for his attacker, already starting to feel the effects of the poison, an ache in his chest or a stiffening of his muscles. He staggers to his feet and, realising that he's dying, what does he do? Surely, a man like Drake would expend the last ounce of his strength trying to get hold of his attacker to throttle him, hook out his eyes, rip at his skin, anything to get some measure of revenge.

Why would the killer risk that?

'Few fatal poisons act quickly enough,' I said. 'And those that do are hard to get hold of. I would guess that the intention was to render him insensible, rather than dead. Chloral or laudanum would do the trick. They work quickly and are hard to detect in a post-mortem examination.' Even my former employer, Mr Hurst, would have been flummoxed. 'Once benumbed, he would be much easier to manhandle.'

Rosie pursed her lips. She knew my history with such stuff and strongly disapproved. In her opinion, no man had any business taking opiates when a woman could give birth to a seven-pound baby with nothing more than chicken broth and gin to ease the pain.

A lamp was lit in the upstairs window and I knew I'd lost her attention. She was thinking of her children, who would need kissing goodnight. I felt a pang of jealousy; of her, not them. The world was large, but she had her place in it, and that place was right here. The shop was humble, but she never doubted it was where she belonged.

'Anyway,' I said, fixing my hat to signal I was about to leave. 'The newspaper will want a couple of hundred words about Drake's murder, so I'll write what we know tomorrow. In a day or two it will all be forgotten.'

I slept soundly that night and set out for my office on Fleet Street just after dawn the next day. I was looking forward to writing my article. My normal fare consisted of announcements about chemical compounds or newly discovered species of frog, so the murder of a wrestling mogul was glamorous indeed. It would have been of greater interest had it not occurred in Whitechapel, a place where the *Chronicle*'s mostly Westminster-based readers generally assumed massacres happened on an hourly basis, but even so there was every chance it would appear on a page number with a single digit.

I was surprised to find Constance leaving the house at the same time. She was thirteen, the daughter of my landlord Alfie, and was rarely known to rise before it was time to cook her father's breakfast.

She had brought Huffam on his lead, scampering along beside her. He'd been my late father's dog and I'd adopted him willingly, until Constance took me to one side and informed me that 'the poor creature is less trained now than when you first got him' and trumped my adoption with her own. Alfie and I were in complete, if unspoken, agreement with this policy, firstly because she was correct and secondly because it provided her with a dumb animal upon which to exercise her well-meaning tutelage, which was preferable to our having to endure it.

'Where are you going?' I asked her, as we strode along pace for pace. She took after Alfie, being tall and long-limbed, and shared his habit of marching everywhere as if late for an appointment. I preferred a gentle amble or, if finances permitted, to take a cab, but I enjoyed her company and didn't want to appear lazy, so I hastened along at her speed.

'Huffam still has that skin infection,' she said, as though it was something we'd previously discussed. 'He can't stop scratching. It's getting worse.'

'I see.'

I did not, in fact, see. One only had to sniff the poor canine to know he came into regular contact with all sorts of malignant substances, so it wasn't surprising he had an irritation of the skin. But how was walking him along a busy street at barely seven in the morning going to help?

Constance appeared to sense my ignorance.

'A veterinary surgeon will know what to do,' she explained. 'He needs a linctus or something. He can't keep worrying at it or it'll spread.'

Now I understood why she seemed to be in such a hurry. She was hoping to get home again before Alfie realised that she'd been gone. He was, by nature, a generous man and his business was doing well, with the pharmacy always popular and a lengthening waiting list for his services as a dentist. But he was saving money to rent a bigger place on Oxford Street and would not be in favour of spending his precious earnings on a poorly dog.

'I don't understand,' I said, and proceeded to prove it. 'Huffam's not a horse.'

Constance lengthened her stride. 'Veterinary surgeons don't just do *horses* these days. They know about all kinds of animal. They have qualifications now.'

Something in her tone piqued my curiosity. 'Have ladies started doing veterinary surgery?'

Constance had, for the past year, spent much of her time and almost all of her conversation advancing her desire to enter the medical profession, gradually weakening her father's resistance to the idea. I would be saddened if, on the brink of success, she was limiting her horizons to becoming a glorified farrier.

'No.' She stopped at the junction of Cambridge Circus, tapping her foot in frustration as a line of carts rattled slowly past. 'A woman is permitted to become a doctor for humans but not for animals. It's absurd, isn't it?'

'Perhaps,' I was considering the topic for the first time. 'But women doctors treat other women. Problems with childbirth and suchlike. Mares don't have opinions about the sex of their surgeon, do they?'

'And what does that say about the relative value of women and horses?' I didn't follow her argument but fortunately wasn't required to reply. 'What do you think of Mrs Thing?'

'Her name is Mrs Gower.'

Constance took a deep breath and strode out into the road, prompting a pony pulling a trap to shy and bare its teeth. 'Very well, *Mrs Gower* then. Do you think she's all she seems?'

I was a little surprised. I had thought Constance and her father's lady-friend had reached some form of truce of late, accepting that the prize they'd been fighting over – viz. Alfie – would otherwise be reduced to a ruin. Mrs Gower had even informed me that, despite her despair at the laxity of the younger generation, she sometimes wished she'd had the chance to be as carefree as Constance. But she'd married young and almost immediately was required to nurse her husband in his illness and eventual death, so all the gaieties and follies of youth had been stolen from her.

'They get on well, don't you think?' I ventured. 'They have a lot in common.'

In truth, I couldn't think of much Alfie and Mrs Gower had in common, save dead spouses, but I wasn't going to say that to Constance.

'Yes, but …' She pursed her lips. 'I like the way we are now. Just the three of us.'

She meant Alfie, herself and me, and I felt a warm glow to be so included. And yet, I knew it couldn't last. Families were created by birth or marriage, not by the weekly payment of rent.

'Things change, Constance. Alfie would never do anything he didn't think was in your best interests.'

We walked on in silence, sullen on her part, until we reached Seven Dials, at which point my route was more southerly and hers straight onwards. As we stopped to bid each other goodbye, it occurred to me that she might be able to help regarding the peculiar method of Mr Drake's murder. She knew everything about medical procedures that could be learned from books.

'I've been meaning to ask your opinion on a matter.'

'Oh yes?'

She stood up a little straighter, eagerly attentive. It was her oft-stated belief that she was not nearly enough asked her opinion on matters.

'I came across a man recently,' I continued, 'who'd been injected with something. The prick of the needle seemed unusually large, easily visible afterwards on his skin. A tenth of an inch or more. Why do you think that might be?'

She pondered the question while Huffam sat obediently at the hem of her skirt, even ceasing to lick his canker when so instructed. Truly, he did seem more content with her than with me.

'A wider needle allows more volume,' she said. 'One that size would normally be used to *extract* things rather than inject them. Blood or bile.'

She spoke with no hint of feminine delicacy. She prided herself on being a female of the new type.

'Could a needle like that be used for a hypodermic injection if one wished to?'

My expertise in medical matters was limited to diagnosing the already dead. I had only the lightest grasp of the techniques used to cure the living.

'Of course, though it would be more painful than with a thinner one. What are the circumstances?'

I didn't want to discuss a brutal murder with her, so I checked my pocket watch. It was seven-fifteen.

'Thank you, Constance, but I have to get to work now. You've been very helpful.'

She frowned, and I would doubtless have been interrogated further had she not been in a hurry. She bade me farewell and strode away along Queen Street with Huffam scurrying at her side.

A fellow of about my age watched her go and licked his lips. I had the urge to poke out both of his eyes. I knew that at thirteen she was not a child, according to the law anyway, but she was utterly unprepared for male attention and had no mother to guide her.

What had I been like at her age? A complete innocent. The way men had looked at me, up and down, down and up, as if assessing a pony they wished to ride or a cut of lamb they intended to eat, was terrifying. I had hidden from it, wrapping myself in scarves, coats and cardigans, and forever professing myself cold or ill, resisting the slightest touch. My mother pleaded with me daily, saying I should at least *try* to smile, speak nicely and be more agreeable. I need not be *quite* so plain, if I would only make an effort.

So much for mothers, I supposed.

My article, as it was printed, was brief. I had written two hundred words, but the subeditor reduced it to eighty-five. It spoke highly of Mr Drake's attention to civic duty, expressed deep regret for his demise and appeared on page nine. I was delighted. It was my most prominent piece since becoming a professional journalist the previous year.

I was hoping to write a further story about the police investigation, but my request was declined by J. T., who said I could add to the body of knowledge on the subject of dead wrestlers when the killer was in court and not before. I pointed out that Mr Drake was the proprietor of the establishment and not a wrestler himself, but J. T. was already engrossed in a paragraph about an exhibition at the Crystal Palace and wasn't listening. I therefore returned to my more customary duties as science correspondent, which on that day amounted to a review of a book by a Mr Paul entitled *Clever Things Said by Children*. I had long come to realise that the elder Mr Whitford held a broad interpretation of the word 'science'.

Nevertheless, the words would not flow, and I had written and rewritten the review three times before hurling my final attempt into the wastepaper basket and heading for home. That evening, a Friday as it happened, I drank whisky with Alfie until late, and by the time I got into bed, I had almost forgotten about the death of Mr Drake. I was thinking rather of the following Sunday afternoon, when I would spend some time with my young friends Aiden and Ciara Cowdery, whom I had rescued the previous year. They lived at the Home for Penitent Females, where their adoptive mother, in fact their aunt, was the matron. She had strong political views and it was her habit to campaign every other Sunday for the Christian Socialists while I took Aiden and Ciara out for a treat. Sometimes we had tea and cakes in a shop and sometimes we played draughts, but on the best days, when the weather was dry and breezy, we carried our kite to Regent's Park and took turns at flying it. Watching the children's faces as they clung on to the string was one of my greatest joys. The last time, Ciara, who was not yet eight years old, had been pulled off her feet by a sudden squall, and the rain drenched us all to the skin.

I was musing on the idea of tying the string to a block of wood so she could hold on to it more easily, when I heard a sound downstairs. Someone was in the yard.

I lit a candle and peeped down through the curtain, but the night was so dark I could only make out vague shapes between the scuttle and the corrugated roof of the privy.

I pulled up the sash of my window.

'Who's there?' I called down. 'This is a private house. Go away.'

There was no reply, but I was certain I could see movement.

My candle blew out and I fumbled on my table for another match, but in my haste, I couldn't find one. Perhaps, I thought, I should call Alfie, but after my cowardice at the penny gaff I didn't want to rely on another man to save me. I should be able to deal with this on my own.

I wrapped myself in my dressing gown and crept down the stairs.

The back room was filled with boxes of remedies stacked five high, looming over me. I groped my way forward to the window, and as I peered out, the blackness of the room gave me an unexpected advantage: I could see the yard more clearly.

Standing in the centre was the Hungarian Lady Vostek.

She approached the back door but stopped, mouth open, lifting a tentative palm in greeting and then lowering it again. It occurred to me that she might be a fugitive from the police. Or, of course, she might have already proven her innocence to Ripley with a straightforward alibi. Or she might have come to kill me. I had no idea.

I found a match in the dresser and lit my candle, and the sudden flame made the window into a mirror. My heart was beating so loudly I could almost hear it, but still I pulled back the bolt on the door. What else could I do? Drake's murder had been my most prominent ever article, and Irina Vostek might be about to confess to the crime or tell me who was the culprit. How could I call myself a journalist if I spurned a revelation like that?

I pushed open the door, shivering in the sudden chill.

She was soaking wet, trailing the damp hem of her dress as she came in.

'I am very sorrowful,' she said, her voice breaking. 'I did not want to make disturbance.'

Her accent was as dense as porridge, but for reasons I couldn't quite identify, her choice of words struck me as peculiar. I wondered whether she was giving the impression of speaking worse English than she actually did.

'What do you want?'

She was twice my volume at least but only an inch or so taller, with a tugboat jaw and a face crowded with features as though they'd been designed for someone built to an even larger scale. In the candlelight, the bruise on her cheek was a kaleidoscope of colours, from yellow to green and mauve. The overall effect was intimidating, to say the least, and yet she wore a contrite expression, as though she was an old chum visiting me unexpectedly for the afternoon.

'Do not be frightened,' she said. 'I mean nothing of harm …' she paused and sneezed explosively, causing me to leap backwards. When she'd recovered, she continued. 'I want speak to Mr Stanhope, journalist at *Chronicle* newspaper.' She squinted at me, examining my face in the flickering candlelight. 'You are sister of Mr Stanhope, yes?'

5

SHE HAD ASSUMED I was female. I felt my face blush pink and was grateful there was no more illumination in the room. It was profoundly shocking to discover that, without my suit and jacket and the other trappings of maleness, a stranger could so easily take me for a woman.

Was my physical reality so thinly veiled?

I was stuck in a cruel quandary. I could either inform her that I was Leo Stanhope and risk her guessing my secret, or I could allow her to continue believing I was not and betray my very self.

But that decision was long since made.

I gathered my dressing gown around my chest and stood up straighter. 'You're mistaken,' I declared. 'I'm Leo Stanhope. We met at the penny gaff, remember?'

She put her hands to her mouth. 'Oh, so sorry. My mistake. My eyes, you know?' She fluttered her fingers in front of her face. 'Candles in the dark. Everything shining and I can't see clear.'

My mother had suffered the same way, among her many other ailments.

'You may have cataracts.' I offered, feeling idiotic. It was a terrible habit, to rest upon scientific exposition to hide my nervousness. And yet I seemed unable to stop myself. 'You can get them treated.'

'Oh.' She looked perplexed. 'Does it hurt?'

'I would imagine so.' I almost shook myself with irritation. 'How did you know where I live?'

She took one of the chairs, without being offered. 'I followed you yesterday.'

'Then why are you here so late tonight?'

She shrugged. 'I had other duties. And I needed time to think. Oswald Drake is dead. Him was murdered.'

'I know.'

She leaned forward and I pushed the candle further away on the table, easing myself into a chair.

'I am not criminal, Mr Stanhope. You must not write that I am a murderer in your *Chronicle*. Was not me. I will go away and not come back, but not because I am guilty of killing Mr Drake.'

'Where will you go? Back to Hungary?'

She folded her formidable arms and I noticed she had a bandage on her wrist. 'Home is not easy for me but is the place I belong.'

'Why run away if you're not guilty?'

'The policemen will look at me and think, I am obvious … what is the word? Someone police accuse?'

'A suspect?'

'Yes, this. A suspect. Mr Trafford tells me I am the first suspect.' She pursed her lips, tears forming in her eyes, though they didn't fall. 'There are things I wish not to tell policemen. Many things. But I don't want hang like Mr

Drake. Mr Drake was a very bad man. Very bad. He deserve to die, yes. But I no deserve to die. It was not me who kill him.'

I was watching her closely, but she didn't falter. If she wasn't being honest, she was a very good liar. But there was still something strange about how she spoke, as though she was consciously picking each word, one at a time.

'What was it about Mr Drake that you didn't approve of, Miss Vostek? Why do you claim he was a bad man?'

'*Claim?* I don't claim anything.' She made a fist and seemed about to pound it on the arm of the chair, which was rickety and might not have survived the assault, but she restrained herself and interlocked her fingers in her lap. 'I say the truth, Mr Stanhope. All men are worthy in the eyes of God, but Mr Drake was less worthy than most, I think.'

I was surprised. Before, she had seemed annoyed by Drake, even angry with him, but now I realised she actually *hated* him. I wondered why. He had seemed … not entirely trustworthy, certainly, but admirable in his way. Why would she harbour such animosity towards a man who pressed farthings into the palms of beggar children and gave them a place to sleep?

'Can you be more specific?'

She sat forward, her elbows on the table, and for a moment her face was lit by the candle. Her eyes were shining with tears.

'No. He is dead and it is done. All finished. I go home and think no more of Mr Drake.'

'Do you know who killed him?'

She shook her head and stood up.

'Perhaps he is sorry for his sins and he hang himself. Or somebody else hang him. What is the word … revenge? Perhaps this.' She nodded firmly. 'Revenge, yes.'

She was looking down at me where I sat, a frown forming slowly on her overbearing forehead. Her eyes flicked to my neck, my wrists, my fingers, which were autumn twigs compared with her own. I squared my shoulders and shrank back further into the shadows.

'Is that everything you have to tell me?'

She nodded. 'Yes. I go now. Goodbye.'

I remained in my seat. By rights, I should have shown her out through the front door, but I couldn't bear the thought of her following me through to the pharmacy, so she left as she had come.

I put my head in my hands, feeling sweaty and breathless. If she'd guessed what I was underneath these clothes, then my secret was no longer safe. I knew what would happen if she told the police. Barely two weeks previously, a woman in Warwick had been sentenced to seven years of penal servitude for pretending to be a man. She wasn't like me, she was simply intent on committing a fraud, but that distinction would count for little if I was arrested. Harry had written the article, sniggering all the while, and the memory of what he'd said was scorched on to my brain:

'How could anyone be fooled by such a claim? What about …?' He mimed a pair of fulsome breasts in case I wasn't sure what kind of problems might present themselves. 'She'll be thankful they sent her to a women's prison or she'd have been ravaged ten times a day.'

He was right about the women's prison. I would be given a dress, a bonnet and whatever name they chose for me. I would never tell them the one I was born with. I'd taken many names in my life, so another wouldn't hurt me. Better that than suffer my sister's sanctimony; such an irony that she felt justified in her condemnation, but she'd been born Jane Pritchard and had become Mrs Howard Hemmings. She'd disappeared as completely as I had.

To calm myself, I started to list all the names I'd ever used, backwards through time: Leo Stanhope, Maurice Stanhope, Maurice Jackson, George … damn, I couldn't even remember the surname. That was my brief period selling books door to door. And before that, Thomas Manly – a foolish choice – and before that … I shivered at the memory. The first name I'd taken while I was still furious with the world, with God, with my father, with anyone who stood in my way: Tom Cobb. That poor, reckless boy, with nowhere to lay his head.

When I was newly born – reborn – and living in Camden, my employer, Mrs Castle, had sent me along to her other shop on the Kentish Town Road. We'd run out of veda bread, so she suggested we split the stock two ways, which meant thirty-four loaves in the crate and a mile walk back through the snow. My arms ached and the sharp edges of the wood bit into my fingers. At the corner of James Street, a man stopped me, someone I knew a little bit. He was a regular customer. Sometimes he came into the shop with his wife and sometimes on his own, usually to buy a bottle of cordial gin. But he seemed sober now and grabbed the other end of the crate, so I couldn't move.

I was sixteen years old.

'Where are you going with all that bread, little Tommy Cobb?'

'Back to the shop. Mrs Castle's waiting for it.'

He pushed the crate hard into my stomach and, icy underfoot, I fell. He stood over me, spitting out his words.

'You act like a girl, Tommy. You're a bloody molly, aren't you?'

He dragged me upright and pushed me against a wall, spitting things, hateful things, about what I was and what should be done to me. I tore his hand from my neck and poked him hard in the eye. He staggered sideways and I kicked him, aiming for his groin, but he twisted away, and my boot caught only his backside.

He surged back at me, grabbing my hair and punching me three times, once in the stomach and twice in the face. The pavement was full of people, but no one stopped him. Through the blood in my eyes I could see their feet scurrying away.

His face was just inches from mine, his stale breath filling my nostrils. 'Answer me, *molly*. You like blokes, don't you?'

'No.'

'People like you are disgusting. Unnatural. You should've been drowned at birth.'

His hand went to his jacket, searching for something, and I was sure it was a folding knife. If it was, he would likely slice me where I stood. But Mrs Castle was a wise old owl and didn't let her staff – her *boys*, she called us – carry her goods around the city unless she knew we could protect ourselves. In my pocket I kept a two-inch bradawl, as sharp as a pin. I pulled it out and, in one motion, stuck him in the guts.

He took a step backwards, his hand to his stomach, blood already leaking through his fingers and on to the snow. He stared at me wild-eyed.

'What have you done to me?'

I left the crate and ran. I didn't stop. I ran past the shop and through the town and all the way to my little room, where I gathered all of my belongings into a bag. I took the road south towards the city with eight shillings and sixpence in my pocket, vowing that I would never again allow myself to become attached to a *place*.

All that was a long time ago. I closed my eyes, my breath steadying.

That Tom Cobb, he was a violent boy. But I wasn't him any more.

I needed to think rationally. Most likely, Miss Vostek had not guessed my physical gender, and even if she had, such an accusation wouldn't deflect attention from herself. My female body made me a less likely suspect, as no one would believe I could overcome Mr Drake and force him into a noose.

And anyway, I told myself, she was intending to go home to Hungary. What was the name of that town she was from? Drake had been right; it was impossible to remember.

I heard a sneeze and realised Huffam was under the table. He usually slept in the box room with Constance, so I was surprised. He climbed to his feet, bleary-eyed, and pressed his nose against my leg. I leaned down to stroke him and felt him flinch when I touched his back. His skin was scabbed and rough.

'Poor fellow,' I whispered. 'The veterinary surgeon wasn't able to help you after all.'

He whimpered, and I crouched down to let him bury his face in my dressing gown. Normally, when I was proven right in a disagreement with Constance, I was delighted to claim cheerful bragging rights, and she likewise over me. But Huffam was so piteous, for once I would've been glad to be wrong.

I wondered whether my father would have known what to do; Huffam was the last of several dogs he'd owned. But it was too late to ask him now; he'd been dead for nine months. He clung on to life for far longer than the doctors had believed possible. I visited him a couple of times before the end, and we talked civilly enough, him wheezing and blind, losing his thread mid-sentence, and me curled up in an armchair, telling him nothing more personal than what I'd eaten for dinner or whether the sun was shining outside. I supposed that suited us both. I'd been tempted to tell him the truth, but it seemed unfair to burden an old man with that knowledge so close to his death. And anyway, it was fitting that he was the final person who believed me to be something other than what I was.

I found my eyes drooping, warmed as I was by Huffam's head in my lap, and so I dozed, sitting on the floor with my back to the wall, only waking when I heard Constance tramping around in her room.

I leapt to my feet and ran up the stairs, setting Huffam to barking. He still had that much energy, at least. I didn't want anyone to see me in my pyjamas and dressing gown, not after Miss Vostek. I wondered how often Constance and Alfie had seen me wearing nightclothes before, and whether they had ever doubted.

It was one more thing I couldn't risk happening again.

I worked on Saturday, arriving late and tired, but not as late and tired as Harry Whitford. He seemed to have fallen out with Miss Chive and spent his time morosely scribbling on his notebook. Our desks faced one another, a design insisted upon by Harry's father who, I suspected, was hoping I would prove a steadying influence on his son.

I started on a brief summary of a conference paper on bowel disease that had even less chance of reaching the newspaper than my usual output, all the while thinking about what might have motivated Drake's murder.

The bells were ringing for three o'clock when I tossed a pencil eraser in Harry's direction.

'You're a wrestling enthusiast, aren't you Harry?'

He didn't look up. 'On occasion. It's a noble sport.'

'I'm sure it is, but … I'm wondering if there's any money in it. I mean, if you were managing a champion, would that make you rich?'

He nodded, putting the finishing touches to a drawing of a soldier who seemed to have taken a bayonet to the chest and was bleeding copiously. I didn't ask why.

'Oh yes, they can do very well. I saw a fight at the Agricultural Hall once where the purse was twenty guineas for the winner. And there are tours.'

'What kind of tours?'

'If wrestlers make a name for themselves, they can travel about the country doing exhibitions. Posing and sparring and so forth. They get decent crowds, I think, but it's not my cup of tea. It's more theatre than actual competition.

They work it all out ahead of time, who gets thrown, who ends up in a neck lock and so on, so no one gets hurt. Where's the entertainment in that?'

'How much money would a business like that be worth?'

'I have no idea.' He looked up at me with a baleful expression. 'Are you planning to see Mrs Flowers today?'

'No, I'm visiting another friend this evening.'

He raised his eyebrows. 'Oh yes? Who is she?'

'*Mr* Kleiner.'

'Hmm.'

He screwed up his picture of a soldier into a ball and thumped it flat on the desk.

When I reached Jacob's shop it was his son, Eddie, who opened the door, clutching an eyeglass to his chest. I guessed he'd been practising, having recently been apprenticed into his father's business making and repairing jewellery.

'Good afternoon, Mr Stanhope,' he said, sounding quite grown up. 'Please come in.'

He'd become sombre since the death of his younger brother, Albie, who'd contracted pneumonia the previous September. Jacob himself had started spending more and more time in bed, claiming he was ill, though it was old age and heartsickness he was suffering from, and I knew of no cure for either of those.

Looking around his workshop, I felt a rush of worry for my friend. He seemed to have abandoned his craft completely. He'd never been a tidy worker, though he was capable of the most intricate work, but now the room was a mess;

gauges, burrs and mandrels scattered across the surfaces, and crumbs of shellac crunching under our shoes.

I found Jacob in his room, and he waved his cane at me as I entered. He kept it near to hand, though he made little use of it other than to gesticulate at visitors or occasionally hammer on the floor for one of his children to bring him another bottle of spirit or empty his chamber pot.

I held up the bag of fruit I'd brought with me. 'Plums,' I announced. 'And some cherries, though they're a little soft.'

He grunted. 'I was beginning to wonder if you'd ever come back.'

He was lying bare-chested beneath the coverlet. I could only hope that the other half of him was more properly clothed.

'It's been one week, Jacob.'

All the same, I thought, I should not leave it so long again. He might fall genuinely ill or soil himself. His wife, Lilya, was blind, so his children would have to clean him, which would humiliate so proud a man.

I pulled up the wingback chair and the little table, and laid out his chess set, giving myself white. These days it took him an age to move a piece, so if I was white at least I knew the game would start. I pushed my queen's pawn forward two squares and accepted a glass of the vicious spirit he favoured. I didn't know its name. Sometimes, I wondered whether the stuff wasn't actually tarnish remover from his workshop.

He grinned at me and waggled his beard, which was now so scanty I could see through it to his pink skin. 'Have you been digging up more gossip for that rag of yours? Or has Charles Darwin done something else of note?'

'He died. Does that count?'

'Truly?' He seemed quite shocked. 'Oh, well that is unfortunate.'

'For him, certainly. I did attend a murder scene, though.'

Jacob huffed and pulled himself into a seated position on the bed, facing the board, revealing that he was, thankfully, wearing drawers on his lower portion, though they hung from him like laundry on a rack. I helped him on with his nightshirt, tugging it down over his uplifted arms. I could feel the narrowness of his bones, the protruding nubs of his elbows and scoliotic curve of his back. I wished with all my heart that he was still as I had first known him: hale, mischievous and wayward with his pawns.

He drained his glass in one gulp and slammed it down next to the board. 'What murder?'

I explained the strange circumstances of Drake's death, resisting the urge to sip the evil brew and wishing Lilya was there to offer me a cup of tea instead. Most likely, she was asleep in the loft room, as was her habit these days. I contemplated making a pot of tea for myself, but by this time Jacob was fully engaged with the events at the penny gaff and I didn't want to interrupt his train of thought.

'A telegram was sent to your office telling you of a murder,' he mused. 'Who would send such a telegram? A man who wants everyone to know about his crime. A *boastful* man.'

'Perhaps. Or a woman. Or someone who knew what had happened but isn't the killer. I explained as much to Detective Sergeant Ripley. Do you remember him?'

Jacob's mouth twitched irritably, and I regretted the question. Our unspoken agreement was that I never asked him what he remembered and what he didn't.

'You're changing the subject. What happened to the telegram?'

I thought back. I hadn't actually seen it. Harry had received it on my behalf and had shown it to his father, who told the police.

'It's probably been thrown away.'

'Why would you be so foolish?' He held up a finger and paused for dramatic effect. 'This could be the exact evidence you need, could it not? And yet you discard it! This is why newspapers are full of nonsense and gossip. You people never understand what's important.'

He hadn't been a supporter of the journalistic profession since *The Times* had declined to print his letter complaining that the silver duty mark was an unfair tax on the jewellery industry. He subsequently visited their offices to make his case in person, only to be told by a junior copy clerk that their readership didn't care about Jewish problems and he should go back to Russia or wherever he came from.

I responded to his move, which had been to match mine, with my king's knight. This was the way our games usually began; a predictable pattern we could follow without thinking. Of late I had begun to wonder whether we had, on occasion, repeated entire games move for move.

'I don't think the telegram contained more than basic facts,' I told him. 'It simply stated that Drake had been hanged, I believe.'

He waved his hand at me as if swatting a fly. 'Bah! It will also say which post office it was sent from. All telegrams have this information. Did you not know?'

'I suppose so.' I pictured one in my mind, a piece of card with printed type. They were so commonplace, and yet I'd never studied one in detail. 'Will it say who sent it?'

His expression soured. 'No, of course not. Why would it? But knowing where it came from might tell you *something*, no?'

'Maybe.'

'*Maybe?*' He lay back down on his coverlet and closed his eyes, his mouth pushed into a childish pout. 'You want answers and I give them to you, but it is never enough. Perhaps you wish me to *sniff* the telegram?' He made snuffling sounds, like a dog at a butcher's pocket. 'I could tell you what the sender does for a living and the brand of soap he uses.'

I frowned, reasoning that telegrams were sent electrically, so the card you received was never actually handled by the person who sent it. But this didn't seem the moment for scientific niceties.

'Come on, Jacob. I'm sorry. You're right, it's a good idea. Let's play chess.'

'Later. I'm tired now.'

He turned away from me, facing the wall.

'Why are you tired? Have you been working?'

'Of course not. It's Shabbat.'

He was not normally so devout.

'But the rest of the week? Have you been in the work-shop? Or teaching Eddie? He needs to learn your trade. You can teach him, Jacob. You're a wonderful teacher when you choose to be.'

He didn't reply, so I sat and waited, listening to the squawks of the magpies outside and watching the gentle rise and fall of breath in his body. The skin on his neck was grey and blotched with liver spots so profuse they were becoming one big spot. I could have left him and gone downstairs, but even in his sulky silence there was comradeship, whether he valued it or not.

My eyes were starting to close when I heard him mutter: 'It's too late for that.'

A few minutes later, he started to snore.

I crept downstairs. Lilya was preparing bread and cheese, sitting at the table with the provender and utensils laid out in front of her, cutting perfect slices and distributing them on to plates so swiftly it was impossible to tell she was blind. She refused all offers of help from me but did accept my bag of plums and cherries.

After supper we ate the fruit with sticky fingers and played charades: Lilya, Eddie, his sister Millicent and me. Of course, Lilya had no idea what actions we were performing and simply called out baseless guesses – 'Milkmaid! Bridle! Cornflour! Engine!' – until we were helpless with laughter and could no longer remember what word we were supposed to be acting out.

It was the first time I'd seen her happy in months, and it fed my heart with gladness.

After the children had gone to bed, I listened to her talking of her youth, when she and Jacob had been forced to flee across Europe from the Ukraine. Her voice cracked as she told me that when they reached Belgrade they slept on benches beside the Danube, lulled to sleep by the sound of the river, certain they were finally safe.

Shortly after St Paul's rang out for ten o'clock, I left the Kleiners, instructing the cab driver to take me to the newspaper office on Fleet Street. I was determined to find that telegram.

Mr Yip, the Chinese nightwatchman, was guarding the lobby. He allowed me inside and grudgingly let me borrow his paraffin lamp. I ran up the stairs to my desk and began sorting through the piles of paper.

I typically received fifteen or more missives a day via the internal system. A few were addressed to me, generally from academic societies – medicine, astronomy and suchlike – wishing me to provide them with free advertising for their latest symposium. But most were sent to other men in the office who, rather than read the contents, simply scrawled 'Stanhope' at the top and stuffed them into my pigeonhole. I didn't object. Having been offered an initial position as an occasional science correspondent, I was now accepted as a full-time member of staff with a weekly pay cheque to match. If the price of that was writing a few dull sentences about road closures and horse shows, so be it.

About halfway down the pile, I found what I was looking for.

Oswald Drake is dead by means of hanging. He was an evil man and deserved nothing less. Seek the truth.

Above that were printed the date and other details. It had been received at our usual telegraph office on Fleet Street and had been sent from the one at Mincing Lane.

My heart sank. Mincing Lane was an unremarkable side street in the financial district of the city, but its post office was one of the busiest in London, swarming with bankers and merchants.

I doubted anyone would remember a single telegram among all those thousands, or the person who sent it.

6

IN THE MORNING, ALFIE was getting ready for church, more out of custom than devotion. Constance was still upstairs, her habit being to postpone for as long as possible the moment when she would have to speak to Mrs Gower, who was seated on the stool in the pharmacy waiting for them both.

Mrs Gower continued to be perplexed about my non-attendance at church, but we generally got on well, having a common interest in watching birds. We'd become quite companionable the previous spring when a thrush had nested in a hedge in the yard. I had been recovering from my burns at the time and was glad to supervise the pale blue eggs on both of our behalf, sending her a celebratory message as soon as the chicks were hatched.

She half bowed her head in my direction.

'Mr Stanhope. I read your article about the awful events in Whitechapel. I hope they find the men responsible and hang them all. Gangs, I'm sure. Or *drunkards*.'

'Or a woman. One of the wrestlers at the place was female.'

Her face took on a strange expression, as though I'd spoken in some exotic tongue she couldn't comprehend.

'A woman would never kill a man that way,' she declared eventually, as if explaining household budgeting to a dullard. 'It's far too showy. She would simply poison his dinner.'

Mrs Gower's outlook on such matters was informed by the books she read – *Lady Audley's Secret* and the like – in which the only person a lady would dream of murdering was her husband.

Outside, her horse and carriage were waiting. It was one of Alfie's great joys, to leave on a Sunday morning with Constance and Mrs Gower and be driven to church. I imagined his arrival there, helping the women down and leading the way inside, perhaps shaking the vicar's hand. For a second, I had the urge to go with them, just to see it. Alfie had been unhappy for most of the time I'd known him, until he met Mrs Gower. She was good for him. Unlike me, he needed a wife.

But even if I'd truly wanted to, I couldn't go to church. I had to go to Mincing Lane.

The bells were ringing as I headed east; first the dull bong of St Anne's in Soho and then the higher, sweeter note of Temple, and finally, drowning out all the rest in a rigmarole of chimes, St Paul's Cathedral, which brooked no competitor for our ears or our souls.

Although the weather was dry, it had rained overnight, and the puddles were soaking into my socks. I cursed the pawnbroker who'd promised me these shoes were watertight. I couldn't buy new ones because any cobbler would notice how small my feet were, so I always got them second-hand and stuffed the ends with newspapers, now reduced to a sodden pulp and squelching with every step.

Despite the day of the week, I knew the post office would be open. The mechanisms of industry did not pause in their ticking, not for God or anyone; bankers and merchants considered the acquisition of wealth to be the holiest of callings, and their success at it to be proof of God's approval.

From the outside, the building was pale and blank-faced, but inside it was quite different: stifling and raucous, containing as many as forty men gathered in a disorderly line, a gaggle of clerks and a telegraph machine that clattered and tapped like a troupe of dancers. Every few seconds, a messenger boy would rush in to be handed a telegram, and rush out again, reading the address as he ran.

For a few minutes I stood behind a gentleman whom I believed to be the last in line, but turned out to be waiting for someone else, so several fellows who had come in after me were now ahead. This, combined with the wetness of my feet, the emptiness of my stomach and the weariness of my legs, put me into a foul mood.

When I eventually reached the front desk, an elderly telegraph clerk in shirt sleeves held out his hand.

'I'm not here to send a telegram,' I explained. 'I'm a reporter with the *Daily Chronicle*. I want to know who sent this one on Wednesday.'

I produced the piece of card and he stared at it as if his mind was so fixed on the normal rhythm of his duties, he was incapable of understanding anything else.

I thrust it closer to his nose. 'It was sent at a quarter past twelve exactly and is addressed to me. Do you know who sent it?'

After what seemed like an age, he shook his head. 'There isn't isn't any way to tell.'

Across the room, a boy was watching us. I glared at him, and he wandered outside, whistling.

I turned back to the clerk. 'Don't you keep a record of some kind?'

'Certainly not.'

The gentleman behind me, who was sporting a tweed coat and one of the highest top hats I had ever seen, tutted loudly.

I leaned forward across the desk. 'Listen,' I said, loudly enough for the whole room to hear despite the racket of the machinery. 'Do you see what the telegram says? It says that a man is dead by means of hanging. Did no one think such a thing worthy of note or enquiry? Are such announcements commonplace here?'

He gave me the thinnest of smiles and spoke as if I was a simple-minded child who would never amount to anything.

'What you don't understand, young man, is that all the telegrams we receive here are of the highest importance. Thousands and even hundreds of thousands of guineas rest on our accuracy and discretion. My responsibility is to copy them out precisely. What they say is none of my concern.'

He beckoned to the fellow behind me, palm upwards for his paper slip. I had already lost his attention.

'Damn you.'

I pushed my way outside.

In my nostrils, I could smell ash. Somewhere across the city, a building was ablaze.

Folks would be gathering to watch the fire brigade employ the steam engine, which would be making as much smoke as the conflagration itself. I put a finger to my cheek, where my skin had lost all sensitivity, as stiff as tanned leather, and imagined my flesh shrinking and cracking like over-grilled bacon.

'Mister?'

The boy who'd been staring was loitering next to me with his hands in his pockets as if we were two old friends deciding where to go for lunch. He had a narrow face, well-brushed hair, and his voice wasn't yet broken.

I found a farthing in my pocket and handed it to him, and would've been on my way, except he seemed to have something further he wished to tell me.

'I'm a messenger boy,' he declared.

'You don't have a uniform.'

'They don't have 'em the size to fit me, sir. I'm small for my age.'

'I see.'

My mind was already pondering on whether Rosie would be finished at church. Her shop was on my route, and I was keen to know whether she had any of yesterday's pies left over.

'I know who sent that 'gram,' the boy said. 'A quarter past twelve on Wednesday. I'll tell you for the right price.'

I was jolted back to the present. 'Really? Who was it?'

He gave me a terse little smile, not unlike the telegram clerk's. 'For the right price, I said.'

'What's your name?'

'Everyone calls me Runt.'

'Children can be cruel.'

He acknowledged the point with an inclination of his head. 'Better small than dim-witted is the way I see it. I keep my eyes open and I'm here every day, rain or shine.'

He was tidy enough and seemed well-fed, but that didn't mean he was honest. He would most likely take my money and give me the name of the last person he delivered to, or one he'd made up. I didn't want to waste my time searching for an address of someone perfectly innocent or who might not exist.

'What did you see?'

He took up a discursive posture, as if about to embark on a lengthy story, for which I didn't have time. A number of gentlemen had tutted as they stepped around us and one had bumped me in the back of the leg with his briefcase, I was quite sure deliberately.

'Well, that's the question, isn't it, sir? It was the kind of thing that doesn't happen every day, so I took note. I thought to meself: Runt, you should remember that, because—'

'You call *yourself* Runt?'

He shrugged. 'Like I said, everyone does. And it's a good thing I did take note because now I have the information and you require it. A shilling seems like a fair exchange.'

'Sixpence.' I extracted two threepences from my pocket and held them in front of his face. 'Half now, and half afterwards, if what you say is credible.'

I felt sorry for the lad and had no desire to torment him, but he could run off with my money as quick as blinking if he chose, and I could ill afford the loss.

He pulled a face. 'How do I know what you'll credit and what you won't? It don't sound like a normal happening, which is why it stuck out. You might think it outlandish and refuse to pay, though it's the God's-honest truth.'

'That's a risk you'll have to take.'

He seemed on the prongs of indecision, but as I started to walk away, he hurried after me, matching each of my strides with two of his own.

'All right, sir, I will accept your miserly offer in the spirit of goodwill, which I hope you'll remember when it comes time to requite the balance. That is to say, pay up.'

I handed him one of the coins, which he rubbed between his fingers. When he was satisfied it was made of metal and of the proper size, he put it into his pocket.

'Here's what I know, sir. It was on Wednesday last and I'd come back from Dunster Court where a gentleman was receiving the price per ton of something, though I know not what. He didn't seem pleased and no tip was forthcoming.'

'Is that relevant, R …' I couldn't bring myself to address him as Runt.

'No, sir. I include the detail as a bit of garnish to my explanation, so you'll understand why I was present at the spot. A quick job, you see. There and back in time to see a certain lady waiting to send her 'gram.'

'A lady? You're sure?'

There hadn't been one female in the room when I'd been in there; not among the customers, the clerks or the messengers.

'Oh yes, sir, she was certainly a lady. Her attire was most distinctive. No mistaking that.'

I wasn't sure what he meant. He took my silence as a prompt to hold out his hand again.

'It might be that I'll remember more specifics when I've got the expectation of a square meal or two in the near future, sir. My memory works best when I know my hunger will shortly be assuaged.'

My own hunger was starting to pinch. We were turning into Eastcheap, a road which would, after a mile and several name changes, go straight past Rosie's shop.

'First, explain to me why her attire was so distinctive. Was she dressed in an especially feminine way?'

'In a manner of speaking, yes, sir.'

He pushed his hand further towards me, and with great reluctance I placed the other threepence into his palm.

'Tell me everything you know about this person. There will be no more money.'

He thrust the coin into his pocket and kept his hand in there also, as if concerned that I might attempt to steal the payment back from him.

'As I say, I was present when she arrived. It was a quiet morning with more lads waiting to deliver 'grams than 'grams coming in, so many of us were stood in the street with our poor bellies rumbling and no chance of a tip. She went in, and I noticed her straight away, so distinctive was she.'

'Please get to the point.'

Normally, his verbosity would have amused me, but I didn't have time.

He breathed in deeply. 'She was a nun, sir.'

'A nun? Like in a convent?'

This seemed ridiculous. Surely nuns didn't visit city post offices in the middle of the day.

He nodded. 'Exactly so, sir. Wearing the full attire of nunhood, which is why the moment made such an impression upon me. We don't get many nuns here, sir. In fact, I surmise she may have been the first.'

I wasn't sure whether to believe him, and yet there was something about his tale that made me think it was genuine. If he'd been lying, he would have said it was a tall man in a flat cap called … whatever name popped into his head. William Gladstone, probably, or General Gordon. But a nun? That was sufficiently ridiculous to have the ring of truth.

'What was her name and address?'

His earnest expression faltered. 'That's not information I possess, sir. I mean, she didn't give it. Surely what I've told you is worth what you paid, and perhaps a tip in addition? I have a sister who'd like to eat also.'

'Did you see what she looked like?'

He took a step away from me, looking rightwards at the lanes leading north.

'Like a nun, sir, more or less. She was a distance away and they all look much the same, which I suspect is their intention.'

'And how do you know she sent this particular telegram and not some other one that happened to go simultaneously?'

He took another step sideways.

'It's possible, sir, but it'd be a coincidence, don't you agree? For her to be so unusual and for you to be searching for a person at precisely that moment.'

I stopped and faced him. 'Perhaps, but—'

Quick as a rat, he was gone, diving between two carts and over the road, no doubt circling back through the alleyways to the post office.

I walked on, unsure what to believe. Could a nun truly have sent me a telegram about a murder?

———

St Paul's was thundering for one o'clock when I reached Rosie's pie shop. Her door was opened by her female employee.

'Hello Alice,' I greeted her, feeling a small burst of pride at having remembered. 'Is Rosie here?'

'We're eating lunch,' she declared, narrowing her eyes, 'though I daresay that's why you've arrived at this hour.'

'Not at all.'

I was drinking in the warm aroma emerging from the shop, which was a combination of fruit, meat, spices and pastry so intense that any greater proximity to the source might overwhelm a person and reduce him to gibbering.

Alice appeared to share that opinion and was disinclined to let me take the risk.

'Very well then,' she said, and went to close the door.

I put my hand on it. 'I just want to speak to her for a minute.'

Alice sniffed and stepped aside. 'You're here more often than her late husband ever was.'

I could hear voices coming from the back.

The counter was empty and spotless, and the racks, where pies the size of a boxer's fist were displayed every other day of the week, were covered with tea towels.

'Who is it?' called Rosie, and her face appeared round the door. 'Leo! Come and join us. Mutton stew and dumplings. There's enough.'

The family was crammed around a tiny folding table, the two youngest children sharing a single chair, and all were holding their plate in their hands except for Rosie's eldest, Robbie, who was attempting to balance his plate on one knee while reading a book. Rosie shooed him to get an extra setting for me, and indicated I should take the poor lad's seat, but I shook my head and remained standing.

I could barely contain my appetite. For one accustomed to meals cooked by Constance – whose stews and pies were almost indistinguishable – it was heavenly.

Before we could start, Albert, Alice's jovial husband, bowed his head, and we all followed suit. Everyone but me crossed themselves in the Catholic manner.

'Bless us, O Lord,' he said. 'And also bless these, Thy gifts, that we're about to receive from Thy bounty. Though soon to be parted, we are always grateful. Through Christ, our Lord. Amen.'

He crossed himself again, and we could start on the food.

'What do you mean, "soon to be parted"?' I asked.

Rosie took Alice's hand. 'They're going to go and live with their son and daughter-in-law in Hastings for the summer. We're going to miss them terribly.'

Alice turned to me. 'We want some sea air, what with Albert's health, though it pains me to leave Mrs Flowers to the mercy of *goodness knows what.*'

Rosie let go of her hand. 'I'm quite capable of looking after myself.' She smiled in my direction. 'Where have you been this morning, Leo? Have you made any progress regarding poor Mr Drake? Tell us everything you've discovered.'

'All right.' I put my plate on the table. I had only consumed one mouthful so far and the anticipation of the rest was agony. 'I visited the post office where the telegram was sent and spoke to a messenger boy who was able to tell me the kind of person who sent it.'

'Well that's good,' she said. 'And what kind of person was he?'

'Not he, but she. A *woman* sent the telegram warning me of the murder.' I eyed my steaming plate and resolved to make my explanation as brief as possible. 'A nun, in fact.'

Rosie's expression hardened. 'A nun?'

'In full habit, apparently. I paid the boy sixpence for the information, but I'm certain he was being truthful.'

A look was exchanged between the other adults, the meaning of which escaped me.

'You're mistaken,' said Rosie firmly. 'Nuns live in prayer and quiet contemplation. They don't go out into London streets and they certainly don't send telegrams.'

'Well, this one did. I intend to enquire at the local convents. Someone must know who she is.'

Rosie shook her head firmly. 'Any woman can put on a habit, Leo. It doesn't mean she's a real nun, does it?'

I waved away her objection, which seemed to me to make no sense at all. 'Why would anyone do that? It would draw unnecessary attention.'

Rosie shoved her plate on the table next to mine and sat back, her arms folded. 'You already know she sent a telegram to announce a murder, so she clearly craves attention. And that's even assuming the boy's telling the truth. More likely he's spun you a fine yarn and you've believed him.'

Everyone had stopped eating now. Alice was giving me a look that would have curdled water.

'Perhaps, but isn't it more likely she was a real nun? It would be the duty of a godly woman to inform someone if she was aware of a crime.'

'But that's not what happened, is it Leo? Whoever she was, she didn't tell the police or a priest, she told *you*, a newspaper reporter. And if you remember, your previous belief was that whoever sent the telegram was complicit, perhaps even the killer. You can't accuse a nun of that.'

'Why not?'

I was considerably perplexed. In any other circumstance, Rosie would be the first to demand answers. She would take nothing on faith.

She took a long, slow breath and then spoke quietly, almost whispering. 'Not everything needs to be proven or disproven, Leo.'

'Well, I suppose we'll have to disagree on that.'

She stood up. 'In that case, I think you've had enough of our Lord's bounty for now, don't you?'

She marched through the shop to the front door, and I had no choice but to follow her. She let me out on to the pavement.

One mouthful. That was all I'd eaten. One single mouthful.

'Rosie—'

She shut the door in my face.

I stood there with my eyes closed for several seconds, wishing I could go back in time like Ebenezer Scrooge. I had been thoughtless. Rosie went to Catholic church every Sunday without fail and her children could recite long passages of the Bible, a feat they had demonstrated on all too many occasions. Unlike me, she cared what God thought of her. No wonder she was annoyed.

I waited for three or four minutes but the door didn't reopen, so I had no choice but to leave. I found a street vendor in the shadow of the viaduct and bought his last pork and vegetable pasty. It tasted like dust and had the consistency of the hairballs Constance's cat was prone to coughing up on the doormat.

It was all I deserved.

That afternoon, I went to the Home for Penitent Females to visit my young friends Aiden and Ciara Cowdery. Their adoptive mother had changed their surnames from Hannigan to her own because, she said, they should not suffer a constant reminder of their pitiful orphandom.

There wasn't a breath of wind, so flying a kite wasn't an option, but I was too distracted by my argument with Rosie to propose any alternative amusements.

'We could walk down to Claremont Square,' suggested Aiden. 'You can hear water gurgling underground.' He cast a sly look at his younger sister. 'One day, it will bubble up and all of London will be drowned.'

He'd almost lost his Irish accent, and had filled out of late too, enjoying his aunt's cooking and the indulgence of the many ladies in the Home.

'That's not true,' I reassured Ciara, who was looking a little uneasy. 'The water is contained underground. It feeds the reservoir, so we all have enough to drink.'

In the absence of a better idea, we set off, stopping for sweet pastries on the way. The two children ate them from the bag while Ciara listed all the bird species she'd learned, ticking them off on her fingers. Always the last of them was a robin because she loved the stories we'd invented together about a boy named Robin who wished he was a bird.

As we were crossing the Euston Road, we had to pause for a group of ladies carrying flags and banners, hogging the centre of the street. There were perhaps fifteen of them, obstructing the traffic, which was backed up as far as The Angel. Their leader was middle-aged and red in the cheeks, her head held high despite the slurs and accusations being hurled at her from the cart drivers stuck in her wake. As she passed, she turned and gave Ciara a cheerful wave.

'Who's that?' asked Ciara, holding my hand more tightly.

I squinted at one of the banners, held by a woman who looked exhausted, close to falling down in the mud. It read: *Forest Gate Ladies' Society. Votes for Women.*

'They're suffragists.' I paused, wondering how to explain. 'They want the things that men have.'

The irony of this definition wasn't lost on me, but I wasn't in the mood for self-analysis.

7

ON MONDAY MORNING, I set out in search of a nun.

I didn't have much information to guide me. All I knew was that Mincing Lane was her nearest post office – and even that might have been wrong.

I started by visiting the excellent cartography shop on Crown Street, where Mr Stanford was able to sell me a folding map of the whole east side of London. Right there in the shop, I laid out the map on a table and drew a line with my finger from Mincing Lane to the penny gaff in Whitechapel. If this mysterious nun had known about a murder there, it stood to reason she had some knowledge of the place. I was pleased to see that it was less than a mile from one to the other, so my search was narrowed considerably.

But try as I might, I could find no convents along that route.

I expanded my exploration to either side, taking in Limehouse to the east and Farringdon to the west, but still, there was no convent for which Mincing Lane would be the nearest post office.

I thumped the table with my fist, prompting one of the shop assistants to ask, in a manner more rebuking than courteous, whether I required any help. When I explained what I was searching for, he shook his head mournfully.

'Not every building of note can be included. There's only so much space on the paper. Your best bet is to make your search on foot. Of course, if you find what you're looking for, we'd be grateful if you'd let us know. We can try to include it in the next edition.'

This seemed a strange reversal of the normal way of doing things, but nevertheless I set out, somewhat reluctantly, as the weather was bitingly cold. I took the longer route to avoid both my newspaper office and Rosie's pie shop which, I knew from experience, would have a queue of customers waiting outside.

Not far from Mincing Lane, I decided to take some refreshment and hopefully regain sensation in my fingertips, and so dived into an ABC tea shop. The waitress brought me a pot of tea, and peeked over my shoulder at the map.

'What are you looking for? I know everywhere round here. Born and bred.'

'I'm trying to find a convent between here and here.' I indicated the two poles of my search. 'It's a route someone takes, or so I believe.'

The waitress scratched her ear. She was very young, but already had a worldly air. The place was quiet now, but I could imagine at lunchtimes these tables would be crammed with commercial men, all keen for her to squeeze closely past them with a tray in her hands.

'No convents in this parish,' she said, and put her finger along the imaginary line I had made, extending it south to

London Bridge, over the river and then eastwards. 'Here though, at the end of Tooley Street. There's a big one. Full of nuns, it is.'

I hadn't thought of looking so far away. If a nun was to walk from that convent to the penny gaff in Whitechapel, she would have to cross the Thames at London Bridge, which would take her further west than the telegram office on Mincing Lane. It was an awfully long way round.

'Are you sure there's no other convent?'

'Not that I know of.'

I finished my tea – no investigation was worth leaving a pot undrunk – and set out, pushing through the crowds over London Bridge and then heading eastwards along the southern side of the river.

Tooley Street was narrow and lined with warehouses and tenements of the most dreadful kind, their walls bowing and breaking apart, opening wounds in the brickwork so wide I could have put my arm inside. The local populace was mostly on the street, having nowhere better to go. The colour of their faces matched the ash-grey of the windows, and their rickets-ridden legs were as bent as the buildings.

As the road curved towards the river, before the houses and warehouses gave way to wharves and jetties, the convent rose out of the squalor like a sun-tipped mountain in a wasteland. Arched windows climbed its sides, reaching up towards a spire that leapt higher than that of the neighbouring chapel. I had developed a dislike for ecclesiastical buildings: their stench of piety and polish, their unquestioned authority and, most of all, their ridiculous height, as if the God of Abraham and Isaac was to be found wafting around in the air above our heads. But even I had to admit it was beautiful.

Looking at the heavy oak door, braced with iron hinges and locks, I realised I had given no consideration to how I might get inside.

———

I knew relatively little about Roman Catholicism. My father had spoken of it occasionally, mostly denouncing Catholics for being in thrall to a foreign Pope, proclaiming that they would betray their country and everyone in it in exchange for a blessing. But he reserved a particular pity for Catholic nuns. He said they were locked away like finches in a cage, prevented from becoming wives and mothers as any decent woman would want and, more importantly, as God's will demanded.

The door to the convent opened and a young lady emerged pushing a perambulator. I dived to catch the door before it shut, but I failed.

She turned and smiled at me. 'Just use the handle. It's always open.'

I was considerably surprised. My father had generally kept his church locked and on the odd occasion he handed his key to the verger or one of his curates, he acted as though it was tantamount to trusting them with his most precious thing; his dog or his pipe, probably. Certainly not one of us.

I pulled open the door and, once inside, stood as still as one of the ghastly statues that surrounded me, my mouth agape.

My father had been quite mistaken. These women weren't sequestered at all. The hallway contained all manner of people, including two young women who were clearly pregnant, a nun and, dominating everything, at least aurally, a baby caterwauling in its mother's arms. Another nun arrived with a glass bottle filled with milk for the infant, and it piped down. The two young women exchanged nervous looks. Yet another nun entered through a pair of swing doors and was about to head up the stairs when she noticed me.

'Can I help you?' She glanced at my skeletal frame. 'Is it food you want, Mr …?'

'Stanhope, and no, thank you.'

It was my rule of life: less food meant less fat, and less fat meant a less womanly form. Rosie's pies were the only exception.

'Then what?'

She was wearing a habit with a black hood and white bib, both somewhat faded, making her look like a dipper I'd once seen pecking for minnows in the New River at home.

'I'm looking for a nun.'

I admit this was a foolish thing to say, but I was stupefied by the conviviality of the place and my brain hadn't yet caught up with my mouth.

She adjusted her spectacles and sighed with the air of one who has had the same conversation many times and was somewhat tired of it.

'Then you're in the wrong place. We're not nuns, we're Sisters of Mercy.' She had a kindly face and I estimated her age at fifty or so, though it was hard to tell. Her garb obscured most of the usual cues. 'We're women religious. Not cloistered.'

'Cloistered?'

She attempted a comforting smile, though I guessed she was unamused by my company and adjudged me a simpleton who'd wandered in by mistake.

'I'm Mother Eugenie Doyle. I'm the Superior here. Our mission is to help those in need. Are you in need, Mr … Stanhope, did you say?'

I shook myself. 'Yes. I mean, no, I'm not in need. I'm a journalist with the *Chronicle* and I'm looking for one of your nuns … Sisters … who sent a telegram to my office last Wednesday. I have a few questions.'

She blinked a few times and wrinkles formed around her eyes. She was older than I'd previously thought; as old as my mother would have been, had she lived.

'A telegram? That's not possible. We don't carry money and have no need of such things. I send letters monthly, but I've never once sent a telegram.'

I wasn't sure how to proceed. If this was the wrong convent, then where was the right one? I had no other ideas.

'Do you or any of your Sisters know the area around Berner Street? Or have any dealings with the people there? It's in Whitechapel.'

'No.'

I had lost her attention. The Sister who'd been giving milk to the baby had stopped and was jiggling the infant on her shoulder. Mother Eugenie tutted and took it from her, briskly patting it on the back as if she was accompanying a jolly tune on the tambourine. The baby launched a mezzo-soprano belch and flopped on to her chest.

She gave the baby back to its mother and returned to me, her lips pursed.

'Why do you ask about a Sister who's familiar with Whitechapel?'

She had become brusque, in my experience a sign that someone knew more than they wanted to divulge.

'It relates to a grievous event. A murder. The telegram was a warning of a kind, and I need to know who sent it. Most likely, it would be someone who knows the area.'

I gave her my most trustworthy expression, but she appeared oddly unmoved.

'This is pointless. We dedicate our lives to helping others.' She gripped her hands together and looked from side to side, speaking in an angry whisper. 'If any of the Sisters knew of a *murder*, they would immediately tell me, and I would inform the authorities. I assure you, none of us knows anything of that kind or has ever sent a telegram.'

'But you do know of a Sister who comes from that area, don't you?'

I hadn't intended to speak sharply, but prising answers out of her was like coaxing Huffam to give up a bone.

She appeared agitated, glancing over her shoulder at the baby, perhaps in the hope it would require her care again.

'Yes, but … I'm quite certain she has nothing to do with any of this. Sister Agnes isn't capable of … you have to understand, she's a special case.'

'Special in what way?'

'She's … gifted, I suppose. And troubled.' Mother Eugenie pulled an expression I found hard to interpret, but perhaps included both exasperation and admiration. 'I only mention her because of the seriousness of the matter. But yes, I believe she is familiar with that area.'

'May I speak to Sister Agnes? It won't take long.'

'She may not agree to see you.'

'I understand. But may I try?'

She fixed her eyes on mine for longer than felt comfortable, and I felt she was making a judgement or perhaps consulting her employer. I wondered what His verdict would be; my tally of well-meaning failures and intentional sins was long indeed.

Finally, she sagged. 'And if I refuse?'

'Then I'll leave you in peace and a man's murder may go unsolved.'

She lifted her chin. 'Very well, you may speak to Sister Agnes. I agree to this only because you seem to be a good man. I believe I can trust you. Many a journalist would have threatened us with some kind retribution if I had declined. Follow me.'

She led me through a low door half-hidden behind the stairs. After the hallway, the ceiling of which was forty feet or more above our heads, I was expecting the rest of the building to be similarly elevated. But the corridor was of a conventional type, one wall broken by arched windows looking out on to the street and the other by doors opening into rooms where women were gathered in groups, talking or praying. We passed a small library where a Sister was reading, and I marvelled at anyone being able to spend their time in such quiet meditation.

Mother Eugenie skimmed down some steps, her feet silent on the stone. She must be wearing slippers, I decided, as my own shoes rapped and echoed behind her, making me feel uncouth by comparison. The lower level was dimmer, lit by high windows and occasional oil lamps, most of which had gone out. I was reminded of the hospital where I had once worked, and felt a shiver run across my skin.

The final door was shorter than the others, fashioned not from oak but a paler wood, beech or elm, with a horizontal lintel rather than an arch. One might have thought it a store cupboard or a maid's room.

Mother Eugenie tapped on the door, her ear close to it, listening for a reply. When there was none, she knocked again, this time more firmly, but still there was no sound from within.

'Are you certain she's in there?' I asked.

Mother Eugenie closed her eyes and placed her hand flat on the wood, almost as if, by so doing, she could commune with the person secluded beyond.

'Of course.'

She opened the door, and the smoke from inside stung my eyes. The windowless room was small and stark, with Jesus dying on His cross on one wall and a candle burning beneath him. Kneeling in front of it was a woman.

'Sister Agnes.' Mother Eugenie's voice was as soothing as a bedtime story. 'This is Mr Stanhope. He's a journalist and has some questions about an important matter. You may be able to help him.'

The woman turned and I recognised her immediately. Her frame, her features and the livid bruise on her cheek were unmistakable.

'I'm at prayer,' said Irina Vostek with no hint of a foreign accent. 'He'll have to wait.'

She looked briefly at my face and turned away, showing no sign that she remembered me at all.

———

There wasn't a chair, so I remained standing, while Irina Vostek, or Sister Agnes, or whatever her real name was, knelt with her head bowed.

Mother Eugenie fidgeted in the doorway, her agitation plain from the scuffing of her slippers.

I decided against saying the truth out loud, that this Sister of Mercy was also a part-time lady wrestler whom I had seen roaring in victory over another lady, and even a man, in a penny gaff crammed with bookmakers and pickpockets. It went to show how much I'd learned over the last few years.

When Sister Agnes had finished her prayer, I opened my notebook.

'May I have some of your time, please? I'd be very grateful for a little information.'

She threw me a chilly glance and pulled her elbows into her sides, making herself as small as possible. Up to that second, she'd seemed uncivilised, a woman with no womanly qualities, and yet I could see that she was unsettled by my intrusion. I wondered whether she suffered from a mental disorder that had driven her into the wrestling ring. If so, she showed little sign of it; no drooling at the mouth or growling in her throat.

I tried again; my voice as gentle as I could manage without veering into a higher register.

'I believe you're familiar with Whitechapel, Sister Agnes. Do you know of a penny gaff on Berner Street? It's important that you tell me *anything* you know. A man was murdered there.'

Mother Eugenie exhaled loudly, plainly thinking I was wasting my time. In the light of the doorway, she resembled a black pawn.

I arranged my face into a solemn expression. 'Perhaps you would leave us, Mother Eugenie? We could pray together for a little while.'

Even I, no supporter of the church, felt a pang of guilt at this lie. One might suppose, after God had presented me with the wrong body, that I would lack faith. But it wasn't the case. I believed in Him completely. I just didn't like Him very much.

'I would prefer not.'

She was clearly reluctant to leave another woman in the sole company of a man, but didn't wish to tell me so.

'She's in no danger from me,' I told her, which was true on more than one basis. I'd seen this prayerful creature stamp on a man's calf and crush his testicles to a pulp.

Sister Agnes stirred, drawing in a deep breath.

'I don't mind,' she said. 'You can leave us, Mother.'

Her Superior appeared to want to say something, but in the end nodded and allowed the door to swing closed. The candle flame flickered briefly and settled.

We were alone in the small room, so quiet that I could hear the air in our lungs.

'You can stop the performance now, Miss Vostek,' I said. 'Tell me why you sent that telegram. And for that matter, why …' I indicated her attire, the room, Jesus, everything. 'Why all this? What are you trying to accomplish?'

Sister Agnes bowed her head, though not in shame. 'You may set your mind at rest, Mr Stanhope. There's no mystery about me. I'm exactly as you see.'

'We both know that's not true. You came to my lodgings, remember?'

She dropped her face lower, staring at her hands in her lap. 'I don't have anything to tell you.'

I crouched down, almost kneeling myself. 'Did you kill Oswald Drake?'

We were so close I could see a stray hair that had escaped her veil pirouetting in the wind of her breath. The temporal vein on her forehead was pulsing.

'Mother Eugenie says that killing another person is a terrible sin, second only to sinning against God.'

She was wearing her religion like armour.

'Do you know who did kill him?'

'I have wondered, of course.' A tiny smile twitched at the corners of her mouth. 'But I have no idea. If I did, I would have told Mother Eugenie immediately. Elspeth deserves to know what happened.'

'Who's Elspeth?'

She lifted her head and, for the first time, properly looked at me. Encircled by a coif, her face looked even more remarkable; crook-nosed, heavy-jawed and over-browed. 'Didn't you say you were a journalist? Elspeth Drake is his *wife*. Or widow now, of course. She's a sweet girl and must be utterly distraught.'

She started fiddling with her hands, rubbing her knuckles together so vigorously that specks of white skin were falling on to the black of her skirts. I wondered whether those knuckles had first been abraded in the ring, clenched into a fist, and whether her current mania was a result of shame or contrition.

'Mrs Drake will inherit the gaff. That must be some compensation.'

She paused in her knuckle rubbing. 'You told Mother Eugenie you wished to pray with me. Was that true?'

I put my fingers to my face where it had been burned. I had prayed twice in the previous twelve years, both times in desperation, and had no intention of doing so again. God's mercy came at too high a price.

'No.'

'I see. You lied.'

She appeared to have none of the conversational traits of most people; she simply listened and answered, neither teetering on the ends of my words, desperate to make her point, nor being overly attentive, calculating her responses. I felt a twist of jealousy; she had as much to hide as I did, and yet she seemed unburdened by her dual life. Was she overly confident, believing no one would ever find out, or did she simply not care?

Or a third possibility: did she not *know*? Perhaps she inhabited her two selves so completely that each was unaware of the actions of the other – even a murder.

If so, I was in danger.

When I worked at the hospital, I had once sewn up the corpse of a man who had died in prison, having been convicted of killing a child. At his trial, he'd insisted that he retained no memory of his alleged crime and that he was, in a sense, two men, one worthy and honourable and the other a monster. Why should the first be punished for the crimes of the second? The alienist who treated him, and who told me this story, said that he'd been unsure even at the very end whether the man was telling the truth or not. Needless to say, the court did not believe him, and neither, evidently, did his fellow inmates at the Holloway Prison, as he suffered an unfortunate and mortal accident in his cell, that of falling on an axe several times.

'We all want honesty from other people,' continued Sister Agnes. 'But very few offer it themselves.' She looked me in the eye. 'Every farmer wants the river diverted to irrigate his own land.'

'Are you speaking in parables now?'

She gave a little shrug and relaxed back on to her heels, seeming more like a normal person than a Sister. The habit she was wearing could be as much a disguise as the drawers and vest she had donned for the ring.

'In that case I'll be plainer, for your sake,' she said. 'You want me to tell you everything, but you abide not in the truth yourself, because there's no truth in you.'

'Quoting the Bible is hardly plain speaking. And please don't say the Bible is the fount of all plainness, or some other aphorism. My father was a vicar, and I know only too well how scripture can be made to suit the needs of the godly, rather than God.'

She climbed to her feet, facing Jesus on His cross. The paint was cracked and shiny, and in the scintillation of the candle, He appeared to be moving.

'Very well, Mr Stanhope. I didn't kill Mr Drake. Is that plain enough? From time to time I experience raptures. Moments of … oneness with the Lord when His will is clearer to me.'

I was losing patience. All this theology was reminding me of my childhood, listening to my father instructing us over the dinner table, lining up salt and pepper pots, serving spoons and gravy boats to illustrate his points, as if their regularity was proof of his righteousness.

Did I honestly believe that this woman was overcome by raptures? If so, was it possible that, while in the grip of such a communion, she had hanged Oswald Drake? She possessed sufficient strength, but why would she do such a thing? Why did she do any of it?

'Did God tell you to become a fake Hungarian wrestler? You still have a bruise on your face.'

She put her hand to her cheek as if becoming aware of the injury for the first time.

'I've answered enough of your questions. Goodbye, Mr Stanhope.'

I looked into her eyes, wishing I had the gift of seeing into another person's soul.

She went to kneel down again, but as she did, the swish of her habit blew out the candle flame, and we were thrown into complete blackness. I could tell that she hadn't moved, and yet a clawing anxiety overcame me, not of her, not exactly, but of this place, this room, with its musty air, cracked Jesus and stifling silence.

I groped across the walls, but the geography of the room wasn't as I remembered, and I tripped over something, falling on to my hands and knees just as the door opened and light came flooding in.

'Are you all right?' asked Sister Agnes, keeping the door open with one foot while relighting the candle.

'I think so.'

She reached out a hand to me and I took it, feeling the softness of her palm and fingers, no larger than my own, no less gentle. She pulled me to my feet with the ease of a mother lifting her child.

I detached myself, feeling breathless and embarrassed, brushing the knees of my trousers and straightening my jacket.

'Goodbye, Sister Agnes,' I said, though I felt certain I would be seeing her again.

8

I STUMBLED PAST THE warehouses on Tooley Street, trying not to run. Above my head, a rope was dangling from a pulley, designed to haul freight up to the precarious doors opening into mid-air on the first and second storeys. The rope was swaying in the light breeze and I thought of Drake's corpse lying pale and limp on the floor. Could a woman of God truly have murdered him? Could she have broken the sixth commandment and afterwards knelt before His cross?

As I reached the crowds on London Bridge, my breathing became more measured, and I slapped my leather-hard cheek with my palm, which caused me more pain than one might suppose. I was being foolish. Religion had nothing to do with this. It was logic that would uncover the killer, and logic was telling me that Sister Agnes possessed the strength to hang a man and that she was leading the strangest of double lives. She was surely a suspect.

But that didn't make her a killer. I needed proof.

It was nearly lunchtime and my feet were walking unbidden towards Rosie's shop. I enjoyed a brief surge of anticipation, not only for one of her pies, but also for that rarest of gifts, the chance to tell her she was wrong. But I desisted. Something told me that Rosie wouldn't be receptive to the truth just yet.

I took a route along the south side of the river and over Blackfriars Bridge, arriving at the newspaper office just as Mr Coxswain was pushing his trolley past my desk. His vegetable soup was lukewarm and glutinous, but it sated my appetite, and I was feeling much better by the time Harry looked up from his typewriter.

'Where've you been?' he demanded, as though he himself was a paragon of punctuality. 'Never mind. Read this and tell me what you think. It's not finished yet. This is just the introduction.'

He pulled the sheet of paper from his machine and handed it to me. I read it with admiration. Amidst his spelling errors and the gradual fading of the ink, he was typically persuasive and erudite.

'I haven't heard of Frederick Lampton before.'

Harry took a sip of his tea, which I noticed was in my cup. He had a habit of taking it whenever his own needed washing, as well as my notebooks, hole-punch, lamp and, on one occasion, typewriter, claiming that an unknown vandal had spilled half a pint of ale over his. I felt a warm glow spread across my chest. This was how it felt to be among the company of men; liking each other, japing with each other, trusting each other. It was all I'd ever wanted.

'He's a Member of Parliament, the new man in Conservative circles. He has the ear of Lord Salisbury and if they win the next election ...' he pulled a face, being more disposed to the Liberals, 'he's in line for a senior post, some even say Home Secretary. He's a frightfully good orator. He says the most awful things, but *brilliantly*.'

'Well, this is very good. I'm sure it'll be the top story.'

I thought our conversation was at an end, but he hadn't finished.

'Why don't you come with me? He's giving the speech this afternoon. Likely to be explosive, from what I hear.'

I looked up at the clock. 'I'm sorry, I can't today. I have a story of my own to write.'

I didn't give him any details. Partly, I doubted it would make the newspaper, as J. T. had told me not to pursue the matter further. Not to mention, I hadn't yet finished my review of *Clever Things Said by Children*, and he was stringent on the matter of deadlines. But more importantly, I was unsure of what to write. Our readers had a taste for eccentric tales from the city peripheries – what Harry called 'colour' – sometimes sending letters to tell us how much more they enjoyed them than the usual dry stuff about debates in Parliament and treaties in the Soudan, but the quotes I'd garnered from Sister Agnes were oblique and theological at best. I doubted anyone would be bothered to read them.

In the end I wrote a succinct hundred words, briefly praising Mr Drake's community spirit and mentioning Sister Agnes's peculiar double life in sympathetic terms. But then I realised I couldn't possibly submit it to the subeditors' desk. I didn't know whether or not Sister Agnes had guessed what I was under these clothes. If she was arrested, she might tell the police, and then I would be arrested too.

Would I ever be rid of this fear of discovery? Must every thought and emotion be rooted in my malformation? I sometimes dreamed that my artifices could become real: the bindings on my chest clinging so tight that my breasts disappeared, the crush of paper in my shoes attaching to my feet, the roll of cloth in my trousers quickening and bonding itself to my pubic region. I could almost imagine it possible. How would it be, to have a torso as strong and upright as an oak and to feel the bristling of hair on my chest and chin? Even my hands could enlarge, a single span reaching from Q to P on my typewriter. I would guffaw and slap other men on their backs as though born to it.

I was too agitated to stay seated, so I stood up and foolishly met the eye of J. T. as he was exiting his office in the direction of the privy. Thinking it best to avoid him in case he asked what I'd been working on, I made a tactical retreat into the stairwell, where I bumped into Harry again. He was wearing his coat and brown felt hat.

'You know, I think I will go with you after all,' I told him.

He grinned. 'Good man. Still haven't completed that book review, I suppose?'

'No. Where are we going?'

I had never before heard of the Beaconsfield Club, and was doubting Harry had the right address even as we approached it. The building was on Pall Mall – that most traditional of streets for such amenities – at the end of a row of larger buildings. On any other street it would have seemed impressive, with roman columns and a shiny brass plaque, but here it was humbled by the grandeur of its near neighbours, the Carlton and Athenaeum, and one might have passed it by without a glance.

Two well-dressed ladies were standing on the stone steps leading up to the door.

'You should be ashamed,' one of them announced.

There was no one else on the pavement so I assumed she must be addressing us.

'We're reporters,' replied Harry, flashing a merry grin. 'Not here to cheer on Lampton, just to write down what he has to say.'

She folded her arms. 'Then I hope you'll be writing that he's an uncaring brute with no regard for others, who might be his mother, sister or wife.'

'Heaven forbid,' the other muttered under her breath.

I wondered what it was about Lampton that might have riled two such ladies. Harry had been circumspect concerning the likely topic of the speech, saying only that I should wait and see.

Once we'd navigated the fellow at the reception, we followed the sound of voices to the bar. Sadly, it wasn't selling alcohol this afternoon, but was laid out formally, with a lectern at the front and several rows of seats for the audience, who had already assembled. They consisted of two very distinct orders of men: wealthy gentlemen on leather club chairs at the front, and reporters on hard wooden benches at the back. Even all together, we were no more than forty, and the applause was patchy as a whiskered fellow stood up and introduced Mr Lampton.

The star attraction was a middle-aged gentleman near as slim as I was, with a neatly cut beard and long, doggish face.

As he surveyed the room, I had the impression he wasn't so much noting who was there as who was absent.

He cleared his throat and made a nervous little cough into a handkerchief he produced from his pocket.

'As you know,' he began, 'I am a great supporter of the institution of marriage. The place of a wife is next to her husband. She has vowed before God to obey him, so what was hers becomes his. As a Member of Parliament and a Christian man I must uphold the evident truth, that once such a vow has been taken, it cannot be untaken.'

His delivery was measured and stern, lacking the histrionic arm waving and lectern thumping of most politicians, and his accent was straight from the grander houses of Mayfair, almost to the extent of parody. My friend Peregrine Black, currently on tour with his theatre company, would have relished mimicking those inhibited vowels.

Lampton raised a finger and leaned forward. 'It is our duty to protect and nurture our wives, just as it is their duty to provide a calm and clean household for us. How can a man better himself if he does not have a good lady at home to comfort him on his return? Make no mistake, it's not money, trade or armies that is the foundation of the Empire, it's the English way of life, and at the heart of that is the sacrament of marriage. The very future of the Empire depends upon it.'

He then spoke at some length about the Empire and the influence of Britain around the world, and I admit my mind wandered. I couldn't shift the memory of Sister Agnes's quiet voice in that windowless room. If I closed my eyes, I was back there again. I could almost smell the smoke as the candle was extinguished.

Harry nudged me, and I took a deep breath to wake myself up.

Lampton was, contrary to Harry's claim, an average orator. What Harry had meant was that his rhetoric would survive transcription to the page in a way most wouldn't, relying less on performance than architecture. If one accepted that families were the cord that held together the Empire and that wives were essential to families, then it followed naturally that we should do whatever was necessary to keep wives in their place. For a few seconds I found myself almost convinced, before remembering that Rosie had been a wife, beaten regularly by her late husband – along with her children – until she'd been driven to plan his murder. It seemed far more likely that what held together the Empire was not marriage but money, of which Lampton had much and Rosie little. From what he was saying, he seemed to believe she should have even less.

'This is why,' he declared, 'I cannot condone the Bill which will shortly be presented to the House concerning married women's property. It would, for example, make wives responsible for their own debts ...' He paused so we could absorb the true horror of this prospect. 'Can you imagine? The next time your wife overspends a little on dresses and hats, as they are prone to do ...' he smiled tolerantly, acknowledging the murmurs of assent from his audience. 'You might never know it has happened. And when the bailiffs come knocking to reclaim the liability, it will be *her* they drag away to debtors' prison. Such an event is unconscionable, a derogation of our duty, and we cannot allow it.'

I found myself strongly disliking this man, who appeared to believe that the sex he would assign to me, if he knew the truth of my physical design, was incapable of understanding the complexities of money or possessions. This was plainly ridiculous. Alfie took good care of his finances now, but always said that his late wife, Helena, was the superior accountant.

I couldn't leave without appearing rude, so I sat and fidgeted, earning irritated looks from my neighbours. Rarely had I felt so out of place, and I'd lived my entire life in the wrong body.

'Furthermore,' continued Lampton, adopting the tone of one who is finally getting to the good stuff, 'I intend not merely to oppose the coming Bill, but also to seek the repeal of the erroneous legislation dating from eighteen-seventy, which started us along this path, dissolving the very principle of masculine authority. It's time we returned this country to the state that God intended.'

I sensed that he had finished, but also that he had over-estimated the familiarity of his audience with legislation from the previous decade. There was some clapping, perhaps more out of politeness than agreement, and then a shifty-looking reporter from the *Standard* asked him, purely for the benefit of others in the room, what the consequences would be if his campaign was successful.

'Wives will no longer be able to inherit property,' replied Lampton. 'It will go to their husbands, as it should. Otherwise, a marriage is little more than a contrivance, an expedient arrangement between two people. It's time for this country to say no to such depravity.'

This prompted some general muttering and hasty scribbling from the journalists. The realisation of what Lampton's plan entailed was slowly seeping into my brain. If he got his way, Constance would be unable to inherit the pharmacy. If Rosie were ever to marry again, her shop would become the property of her husband, no matter that it had been founded by her grandfather. No matter that her last husband had whipped her bloody with his belt.

Without being aware of what I was doing, I stood up.

'That's monstrous,' I declared.

Everyone looked in my direction.

'Who are you?' asked Lampton, with a predatory glare.

'Stanhope from the *Chronicle*.'

'I've never heard of you.'

'What about husbands who are vicious, wicked and drunken? Should women be in thrall to them for ever? Is that their Christian duty?'

Lampton placed his elbows on the lectern. He had a habit of interlocking his fingers and fluttering them, as if his hands were a butterfly drying its wings.

'Yes,' he said.

He nodded to a large fellow standing behind him, who fixed his eyes on me and cracked his knuckles.

———

Afterwards, as we were standing on the Pall Mall pavement, Harry clapped me on the back. 'Well, that was quite a scene,' he said. 'The first time I've ever been thrown out of a press conference.'

'I'm sorry. I don't know what came over me.'

'No need to apologise. It was quite splendid. And don't worry, I won't mention it to the old man.'

I hadn't considered what would happen if J. T. discovered I'd told a prominent Member of Parliament that his ideas were monstrous. I might lose my position at the newspaper, though it was equally possible he would laugh and offer me a glass of whisky. He wasn't an easy man to predict.

When I got home to the pharmacy, Constance had cooked something she claimed was potato hash. Afterwards, I complimented her on her culinary skill, which surprised her and baffled Alfie, but I was feeling all too aware of the work that women endured on men's behalf and hoped she might improve with some encouragement.

As evening fell, Alfie and I shared the dregs of a bottle, while Huffam – no epicurean, he – noisily devoured the last of the potato hash. Afterwards, I went to bed, certain that tomorrow would be a better day. I would finally finish my review of *Clever Things Said by Children* and was planning to visit Rosie at lunchtime, hopeful that my previous tactlessness would be forgiven, especially as I had been proven correct about the convent.

And yet, when I was lying on my bed that night, I found myself unable to sleep. I kept turning the same question over and over in my mind: was Sister Agnes a real person and Irina Vostek a creature of her imagination, or was it the other way around?

———

The following day, before I had even sat down at my desk, J. T. approached me, clutching the day's newspaper in his hand.

'Where's my son?' he demanded, pointing at Harry's empty chair.

His gruffness was actually a good sign. He treated Harry and me like puppies in need of training, and worried that if he ever succumbed to the more agreeable side of his nature we would scurry away and get ourselves into even more trouble.

'I'm sure he'll be in soon.'

This was optimistic. When we'd parted the previous day, Harry had said he intended to return to the office to finish his article about Mr Lampton. He thought it was certain to make the second page. Afterwards, I had no doubt, he headed to the bar for an early celebration, and was likely now to be sleeping it off. But I couldn't let him down; his father already believed him to be the more feckless puppy of the two of us and had threatened to chain him to his desk if he didn't learn how to behave.

J. T. grunted. 'Christ. He writes one decent story and takes a week to recover. Right, we need to have a word about this article, Stanhope.'

'Which one?'

He prodded the newspaper. 'Which one do you think? The nun. Is what you wrote about her true? I won't blame you if you made it up, but you need to tell me.'

I stared at the page, unable to believe what I was seeing. My article was there, printed in black and white. And I hadn't even submitted it.

Of course: *Harry*. He was forever taking my things. He must've spotted the article on my desk and submitted it on my behalf. Damn him.

J. T. tapped the newspaper again. 'Well?'

'Yes,' I stammered. 'Of course, it's all true.'

'Then why did you bury the best bit in the fourth paragraph? Thank God the subeditors did their job, or no one would ever have found out about Sister what's-her-name and her double life.'

'Agnes. And she's not a nun, she's what I believe they call a "woman religious". Specifically, a Sister of Mercy.'

He stared at me with an expression of incredulity. 'Don't tell *me*. I don't care. Get yourself back down to that convent right away.'

I rubbed my eyes, trying to gather my thoughts. The article was printed on page five, making it the most prominent I'd ever written.

'Why?'

He shook his head despairingly. At moments like this, his northern accent became more pronounced.

'Because she's the bloody story, you idiot. Go and find out where she's from and how she became a fighter. How she squares that with being a nun and if she intends to continue. And whether she's a murderer. Go and be a *journalist*, for God's sake.'

When I arrived at the convent, a group of fifteen or twenty people was waiting outside on the pavement. Some of them seemed to be locals or passers-by, but others were clearly reporters, clutching notebooks and waiting by the door. These weren't the affable fellows I knew from my usual beat, who sat with me through arid announcements about newly discovered cures for warts or the exact movement of Venus, and who would willingly share spare pencils and cigarettes. These were weathered professionals with greasy skin and down-turned mouths. One was picking at his gums and another was hacking phlegm into his handkerchief.

'What's going on?' I asked.

The gum-picker shrugged, breaking off from excavating his molars with his forefinger to let his tongue take a turn.

I turned to the phlegm-hacker, but he was more concerned with the contents of his handkerchief and wouldn't meet my eye.

I tried the door. It was locked.

Having no alternative, I slouched against the wall next to them. Journalism might sound thrilling to those not in the business, but most of it was just waiting for something to happen. There were times when I missed the raw excitement of being a hospital porter.

After what was probably only ten minutes, but felt like forty, the door was pushed open and a young, blond constable came out.

'Stand aside everyone,' he bellowed, as if we were a horde of thousands.

A sergeant emerged, followed by a sad sight indeed. Sister Agnes was being led out between two further policemen. Her expression was one of bewilderment.

The journalists immediately started yelling questions.

'Are you a real nun?'

'When did you decide to murder him?'

'How many men have you wrestled?'

And then, as they saw her more clearly.

'Are you an actual *woman*?'

She glared from side to side, blinking in the sunshine, but didn't reply. The policemen steered her towards a side street where, I now saw, a Black Maria was waiting for them. The street ran parallel to the railway, and the clatter of a train drowned out the reporters' pestering.

She looked back and caught my eye, but I wasn't sure if she recognised me.

As they approached the Black Maria, she slowed. The blond constable gave her a push in the small of her back. 'Get a move on.'

She flinched away from his touch. 'But I haven't done anything wrong. Where are you taking me?'

She slowed further, almost to a stop, and stared back at the spire of the convent chapel climbing into the blue sky.

'Why did you kill Oswald Drake?' called one of the reporters, prompting another avalanche of questions, impossible to distinguish and rising in volume until they were practically being yelled at her. 'Over here! Look at me! Tell us … my darling, look at me? When did you … look at me!'

When she reached the carriage, she leaned against it, gripping the roof-rail. The constable tugged on her wrist and, when he was unable to dislodge her hand, beat down on her forearm with his fist. She cried out and gritted her teeth, but still held on. He swore loudly and fumbled for his billy club.

Before he could pull it out, she spun and grabbed his neck, shoving him backwards against the dumb-iron of the carriage. His hands flailed as his helmet flew off and bounced across the dirt. Another constable attempted to pull her away, but it was like trying to uproot a tree. The first constable's veins were standing out on his florid face and his eyes were wide with fear.

The sergeant clutched the back of her tunic and struck her on the head with his club. She fell to her knees in the mud.

For a few seconds, no one moved. Then, she took a deep breath and clenched her fists.

The sergeant raised his club above his head.

'No!' I shouted to her. 'This isn't the wrestling ring. They'll kill you.'

Our eyes met and I could see her fury boiling. She did not like to lose. But eventually, she bowed her head, clutched her hands together and climbed into the carriage.

The young constable was rubbing his neck. 'Bloody Catholic bitch.'

None of them seemed keen to get in beside her. The sergeant and one of the constables clambered up next to the driver and the other two stood on the steps, holding on to the roof-rails.

With a shake of the reins, they were gone.

9

THE JOURNALISTS WERE LEFT standing and scratching their heads, but as soon as the carriage was out of sight they started scribbling busily in their notebooks.

I supposed they were accustomed to such drama, but I was forced to lean on the wall to recover, my chest heaving. For a moment I thought I might be sick. Up until that week, I'd only written articles about science or odd topics no one else wanted to cover. I was used to days going by when nothing of mine was printed in the newspaper at all, and I always started at the back when searching for my work. But now, thanks to my article, a woman had been hit on the head with a cosh.

My God, they could have killed her.

The ground seemed to spin and lurch, and I was aware I was falling, but I couldn't have said in what direction. The pavement loomed up and my palms stung. I blinked, trying to focus on the tiny pebbles and rutted dirt, and the foulness of it filled my throat, jolting me back to my senses.

I climbed gingerly to my feet and brushed myself down, picking grit out of my skin and mourning the holes in the knees of my second-best pair of trousers. As I was heading back to the convent, the sun emerged from behind a cloud and cast the shadow of the spire along the pavement. I looked up, shielding my eyes from the glare, and in one of the tall upstairs windows, Mother Eugenie was staring down at me, white-faced. I waved and pointed to the door, and a moment later I heard the bolt draw back and she opened it, beckoning me inside. I made it through just as the other journalists began running towards us.

Mother Eugenie swiftly closed the bolt and leaned against the wall, withstanding the indignant bangs and shouts from outside.

'I hate to shut anyone out,' she said in a low voice. 'It's our ministry to help people, not turn them away.'

'You did the right thing.'

'I pray so.' She clutched the silver cross hanging around her neck. 'Are you all right, Mr Stanhope? I saw you fall.'

'Yes, I … I'm fine, thank you. I'm sorry about Sister Agnes, that's all. I didn't mean for any of this to happen.'

She shook her head. 'It's not your fault.' I could see her reconsidering. 'Not entirely, anyway.'

Another Sister came into the hall, her shoes click-clacking on the stone floor. She had a furrowed brow and purposeful manner, and was in her thirties, as far as I could tell. I caught her sharp eyes as she approached and was reminded of someone I knew, though I couldn't call to mind who it was.

'Have they gone yet? Who's this?'

I gave the newcomer a little bow. 'Leo Stanhope. I'm a journalist with the *Chronicle*.'

She looked briefly upwards towards the rafters in a manner I took to be asking God for strength. I wondered whether her obvious mistrust would cause her to withhold her name, politeness be damned, but eventually she muttered: 'I'm Sister Nora. Why are you here? Haven't the press caused enough trouble?'

'My article about Sister Agnes was submitted by mistake,' I said. 'I'm sorry it was printed.'

The two women shared a long look. From her demeanour, I guessed that Sister Nora was second in seniority. Her chin dropped a little.

'Very well,' she said quietly to Mother Eugenie. 'I'll be at prayers. I'm sure we'd all be *delighted* if you'd join us when you're ready.'

She bustled away without looking back. As the door thudded shut behind her, Mother Eugenie gave me a tense nod, bordering on the collusive.

'I have a task for you,' she said. 'It's the Lord's work.'

'I don't much like doing the Lord's work.'

I felt as though I was confessing a terrible secret, though it was obvious to anyone who knew me that the Almighty and I had parted ways long ago.

Her expression didn't waver. 'That's the thing about the Lord's work. It doesn't matter whether you like it or not, so long as you do it.'

Instead of going along the corridor, as we had last time, we went up the stairs and then back on ourselves. I looked out of the tall, arched window, realising that this was where Mother Eugenie had been standing when I'd waved to her to let me inside. The pavement was empty now, the journalists having gone back to file their stories, much as I should probably have done.

I wasn't used to such silence. In all my usual places – my room, the newspaper office, Jacob's house or Rosie's shop – the hustle and hum of the city was with me. It was like the sound of my own breath or the beating of my heart. But I could've heard a flower die in the quietude of the convent.

Mother Eugenie indicated a grand door. 'This way.'

Inside, the room was spacious and well lit, with a fire popping and crackling in the hearth. I eyed it warily, feeling the skin on my cheek pinch and itch.

'Are you sure you're all right?' she asked. 'You're looking peaky.'

'Thank you, I'm fine.'

I forced myself to look around the room and was briefly reminded of my father's office at the vicarage, but then realised I was making unfounded assumptions. The bibles and concordances were familiar enough, but there was no smell of dog hair or pipe smoke, no open books face down on the table, gradually splitting their spines, and no braided chasubles hanging on display, arms outstretched on their poles like angels sent to judge us. This was a simple room for reading, praying and making conversation.

Mother Eugenie lowered herself on to one of the two sofas, not troubling to tidy her skirts. I supposed the benefit of wearing a habit is that one doesn't have to bother.

'I was in the Crimea once, nursing men back to life. Or helping them to die.'

'I see.' I must've looked confused because she raised her eyebrows impatiently.

'I was doing the Lord's work, but I didn't *like* it. Do you see? Holding a boy down so a surgeon can saw off his leg wasn't *pleasant*, but it had to be done.'

'Were you with Florence Nightingale?'

I felt a brief shrinking in my stomach, realising I was giving in to one of my less worthy impulses: saying the only thing I knew about a topic in the hope it would make me appear well informed.

Mother Eugenie flicked a grey hair off her sleeve. 'Miss Nightingale was there also, yes. Her contribution is well remembered, I think. Perhaps more so than ours.' She gave herself a little shake. 'Quite the story, a wealthy woman like that, finding herself among the blood and filth of a war. But she did some good, I'm sure.'

Somehow, she made it sound like a criticism. Now *that* was far more like my father.

I wanted to appear at ease, and so sat down on the other leather sofa – or rather, *in* it, as it swallowed me to the extent that my knees were higher than my waist. I tried to edge as far from the fireplace as possible, but the thing had me in its grip.

'Poor Sister Agnes,' the Superior continued, closing her eyes briefly. 'She wasn't born for a life of service. Her mother was foreign, from an affluent family, and her father was in the army, a junior officer who never rose. He lost all their money on bad investments. When he was killed, there was nothing left. Her brothers joined the army themselves and her mother believed no man would ever marry Agnes, so she was sent here, barely more than a child.'

'Perhaps it was for the best,' I suggested, trying to speed up the conversation.

'If so, then at present I'm at a loss to see how.' Mother Eugenie angled her head towards me. 'Though the Lord has been known to withhold his plans from me, on occasion.'

'Were there any signs then of what she would become?'

She looked up at the cross on her wall. 'Perhaps, at the beginning. When she first came to us, she was headstrong and troublesome, forever objecting to the rules we observe here. And she had a terrible temper. She used to throw things when aggravated and once broke a crucifix over her knee.'

'That's not very holy.'

She smiled thinly. 'No, but a crucifix is just a thing. It can be replaced.'

I was surprised by her pragmatism. If I'd broken a sacred object in my father's church, he would have acted as if I'd spat in God's face.

'And then, I assume, something changed?'

She smiled, acknowledging the predictable passage of her story. 'Yes, quite. One day, finally, she began to listen to what the Lord was telling her. She'd been a hair's breadth from expulsion, but overnight she became the meekest novitiate I'd ever seen. She was quiet and cooperative, doing as she was told without complaint. I gave thanks. Frankly, we all did, though of course we didn't know what would happen. Not exactly.'

'Ah.' I nodded, finally understanding this lengthy preamble. 'Sister Agnes's other career as a wrestler wasn't a surprise to you. You knew already.'

She looked away, not meeting my eye. 'After she took her vows, she claimed to be getting … raptures. She called them that and, as devout as she was, we didn't doubt her. She said the Lord was speaking to her directly. She prayed day and night, and at the same time, she withdrew from our work with the sick and mothers-to-be. Sometimes we didn't see her for days. And then I realised that, some evenings, she was leaving the convent altogether.'

'Is that not permitted?'

'We're not *cloistered*, Mr Stanhope. I thought I'd explained that to you. We can leave if we wish. But it's unusual to go out after prayers and without telling anyone. And there were injuries too; cuts, bruises, even a sprained wrist. It wasn't normal. So, I decided to follow her.'

'When was this?'

'January, I think. Her prayer room is next to the back door and I was in the corridor and heard her moving about. I kept quiet, in the shadows, you know, and when she appeared, she was wearing …' she paused. 'Well, she was wearing clothes unsuitable for our calling, let's say. I followed her to a ghastly street and a building filled with men. I couldn't go inside, of course.'

'But you feared the worst.'

'Yes, indeed.' She swallowed hard and steeled herself. 'I feared she had fallen into … sins of the flesh. And yet, I could not believe it.'

I rolled my eyes. 'No, me neither.'

Mother Eugenie gave me a sharp look. 'When we met before, you gave me the impression you were an honourable man and I allowed you entry on that understanding. If I was wrong, and you're as vulgar and callous as every other member of your profession, then we have nothing further to discuss.'

I felt ashamed of my unkind joke. I prided myself on my good nature, but since starting at the *Chronicle*, I'd become infected by my colleagues' indelicacy, at least according to Rosie, who paid keen attention to my conduct and was ever willing to propose improvements. I supposed I had been trying to fit in.

'I'm sorry,' I said sincerely. 'I don't wish to be as other men are.'

Inside, some small, bitter part of me laughed.

'Well then.' Mother Eugenie sat back. Had she been a man herself, she would've lit a cigar. 'Let us continue. The following day, I spoke to Agnes about it and she denied everything. She said she'd been experiencing a rapture and was quite unaware of what she was doing. I didn't know whether to believe her, so …' she clasped her hands together. 'So, I did nothing. It was a mistake. Having allowed her to take her vows in the first place, over the objections of others, I was perhaps overly lenient.' She fiddled with her hands in her lap. 'We have so many duties, it's easy to let things slip. One day becomes three and four, and then a week and a month.'

I felt sorry for the Superior. She was bent beneath her responsibilities, blaming herself for the sins of others. At least there was a way I could help her.

'And you want me to write an article about all of this?'

She shook her head. 'I'm not expecting as much, Mr Stanhope. I'm simply explaining it to you, so you understand. Agnes isn't a killer. I'm certain of it. I would be grateful if you'd make that clear in whatever you write.'

Just a few days previously, I had watched Irina Vostek bellow at the crowd like a bear.

'You haven't seen her wrestle. She's as aggressive as any man.'

Mother Eugenie pursed her lips and gazed into the fire. 'I know. I read your newspaper. The truth of what she was doing was almost as bad as what I'd feared; a Sister wrestling other women – and men as well – it's inconceivable. And yet, it's not murder, is it? Not even illegal.'

'That's true.'

I attempted to stand but couldn't summon the necessary leverage and found myself sinking back into the sofa. I tried again, finally gathering enough heft to tip forward and stagger to my feet. Mother Eugenie rose from the furniture with the elegance of a hot air balloon.

'Will you do as I ask, Mr Stanhope?'

I wanted to say yes, but something was nagging at me. Some detail lost among everything Mother Eugenie had explained.

'Where did Sister Agnes get those unsuitable clothes from, the ones she was wearing when you followed her?'

She peered at me for a moment, her face blank. 'I don't know. I didn't think to enquire.'

'In that case, if you want my help, you have to let me search through her belongings.'

Mother Eugenie refused to allow me into the dormitory, which she said had not seen a man since it was built and would not be seeing one now. In any case, Sister Agnes's possessions amounted only to her religious clothing, which was stored in a shared wardrobe. It would be somewhat obvious if a bright yellow dress had been hanging alongside all the plain tunics and scapulars.

Our compromise was that I could search the small prayer room in which Sister Agnes spent most of her waking hours. I asked Mother Eugenie for a portable lamp, rather than lighting a candle. The memory of that sudden blackness, the oppressive silence and the stink of smoke was still sharp in my mind.

As I opened the door, Jesus on His cross seemed to flicker and turn. I told myself I was being foolish; it was nothing more than a trick of shadow and lamplight. This was just a room like any other; four walls, a floor and a ceiling. The Lord was no more or less powerful here than in my bedroom or the reeking privy of the Blue Posts pub.

I tapped the plinth with my foot, realising it was what I'd tripped over the last time I was there.

'Was she in this room when the police arrived?'

'She was.' Mother Eugenie's voice was halting and thick. 'I pray for her swift return. It would be awful to be one short at vespers.'

'I'm sorry, but … it may take longer than that.' I looked into her eyes, wishing I didn't have to break this news to her. 'It may be days or even weeks.'

If she was *ever* released.

She took some time to reply, her mouth curling downwards and her chin starting to wobble. 'I don't understand, truly I don't. Agnes has done nothing unlawful.' She clasped her hands together, shaking them in exasperation. 'She struggled with our life here in the past, it's true, but she's incapable of killing another person. *Incapable*. Surely the police will understand that?'

Rather than tell her that the police would certainly *not* understand that and would gladly see her hanged, I changed tack.

'Did they search in here?'

'Yes. There was nothing to find.'

I admit I was surprised. The room was much as I'd last seen it. Our boys in blue tended to prioritise thoroughness over tidiness and I would have expected the few items in the room to have been tossed on to the floor: a dozen or so books, three candlesticks, some spare candles, a half-finished glass of water, a small plate and a fruit knife.

'Does she have any other private space than this one?'

'No. Even this isn't private, strictly speaking. Any of us can use it.'

'But you don't.'

She bowed her head a little. 'No. It was a storage room before Agnes decided she needed somewhere for her raptures. We don't intrude.'

I moved the lamp to the shelf at the furthest end of the room, and Mother Eugenie became a silhouette in the doorway, a halo shining around her head. I smiled at the sight, but I knew very well that taking a religious title and wearing vestments didn't make a person holy.

There was nowhere to hide anything in this room; no chest or cupboard, no padlocked alms box. And yet, she must have kept her clothes *somewhere*. I sat on the kneeler with my back to Jesus, inhaling the bitter stink of camphor and beeswax.

As a child, I had been messy, leaving my books and drawings strewn across the floor and underclothes spewing out of my wardrobe. My mother despaired, and my sister, who shared the room with me, more so. Once, after treading on one of my chess pieces in her stockinged feet, she had gathered up all my things and thrown them out of the window, and then barricaded the door. But she allowed me back inside after an hour. She had loved me, then.

In truth, I'd never cared much about my possessions, anyway. I was the offspring of a vicar in a wealthy parish and had been brought up to expect occasional gifts of books and clothes and chess sets, so I never valued them as much as I should have, young fool that I was. What I valued were the threepences I earned teaching sums to local children, saved up so I could leave the vicarage to become the person I was always meant to be. I kept the money in a purse under a loose floorboard.

What if Sister Agnes had hidden her secret in the same place that I had hidden mine?

The wooden plinth was made of planks running from edge to edge, raised perhaps eight inches, a tiny stage on which to pray.

I crawled across it, rapping my knuckles on the wood. The boards all sounded the same except one, which was dull, like a loose drumskin. I pushed my fingernail under the board but couldn't move it. I grabbed the fruit knife and pushed the blade into the crack, levering the board up and revealing a space beneath.

'What are you doing?' asked Mother Eugenie.

I put my hand into the hole and groped around on the cold floor, feeling some kind of soft material with my fingertips. I pulled on it, and out it came, a yellow dress, neatly folded. Next, I recovered a black jacket, a rolled corset, a purple ribbon and a bonnet. The last item was a petticoat in some kind of linen, with a coarse horsehair tournure still buckled into the waistband.

'Mother Eugenie breathed deeply. 'Those don't prove anything,' she said. 'I've already told you she had secrets.'

I pushed my arm further into the gap, almost at the limit of my reach, and felt something else, long and metal, the width of my finger. I pulled it out and held it up to show her. It shone in the candlelight.

She put her hand to her mouth.

'Oh no.'

It was a hypodermic syringe.

RATHER THAN GO STRAIGHT to the police station, I detoured
to my office, though I'd already missed my deadline and
could hear the clink and clank of the type being set by
the compositors in the next room. No matter. Our readers
would learn about Sister Agnes's arrest the day after tomorrow, along with three paragraphs about the good works of
the convent. I was a man of my word, though I doubted
those particular words would survive the subeditors, who
had a tendency to remove what I called 'relevant back-
ground information' and they called 'extraneous verbiage'.
They would be more interested in her garish clothing,
which I laid out on the floor, and of course the hypodermic syringe, which I set on my desk, so it rattled as I
hammered, two-fingered, on my typewriter.

By the time I got to the police station on Whitehall, it
was early evening. I knew the place well, what with one
thing and another, and greeted the constable on the desk
like an old friend. He went to fetch Pallett, treating him
with a curious deference, though they were the same rank.

Pallett accepted the bundle of ladies' clothes with an air
of discomfiture. 'Very interesting, Mr Stanhope. Detective
Ripley will be wanting to see these.'

I had hoped to avoid seeing Ripley but supposed it was necessary if I was to get what I wanted. When he arrived, he was munching a pasty which smelled fatty and overcooked.

'Did you find these in Agnes Munro's room?' he asked.

I hadn't previously considered that she would have a surname.

'*Sister* Agnes Munro's prayer room, yes.'

He spoke with his mouth full. 'She's plain Agnes Munro to us.'

'Would it be different if she was Anglican? I'd like to speak to her.'

He shrugged. 'No press men in the cells. If we allow one in, we'll be overrun. Got enough rats as it is.'

Something in his tone struck me as unusual, at least for him. He sounded *embarrassed*.

'Very well.' I offered him my most polite smile. 'Then you won't be interested in the proof I've found that she's guilty, will you?'

I started to leave, knowing he would stop me. After I'd taken two steps, I slowed down, intending to give him every opportunity to mentally process what I'd said before calling me back. By the time I'd reached the door, now creeping at a snail's pace, and he still hadn't said a word, I had no choice but to turn round.

He was still standing in the same spot, ruminating on his pasty.

I threw up my hands. 'Don't you want to know what the proof is?'

He spoke with his mouth full. 'It's against the law to withhold evidence. If you'd gone through that door, I'd've arrested you, searched you and dragged you down to the cells for questioning.'

I wasn't sure whether to believe him or not. He was impossible to read.

'At least then I'd be able to speak to Sister Agnes.' I was sounding more petulant than I'd intended.

He took another bite and wiped his free hand down his jacket, leaving a trail of grease like a slug. 'Your choice.'

I folded my arms. 'Detective, I think it's quite reasonable that as I've done your job for you, you should help me do mine. I only want to talk to her for a few minutes.'

'Show me this proof and I'll think about it.'

I carefully withdrew the syringe from my pocket and removed the cork I'd stuck on to the point of the needle, disinterred from Harry's desk.

'I found this among her clothes.' I pulled on the plunger. Inside, the barrel was dry, but still held the faintest aroma. 'Morphine, to render Drake insensible while she fitted the noose.'

Ripley took it from me and rotated it in his fingers. 'When you looked at the corpse, you said the bore of the needle was wide.' He touched the tip, raising a tiny dot of blood. 'This is sharp.'

I shrugged. 'There must've been a struggle before the drug took effect. The hole was made bigger.'

I wondered if Drake had been aware of what was being done to him, the coarse rope tugging at his neck and the sudden constriction. I hoped not.

Constable Pallett cleared his throat. 'It can't hurt to have a confession as well, sir.'

Ripley ate the last of his pasty and licked his fingers. 'She's a bloody Catholic. You'd think she'd be used to confessing things. All she'll say is she's a good Sister and it's a sin to kill. Anyway, now we have this, it doesn't matter. She'll hang anyway.'

Of course, it was true. This small thing I'd found would lead to a woman's execution. I supposed some retribution was required for Drake's death, yet I felt no craving for it. I could scarcely bring his face to mind. Instead, I was imagining Mother Eugenie back at the convent, waiting for Sister Agnes to come home for vespers. Was it asking too much that she should be allowed to do so, all sins forgiven? Just this once, could the law require no eye for this eye and no tooth for this tooth?

'We had a deal, Detective. Unless you want me to deny where that syringe came from, you'd better take me to her cell right away.'

The police jail had been renewed since I was last down there. It had previously been two large cells, but was now six smaller ones in a row, separated by brick walls.

'We keep the real bastards apart now,' explained Ripley. 'Fewer killings.'

Three of the cells contained men sitting sulkily on the floor or leaning against the bars. One of them was scrawny and rabbit-faced, and he grunted that he'd like to get more closely acquainted with the nun, or words to that effect. I almost wished he could get his way, because, I suspected, such an acquaintance would end up with both his arms being broken, if he was lucky.

Sister Agnes was in the last cell.

Ripley unlocked her door, and I entered. She'd been granted a pinewood chair but was instead choosing to kneel on the ground facing the wall. It was a comfort for her, I supposed, the constancy of those hard, cold bricks. But there was no Jesus hanging above her head now. She had to imagine Him.

I sank down on to the chair, attempting to calm my breathing. I couldn't afford my voice to squeak. Ripley might close that door and turn the key, and I would be trapped. Or worse, he might throw me in with one of those other men. I knew my fears weren't rational, but I couldn't completely dismiss them. They hovered on the edge of my perception, snapping at me like vicious little birds.

Eventually, I knew I had to say something. The silence was unbearable. But it was Sister Agnes who spoke first.

'You again?' Her voice was soft, barely above a whisper.

She looked up at me and her face was a ruin. Her lip was split, her cheek was cut to the bone and her nose was crooked and purple. One of her eyes was torn from lid to brow, and the other was so swollen she could not possibly see through it. Her left hand, pressed to her right in prayer, was marked with a black curve; the shape of a boot heel. Her habit was ripped at the shoulder and the pure white of her bib was splattered with blood.

Ripley cleared his throat. 'She resisted arrest, so I'm told.'

I turned to him, furious. 'No, this was revenge. Your men did this to her. Look at this.'

I pointed at the stone floor, which was smeared with red in great sweeps, left and right, as if someone had been dragged from side to side while bleeding.

Ripley put both of his hands in his pockets, an uncharacteristic gesture. 'She resisted a lot.' I stared at him and he lowered his eyes. 'Look, I don't condone it, but she had it coming. You can't do that to a copper and expect there not to be consequences. If you ask me, they went easy on her, being a nun and all.'

'Go and fetch some medical supplies. Needle and thread, bandages, balm, whatever you have. I'll be including this in my article for the *Chronicle*.'

He rolled his eyes. 'Yes, I'm sure the good people of London will be furious at how we treated a liar and a murderer.'

'They ought to be.'

He patted his pockets, looking for his cigarettes. He liked to use them as punctuation, slowing and pausing the conversation as he inhaled and exhaled the smoke. But he couldn't find them, and eventually settled for chewing his nails instead.

'I'll have to lock you in.'

I felt a cold shiver in my stomach.

'Why?'

He excavated the pith of his fingernail before answering.

'Can't have visitors wandering around in here. If you want to be alone with her, you're in the cell.'

'Do you promise to come back promptly with medical supplies?'

'Probably.'

He grinned and my skin started to itch all over. What if he forgot about me? Or left me there for his own amusement? I would have to stay all night. I would have to share the pail with Sister Agnes.

The lock turned with a sound like a rifle breech being closed.

'As quickly as possible please, Detective. I don't want to be in here a minute longer than necessary.'

He may have replied, but if so I couldn't hear him over the jeers of the men in the other cells.

Sister Agnes was hunched over, her face hidden.

'Let me see,' I said to her, but she flinched away.

'Did Mother Eugenie send you?' Her voice sounded congested and pained. 'Have you come to take me home?'

I wished I could. She didn't belong in this place. 'No, I'm sorry. But she does believe you're innocent.'

Sister Agnes was thoughtful for a moment. 'She's concerned about the reputation of the convent.'

It was the first thing I'd heard her say that seemed connected, by even the most elastic strand, to reason.

'Yes, she is. Why did you pretend to be Hungarian? Shouldn't someone like you be more concerned with God than wrestling?'

She tried to smile, though the expression quickly twisted into a wince. 'You care a lot about my duty to God, do you? You, who refused to pray with me?'

Her voice held a trace of Irina Vostek's lilting intonation. Perhaps, I thought, unlike me, she wasn't one thing rather than another, but was two things at the same time; both a wrestler and a woman religious. I wondered how it felt to be so resolved.

I wished I knew if she had deduced my secret, and what she would do if she had. I couldn't be sure whether she would betray me, pray for me or pull off my arms and legs and swing them over her head as trophies.

'Will you tell the police anything I might not want them to know?'

I couldn't ask her more directly without giving away my reason for the question. It was infuriating.

She looked at me with her one open eye for what seemed like a long time, and then turned back to face the wall. She held a potency, a pressure, like a vast rock on the brink of cracking. I had the impulse to run away, out into the street, where I could lose myself among the crowds on Whitehall. But of course, I could not. Ripley had locked me in.

'I'm not interested in you.'

'Good.' I resisted the brief rush of relief. I didn't trust it. 'You said before that Mr Drake was evil, but everyone else seems to think he was an upstanding citizen. The wrestler, Mr Trafford, told me that Drake always insisted on lawful behaviour. Quite honestly, I think he worshipped him.'

She nodded and I saw a hint of humour around her mouth. 'Mr Trafford's a decent fellow and a good wrestler ...' She mused for a second or two. 'An *average* wrestler, anyway. But does he seem to you to be an *intelligent* man? Is he possessed of a large brain?'

'I couldn't say. I know he's very brave.'

'Yes, that's true. Mother Eugenie went to the Crimea in the war, did you know that? She was a nurse on the front line, patching up the soldiers to go back to fight and die.'

'She may have mentioned it.'

Again, that hint of amusement. 'Yes, it does crop up in her conversation from time to time. Bert Trafford's the kind of man you'd want with you in such a war. He would do as he's told and thank the officers very politely when they commanded him to run into enemy fire. But you wouldn't want him planning troop deployments, I don't think.'

I fished in my jacket pocket for my notebook. 'You mean there were things going on that Mr Trafford didn't know about.'

She nodded. 'He grew up in poverty and he's naturally grateful to Mr Drake for rescuing him. He found a profession in the ring and an income. A wife, as well. He had no reason to doubt his master.'

'What do you suspect Drake of having done?'

She did not immediately reply, remaining still and silent for so long that, had she been anyone else, I would have thought her asleep. And yet I knew she was not. Neither was she praying. She was *thinking*, not yet decided on a course of action. Once she did decide, I surmised, she would commit absolutely. This woman did nothing by halves.

'Can I trust you?'

She crossed herself and climbed slowly to her feet, pausing before straightening up. I waited for her to unclench her fists as the pain passed, trying to ignore the prickling in the soles of my feet.

'Yes, absolutely.'

'Very well. What is your purpose, Mr Stanhope?'

'My *purpose*? In what respect?'

'Obviously, I'm asking ...' She closed her eyes and I realised she was counting to five, regathering her lost patience. 'I wish to know what gives your life meaning. How is the world different, better, because of your existence in it?'

'I ... don't know. I've never considered such a thing.'

In my daily life, almost all my attention was occupied with keeping my secret. There was little time left for spiritual musings.

She nodded. 'Well, perhaps you're lucky. I think of little else. I know that my calling as a Sister of Mercy should be sufficient, but I find myself wondering if God has some other plan. His will isn't clear to me. And yet, I believe I understand *your* part.'

'My part? What do you mean?'

'You're a journalist, after all. That's why I sent you the telegram telling of Mr Drake's death. I couldn't bear the thought of his crimes going undiscovered. I believe the Lord has chosen *you* to expose the truth.'

I admit, that idea dumbfounded me. If God had a plan, I would have preferred He kept it to Himself. And why share it with me now? I had spent countless hours in my father's church, less a spiritual haven and more a meeting place for decent people to confirm to each other how very decent they were; Sunday best clothes and pews in order of wealth, from shiny top hats at the front to bowlers in the middle and flat caps at the rear. I felt the authority of my father well enough: his booming sermons, baleful prayers and furious sidelong glares whenever I yawned. But I never once heard the voice of God.

'Surely, we have free will, don't we? Isn't that the whole point? If we're just working to God's whims, we're nothing more than ciphers. No one can be blamed for anything. Even murder.'

'Both can be true, Mr Stanhope.' She angled her head towards me. I sensed that she was well practised at this argument. 'The Lord has a plan, but we choose whether or not to follow it.'

'I think you're avoiding responsibility.' I stumbled over the words, unsettled by her dogma. 'You're saying Drake deserved to die, but you won't tell me why you killed him.'

'He deserved death, yes, but the Lord didn't demand that I give it to him.'

I was brimming with frustration. Despite all good sense, I had a reluctant admiration for this woman. And yet, and yet … I knew for a fact that murderers could be likeable, even honourable. Had I been gulled by her clothes and her devotion; all that kneeling and praying?

She carefully lowered herself again, each movement laborious, tested for its price in pain. We're never so aware of the mechanics of our bodies as when they're damaged.

I remained standing.

'How can you still proclaim your innocence, Sister? Surely you must see that your best defence is to admit your guilt and claim you didn't know what you were doing during one of your …' I could scarcely bring myself to say the word: '… raptures.'

She bowed her head. 'I can't do that. It's not true.'

'I'm sorry.' I had no desire to be cruel, but she deserved to know what would see her convicted. 'I found the syringe you used to inject Oswald Drake with morphine. It was under the boards in your room.'

For the first time, she had no answer; no godly prating, no circumlocutions.

I took a deep breath and imagined what J. T. would say when I brought this story back to him.

The door at the far end of the room burst open and I could hear footsteps hurrying towards us.

Sister Agnes looked up. 'If you see Mother Eugenie, please … I need her to know that I'm sorry.'

I had the urge to tell her that no remorse could bring back the dead, but she was so pitiful, with her bruised face and lacerated eyelid, I couldn't bring myself to do it.

'Of course.'

Ripley appeared at the bars, seeming unusually harried. He was empty-handed aside from the key, which he rattled in the lock of the cell, initially failing to engage it and swearing under his breath. When he finally succeeded, he threw open the door and dragged me out.

'Time's up. Quickly. I need you gone.'

'Where are the medical supplies you were supposed to bring?'

He slammed the door shut. The clang of it reverberated around the room.

'There's been a development. I never should've let you in.'

He marched me to the main entrance. 'Did she tell you anything useful?'

'Only that she was sorry.'

He rolled his eyes. 'They're all sorry, Stanhope, once they've been caught.'

Outside, night had fallen. I was surprised to see a group of eight or nine men gathered on the steps. They were muttering to each other and seemed angered by something. I lowered my face and walked swiftly past them, having no desire to find out what it was.

On my way home, I stopped in Trafalgar Square, where a vendor was crying the title of his newspaper, minus any discernible consonants. He was standing in the shadow of the statue of George IV, whose smug expression was matched by that of his horse.

'Almost sold out,' the fellow informed me as he took my penny. 'Big news today. Been a right rush, it has.' He grinned toothlessly. 'At least I get to knock off early, eh?'

I wondered what could be so important that the *Evening Standard* was in high demand.

I opened it under a streetlamp and could hardly believe my eyes.

11

'WHAT DO YOU MEAN, you missed the deadline? Is that why every other newspaper has the story and we haven't?'

I'd left the house at dawn and arrived in the office before St Clement had chimed for seven o'clock. I had been looking forward to my breakfast of bread and nuts at my desk but hadn't yet eaten a mouthful.

J. T. slammed his copy of the *Evening Standard* down in front of me, where it joined two other newspapers, neither of them ours. He prodded at one of them.

'According to this, she's seven-foot tall with a face like a gargoyle. You never told me she was a bloody giant!'

'She's taller than average, but that's ridiculous. And anyway—'

'She murdered Oswald Drake for sport. And him a decent businessman who cares for the welfare of local kids.' He paused, but this time I didn't respond, sensing he was waiting for me to do so in order to interrupt again. 'She prowls around at night searching for men to string up, and all in the name of God, apparently. They're calling her ...' he picked up the newspaper and scanned down the text '... the "Angel of Death". They're saying folks in the East

End should be grateful that this vengeful killer's been locked up. They're saying the monster should be executed and they don't seem too interested in whether there's a trial first.'

I put my head in my hands. I was certain he was about to fire me and had the urge to weep. This would be the third position in a row I'd been fired from. I should have stuck to science stories. I was good at those, and no one cared much if they were filed on time.

J. T. drew in a huge breath and exhaled slowly through his nose. 'My missus says I'm too stressed. She thinks I need to relax more. But how can I, with you two?' He pointed at Harry's empty chair. 'One of you would make a decent journalist if he could be bothered to turn up, and the other wouldn't recognise a story if Gladstone himself ran past naked singing "The Good Ship Venus".'

'They've exaggerated everything.' I was trying to keep my composure, with limited success. 'She didn't start the fight with that constable and she certainly didn't nearly kill him. He pushed her first.'

J. T. wasn't listening. He pointed at another of the newspapers. 'This one's calling her "the Beast of Berner Street".'

'It's not true. She's not a *beast*. She killed Drake for a reason.'

'Which is?'

'I don't know yet. Something to do with God's plan. But I did find the syringe that she used to poison Drake in her room. That's what I was doing when I missed my deadline.'

J. T. gave a low whistle. 'Is the syringe the murder weapon? Does anyone else know about it?'

'Only the police.'

'Good.' He patted me on the shoulder. 'Then it's an exclusive. We might make a reporter of you yet.'

———————

I wrote two hundred words about my discovery of the syringe, explaining in vivid prose how Sister Agnes had used morphine to subdue Oswald Drake before hanging him. When I handed the story to the subeditors, they started work on it immediately, which they had never once done for my reports from the Royal Geographical Society.

My relief at not being fired had made me hungry, so at noon I set out for Rosie's pie shop, hoping that the passage of time had mollified her ire.

There was a queue stretching along the pavement, and I was amazed to find Harry in it. I joined him, ignoring the muttered complaints from behind me.

He grinned like a loon. 'You've been having a time, haven't you?'

'Your father wants to know where you are.'

'No, he doesn't.'

'He definitely does. He was insistent on the point.'

Harry shook his head. 'He *thinks* he does, but how would it benefit him, eh? If he knew I was here, he'd be even more annoyed than he is now. It's not good for his heart, believe me. He's better off living in ignorance.'

When our place in the queue reached the inside of the shop, I smiled at Rosie, who pursed her lips in response.

'Have you come to your senses yet, Leo Stanhope?'

I was conscious of Harry standing beside me, one intrigued eyebrow raised. But my pride counted for little compared with my desire to be back in Rosie's good books.

'I have. I'm sorry I was tactless before. I know your religion is important to you.'

She nodded, attempting a smile. I could tell that I hadn't said entirely the right thing, or had missed some nuance, but she seemed to take my apology as, at the very least, well intentioned.

'Perhaps I was a little too harsh,' she said. 'I know you're not one for church.'

She met my eyes and I knew that she truly did understand: how could I kneel at the altar rail and give thanks to God when He had so corrupted my design?

She turned to Harry and favoured him with an expression I hadn't seen before, at least not on her face: a sort of *agreeableness*.

'Leek and ham, Mr Whitford, same as usual?'

He grinned. '*Harry*, please. And may I call you Rosie?'

'You may, Harry.'

She pulled a pie from under the counter, already wrapped up, and Harry breathed in the aroma. 'You are the queen of bakers.'

I looked from one to the other in amazement. He'd only met her a few days previously, and yet now he had a *usual* pie, kept under the counter in anticipation of his arrival. I didn't even know one could have a usual pie and I'd been coming here for two years.

'I'll have leek and ham as well, please.' I was tempted by the smell of Harry's.

Rosie looked a fraction sheepish. 'I'm sorry, Leo, but that was the last one. We have pea and ham instead, if you'd like?'

I nodded, though it seemed like a poor substitute and turned out to be the first of her pies I had ever not completely enjoyed. I found myself unable to shift the idea that leek would've been a tiny bit nicer than pea.

Harry and I ate them sitting on the wall outside, watching the carts and carriages parade slowly past us.

'Did you finish that article?' he asked. 'About the Butcher of Berner Street?'

'Beast.'

'What?'

'They're calling her the *Beast* of Berner Street.'

'Hmm.' He thought about it, chewing on his mouthful of probably excellent leek and ham pie. 'I prefer "Butcher". Beasts are too … mythical.'

'What on earth do you mean?'

'Mythical is perfect for the time *before* a killer is caught. Everyone loves a monster that goes around murdering people, evading the police by seemingly supernatural means.'

'Truly?'

It seemed unlikely, but he was adamant.

'Of course. But once they're caught, they can't be mythical any more, do you see? They're not a beast, they're a person, with a name and a face.' He nudged me with his elbow. 'They're just like you and me, except lacking all conscience. To make them properly scary, you need to make readers imagine the blood-soaked apron and piles of entrails as she chops up her victims. They have to smell the bile. That's why *Butcher* of Berner Street is better. Much better.'

'She didn't chop him up, she hanged him. And she's not a butcher or a beast, she's a Sister in a convent.'

I thought of Agnes; her over-large nose and looming brow, her kind, quick eyes and gentle smile. Giving her such a brutal nickname was cruel, and yet Harry seemed certain he was right.

'What could be more terrifying than a murderous nun?' He swept an arm in front of him like an actor in the final scene. 'The *Butcher* of Berner Street, slaughtering innocents in the name of God, a woman without feminine instincts, driven by an unnatural lust for blood.'

I rolled my eyes. 'All right, but I'm not sure how innocent Drake was. She said he was an evil man who deserved to die.'

'Revenge, then. Has she admitted she killed him?'

'Not yet, but I found proof: the syringe used to subdue him. It's an exclusive.'

'Hmm.'

He remained silent for several seconds, which was unusual. He generally loved to talk, and I generally let him. Silence was safer for me. We had enjoyed many lengthy conversations during which I said nothing at all.

Eventually, he licked his lips. 'To fully own the story, to lead it, we need to know more about this Drake fellow. A nun doesn't just decide to string someone up for a jape. He was a handsome man, I gather. Was she in love with him, do you think?'

'I highly doubt it.'

'What, then? I've heard nuns are all a bit … you know. Shut up in a convent their whole lives. Who knows what goes on? I've always wondered what they wear under all that clobber. I wouldn't be surprised if it was nothing at all and they're exposed to the fresh air like newly-opened tulips.'

I sighed. He was an excellent, though unreliable, journalist, but his mind ran on railway tracks. If it wasn't lust, it was power, and if it wasn't power, it was money. Harry could no more see the myriad complexities of human behaviour than a train could chase rabbits across a field.

'She's not that kind of nun. Or any kind, actually. Anyway, I don't see it. She wouldn't be impassioned by matters of the flesh.' He opened his mouth to speak, but I forestalled him. 'Or money, either.'

He raised an eyebrow, considering me naïve, but he didn't press the point.

'Very well. You have a good story for tomorrow's edition with the murder weapon. But what about the day after? You've got *how* she killed the fellow, but not *why*.'

We walked back to the office together, and I waited at the subeditors' desk until one of them, an older fellow named Horace, looked up. He had been, according to unanimous opinion, the best journalist in London until he lost both his feet in a carriage accident. Now, his job was to improve the copy produced by the likes of me, which must have been galling, to put it mildly.

'Stanhope. Do you have another piece?'

'No, I want to make a change to the last one. Am I too late?'

He shook his head. 'We can always change the lead story, right up until it hits the presses. Congratulations. Your first, isn't it?'

I couldn't speak for a few seconds. The lead story!

'Yes, it is. I want to add something. Can we describe Sister Agnes as "The Butcher of Berner Street"?'

He nodded, and I could see him visualising the words in the newspaper, how they would look in type and flow over a line.

'The Butcher of Berner Street. Yes, I like that. Well done, Stanhope. Well done.'

As I walked away, I was surprised to find my hands were shaking.

I told myself I shouldn't care. I should be like Harry and J. T. and all the other men of the office; battle-hardened with a heart of leather.

But still, I couldn't get Sister Agnes's face out of my mind.

———

That afternoon, I set out again for the penny gaff. Harry was right, I needed to learn more about Oswald Drake and what he'd done that had led to his murder. I hoped someone would be there, perhaps the widow, but I was disappointed. It was all locked up without a soul in sight I recognised, though there was a collection of cigar ends, food wrappers and piss trails on the pavement that told me some others of my profession had recently visited.

I could wait, of course, sitting next to the two ancients on the step opposite smoking bacca pipes, talking behind their hands, their unbelted trousers gaping at their waists and their grey chest hair billowing over their vests. Or I could go somewhere else.

I pulled out my map, and spread it against the penny gaff's window, as if I was adding one more poster to those already festooning it; faded pictures of the great George

Steadman in his sports kit, poised for action, and Charles A. Sampson, billed as the strongest man in the world.

I needed a moment to find what I was looking for: the Church of the Martyrs, only a short stroll away. Maybe the young deacon could tell me something useful.

The walk was pleasant, past rows of identical cottages, each with a door on to the pavement, a window beside it and another above, the whole house ten feet wide at most. I guessed the men who lived there worked on the docks and were absent at this time of the afternoon. Only the very old and the very young were crammed together in the doorways, watching me as I passed.

The last few yards before I reached the church went through an alleyway alongside a school, and the children were finishing for the day, rushing for the exit with their satchels over their shoulders. I felt an overwhelming burst of jealousy. When I was their age, school had been a respite from my father's vigilant eye. I used to run into my class-room every morning just as my teacher was unlocking the door and stay until dusk, when the caretaker threw me out. If I could, I would have hidden in the library among the stacks, breathing in the smell of paper until everything was quiet, and then read all night by the light of a candle.

But girls didn't stay in school. My sister Jane and I were evicted at eleven years of age. My brother Oliver, of course, had stayed on until he was seventeen despite knowing nothing of long division and never having read a book all the way through in his life.

As I approached the Church of the Martyrs, a flock of pigeons lifted from the graveyard and settled in the trees and on the roof, scratching and bickering. Without them,

I might have missed the church altogether. It was the kind of place one might pass every day for a dozen years and still be surprised when someone pointed it out: bulky and squat, with ugly lancet windows, brown brick walls and an offset spire that gave it a lopsided look. If it was truly God's house, He should have a stern word with the architect.

Inside, it was of a conventional design: pews, columns, altar, the usual arrangement of hanging lamps. My father would never have admitted it, but he would have liked this church. It was honest in its conformity. Even the votive candles and Catholic pictures of Christ and Mary would have met with his grudging approval; he had a weakness for pageantry. But of course, he was gone now. The last time I'd seen him, his voice, that bass instrument more suited to fire and brimstone than the line-by-line biblical analysis he favoured, had been reduced to little more than a whisper.

'Can I help you?'

I was jolted from my memories by an elderly fellow with wisps of white hair clinging to his pate as if he'd recently walked through a cobweb.

'I'm looking for Mr Sutherland.'

'Oh.' He seemed disappointed.

'Are you the priest here?'

'I am. Sutherland is my deacon.' Something in his tone suggested the words: *and nothing more.*

Behind him, the man himself appeared, as serene as when I'd last seen him. The elderly priest harrumphed and wandered off towards the right-hand transept, straightening a hymnbook as he passed. Sutherland waited until we heard the door open and shut before he spoke.

'You're the journalist,' he said.

'Stanhope.'

I shook his hand. His grip was firm, and he met my eye squarely. He would probably be considered handsome, though rather in the manner one might draw a picture of a handsome man, with a flawlessness that was essentially bland.

He indicated the front pew, and I sat beside him.

'How can I help you?' His voice was like silk.

'The police have a suspect in the murder of Mr Drake.'

He angled his head in acknowledgement. 'Yes, a Sister from the convent on Tooley Street. I know the place well. We offer the Eucharist there.'

'How well do you know Sister Agnes?'

'Only a very little. I've met them all, but I don't know any of them well.' He coloured a little. 'I can't remember ever having spoken to her.'

'Can you think of any reason why she might have killed Mr Drake?'

He pushed his fingers through his lustrous hair, and I thought to myself: he's trying to work out what I've already uncovered.

'No, of course not. Drake was well respected. He and Elspeth came here every Sunday without fail. Their son was baptised here.'

He was trying to give an impression of probity, but he didn't know who he was talking to. I'd been deceiving people – even those I loved – for years. I knew a liar when I heard one.

I decided to change tack. 'Why did you come to the gaff that morning, when we last met?'

His face flinched, ruining its symmetry. 'I heard about the murder from one of my parishioners. It's my duty to attend and help anyone who requires it. If I remember correctly, you had cause to be grateful I was there.'

'Yes, quite. The locals seemed ... quick to anger.'

'They're protective of their own. This isn't a wealthy area and people stick together.' He smiled, faking amiability. 'What's your interest in all this? The police have the killer in custody, so the matter's closed.'

'Perhaps.'

'You seem doubtful.'

I took a deep breath, finding that I did not like this deacon. His saintly manner and oh-so kindly smile reeked of sanctimony.

'I'd like to speak to the widow. Do you know where I might find her?'

He looked stunned, as though I'd suggested spending our afternoon ringing the church bells out of sequence. 'Elspeth is in mourning. She needs comfort and prayer, not a newspaper reporter asking questions. It's utterly impossible.'

'I have no wish to upset her, I assure you. But Sister Agnes deserves the truth to be told. She might be given leniency and avoid the noose.'

'I'm afraid I place the needs of the widow above those of her husband's killer. Now I really must get on.'

He headed towards the transept door, bowing briefly towards the cross, his head otherwise held high and his pace seeming calculated to be neither fast nor slow.

'Mr Sutherland,' I called after him. 'Oswald Drake took over the penny gaff quite recently, didn't he?'

He turned. 'Yes, I believe so. What of it?'

'Previously, he was doing a strongman act, and then he became the owner of his own business. Quite a rise, wouldn't you say? I was wondering where he got the money to invest.'

Again, that flinch. It was as well that clergymen weren't permitted to gamble as this supercilious deacon would be hopeless at three card brag. He strode towards me, this time at speed. I backed up until my thigh was pressed against the wooden seat of the front pew.

'You shouldn't be throwing accusations around.' His voice had been stripped of its godly veneer. 'The wrestling gaff on Berner Street is a place for honest working men to relax and enjoy some sport away from their wives. Have you ever made anything of value, Mr Stanhope? Do you ever stick your own neck out, or do you simply leech off the achievements of others?'

I produced my notebook from my pocket. 'I only want the truth.'

'The truth is that people around here don't like interference from the likes of you. They resent it. You'd do well to write your articles about something else from now on.' He prodded my sternum with his finger. 'Don't fly too close to the sun, Mr Stanhope, or I guarantee, like Icarus, you'll fall and die.'

With that, he turned and stalked away.

Had he been warning me, or threatening me? I couldn't tell. Perhaps he wasn't sure himself. He clearly wanted me to cease my investigation. But why? And what would he do if I didn't?

I looked up at the stained glass window, but no prayer came to mind. I didn't believe the Lord had a plan for me or Sister Agnes. She was deluding herself. He was as indifferent to our fates as I was to the pigeons on the roof, and our prayers were nought to Him but the scratching of claws on tiles.

12

I SAT FOR A few minutes to catch my breath, and then got to my feet and surveyed the church. I'd spent hundreds of days in one much like it, and not just Sundays either. I was sent there constantly, to fetch and carry, lay out hymnbooks, sweep the floor, clean the altar, check the rat traps and examine the cushions for holes. There was no end to it. As a punishment, I was made to polish the wood or clean wax off the candlesticks or dust the books of baptisms, marriages and deaths. And I was punished a lot, so I knew that church better than any other human, and almost as well as the cat.

I understood how churches worked.

Treading quietly, I did a full loop of the nave and then the transepts. In the left-hand one, the parish chest was pushed up against the wall, piled high with folds of cloth that turned out to be curtains awaiting repair. The chest was of a similar design to my father's, solid and heaving, with a clasp and padlock on the front. And, just like my father's, the padlock was hanging open. After all, who would steal a parish record?

I lifted the lid, wincing at the creaking of the hinges. Inside, the books were carefully arranged. Apparently, Catholics cared as much about these things as Anglicans.

The books of deaths were of no interest to me as I doubted Drake's was yet recorded. I ignored the books of marriages too; they didn't include the groom's address. I knew this from my idle hours spent making up grisly stories about newly wedded couples – fatal accidents and vengeful lovers – when I was supposed to be putting the books back in order and checking the chest for mouse droppings.

No, it was the baptisms I was interested in.

How old was Drake's son? I'd seen the infant briefly in his mother's arms at the penny gaff, but I was no expert at ageing babies. I pulled out the latest book of baptisms and flicked through the pages, going backwards in time. I was so absorbed, I didn't initially hear the footsteps, and he was almost standing over me by the time I looked up.

'What are you doing?'

It was the elderly priest. He was frowning.

I swallowed hard. 'I'm trying to find the address of one of your parishioners. His child was baptised here.'

'Who?'

'Oswald Drake. He was killed recently.'

The old man nodded, brushing a few strands of hair from his forehead. 'Yes, I heard about that. Terrible business. Did Sutherland give you permission to look in there?'

I couldn't dissemble. My usual deceit was to keep myself safe; it wasn't my fault I'd been created awry. But I'd been feeling guilty about lying to Mother Eugenie and wasn't inclined to repeat the mistake.

I replaced the book in the chest. 'No. The information might help gain leniency for a Christian woman, but Mr Sutherland said he wouldn't help me. He suggested I should leave.'

'I see.' The old man rubbed his chin and glanced hastily over his shoulder. 'Well, it really isn't his decision to make. Sutherland has been known to, shall we say, overstep his authority? I'm the priest of this parish and have been for eighteen years.'

I adjusted my face to a deferential expression. 'Of course. You're the senior man.'

'Exactly. And in *my* opinion, it's a reasonable request.' He took the book from my hands, licked his thumb and turned a few pages, scanning down the columns. 'Here we are. Reginald, son of Oswald and Elspeth Drake, baptised on the seventeenth of November eighteen-eighty. I remember the day well. We did it right after the service and everyone stayed. Mr Drake provided a cold lunch—'

'The address?'

'Oh, yes, of course.' He squinted at the book again. 'Number eight, Cressy Place. Just off the Mile End Road. It's a ten-minute walk, if you don't dawdle.'

———

After the smoke and dirt of Whitechapel, Cressy Place was extremely pleasant. It was a narrow lane, one side of a triangle with two other roads. Along a passageway I could see a scrubby park where an apple tree was struggling to bloom. That square of grass would be the playground for young Reginald Drake when he was older, I supposed. He would climb the tree and ponder on what kind of man his father had been.

Number eight was much like the others: a small front garden filled with roses and a chessboard pathway leading to a brightly painted front door. It was the kind of house I dreamed of living in.

I knocked and waited, but there was no reply. I cupped my hands around my eyes and peered in through the window. The front room was dim, containing only a few pieces of plain furniture. No books or pictures, no flowers or ornaments. Despite the owner's recent demise, there was no wreath on the door.

A finely dressed lady came in through the neighbour's gate carrying a basket of flowers. She blinked at me solemnly.

'Are you looking for Mrs Drake?'

'Yes. Do you know where she is?'

She sighed and put down her basket. 'Elspeth had to leave rather suddenly, poor love.'

'Why?'

'It's not for me to say. But I'll tell you this: the poor girl doesn't deserve any of it. Not one bit. I'll miss her, is the truth. We used to play backgammon. I taught her, but she was better than me in no time.'

'Do you know where she went?'

She gazed at me, sizing me up. 'You don't look like a debt collector.'

'I'm not. My name's Stanhope. I'm a reporter for the *Daily Chronicle*. I'm investigating what Mr Drake was doing that led to his murder.'

'Aye, well, that's a good question, isn't it? Some might say he got what was coming to him.' She glanced hastily up and down the street. 'Wait here.'

When she came out again, she was holding a piece of paper, which she gave to me. 'It's Elspeth's new address. She didn't want me to have it. I think she was ashamed. But I insisted.'

'Labour in Vain Street,' I read out loud. 'Is that really what it's called?'

'Apparently so. By the wharves, she said. Don't tell anyone else how you got it.' She shook her head sadly. 'If you see her, tell her Mrs George sends her kindest wishes. The very kindest. She's always welcome here for a pot of tea and a game of backgammon. And baby Reggie too, of course.' She wiped her eyes and sniffed. 'And tell her to take care of herself, if she's able.'

I thanked her politely and headed south, occasionally consulting my map. Most of the journey was tolerable enough, along streets lined with houses and shops, including a newsagent with a billboard outside: *Nun Arrested for Vicious Murder*. But as I crossed over Commercial Road and headed south towards the docks, the greenery of Cressy Place quickly became a vague memory, replaced by high-walled warehouses and, behind them, booming factories sending black clouds of smoke into the air. I could smell the river too: oil, silt, rotting waterweed, excrement and fish.

How did Mrs Drake end up here, after the calm and prosperity of Cressy Place? I knew how I would feel if I lost my lodging with Alfie and Constance, and this poor woman had lost her house and husband both, with a babe in arms to care for as well. She must feel desolate and abandoned, as if her life had ended at the same moment as Oswald Drake's.

The road sloped down, passing alongside the docks at Shadwell, a sorry slum stained white with salt. Four stevedores were staggering under sacks and crates, shoulders broad and shoes heavy, unloading their burdens on to barrows. I couldn't imagine what such work would be like. After a few years of it, a man of my age would look fifty, and a man of fifty would probably be dead.

As I watched, one of the crates started to move; the slats of its wooden side were being prised apart from within. A tiny brown hand appeared and then a face, peering through the gap, disturbingly human-like; a monkey, no bigger than a cat. I'd seen such creatures before at the zoo. One of the stevedores cried out and pointed, but before he could stop it, the beast had squeezed out and bounded along the jetty, tail in the air. The fellow gave chase, but he was hopelessly out-classed. The monkey looked once over its shoulder and danced up the wharf building, leaping along the gutters and perching briefly on a pulley arm before disappearing from view. The entertainment didn't stop there. Back at the crate, another face was already peeping out. The stevedores lost three before deciding that their time was better spent repairing the crate than chasing the animals around the dock.

The appropriately named Labour in Vain Street ran close to the basin. The water was high after the spring storms, lapping over the quays into great muddy pools.

The number I wanted was scrawled on to a concrete pillar next to a short stairway descending to a basement door. Looking down, I could see a baby in a basket through the grubby window, and then Mrs Drake herself. Her mourning frock was finely embroidered, but her hair was straggling out of a too-large mob cap, making her look more like a junior housemaid than a lady who'd recently been living in Cressy Place.

Unaware she was being watched, her expression was one of simple adoration, gazing down at her son as if unable to believe that such perfection could exist. I had the impression she could watch him for ever, and in truth I could have watched her watching him for ever as well.

She had a blanket in her hands. I thought she was about to tuck it around her baby, but instead she started to fold it, first in half, then a quarter, then an eighth. As I watched, she gently placed it over the infant's face and began to press down with both hands.

By the time I reached the bottom of the stairway, she had whipped the blanket away and thrown it on to the floor. The baby began to emit a thin, piercing wail, followed by an intake of breath and then another wail, even louder. I'd never felt so delighted to hear a baby's cry.

I hammered on the door and she opened it. Only some strange sense of decorum prevented me from pushing past her and gathering up the child in my arms.

'What were you doing?' I demanded.

She started to shake, covering her eyes with her hands and sobbing. After a moment, she hunched forward and buried her face in my shoulder, weeping fit to burst, and me a stranger. I didn't know what to do, so I patted her gently on the back and waited for the eruption to subside. I couldn't imagine what anyone would think if they saw us, embracing in the doorway in full view of the pavement above.

Thoughts flew through my mind. I couldn't leave the child with her, as she was clearly a danger to him. Should

I call for someone to fetch a policeman? Should I steal the child away? I knew of an orphanage where boys were given decent food and discipline in preparation for a life in the army, and the owner wasn't above taking a bribe if you didn't want questions asked.

Eventually, she prised herself away. Now I could see her properly, I realised her face still had its adolescent bloom. She was eighteen or even less and had been married to a man old enough to be her father.

'I'm sorry,' she stuttered. 'I must've given you a fright. I wouldn't hurt him, not really. I stopped before any harm came. You saw that.'

I was concerned she might fall to weeping again, so I took half a step backwards, putting my hand on the outside wall of the building. It was wet, but not from the rain. In the room behind Mrs Drake, damp had spread in a great stain across the ceiling and was beading on the windows and glistening on the floor. The stink of mildew clogged my throat. I poked at the sill and it separated under my fingers, revealing a plump woodlouse underneath.

'Do you remember me?' I asked, as gently as I could. 'I was at the penny gaff after your husband ... after he was found. My name's Stanhope, I'm a reporter with the *Chronicle*. May I ask you some questions?'

She nodded. 'But you can't come in. I don't want any gossip.'

This seemed a fine insistence on propriety after she'd wept on my shoulder in full view of anyone passing, but I supposed it was her choice to make.

'The police have someone in custody,' I said. 'Do you know Irina Vostek? It's her, except ... well, it turns out she was living a double life. Did you ever have reason to believe she wished ill on your husband?'

Her expression was blank, as if I'd mentioned that today was warmer than yesterday or that I'd recently bought a new pair of socks. You would never believe I'd just told her the name of the woman who had made her a widow.

'That's a great shame,' she said eventually. 'Irina was always very kind to little Reggie.'

She picked up her child and began to rock him gently as if she had a slow song in her head and was keeping time.

'I went to Cressy Place. Mrs George sends her regards. Why did you leave there?'

'For this palace, do you mean? I was evicted. Oswald hadn't paid the rent. Once the landlord found out my husband was dead, he came knocking, and I didn't have enough. Everyone thinks I've inherited a fortune, but the only thing I got was debt.'

'When did you realise?'

She pulled at her lace collar, as if it was constricting her. 'Only after he was dead. Turns out, he was stringing everyone along, making promises, you know. Trying to keep our noses above water. He could talk the angels down from heaven.' She ran a finger down the condensation on the door jamb and it formed a rivulet, dripping on to her step. 'No one'll loan money to a penniless widow, will they?'

I pulled out my notebook and pen, delighted that someone was finally willing to provide me with some information. 'Do you know who made the investment in the gaff? It might be—'

She interrupted me. 'I don't know anything about that, Mr Stanhope.'

I was disappointed, but it made sense. A man like Drake wouldn't share his affairs with a woman, let alone one so young. If she was eighteen now – and she hardly looked even that – she couldn't have been more than sixteen when she gave birth.

'How did you meet your husband?'

She gave me a sharp glance. 'At a society ball, of course. He requested the first dance and we kissed on the balcony. The Duke of Whitechapel invited us.'

Like an idiot, I'd almost begun writing that down before realising she was mocking me.

Judging from her age and accent, there was a more obvious answer. 'You were a pauper. He took you in with the others.'

She smiled, but it was bleak. 'I was a pauper before and I'm one again now. Almost makes it worse, wouldn't you say? Seeing what life's like when you have money, and then having it taken away.'

She put a hand to the back of her neck, massaging her skin, and I wondered if he had beaten her. She was inches shorter than me with a waist smaller than one of his biceps.

'And what now, Mrs Drake? Or may I call you Elspeth? Will you be staying here?'

She shook her head. 'I can't even afford this place beyond today and I can't go back to having nothing. That's why …' She gazed down at her baby now sleeping peacefully. 'Maybe we'll go for a little swim tomorrow, just him and me. Go together.'

I recognised it in her, that despair. It called to me like an old friend, drew me in, wrapped itself around me. There are few things more comforting than despair.

But she didn't know how hard it was to drown.

'There's no need for anything like that. I know of some-where you'll be safe, I promise. It's a Home for Penitent Females and they'll take you in. And little Reggie too. The matron is a decent woman.'

I was determined that she and her baby should come to no harm. None of this was her fault.

She shook her head. 'I don't want a handout.'

'It's not, I assure you. You'll work for your board.'

She looked up and I detected a glimmer of hope in her eyes. 'Is that true?'

'Of course. Get your things. We'll go straight there.'

It had to be now. I couldn't leave her behind, not even with a promise to return. I didn't know what she'd do in my absence.

'What if they turn us away?'

She clung on to the door jamb and I could see that she was reluctant to leave her dank little basement, no matter how ghastly it was. Even having so little, one can still fear having less.

'They won't, I promise. Look, Mrs Drake … Elspeth … sometimes, you have to move on. Everyone does. I've left places myself, places much nicer than this, and I've never regretted it.'

She gave me an almost imperceptible nod. 'Very well, Mr Stanhope. I want no charity on my own behalf, but for Reggie's sake I'll put my trust in you.'

She spent a minute or so stuffing her meagre possessions into a cotton sack, and then looped Reggie's basket over her arm and hoisted Reggie himself on to her hip. We were about to climb the steps to the pavement when a shadow of a man appeared against the sun, now low in the sky.

He was holding a cane, which he pointed at me. 'You again?'

I recognised his voice. It was the dandy, Coffey, who'd accused me of Drake's murder at the gaff.

Elspeth squinted up at him. 'What are you doing here, Nick?'

'I came to find you, of course. Why didn't you tell me where you'd be? I had to get it from your neighbour.' He tapped his cane on the top step. 'Took a bit of persuading.'

'You wasted your time,' I said firmly. 'She's coming with me.'

I ushered her towards the stairs, intending to guide her past Coffey before he could come down, but he blocked the gate.

'We need to talk, Elsie.' He sounded almost plaintive. 'Oswald's dead and he ain't coming back. I keep thinking I'll pop along and see him, but I can't. It's just you and me now.'

'I miss him too,' she replied. 'It's hard to believe I'll never hear his voice again. But there's no money, Nick, if that's what you're hoping. There's nothing. He was in debt up to the crown of his head.'

'It ain't that, honest it ain't.' His voice cracked a little and he wiped his face. 'I've had my eyes opened of late. I was living in his shadow is the truth, but there's a better world coming, and I'm going to be part of it.'

'What are you talking about? You're not part of any better world.' She gestured at his empty sleeve. 'You can't even scratch your nose and your backside at the same time.'

I couldn't see his expression, silhouetted as he was, so was surprised when he laughed. 'That's a good one, that is.

Scratch my nose and my backside, I'll have to remember that.' He beckoned to her to follow him. 'Come along. You don't want to stay with *him*, do you? He ain't one of us. You belong with your own, and Reggie too.'

'Where would we go?'

He shrugged. 'I got plans, Elsie. Don't you want to see?'

I caught her arm. 'What about my offer? The Home for Penitent Females will take you and Reggie in, I'm sure. There's no charge.'

She pulled her arm away. 'It's been my experience that there's always a charge, Mr Stanhope. Nothing's for nothing.' She slowly climbed the steps and handed her cotton bag to the dandy. 'All right, Nick, Let's see this better world you're talking about.'

I tried to follow her, but Coffey jumped down the steps, lifted his boot and thrust it into my chest, shoving me backwards through the still open doorway. My heel caught and I sprawled on to my behind, sending jolts of pain through my back. He followed me, raising his cane above his head, and I curled away from him, covering my face. But the blow never landed.

'Leave him, Nick,' I heard her say. 'He was trying to help. Let's just go.'

By the time I had got to my feet and climbed the steps again, they'd disappeared. The only creature in sight was a monkey, crouching in the centre of the street with its tail held high, scooping puddle water into its mouth.

13

I searched Elspeth's tiny room, which had space for a bed and a chest of drawers, or, strictly, *drawer*, as all but one were missing. Nothing was left except black mould and insects, so I took a cab home.

In my room, I lay on my bed, for once not resenting the trough that ran down the centre. I was, at least, warm and dry. But still, I was unable to get comfortable. My ribs seemed to be bruised rather than broken, but they hurt like hell. Worse, the sole of Coffey's boot had caught my right breast. When I unpeeled my binding I almost cried out.

Sleep would not come. Every part of me was aching, and my mind was consumed with concern for Elspeth Drake. She seemed to lack all faith in her future and had gone with Coffey willingly when he asked. Of course, she'd been willing to come with me too, so perhaps that's just how she was. Perhaps that's why Drake had married her; a biddable plaything who would do as she was told and could always be replaced if the mood took him. I wondered if she knew that. Probably she did; there wasn't much that girls who'd lived on the streets didn't know about men.

At dawn, I raised myself and squatted over my chamber pot, bent forward with my hands on the floor. It took me a further five minutes to stand up and another ten to wrap myself in a clean binding – my cilice, I called it, after the shirts worn as a penance by monks, though they should've tried strapping one over a bruised breast if they truly wanted to know what God's punishment felt like.

To cap it all, my monthly blood had arrived. As ever, I'd prepared a sanitary cloth in advance, but still my nightshirt was tainted with a stigmatic red smear.

I cleaned between my legs with cold water from the basin and used the same water to wash my nightshirt and cloth. By the time I came downstairs to where Constance was preparing breakfast, I felt as though something with teeth had hatched inside me and was trying to chew its way out.

Alfie handed me the morning's *Daily Chronicle*. 'Congratulations.'

There was my story, at the top of the second page, the first one after the advertisements. I would have glowed with pride, were I not crippled.

Constance snatched it from me and started reading. '"The *Daily Chronicle* has uncovered new evidence of the guilt of Sister Agnes Munro in the vicious murder of Oswald Drake at his wrestling club on the tenth of May." Gosh, Mr Stanhope, is this you? Did you really write this?'

'I did.'

I opted not to mention that it wasn't quite what I had written, the subeditors having excised the word 'brilliantly', before 'uncovered'.

She continued: "'Our correspondent was the only person permitted into the rooms at the Convent of Mercy, where he found a disguise and a hypodermic syringe hidden beneath a floorboard. Mr Drake was drugged with morphine prior to being hanged, so this new evidence will surely result in the conviction of Sister Agnes Munro, the Butcher of Berner Street.'"

Alfie put his hand out for the newspaper, a broad grin spreading across his face. 'My word, Leo. You're becoming quite a man of note, aren't you?'

I modestly demurred. 'I don't know about that.'

Constance seemed about to argue with me, but an acrid smell was emerging from her pan of porridge and she had to attend to that instead.

'Who's this fellow, Lampton?' asked Alfie, having turned the page of the newspaper.

'A politician.'

His eyes widened as he read. 'One who seems to have *opinions.*'

He said this rather in the manner one might say someone had scabies. Alfie cared little more about affairs of government than I did.

'That's what politicians do.'

Alfie shook his head. 'No, I mean he has opinions about this murder. He's quoted here.' He scanned down the page. 'I suppose he does have a point. I mean, it's not natural, is it, ladies wrestling.'

'Sister Agnes seemed quite good at it.'

He didn't look up from the newspaper. 'Look, I'm in favour of them being allowed to do more, I really am. There are ladies in my profession who I'd gladly hire to work on the female products. They're better at some things and men are better at others, and that's just how it is.'

Constance carved a lump of charred porridge from the pan and thumped it on to his plate.

'Breakfast,' she declared.

We ate in tense silence until Constance's curiosity got the better of her.

'You were asking about a syringe before, Mr Stanhope. Was it for this investigation?'

She seemed thrilled by the possibility.

'It was.'

I glanced a little nervously at Alfie, who had strict views on what his daughter should and should not be permitted to know about, which certainly excluded murder weapons. Fortunately, he was engrossed in a report about football.

'It was a wide needle then, like you thought?'

I had forgotten we'd discussed that topic.

'The hole in his skin may not have been made by a wide needle after all,' I explained. 'I now believe it was a narrow one, but waggled about.' I made the motion with my hand, as if stirring a cup of tea.

'Why on earth would the killer do that?' she asked.

Then Alfie did look up, frowning at the two of us in turn. 'I'm sure Mr Stanhope has to go to work now, don't you Leo?'

'Of course.'

I climbed gingerly to my feet.

'Are you all right?'

'Someone kicked me yesterday. Perils of being a man of note.'

Constance clicked her tongue. 'Let's get you something for the pain.'

She filled a cup with water and beckoned me to follow her into the pharmacy, closing the door behind us.

'I'm investigating Mrs Gower,' she whispered.

'What?'

'I'm quite certain she isn't as she appears. Did you know that her husband died with no money?'

'How could you possibly know that?'

'One of the clerks at the bank told me. He's a friend of mine.'

She busied herself stirring a teaspoonful of salicin into the cup and stood watching me drink it like a mother with a sickly child. It was ghastly stuff and made me shudder when I got to the dregs.

I wiped my mouth. 'Constance, you must desist. It isn't your business.'

'It *is* my business,' she said firmly. 'He's my father.' And then more loudly. 'There. You'll feel better soon, Mr Stanhope.'

———

I was late to the office. I'd made the mistake of returning to my bed for a few minutes to soothe the pain and ended up closing my eyes for an hour, so by the time I walked in, Mr Coxswain had already completed his first tea round. I eyed with envy the steaming cups and plates of shortbread biscuits on my colleagues' desks.

Before I could sit down, I was greeted by a fellow whose name I couldn't remember, if indeed I'd ever known it.

He punched me lightly on the shoulder, grinning broadly, taking no notice of my agonised groan.

'Stanhope! The man of the hour!'

I staggered to my desk and put my head in my hands, ignoring Harry, who was leaning back in his chair with his hands behind his head. Others were arriving at my desk too: reporters, copyboys and advertising men, all nodding and leering at me as though about to break into spontaneous applause.

'Two editions already,' said Harry.

'A third on its way,' added one of the men. 'Sold out everywhere. We've had to keep the lads back in case we need a fourth. Never needed a fourth before, not once.'

'Only seen *three* editions a couple of times,' said another fellow. 'Last time must be five years ago when Father Tooth got himself arrested.'

Harry rubbed his hands together. 'You've done it now, Leo. The Butcher of Berner Street has caught the public imagination.'

'You named her that, not me.'

He bowed with fake humility. 'My minor contribution to your masterpiece.'

J. T. joined the party, his mouth stretched into a shape I hadn't seen before: a smile. He vigorously shook my hand.

'Good work, Stanhope.'

I thanked him, and whether it was the glow of his approval or the salicin finally taking effect I couldn't have said, but the pain seemed to have dissipated almost completely.

After five minutes of merriment, including a fresh pot of tea and three shortbread biscuits fetched specially from the kitchen by Miss Chive, J. T. clicked his fingers at us, his expression sagging into a more familiar scowl.

'You've all got work to do. Best get back to it. Harry, you can take Stanhope with you.'

'To where?' I asked.

Harry picked a piece of paper off his desk and waved it at me. 'Lampton's people are handing out these flyers. He's going to give another speech, apparently, inciting the masses, that sort of thing.' He winked. 'Let's avoid getting thrown out this time, eh?' J. T. seemed about to ask what he meant by that, but Harry leapt to his feet. 'We mustn't be late. There's likely to be quite a crowd.'

When we got outside, he turned eastwards.

'Where is this speech?' I asked.

He pointed back over his shoulder. 'Whitehall.'

'Then why –?'

'It's not until this afternoon. I thought we could have a celebratory ale and pie in the meantime. It's a sin to sit around in the office on a lovely day like this.'

He was right, the sun was beating down on us. Gentlemen were coatless, some even in shirt sleeves, carrying their jackets over their arms. Ladies had dispensed with scarves in favour of open-necked frocks and straw hats.

The short walk to Rosie's shop raised my spirits and loosened my muscles. I was sure now that my ribs were only bruised, not broken, and even my right breast seemed to be recovering a little, though I had to walk with an unnatural, stilted gait to avoid my cilice chafing against my grazed skin.

As we emerged into the light from under the railway bridge at Ludgate Circus, Harry stopped and turned to me.

He seemed boyish and awkward, and I was reminded that he was younger than me by three or four years.

'Mrs Flowers is a widow, isn't she? Did you ever meet her husband?'

'I saw him, once. I spoke to him briefly, as I remember.'

No need to mention that Jack Flowers had been dead at the time.

Harry scratched his beard thoughtfully. 'Do you know if she has any suitors at the present?'

'I'm afraid I don't. We never talk about that sort of thing.' Though I couldn't imagine it. Where on earth would she find the time?

'Does she like going for walks, do you think?'

'Oh yes, she walks everywhere. Hates taking cabs. It's infuriating, quite honestly.'

His expression was one of frustration. I had the feeling I was missing his intent.

'I mean, would she like going for a walk *with me*? I was wondering about taking her to see the gardens at Kew. Some flowers for Mrs Flowers, that sort of thing. Would she be amused, do you think?'

'She might enjoy that, yes.'

I was aware that my tone was unhelpfully non-committal, but in truth I didn't know how to react. Rosie was … she was just Rosie. Always Rosie. She was like your favourite pair of shoes that might pinch once in a while, but will go with you on every journey, no matter how far. I was certain she wouldn't appreciate that comparison, but there was no higher compliment I could think of. I was her shoes too. I would go anywhere Rosie wanted to go; no hesitation, no equivocation.

Of course, I was dimly aware that she was a woman and might one day entertain romantic feelings towards a man. But Harry? All at once, I had a picture of it: the two of them among the buds and butterflies, arm in arm, leaning in to murmur a coy remark, sharing a joke and gazing into one another's eyes as they laughed. He was tall, was Harry, with blue-eyed charm and an easy smile. Women liked him. No matter how much he'd drunk the night before, he was always well groomed and quite rarely stank. But he wasn't what one might call *reliable*. He fell in love at the drop of a handkerchief and fell out of it just as quickly; almost as quickly as he fell out of bars, and with rather less of a hangover.

He gave me a concerned look, his head cocked to one side. 'I'm sorry, Leo. I thought you were simply friends. Do I have that wrong?'

I could have told him that Rosie had murdered two people, one she knew about and one she didn't, and I'd never told a soul about either of them. Or that she'd saved my life and I'd saved hers. I could even have used the shoes metaphor, but decided against it, especially as my actual shoes were taking in water like holed dinghies. In the end, I just clapped him on the shoulder.

'Of course we're simply friends. Come along, I'm getting hungry.'

Rosie herself was wedging open the door as we arrived, her first customers of the day. The plumes of steam flowed over us; heady meat and pumpkin, sweet pastry and sugared dates. I could have stood on the pavement for hours just breathing it in.

'We're dodging work,' I announced to her in as cheery a manner as I could muster. 'We decided we'd rather eat your pies than sit in the office.'

Harry added what was, to him, the more salient detail. 'And drink some ale.'

Her mouth was set flat, like a minus sign.

'You're proud to be taking a wage for doing nothing, are you?'

I suppose I had been a trifle insensitive. She had probably been baking since dawn.

'Believe me, I've earned it today. I've had a success. We're celebrating.'

'What would that be, then?'

'An article in the newspaper. You were wrong about that convent. Sister Agnes *is* the killer.'

We followed her into the shop, but rather than serve us, she went into the back. Alice appeared instead. She explained to Harry that his usual leek and ham pie hadn't been made that morning for some reason, and they spent several minutes exchanging opinions about fillings while I mused on what could have made Rosie so peevish. She had no right to be cross with me for taking an early lunch, and she *had* been wrong about the convent. Rather than stalking off with scarcely a word, I was of the opinion that she should apologise.

Harry bought us each a gammon and broccoli pie and a glass of ale, and Alice was giving him his change when Rosie came back into the shop. Under her arm, she was holding a copy of today's *Daily Chronicle*, which made her present incivility all the more remarkable. One might have expected her to congratulate me and perhaps offer us the ales on the house.

'This is your work, is it? Your *success*, did you call it?'

'Yes.'

Something in her expression made me think that congratulations were not about to be forthcoming.

'You've decided this Sister Agnes is guilty then. You called her a *butcher*.'

'We found compelling evidence.'

She nodded, but it wasn't agreement. It seemed more like confirmation of her low opinion.

'And you've presented it to her, I suppose? You've heard what she has to say about this evidence.'

I folded my arms. 'Yes, I have. All criminals claim they're innocent, Rosie.'

She looked at me as if I was the meanest creature on God's earth.

'She's a *nun*.'

'She's not actually a nun, she's a ...' I realised the point was probably moot and chose a different line of argument. 'I'm investigating every aspect of the story, believe me. I visited Drake's widow and she told me he'd spent all of their money. There's something peculiar going on at that gaff, I'm sure of it.'

She prodded at the newspaper. 'But this doesn't mention any of that.'

'I only found out yesterday evening. You clearly don't know how journalism works.' She frowned deeply, so I opted to explain. 'It's always a day out of date. We write the news one day and print it the next.'

'So, you wrote this *before* you knew all the facts? You're happy to write something untrue and change your mind later.'

I opened my mouth to speak, but no words came out.

Harry took a sip of his ale, watching the two of us. 'Seems she does know how journalism works after all.'

Rosie briefly narrowed her eyes at him, before turning back to me. 'You should be ashamed of yourself, Leo Stanhope, instead of standing there smirking like an idiot.'

'I'm not smirking.'

'You are smirking. You like to smirk when you think you're clever. But there's nothing clever about calling a woman a *butcher*.'

'I know.'

I glanced at Harry. After all, *the Butcher of Berner Street* was his idea. But he chose not to volunteer that information.

Rosie followed my look. 'And as for you, Mr Whitford, are you the co-author of this figment?'

He hastily shook his head. 'No, not at all. I wrote the article on page three about Mr Lampton. He's opposed to wives having financial independence, or any independence really.'

She nodded. 'Now there's a subject worth writing about. That bloody man telling women how they should behave. He's a pompous bully, is what he is.'

Harry smiled. 'I'm doing my best, Mrs Flowers. We were on our way to watch him speak this afternoon, and I'll be looking out for any sign of pomposity or bullying, I assure you.'

She turned back to me; her eyes fiery. 'There. You see? You can learn something from Mr Whitford.'

The sheer injustice of it was dumbfounding.

I could tell from Harry's smile, twitching his moustache at the corners, that he was about to press home his advantage. 'Actually, Rosie,' he said. 'It's a topic I'd love to discuss with you further. I was thinking we could go to Kew Gardens on Saturday evening, and you could tell me your ideas on the matter?'

She looked at him, her chest still heaving with rage at me, and I thought she would laugh bitterly or just shake her head. But she didn't. She drew herself up to her full almost five feet and shot me a single, piercing glare.

'Yes, Harry, I *would* like that very much.'

———

I insisted on taking a cab, pleading that my injuries demanded the gentlest treatment, and gazed out of the window as we described a gentle arc along the Strand, around Trafalgar Square and down Northumberland Avenue. There, we halted, and the driver called down to us that we could go no further because a crowd had gathered with, in his opinion, the specific intention of preventing hard-working cabbies from earning a living.

'I suppose this is it,' grunted Harry, and we got out.

The crowd was two hundred strong at least, and mostly men, spreading across the lawns of Whitehall Gardens and on to the Embankment itself, gathering in groups and leaning against the river railings, blocking anyone from walking past. One might have thought they were here for a picnic or some other pleasant diversion, but for the dourness of their faces and earnestness of their conversations. The fog was sitting heavy on the Thames, making the gardens seem other-worldly and isolated, an island set apart from the streets and houses of London. It was a world away from the cosy intimacy of the Beaconsfield Club.

'So many people.'

Harry laughed. 'It's a *movement* now. That's what makes it news. Come on.'

I followed him into the throng as he held up his card and barked 'reporters coming through' at anyone who got in his way. We joined our fellow gentlemen of the press at the point where the gravel paths intersected at the centre. They were a sallow-looking bunch in heavy coats despite the warm weather; evidence of their natural pessimism.

For half an hour or so, we performed that most typical of journalistic functions, we waited. In my case, I spent the time sitting on a bench, hunched over because, I told Harry, my bruises hurt like hell. This was partly true, but the greater agony was from the injury God had caused me: the cramping from my monthly blood. I could scarcely keep myself from curling up on the ground. It was not normally this bad, and I wondered whether He was punishing me more than usual. Perhaps my article accusing a Sister of Mercy of murder had vexed Him.

Eventually, a murmur flowed through the crowd and Lampton appeared, flanked by two large fellows, one of them the upmarket thug who'd tossed Harry and me out of the Beaconsfield Club. They processed to the centre of the gardens, accompanied by whooping and cheering as if Lillie Langtry herself had arrived wearing nothing but her underclothes. Lampton raised his arms for quiet and was about to speak, when I noticed two familiar figures in the crowd: a man in a silk top hat and a lady in a black taffeta dress and black bonnet, a veil covering her face and a bundle held in her arms. The man was the last to finish cheering, and I realised he was Nicholas Coffey, his expression agog, drinking in the moment like a rosebud opening in the sunshine.

And the woman was Elspeth Drake.

14

I STARED AT ELSPETH, willing her to notice me, but she seemed entirely preoccupied with baby Reggie, who was wrapped in a woollen shawl. At least she seemed to be safe and in good health. I couldn't imagine what she was doing here.

Lampton held up his hand for silence.

'Thank you!' he shouted. 'What I have to say is extremely important. All of our futures are at stake.'

He waited for further applause, but the limitations of the location quickly became clear; even on such a still day, a man's voice would scarcely carry much further than the inner path. Perhaps an especially broad-chested fellow might do better, but Lampton was not that fellow; he was wan and slight, with shoulders as narrow as my own. Anyone more than thirty yards away couldn't hear a word he was saying, so rather than a rapturous roar, as he no doubt expected, the clapping moved backwards through the crowd like ripples on a pond.

But still, I had the feeling that the assembly was less interested in what he actually said than the fact that he was there. I watched their eyes. They were transfixed.

Lampton thumbed over his shoulder. 'Behind me in Scotland Yard, a woman is housed of such unnatural constitution that she denied her very being. Can you imagine? She wore the mantle of a godly person living a dutiful life, but all the while she was harbouring a secret. For there is no goodness in her. She murdered a man, an honest and successful man, in the most hideous fashion. She drugged him and she hanged him not three miles from this spot. Well has she been called the Butcher of Berner Street.'

Lampton stepped back, nodding, as the cheers welled up around us.

I felt sick.

The other journalists were scrawling in their notebooks at a rapid rate, occasionally sucking on their pencils or scratching their beards.

'In truth, she's scarcely a woman at all,' continued Lampton, his voice reedy and straining. 'She is a horror. A monster. A goliath.'

'And a Catholic!' yelled one of the men at the front.

'Indeed.' Lampton nodded as though the thought hadn't previously occurred to him. 'And a Catholic. So grotesque is she that ... well, it's hardly a surprise.' He rolled his hands as if winding wool. 'I won't say what I think.'

His audience shouted their encouragement and the man at the front yelled: 'Go on!'

The baying grew in volume – both men and women – until Lampton laughed and held up his hands in surrender. 'Very well, I will say this. She would not be my first choice for an evening. May I leave it at that?'

The audience hooted wildly. Fellows with glasses of ale clinked them together.

Lampton appeared buoyed by the response and reached out as if to embrace the whole crowd. 'Or the second or third, if I'm honest. In fact, if God saw fit to expunge every woman in England but her, I would sooner be celibate!'

This was met with such uproarious gaiety that I was unable to hear his next few sentences despite being no more than a few feet away. Men were slapping each other's backs and loudly concurring, even those from different parts of society – patched jackets and flat caps gloating like old friends with frock coats and bowler hats – their wet mouths agape for the next belly laugh. I felt as if I could pass among them unnoticed like a wisp of smoke.

Lampton paused for quiet, his fingers fluttering.

'He isn't using a script,' Harry whispered to me. 'We can't get a copy of his speech later, so we'll have to write it down as he talks and compare notes afterwards. You can't stand there daydreaming, Leo.'

'I'm not.'

'You are. This isn't an announcement about postage stamps, or whatever it is you usually do. He's a national figure.'

I opened my notebook again. I hadn't yet written a single word.

Lampton shook his head sadly. 'I don't blame that blighted woman. It was not her fault. How could it be?' He gazed up and down the street, catching the eye of several of his audience. 'She is but one part of a greater sin, a poison in our nation. I speak, of course, of women claiming the rights and roles of men. We all know the Lord's will in this. He gave men the authority for a reason, knowing that the female mind was gentle and subject to vagaries of temperament, moved always by pity rather than strength. Her body, through God's holy design, is likewise weak and soft, the better to birth and nurse children, to thrive within a purely domestic sphere. Without masculine authority, she is a slave to her basest emotions. We must return this nation to Christian values. It is our duty as men.'

The fellows around me had started to grow agitated. The laugh-along cheers from the start of the speech were hardening into angry shouts. A young constable standing near us took a tighter grip on his billy club.

A sharp squeeze of my insides forced a groan out of my mouth.

'Are you all right?' hissed Harry.

I nodded and made my first notation: *Our duty as men? What does that mean?*

Harry looked over my shoulder. 'It doesn't mean anything, just sounds commanding. He's an opportunist, that's all.'

'This,' continued Lampton, 'is the danger we all face. It is unconscionable. Do you realise that if the Bill shortly to be placed before the House passes, wives will be held responsible for their own debts? Can you imagine?'

He paused again, glaring at the crowd, one or two of whom – those with an ounce more intellect or who hadn't been indulging in quite so much ale – seemed to be considering the pros and cons. Perhaps the idea of their wives, rather than themselves, being dragged off to debtors' prison wasn't as unappealing as Lampton was hoping. Even the drunker members of the audience were growing restless; the part about the giant murderess had been rollicking fun straight from the penny dreadfuls, but these legislative niceties held far less interest.

Lampton seemed to realise that his own obsessions weren't shared by the common men and women. He clapped his hands together. 'Well, I must get back to the House. Rest assured, I will work tirelessly to turn back the tide of depravity in this country.'

The crowd shouted his name and clapped their hands above their heads as he strode away towards Westminster.

No sooner had he left than, to everyone's surprise, another voice rang out. 'Ladies and gentlemen!' It was Nicholas Coffey, waving his satin opera hat. 'Ladies and gentlemen! If I might add to the words of the good Mr Lampton, I would like to present to you the two contrasting visions of womanhood.' The crowd turned to face him, displaying the kind of indifferent curiosity borne of having nothing better to do. 'As my good friend said, behind us in jail we have the monster, the butcher, who cruelly took the life of the best man I've ever known, Oswald Drake. She's destined for the rope. While here, in our company, we have her opposite in every way.' He took Elspeth Drake's arm and pulled her next to him. She resisted, seeming unprepared for the sudden attention, but he gripped her harder. 'Look upon the angel to the butcher's devil, a picture of everything that's good and right in womanhood. The widow of Oswald Drake!' He pulled back her veil, and she hunched her shoulders, staring left and right, hugging Reggie closer. The men watching were oblivious to her discomfort, craning their necks as though she might be about to perform a dance for their benefit. One of them whistled.

'Let's go,' Harry hissed at me. 'This is nonsense.'

'No. I want to hear what he has to say.'

Coffey took a deep breath, casting his hand across the crowd as if scattering seeds. 'See how gentle she is? How compliant? How motherly she is towards little Reginald, now half orphaned by the unnatural bloodlust of a killer. Who would you rather come home to, my friends, after a hard day's labour? Her or the Butcher? A wifely kiss and a pleasant meal on the table, or a knife in your belly while you sleep?'

This was met with a half-hearted cheer. A fellow near me, who'd been drinking steadily since we arrived, shouted out: 'You're a faker! She's a dollymop from the docks!'

Elspeth drew in a sharp breath and cast a fierce glare at Coffey, seeming on the brink of giving him a piece of her mind. But he didn't take any notice.

'No, no, no! She really is Drake's widow. It was a tragedy her husband was taken from her so suddenly, so brutally. Hanged by the neck, thrashing and bleeding, yet unable to free himself or cry out for help. Can you imagine the agony and terror? Can you picture the scene? Well, ladies and gentlemen, you are in luck.'

Several conversations broke out at once, and Coffey was unable to make himself heard. The general view seemed to be that a pitch was coming, and we needed to hold on tightly to our wallets. One fellow muttered that Coffey probably had a dozen such widows in different parts of London, all ready to play their part.

'I can prove every word!' Coffey yelled. 'The very gaff where the murder took place will be reopening tonight. You will lay eyes upon the exact spot where Mr Drake took his last breath. His blood is still wet on the boards and the Butcher's rosary beads are still scattered across the floor.

The stink of death hangs in the air.' A surprised murmur went through the crowd. Impressed looks were exchanged. 'Berner Street in Whitechapel. Doors open at eight o'clock sharp for a tour, with three wrestling bouts to follow for your amusement and wagering. No ladies allowed and no bringing your own ale.'

This was the last straw for Elspeth, who had clearly not expected to form the centrepiece of Coffey's advertisement. She tore her arm from his grasp and cuffed him across the head, knocking off his hat. Little Reggie immediately woke up and began to wail with the kind of volume and potency Lampton could only envy. Elspeth stormed away, and Coffey picked up his hat and followed her, going red in the face as the catcalls rang around the gardens.

'Where are you going?' Harry called after me. 'We should leave together. We have to compare notes.'

I didn't reply. I was fixated on the sound of Reggie's diminishing wails and the sight of Coffey's opera hat bobbing among the bowlers and caps.

The wind had picked up, and squalls were chasing each other along the river among the ships and dinghies. On the opposite bank, the wharves hunched fatly like crows who'd eaten their fill of carrion, and above my head the unlit streetlamps were buzzing as if a million bees were trapped inside.

I spotted Coffey and Elspeth ahead of me. He had caught up with her and now had his arm linked with hers, so they seemed much like any other couple out for an evening stroll, unless you looked closely. He wasn't accompanying her; he was forcing her along. I hurried to catch up, trying to keep the loose soles of my shoes from slapping on the pavement.

They were almost at the junction of Northumberland Avenue when a grocery cart lurched around the corner and Elspeth bolted out in front of it, baby Reggie in her arms. I turned away, imagining them both crushed beneath the hooves and wheels. I'd seen it happen once before, a boy not looking where he was going, stepping out into the street. He didn't even have time to cry out.

Elspeth was luckier, ducking sure-footedly under the animal's head and dashing out of sight. Coffey was caught unawares. He attempted to pursue her, but had to negotiate the cart and its horse, now blocking the street, so by the time he reached the pavement on the other side, all he could do was stand and scratch his head, turning each way in turn.

I lowered my bowler over my eyes and strode as quickly as I could without doubling over from the grabbing pain in my lower belly.

Near the bridge, the path grew crowded with fellows proposing various entertainments, gambling and dancing, the noisiest of them offering couples trips up and down the Thames on his rowing boat – guaranteed to soften a lady's heart, he promised. I tried to dodge past him, but he stood in my way, explaining with a wink that, for an unaccompanied gentleman such as myself, he could supply a romantic partner for a very reasonable fee, noting that he faced backwards while pulling on the oars and so would be unaware of any goings-on provided they didn't get too energetic and cause a capsize.

By the time I'd convinced him I wasn't interested, Coffey and Elspeth had gone. Worse, my pains were chewing at me from within as though I was trying to pass an undigested thistle. A few dozen yards further on, there was a bench, and I staggered towards it, gathering my jacket tightly around me, planning to lie down for a while, or possibly for ever. That was where I found Elspeth Drake, hunched forwards, tears falling silently into Reggie's blankets.

She noticed me coming towards her and jumped up, hastening south again along the pavement. I followed her as she threaded her way between other pedestrians, occasionally looking back over her shoulder. We made a strange pair, hunter and prey, me groaning at my cramps and bruises and her in full mourning weeds, including a veil, carrying a baby that had started wailing again, a siren anyone could have located with their eyes shut.

She took a sudden left turn at the Whitehall Stairs and I spotted her bonnet as it disappeared below the level of the parapet alongside the river. I rushed to the spot and was relieved to see a tidal beach where the red fireboat was slumbering on one chine, grounded on the stones.

Elspeth was trapped. The beach narrowed to nothing at either end where the river lapped against the wall. She hesitated at the bottom of the steps and looked up. I suffered a rush of fear that she'd make good on her threat to swim out with Reggie and drown both of them, but instead she slowly climbed the steps again and stood in front of me, her expression both resolute and exhausted.

I was struck again by how small she was, and how young. With her veil pulled back, her skin was the colour of peroxided bone and her eyes were like slate, as if God had intended to make them blue but had run out of ink. Her arms, enfolding Reggie against her meagre chest, nowhere near filled her sleeves, which hung like tents come adrift from their guys. She was little more than a child, with a child in her arms.

Reggie was giving it full blast, so we had to shout over the racket, attracting some strange looks from passers-by.

'What do you want, Mr Stanhope?'

'Just to talk to you. Can we sit down?'

I indicated a bench under a streetlamp, as though inviting her to tea in my own parlour. She followed me and sat very neatly at the other end, both of us looking out over the river.

'I'm very popular these days. When Oswald was alive, no one noticed me.'

I wondered if she preferred not being noticed. She'd married a charismatic man, and life in his shadow must have felt very safe for a former street urchin.

'People are angry about his murder. In a way, that must be a comfort.'

'Must it?' She rolled her eyes. 'They seem more ghoulish than angry.'

'I'm not a ghoul, I'm a journalist.' Some part of my mind was laughing at that. 'And you're poor and desperate.'

She lifted her chin. 'Not at all. I'm due to inherit a fortune from my Great Aunt Beth, who a has a big house in Surreyshire. But the woman refuses to die. She's a hundred and forty now and still goes riding on her pony every day.'

'What an inspiring tale.'

'Isn't it?'

I didn't have time for this jibing. In the distance, bells were ringing for four o'clock, and I was on a deadline.

'Do you think I know so little of your life? Is that why you taunt me with silly stories?'

She looked away, to where the steamboats were chugging and growling against the docks, their voices so deep I didn't so much hear them as feel them through my feet.

'I see what you are, Mr Stanhope, with your newspaper and your fine clothes and your education. You're a sightseer. You watch us, you judge us and then you leave.' She rocked her son gently as he fell quiet. 'We don't need pity from people like you.'

I folded my arms, unsure whether she was right. Was I just a sightseer? I decided I would think about it later, and then realised that was precisely what a sightseer would do.

'Very well. No pity then. Why did you run away from Mr Coffey just now?'

She shrugged and shook her head. 'I've known Nick Coffey a long time. We're the same, him and me. You wouldn't understand.' She hugged Reggie closer. 'He used to be a good man, in his own way, but Oswald's death changed him, 'specially as it was someone he knew who did it. He liked Irina well enough and never guessed she was a killer.'

'In what way has he changed?'

She bit her lip, unsure whether to tell me. Eventually, she sighed. 'He thinks ladies have overstepped. He says he's going to reopen the gaff and be like Oswald used to be. A big man, you know. But he can't do it, can he? By rights, the gaff should be mine.'

'Coffey and your husband were close, weren't they? How did you meet them?'

She gave me a wan little smile. 'That's no secret. I was thirteen and my friend Peggy was twelve. We sneaked into a show together.' Her face brightened a little. 'It was magical; clowns, jugglers, trapezes and all sorts. Nick was taking tickets on account of his hand, though he'd been an acrobat before. Did you know that? He grabbed me and I thought he'd throw us out, but he sat us in the front row, best view in the house. Oswald was a strongman, bending bars and lifting barrels above his head. He was so handsome; me and Peggy both thought so. He invited us back the next day and gave us food and somewhere to lay our heads. We was very grateful.'

'And did Drake … did he demand anything from you in return?'

She shrugged, as unbothered as if I'd asked whether she liked sugar in her tea. 'It was a small price to pay. No price at all for me. I became his wife and I miss him every minute.'

She seemed sincere, almost tearful, talking of the man who'd molested her at the age of thirteen.

'What about your friend Peggy? Was she …'

But I couldn't continue. A pool of blackness had opened up in front of me, pulling me downwards. I could almost taste the oil in the water. Always it was this way; a word, a smell, a drop of sweat, a slanting shadow on an attic wall. Or a sudden realisation. At that second, I knew as certainly as I knew my own name that her friend had been molested too, just as Elspeth had. This was what Sister Agnes had hinted at; Drake abused the girls who slept under his roof.

'Are you feeling all right?' Elspeth was peering at me. 'You came over all queer.'

'Yes, thank you.'

She nodded, but it wasn't exactly sympathy. More a kind of fellow feeling.

I gathered my jacket closer to my chest. 'Where is Peggy now?'

She took a few seconds to reply, blinking back tears. 'Peggy's dead. She died of seizures a few months back.'

'Oh. I'm very sorry.' It was an impossible question, but I needed confirmation. 'And the other girls in the gaff? Did your husband … demand a price from them too?'

'I think I've answered enough questions.' She set her mouth tightly and stood up. 'I have to leave now. I'm expected.'

'Who's expecting you? And what about the other girls? Please tell me.'

'Goodbye, Mr Stanhope.'

She turned to walk away, and I followed her. 'Elspeth, I can still help you and Reggie. That place at the Home for Penitent—'

A male voice broke into our conversation. 'Are you in need of assistance, madam?'

He was a stout fellow, I would guess in his forties, accompanied by an equally stout wife. Both were eyeing me with suspicion.

Elspeth gave them a pretty curtsy. 'Only a few coins, sir. I needed to get home and asked this gentleman if he would be so kind. He was telling me what he wanted in exchange for helping me, using words I've only heard before in the mouths of navvies. I was shocked, if I'm honest, and my poor Bertram's only been in the ground three months.'

The fellow turned towards me, his whiskers bristling. His wife put a sympathetic hand on Elspeth's arm.

'None of that is true,' I said. 'Not a word.'

But I could tell they'd already made up their minds.

'How much do you need?' asked the fellow, steering Elspeth towards Westminster.

The last thing I heard her say before she disappeared from earshot was: 'Two shillings should be enough, sir, though half a crown would be a boon, to buy some food for little Timmy. We ain't eaten in a week.'

I sighed and started walking in the opposite direction, northwards towards my office. I had less than an hour to get there, write my article and submit it. I was so preoccupied that I didn't hear footsteps behind me until I felt the prick of a blade against my back.

A voice hissed into my ear: 'Where is she? Tell me now or I'll open you up like a fish.'

Coffey propelled me along the pavement, leaning into me as if we were pals who'd had too much to drink. I could smell the gin and peppermint on his breath.

The point of the knife had penetrated through my jacket and shirt and was pressing against the hardier fabric of my cilice. One small push and the blade would pierce my skin. Just stopping suddenly would probably be enough. I kept walking, watching my step on the paving.

'Where is she?' he asked again. 'What have you done with her?'

'Do you mean Mrs Drake?' My voice was quivering and pitching upwards. 'We spoke, that's all. I tried to help her, but she left with two strangers.'

Surely, I thought, he can't kill me here, with so many people around us. I might be better served by refusing to go any further, daring him to stab me, rather than being led obediently away to die in some alley.

But I wasn't brave enough.

I felt the pressure in my back ease and then disappear. Coffey wiped his empty sleeve across his face.

'She shouldn't be on her own,' he mumbled. 'It's not safe. I only want to know she's all right.'

'She seems able to look after herself.'

He gave me a look that said he thought me naïve and foolish. 'You don't get it. Underneath all that jibber-jabber, she's frightened of her own shadow. If it wasn't for me, she'd be …' he stopped himself and closed his eyes. 'It's like Mr Lampton says. Ladies need the help of a gentleman to shore up their delicate natures.'

I'd just seen Elspeth Drake extract half a crown from a stranger as neatly as a starling pecks a caterpillar out of a log. Her nature seemed anything but delicate. And what of Rosie and Constance and my sister Jane and the only girl I had ever loved, with curly hair, a mark on her face like black-berry juice and heels that thump thump thumped against the frame of the bed? Not one of them possessed a delicate nature as far as I could tell. Not to mention Sister Agnes.

'You saw the wrestling. Did Irina Vostek seem weak to you?'

Coffey rolled his eyes. 'She's not as strong as she looks, believe me. Making women wrestle is an offence against God.'

He shoved me away, slipping the knife quickly into his pocket, though not before I could see its design, which was stubby and brutal, fitting between the fingers of his fist like a corkscrew. If he had punched me, I would have been gouged to shreds.

'What will you do now?' I asked him.

He bit his lip, looking both ways along the pavement. 'I'm reopening the gaff tonight. Come along if you want.'

He had the decency to look sheepish. 'I hope you'll forgive me my hastiness just now. No hard feelings. I'm worried about Elsie, that's all. It's men like us have to look out for girls like her.'

He puffed out his chest and some perverse part of me was tempted to tell him the truth about myself. It would be suicide, but in the brief second before he stuck me with that knife, I would enjoy seeing his expression.

He turned to go, but something was still bothering me.

'Wait! Mr Coffey!' He looked round with a furtive glance, and I had the impression he didn't like his name being used in public. 'Mr Coffey,' I repeated more loudly, getting my small revenge. 'What you said about Irina Vostek – Sister Agnes – being weaker than she looks. What did you mean by that?'

He picked at his tooth, clearly wondering whether to tell me. 'Her wrist,' he said eventually. 'She has a sprain that won't heal. It swells up like a spud and I have to drain and bandage it after every fight. Tender as a flower and no use in the ring at all. But she's clever, see; favours her other hand and kicks hard and quick, finishing her opponents before they work it out.' He held up his sleeve. 'She can no more clap than I can.'

I watched him go, weaving nimbly through the early evening crowds, while my mind fumbled with this new information.

If Sister Agnes only had one strong hand, how did she hang a man from a rope?

———

Following the arrest of Sister Agnes Munro, fresh evidence has emerged concerning the affairs of Mr Oswald Drake, which casts his murder into a new light. Far from being a man of fine qualities, as some have insisted, Mr Drake was significantly indebted. Since his death, his penniless widow has been evicted from her home at eighteen years of age, with their infant son in her arms. It seems likely that, prior to their marriage, she was one of many poor girls he allowed to sleep in his property, for reasons I am sure our astute readers can surmise.

On Thursday, Mr Frederick Lampton, the Conservative Member of Parliament for Chippenham, gave a speech in Westminster condemning Sister Agnes Munro in the strongest terms, garnering strong support from onlookers, estimated at over two hundred men and women. What are we to make of this new

'Leo?'

I looked up from my typewriter at Harry, his face too close for comfort. His lips were moving as he read over my shoulder.

'Your first sentence is quite wrong,' he declared. 'To start with, you've called her by her name and title, which is far too dull. No one's afraid of a nun. Call her the Butcher of Berner Street. And "arrest" is too civilised as well. Following the *capture* of the Butcher of Berner Street, new evidence has … no, not "emerged", it sounds like something washed up at low tide. Our reporter has discovered, no, *uncovered* new evidence – you see how much better that is? – that Mr Oswald Drake was not as saintly as some, such as Mr Frederick Lampton, Conservative Member of Parliament for Chippenham, et cetera, et cetera.' He nodded, agreeing with his own corrections. 'You have to grab their interest right away, you see? Force them to read on.'

I folded my arms. 'I'm starting to think she might be innocent.'

'So? It's not up to us to decide who's guilty and who isn't. Our part is to inform the public of the facts. Except the public has the attention span of a kitten, so we dress it up a bit. Better they read something rather than nothing, wouldn't you say?'

I shrugged. 'I suppose so.'

The gap between *dressing it up a bit* and outright lying was narrow indeed. Harry didn't share my concerns.

'Of course it is.' He clicked his fingers, dismissing the entire question in a single gesture. 'Where did you run off to yesterday, anyway?'

'I wanted to talk to the widow.'

'And leave me to write up Lampton's boring speech? Very clever. I suppose you'll get the top story again and my piece will have to go underneath. I'm just your opening act these days.' He smoothed his hair over his ears theatrically and spoke to an imaginary person to his left. 'Yes, I used to work with Sir Leo Stanhope long before he became wealthy and famous. Back then he was a humble science reporter who couldn't write a decent first paragraph and never finished his book reviews. Now, only interviews with Prime Ministers and Princes are worthy of his time.'

'I have to finish this.'

I started typing again, hammering on the keys as loudly as I could.

He grinned and continued his pretend interview, this time at greater volume. 'In those days, Mr Stanhope had a sense of humour, sadly now drained away to nothing. I remember one occasion when he replaced the cheese in a bread roll belonging to the then Assistant Editor, Mr Terence Aubyn, with a large dollop of potted herring, causing the aforementioned Mr Aubyn to come out in an allergic rash.'

'That was you, Harry.'

'You were my accomplice. In fact, it was you who supplied the noxious substance.'

Mr Aubyn had been self-important and choleric, and he deserved a little pricking. We had conspired together in whispers before executing our plan to perfection. I didn't feel guilty. Just for that afternoon, I was one of those rascal boys, getting up to ruses and dodging the blame, just like Harry, who possessed an impish capacity for coaxing other people into mischief.

I wondered what would Rosie do when the full power of his charm was turned upon her?

He sat forward, becoming serious. 'What's wrong, Leo? You look like you've lost a bet. Are you worried about Sister Butcher?'

'I am. There's more to this murder than meets the eye. I believe Drake beat his wife and molested the girls who slept in the gaff. Frankly, I'm beginning to think he deserved what he got.'

I finished the article and submitted it. The subeditor, Horace, read the whole thing in front of me, grumbling about junior reporters who lacked the sense to pick a nickname for a murderer and stick with it. Afterwards, I went to the privy and changed my sanitary cloth, folding the old one and drop-ping it into the waxed paper bag I'd brought with me.

At five o'clock, I dashed out of the door before anyone could argue.

The walk was brisk in the early summer rain. I lifted my jacket over my head and stepped over the puddles, trying to avoid the washes of muddy water cast at knee height by passing carriage wheels. My shoes were leaking worse than ever, and I was squelching loudly by the time I reached Jacob's house, ironically on Shoe Lane.

There was a time when we spent every Thursday evening at our chess club; thirty or forty men hunched in smoke so thick so you could scarcely find your way back to your board from the bar. We used to drink ale and whisky, play chess and laugh so hard we couldn't draw air back into our lungs. I still enjoyed his company, but our contests lacked variety these days. Even the finest steak can become tedious if it's all one has to eat, and Jacob's game was not the finest steak.

Again, it was young Eddie who opened the door. He greeted me politely, enquiring after my health and reply-ing, when asked, that he too was quite well despite the damp weather. I fervently wished that he hadn't chosen to construct this carapace of adulthood around himself at twelve years of age. I would rather he had raged and screamed at God and the world for taking his little brother from him.

Lilya and Millicent were cutting dough into rolls, a regu-lar delight since they'd acquired their own oven, an iron beast crouching in the corner blasting heat and smoke into the room. Not being one to remove my jacket in company, I had no choice but to suffer and sweat.

'Leo!' exclaimed Lilya, holding my shoulders in her floury hands.

'How are you?'

She gave me a bleak smile, her irises flicking from side to side behind the mist. 'I continue. That is all. Today, tomorrow. Afterwards, who knows?'

She sometimes claimed that she could still see things: long-dead faces, faraway houses and a donkey she'd once ridden, as whole and real as when she was a girl. She once asked me if I thought these visions could have been sent by the angels because she was blind. Perhaps everyone received them, she suggested, these gifts from heaven, but the light shone too brightly in most people's eyes for them to see. I replied that it might be so, but I was lying. They were nothing more than hallucinations created by her brain to make sense of her newly blank world. But they comforted her. Who was I to take that away?

'You will have dinner with us, Leo, yes? Perhaps persuade that old fool, my husband, who is a blessing every day, to raise his lazy backside from his bed and eat at the table. He has two children here who miss him.'

Millicent and Eddie exchanged a look that I chose not to interpret.

'Of course. I'll see what I can do.'

Lilya slammed her ball of dough down on to the board. 'He sleeps and I make bread. Every day the same. I throw away half the bread because he will not eat it. He will not eat anything. He will not repair jewellery. He will not go out.' She pinched her nose and spoke in an adenoidal drone. 'He will not wash himself. He is disgusting.'

I was not overbrimming with optimism. Jacob was as stubborn as an ulcer.

He was lying on the coverlet facing the door.

'Ah!' His voice was dry and thin. 'Is it Thursday already?'

I nodded, thinking that Lilya had been right; the room needed airing and everything in it needed boiling, including Jacob. It wasn't the chamber pot – I assumed Millicent took care of that – it was the stench of indolent humanity that filled my nostrils; bedclothes saturated with sweat, and underclothes stained grey and, in places, yellow, hanging off his bones like a half-shed snakeskin.

'Lilya wants you to come down for dinner.'

He flicked his hand impatiently. 'She thinks it's important for me to do these things. Breakfast and dinner and work. She thinks it will solve everything. It will not.' He sat up, wiggling his bare toes, scratching his overlong nails across the floorboard. 'Will you be white or black?' He didn't wait for a reply but pulled the table towards him and started setting out the pieces, making himself white. 'Now, tell me, what do they have you working on? The usual dull stuff, or has Charles Darwin discovered something new? Are we all descended from frogs now?'

'No, nothing new from Darwin. Neither will there be. He's dead.'

By my reckoning this was the fourth time I'd told Jacob this news, and yet he seemed no less surprised each time.

'Oh! Well, that is unfortunate. Such an intelligent man.'

He moved his queen's pawn two squares forward in a standard opening. It had been some time since we'd actually finished a game and I held little hope that this one would be any different, but still I matched him with my own pawn. Perhaps, I thought, I should play deliberately badly. He might find some pleasure in remembering that our contests could be won or lost.

'For Lilya's sake,' I reminded him gently, 'you could make more effort.'

'And you're the person to advise me of this, are you? You will instruct me what I should do for her sake, for your sake, for everyone's sake. All except mine. My sake does not count. This much we know already.'

It was an old argument, oft repeated but never concluded.

'I've apologised already, Jacob. You blame me for not coming more often when Albie died, and you're right. I was still recovering, but ...' I put a hand to my cheek. It was hard and unfeeling, glazed by the flames. 'I know I was selfish. I regret it very much now.'

He moved his king's knight and I matched him. He quickly moved his queen's pawn two spaces forward and scratched his head, cascading dry skin on to the board.

'A little understanding is all I want. You spend your time worrying about ...' he swept a finger up and down. 'About what you are, who you are, whether you have this part or that part. Believe me, when you're old it ceases to matter. Everything shrinks and sags. Do you think Lilya is the same as she once was, with bosoms like puppydogs straining at the leash? Goodness, she was *magnificent*. Now, you can hardly tell the difference between us unclothed.'

'She's still beautiful,' I said. 'And it's much to her advantage that she no longer has eyes to see what *you* look like.'

'Hm, perhaps. Fortunate for us both.' He licked his lips. 'What I'm saying, Leo, is that you think too much about yourself. All the time, like an obsession. What you *lack*, rather than what you *have*. I would have thought … no, let us just play. Whose move is it?'

I felt a coldness creeping across my skin. I was well used to Jacob's critiques – my impulsiveness, my diffidence, my choice of profession – but this felt different. He seemed to be *angry*. Rather to my own surprise, I realised I would give a great deal to regain his high opinion of me.

'What were you going to say?'

'You're like my own child. You know this.'

'Yes. I'm always honoured.'

He held up one finger. 'My child, but not my son, hmm? Not anyone's son.' He met my eyes, peering under the bushes of his eyebrows. 'Don't look at me that way. It's still a woman's blood that flows in your veins, and I would've thought …' he ran his hand across his hair. 'You know. I would've thought you'd possess a woman's *consideration*. A little gentleness, to take care of an old friend. Instead, you seem determined to prove yourself as tough and heartless as any man.'

'Jacob …'

I stood up, unsure what I was intending to do next. Had anyone else spoken to me in that way, I would've walked out and probably never come back. But Jacob was Jacob. After I'd been burned, before Albie became ill, he visited me every second day with fruit tarts and cakes, cutting them into tiny pieces when my throat was too raw to swallow anything larger. He fetched my ointment, fixed the bandages on my hand and even gave me a new bowler hat to replace the one that was lost, with a high crown and narrow brim just like the old one. He'd shown far more consideration than I ever had.

He looked out of the window, his chin beginning to wobble.

'You know I don't care what you are, what you wear. I don't ask why or when. Leave if you must. I don't need you. None of this is your business.'

'Of course, it's my business. You're like a father to me, far more so than my real father ever was. You can't drive me away just because you're stricken by grief.'

He gave a petulant shrug. 'It would be better if you went. I have things to do.'

He cast a swift, guilty look at the drawer in his little table, where the box of chess men was kept when they weren't being used. I followed his eyes, and he reddened. I shot out a hand for the drawer and he tried to stop me, but I was quicker and stronger. I pulled it open, and inside was a cigar box.

'What's in this, Jacob?'

But he wouldn't reply.

I emptied the contents on to the chess board: a brass hypodermic syringe and a paper bag half full of white crystals. I put a few grains on my finger and tasted them. They were as sour as lemon rind.

'This is morphine,' I said.

He closed his eyes. 'Perhaps it is. I forget.'

I glared at him, infuriated. I had declined all morphine and chloral when I was recovering from my burns, not wanting to sink again into that black water. I could well remember how it was; phantasms of men with wolves' heads and a ghastly humming I couldn't abide. I would rather remain conscious and suffer the agony. And now here was Jacob, using the stuff to escape into nightmares of his own, avoiding the truth that his precious boy was dead and there was nothing anyone could do about it.

But in truth, what would I do, I wondered, if Aiden or Ciara or Constance were taken from me that way, by a sickness that lasted a mere four days from the first cough to the last breath? I would be the first to reach for a syringe. Damn it, I would be standing on Westminster Bridge where my name waited for me still, scratched into the paintwork under the handrail. I could almost hear the roar of the river and feel the wind against my face, the sudden rush and the slam of water shutting out the sky.

I sat down.

'Please, Jacob, let's just play chess like we used to. I miss those days. It's your move.'

———

When I got home, much later that evening, I emptied my pockets on to my bed: a cigar case containing a syringe and a bag of morphine.

For a few seconds, I felt overwhelmed by temptation. I almost did it. My hand was on the bag and my mind was calculating exactly where in the pharmacy Alfie kept his pure alcohol. How sweetly the crystals would dissolve and how easily I could slide that liquid into my veins.

I turned back before I reached my bedroom door.

If I injected myself with morphine, I would be lost. There would be no coming back a second time.

I lay down, listing all the names I'd taken for myself, trying not to think about how it would feel, not to feel.

I started at the beginning this time. The first name always made me shudder; Tom Cobb, that desperate lad. Next, I was Thomas Manly and almost went to debtors' prison, saved by my sister, Jane. Then George Harding, Maurice Jackson and Maurice Stanhope, a surname borrowed from the London street. I liked that it included the word 'hope'. And then one day I went to the menagerie on the Strand and saw a toothless lion with drool in its mane and fur like an old curtain. But you could see how he might have been in his prime: a taut mass of muscle and death. The sign called him: *Panthera Leo*, and that was that.

I had become distracted.

Something was nagging at me, but I couldn't focus. Some connection I ought to make.

I looked at the syringe and it came to me. Sister Agnes had kept one much like this hidden in her prayer room. What if it was for the same purpose?

Raptures was the word she'd used, for those moments of oneness with God.

But what if those moments weren't so much spiritual as *chemical*?

What if the reason Sister Agnes kept a syringe wasn't to poison Oswald Drake, but to inject herself?

16

THE FOLLOWING MORNING, I collected a copy of the *Daily Chronicle* from the seller in Trafalgar Square, delighted to see that my article was the top story.

I headed to Rosie's pie shop as quickly as I could, trying to ignore the cramping in my guts.

The glow of her oven shone against the window. I tapped on the glass and her face appeared, and even through the soot I could see her pursed-lipped expression as she made up her mind whether to admit me or not. In the end, curiosity won over disapproval.

The locks clanked and the door opened a crack.

'What do you want?'

'I'm not certain Sister Agnes is guilty now.' I handed her the newspaper. 'I've written a new article. I need your help.'

She read it while I clasped my fingers together so tightly I was sure the skin would break. Finally, she looked up and half smiled. It was like the sun appearing from behind a cloud.

'That poor woman,' she said. 'What are any of us supposed to do? It's either marriage or the convent. Certainly, I'd never get married again with the law as it is.'

'Quite right.' I looked at the sign, still just about visible on the door: *Dolan and Son*, her grandfather and father. 'Your husband would take ownership of all your money and this shop as well. How could you place that amount of trust in any man?' I laughed at the absurdity of it. 'Even someone like me?'

Her eyes met mine, a trace of a frown forming on her face.

'What is it?' I asked.

'Nothing.' She beckoned me inside. 'Don't stand there like an idiot, I've things to do.'

She led me into the back room, where I sank gratefully into a chair. I'd hardly had a minute's sleep the previous night, having lain awake putting the parts together. Sister Agnes had loathed Drake and wished him dead. She had lied about her true identity and had competed in a sport that some might say was against nature. But none of that was a crime. She might be a user of morphine, but that didn't make her a murderer.

I explained all of this to Rosie while she cubed beef, fed sliced apples and cornmeal to her two younger children, stirred her washing and noted yesterday's take in the ledger. Twice, she had to leave the room with an armful of dripping laundry, and I marvelled at her industry. While she was gone, I showed Samuel, her youngest at four years old, how to place apple slices on top of his cornmeal and push them around his bowl like little sailing boats. When Rosie returned, she rolled her eyes indulgently and tossed me a wet cloth to clean the floor and my trouser leg.

'Can you prove it wasn't Sister Agnes?'

'I don't know. But she has an injured wrist, so would've had a lot of difficulty raising a man on a rope. We need to talk to her.'

Rosie looked doubtful. 'Is that what you intend to say to the police? "Look at her poorly wrist."'

She rattled her pan on the stove, causing flames to leap, and I sprang from my chair towards the door. The fire died almost instantly, hissing and smoking, and I tried to disguise my panic by acting as though I'd simply chosen to stand at that moment.

'Are you all right?' she asked.

'Yes, of course.' I drummed my fingers casually on the shelf. 'I know the police won't change their minds on my account. But they might let us visit Sister Agnes. You're a woman and a Catholic, and I'm neither. She might talk to you.'

Rosie wiped her hands down her apron. 'Also, you named her a butcher, which she'll doubtless remember.'

'I'm trying to make amends.'

'Aye, well. You've got yourself into a pickle and no mistake.'

She placed a large bowl of potatoes and two peelers in front of her children, and they set to work with well-honed efficiency.

'Where's Robbie?'

Jacob's loss of Albie had made me anxious.

'School. He can already read, which is more than his father ever learned how to do.'

I could tell she was blooming with pride. She'd taught the boy to count when he was only five, and had insisted I listen to a demonstration, having the gall to scold me when I pointed out he'd gone directly from nineteen to thirty.

'Will you come with me or not?'

She sighed. 'All right, I'll come once Alice is back from the market. I have to stay here for Albert until then.' She pointed towards the ceiling. 'He had a bad night. In the meantime, do you want a pot of tea and something to eat?'

It was the best question I'd ever been asked.

The traffic was backed up along Whitehall and everyone was wilting in the heat. A horse had collapsed, snapping the splinter-bar of its carriage, and a group of men was standing around it, scratching their heads.

The police had erected a wooden barrier outside their headquarters, and within the perimeter, a small group of women were singing, though I couldn't hear the tune over the noise from the crowded street. Their leader was around sixty years of age and of significant girth, full of vim, turning around from time to time to encourage the others. She was holding a banner on which was written: *Free Sister Agnes*.

Rosie craned her neck to see. 'Suffragists.'

'What do you think of them?' I asked. 'Votes for women and all that.'

She cast a wary look at the singers. 'I'm too busy putting fillings into pies to take much notice. But I wouldn't mind not getting punched or pinched by a man ever again. If they could achieve that, it would be nice.'

Two police constables were standing nearby, trying to be inconspicuous but clearly observing the protesters from under their helmets. I wasn't sure why they were so concerned. These ladies seemed less like revolutionaries than wives and mothers of the sort one might see haggling over the price of haddock at the market or scolding their husbands before church.

There was a noise on the opposite pavement as a hungry-faced fellow in an opera hat climbed on to a stool. He pointed his hand towards the suffragists, and I realised with a pinch to my guts that it was Nicholas Coffey, once again attempting to address the citizens of London.

'Gentlemen! The time has come to draw a line! Enough is enough!'

'Mother of God,' muttered Rosie.

We weren't the only ones listening to him. Three men had stopped, one of them a bone-picker with a sack on his back. Another fellow nodded and gave a thumbs-up as he walked past.

Coffey raised his voice as if they were a horde of thousands. 'My dear friend Oswald Drake was murdered in his bed, strung up like meat, and those women over there are claiming the killer should be freed! What should we do about that, eh? Are we going to stand for it?'

His tiny audience shook their heads and one of them clapped.

Coffey waved his arm, taking in the whole street. 'Send out word to all the working men of London. Gather them all here with me. We must stand up for our rights as husbands and fathers. Send out word to every Christian man who's had enough! Gather here! Gather now!'

'Come on,' I said to Rosie. 'No one's stupid enough to take any notice of Nicholas Coffey.'

The suffragists were finishing their song, which I now recognised as 'Hail, Queen of Heaven'. Their leader waved her flag and bellowed at her followers: 'Free Sister Agnes!'

When she turned back, she was surprised to find me standing in front of her. 'Who are you?'

'My name's Stanhope. I'm a journalist. May I ask you a question, please?'

She blinked three times in quick succession. 'Of course. Always happy to gain publicity for our cause.'

'Thank you. What makes you think Agnes Munro is innocent?'

'Ah, well.' She prodded me in the shoulder with her finger in a most unladylike fashion. 'She might be innocent, and she might not. But I do know that if she were a gentleman, she'd get a fair trial. But a lady? She's already condemned. No one cares how a gentleman looks or what he does in his spare time, but for a lady, it tips the balance. We're guilty before the judge walks into the courtroom. You fellows in the press see to that.'

The other ladies struck up another song, this one brisker, with a tambourine accompaniment. I squared my shoulders and shouted over the din.

'I'll do my best to report with absolute impartiality, I assure you. I want to see justice done.'

She clapped me hard on the upper arm. 'Good for you. But you won't succeed. A *butcher*, they called her. What chance does she have after that? She'll hang as sure as I'm standing here.'

She had the faint trace of an Irish accent and a peculiar directness in her manner that reminded me of my childhood. Back then, girls spoke to me that way all the time, believing me to be like themselves. But since I'd begun living as myself, women spoke differently to me, avoiding my eye, maintaining physical distance, withholding absolute candour. It was as though I'd left a club I hadn't known I belonged to.

Rosie took my elbow. 'Enough, Leo. Let's go inside before your idiocy gets you into any more trouble.'

Rosie, of course, was the exception to every rule.

The waiting room was quiet for once, the benches standing empty and the dust swept into curves on the floor. There was one fellow ahead of us and a single constable behind the desk, who jumped and glanced nervously at Rosie. I supposed he was unused to battalions of ladies protesting outside his door.

The fellow turned and it was Iain Sutherland, the deacon from the Church of the Martyrs. He tipped his hat to Rosie.

'Mr Stanhope and Mrs Flowers. Have you come to see poor Sister Agnes? Your next article, I daresay. The murderer brought low by the heroic police, that sort of thing?' He winked conspiratorially at the constable, who hadn't been listening. 'Anyway, you did well to come inside before the trouble starts.'

Rosie looked nonplussed. 'What trouble?'

He smiled gently, as if asked for an explanation by a child. 'Tempers are running high, Mrs Flowers. People shouldn't inflame them.'

'With singing?' Her voice had taken on an acerbic edge.

He didn't appear to notice. 'Yes, indeed. They should go home and tend to their husbands and children. Now, would you like me to take you in to see Agnes? They've already said I can meet with her.' He touched his dog collar. 'Privilege of the clergy.'

He had a collusive manner, as if we were all indulging in a private joke. It made me want to poke him in the eye. Instead, I punished him with politeness. 'Thank you, Mr Sutherland. But as I remember, last time we met, you compared me to a leech.'

He barely flinched. Truly, he was as smooth as goose fat. 'Yes, I'm sorry about that. The thing is, Whitechapel's a poor area, and nobody gives us any help. We stick together. We don't like outsiders telling us what to do.'

'Are you a local, then?'

I didn't believe he was. His accent was far too refined to have been milled in the slums of Whitechapel.

He gave me that fake half-smile again. 'I've acclimatised.'

'Have you come to offer Sister Agnes confession?'

He straightened his collar and pulled himself up to his full height, reminding me what a physically powerful man he was. 'No, though I have no doubt she has much to confess.'

Rosie pulled herself up to her full height also, coming almost to his shoulder. 'It's not your place to judge.' She turned to me. 'He's a deacon, Leo. He can't offer confession.'

Sutherland interlocked his fingers in a manner that might have seemed patient and pious. But his knuckles were white.

'Mrs Flowers is quite correct, of course. I'm not yet a priest. Nevertheless, I can pray with the Sister for the Lord's grace.'

There it is, I thought. A shroud of forgiveness covering the stinking corpse of contempt and condemnation.

'You're sure she's guilty, then?' I asked him, through clenched teeth.

He looked at each of us in turn. 'If not her, then who?'

It was Rosie who answered. 'Mr Coffey's making a lot of noise. He's out there now, pointing the finger at Sister Agnes. He's very keen to direct blame towards others rather than himself.'

Sutherland scoffed. 'You can't possibly suspect Coffey. He's naturally upset, that's all. He knew Oswald when they were children.'

'He might be in love with Drake's wife,' I said. 'That would be a motive.'

Sutherland's face flushed. 'Elspeth? I wouldn't have said so. Certainly, I'm sure she never gave him any encouragement in that regard.'

Rosie gave him a sly look. 'She's a pretty girl, isn't she?'

'Yes, she is.'

'But very young.'

He adopted a benevolent expression. 'I'm simply describing how Coffey might perceive her. He's a lesser man than Drake was, and I suppose he might have succumbed to envy. A deadly sin.' He inclined his head. 'Shall we go inside?'

———

As we entered the corridor, we could hear the women outside, their singing now grown louder and more insistent. I hoped Sister Agnes would be comforted to know she wasn't forgotten.

Yet now, there were masculine voices as well: shouts and angry insults.

The duty sergeant unlocked the door to Sister Agnes's cell, and she stood up as we entered. She was wearing a brown cotton dress and an apron, with a mob cap perched precariously on her head, making her look more like a well-built stable girl than a woman of the cloth. Her wounds had started to heal, and someone had stitched her cheek, but still, she looked a sight; half-blind, fat-lipped, rough with scabs and, as she smiled a greeting, lacking at least two front teeth.

Rosie gasped when she saw the Sister but recovered and looked her in the eye as she introduced herself. 'It's a wickedness, what they've done to you.'

Sister Agnes attempted a smile. 'It's certainly been quite unpleasant.' I felt a twist in my stomach at her bravery; trying to console us while she was in agony herself.

'We've found new evidence,' I told her. 'We think Nicholas Coffey might be guilty.'

She didn't react to this good news. She seemed numb. I knew how that felt. After a couple of days in a cell, she had wept all the tears she could, suffered all the torments and shivered all the shivers her body could bear. All that was left was this: skin, muscle and bone, empty of all feeling.

Eventually, she shrugged. 'You're the one who said I'm guilty. You called me a beast.'

'Butcher,' Sutherland corrected her, a tad unnecessarily, I thought.

The ladies outside had stopped singing, though the drum could still be heard. A shout went up; male voices.

'Your wrist is sprained,' I said. 'You've had it for some time, haven't you? I don't believe you could haul a man up on a rope and cleat it off.'

I blanched as I remembered what Coffey had said; that at times her wrist had swollen to the size of a potato and needed to be drained. Constance had told me that needles used for extraction usually had wide bores. Could the same syringe have been used both to drain Agnes's wrist and to inject morphine into Drake's neck?

Sister Agnes smiled regretfully. 'Somehow, I don't think that will help.'

She pulled back her sleeves, one at a time, and her forearms were blue and yellow where the police had beaten her. Any previous injury would be impossible to detect.

'There's more. I'm not convinced the syringe we found among your possessions was used to poison Drake.'

These were the times I loved the most, when I had manoeuvred every piece into position, closed off every exit and had only to make that final move. I savoured the moment. The game was about to be won.

Sutherland frowned. 'Explain what you mean.' He seemed to think he was in charge.

'Admit it,' I said to the Sister, my voice taking on a metallic edge. 'You're a morphine user, aren't you? What you call raptures aren't raptures at all, they're stupors. But the good news is, if the syringe was for your own use, there's no real evidence against you. All you have to do is tell the truth. Your sin will set you free.'

We were interrupted by the sound of the door at the end of the corridor opening. Detective Ripley appeared, his jacket smeared with grease and a cigarette glowing serenely in his mouth.

'I heard you were here,' he mumbled, addressing me. 'Causing unrest again.'

'What unrest?'

He nodded towards the high window. 'Your accusations have stirred people up. Miss Munro has become a *cause*.' He peered at Sister Agnes, one of his eyes almost shut. 'You're dividing opinion, madam. Husbands and wives on different sides.'

'Different sides?' Sister Agnes gave him the same beatific smile I'd seen immediately before she dropped a knee on her opponent's groin. 'You make it sound like a battle.'

Ripley nodded towards the window, smoke drifting from his nostrils. 'There's going to be a battle out there soon enough, believe me. Some of those blokes are spoiling for …'

He trailed off, squinting curiously at her from under his brows. She was motionless, as though metamorphosed into stone, hands clasped in front of her, eyes closed, though not in sleep. Rather, she seemed tense, lines forming around her mouth and temples, lips thin and pale. She remained that way for half a minute, until her face softened and relaxed, becoming so peaceful that when she finally opened her eyes, we all jumped.

She exhaled slowly. 'You see, Mr Stanhope? When the Lord wishes, He speaks to me without …' she had been going to say *morphine*, but instead she straightened her collar, set her shoulders and addressed Ripley in a voice as cool as butter. 'It cannot be a battle, Detective. The sides are not evenly matched.'

I'd never seen him so flustered. Her brief reverie and steady gaze seemed to have utterly unmanned him. He took a brief, strong pull on his cigarette. 'I don't know why these ladies get so bothered. My missus is in charge in our house. I can scarcely get a word in. Seems to me—'

'It doesn't matter,' I interrupted, feeling that the conversation was getting off track. 'The point is there's no proof the Sister did anything wrong. She should be let out immediately. We have new evidence.'

'What evidence?' asked Ripley.

He was recovering his composure, heartened to be the one demanding answers.

I nodded to Sister Agnes. 'Tell the detective,' I instructed her. 'Tell him what the syringe was for.'

This was the moment. All she had to do was admit the truth and she could return to the convent for vespers with her Sisters and Mother Eugenie. *Just say it.* The words in my head almost leapt out of my mouth. *Tell him that you injected yourself with morphine.*

Sister Agnes inclined her head towards me. 'I'm sorry, Mr Stanhope, but I can't do as you wish.' She turned to Ripley, her chin lifted and proud, exactly as she'd been when she stood over her defeated foe in the ring. 'I'm changing my plea. I confess to the murder of Oswald Drake. I'm guilty and I deserve to be hanged.'

17

Rosie and I stumbled out into the corridor.

'Why did she confess?' she demanded, waving her arms. 'Has she been sent mad by being in that cell? Was it the beating?'

I scratched my head, still unable to believe what I'd heard. 'I don't think so. She told me before that God has a plan for her.'

Rosie rolled her eyes. 'Some plan, to be hanged for something she didn't do.'

We had stood in that tiny cell begging Agnes to recant her guilty plea. I'd explained that even if she was too ashamed to admit to using morphine, that didn't mean she had to confess to *murder*. But she was resolute, facing away from us and refusing to answer. She didn't even react when she was told that the following morning, she would be transferred to the City Prison. I could only assume she wasn't aware of its reputation.

In the end, Ripley threatened to have us removed, allowing only Sutherland to remain so he could pray with the condemned woman.

'It's my fault,' I mumbled, more to myself than to Rosie. 'I was the first to accuse her.'

I felt a twinge in my belly that made me want to double over, but instead I straightened my back, sending a lightning strike of pain through my bowels and outwards to my skin.

'You can't blame yourself.' Rosie squeezed my arm, a gesture so unlike her I felt sure she secretly blamed me too. 'You didn't force her to change her mind.'

'No, but if it weren't for me … oh my goodness!'

As we emerged through the doors into Whitehall, we saw that the scene in front of us had changed utterly.

The suffragists had been backed into the yard beside the police headquarters, a cordon of constables strung out in front of them. We could still see the ladies' flags waving and hear their drum beating, but now their voices were drowned by the shouts and stamping of the men crowding the street. They were perhaps three or four hundred strong, not tightly packed but milling about, fingers twitching as if they were waiting for a signal. I didn't like the look of some of them; dark brows and hard mouths, arms locked to their sides, and jackets buttoned up despite the weather. I could feel my right cheek draw tight and begin to itch.

We climbed down the steps, keeping close together. A couple of the men were watching Rosie, swigging ale and muttering to one another behind their hands.

The two constables were still standing on the pavement, as skinny as reeds. I approached one of them and pulled out my notebook.

'I'm a reporter for the *Daily Chronicle* and this is my … assistant reporter.' Rosie shot me a look, but I ignored her. 'This is a public thoroughfare. Why are you allowing it to be invaded by these men?'

He opened his mouth, his eyes flicking from side to side as though the explanation might be written on the flagstones. Eventually, he mumbled: 'I was told ... I mean, they just arrived, and we don't have the manpower. It's not as if ...'

'Can I quote you on that? What's your name?'

'Perhaps you should speak to the sergeant.'

He pointed a shaking finger at a substantial fellow striding towards us, and I was amazed to see it was Pallett, with another six policemen in his wake.

'Are you in charge here, Constable?'

'Sergeant now, Mr Stanhope.' He indicated his sleeve, where three stripes were proudly displayed in a V-shape. 'You two shouldn't be here. It's not safe. I'll ask you to leave, please.'

He didn't wait for a reply but set off towards the ladies in the yard, shoving men out of the way with a politeness only he could muster.

We attempted to go in the opposite direction, towards Trafalgar Square. I led the way, but it quickly became difficult. The crowd, which had been relatively dispersed and fluid, was becoming compressed as it grew. We were struggling against the flow and soon found ourselves carried backwards, so we had no choice but to turn, squeezed together, shuffling towards the suffragists in the yard, soon locked so tight we were treading on the heels of the men in front. My arms were being pushed tightly against my chest, which was tender and sore enough without being pummelled by other people's elbows.

Rosie put her hand in mine. 'Stay together, all right?'

Breathing was becoming difficult and I couldn't see past the hats and shoulders. Arms were being raised and ale spilled. The man beside me yelled: 'Get back to your kids!'

Someone fell, grabbing at my jacket. I let go of Rosie and turned to haul him to his feet, but when I turned back, she'd disappeared.

'Rosie!' I pushed men aside, swimming through the crush. 'Rosie!'

'Leo!'

She was ahead of me, but I couldn't see her. 'Try to get to the back!'

'I will!'

I caught sight of her skirts as she was squeezed between two oafs who were yelling insults and stretching their necks. And then she was gone again.

The crush stumbled forwards, forcing me along with it. The noise was becoming overwhelming: roaring, stamping and clapping. The fellow next to me produced a bludgeon from his jacket and waved it, screaming that these ladies were too ugly to deserve husbands. That idea seemed to catch on quickly, and soon lots of them were shouting insults, even threats. A bottle was thrown from behind me, arcing over our heads towards where the ladies were singing, and I heard it hit the ground with a percussive crash. I put my palms over my ears and shut my eyes as I was buffeted from side to side, jostled in the back and in the chest, clouted in the face as someone raised an arm in protest. I no longer had any control. I was a twig on a busy river, spinning from rock to rock, settling for a brief moment, only to be whisked away again by the current.

It was almost a relief.

When I opened my eyes, I had been pushed close to the line of policemen separating the men and women. The suffragists were singing fiercely and waving their banners: 'Free Sister Agnes', 'We Stand Together' and 'Votes for Women'.

Pallett was facing them, holding up both his hands. 'Stay back, ladies. We can't ensure your safety otherwise.'

I felt an arm around my neck, clutching me closely, and a face inches from mine, alcohol on his breath.

'Them coppers can't stop us,' he muttered. 'When I give the word, we'll charge 'em. You and me. You ready?'

He went to pat my chest with his other hand, and I couldn't allow that. I twisted away from him and barged into another fellow in front. As he turned, I dived into the gap. The drunkard who'd spoken to me was enraged by my sudden exit, and I heard his yell and felt his hand grab for my collar. But I was too quick. I shunted another man out of my way and found myself disgorged from the mob against the police cordon, where a bulky constable was gripping a billy club in his fist.

'Leo!' called a familiar voice, and I was relieved to see Rosie a few feet away along the line.

'Please,' I said to the constable. 'We're not part of this. We need to get out.'

Pallett turned and caught my eye. He nodded to the constable, who allowed us to pass in front of him and on to the next copper, and so on until we were spat out at the edge of the crush. More policemen were arriving as reinforcements, some of them with pistols in their hands.

We skirted around the police headquarters and hurried as fast as we could up towards Trafalgar Square, and civilisation.

Rosie was rubbing her cheek below her left eye.

'Did someone hurt you?' I asked. 'Let me see.'

'An elbow, that's all. I don't think he knew I was there.' She straightened her neckline and tugged her bonnet down on her head. 'I've had worse.'

I heard a hail behind us and kept my head down. I was too exhausted to cope with anything further. But the hail came again, and then the sound of pounding feet.

'Hey, Mr Stanhope!'

Trafford, the wrestler, was loping towards us, with four others in his wake. They were enough like him to be brothers or cousins, and I didn't like the look of them.

'What are you doing here?' I pointed towards the mob. 'Are you part of … all that?'

'Of course.' He puffed himself up like a rooster. 'Mr Coffey asked us to come. We're demanding justice for Mr Drake. Without him I'd be begging on the street. You called it, Mr Stanhope. A butcher is what she is, and she should hang for it.'

'I didn't know you and Coffey were close.'

He twitched. 'We've had our differences in the past, but he's right about this. He says we need to stick together.'

I looked at his eyes and saw, not anger or passion or a burning desire for justice, but *relief*. He needed to follow someone. Now Drake was dead, he'd cleaved to Coffey.

'And you're prepared to use violence to achieve that aim, are you?'

'No worse than after hours at the King's Head, is it?' He leaned in towards me. 'Me and the lads've been talking.'

He cast a sour look in the direction of his companions. 'They don't believe me, as it happens, but now you can tell 'em. We're mates, ain't we?'

One of the other men, resembling Trafford if he'd gained four stones, none of it in muscle, stepped towards us. I heard Rosie's intake of breath. *I've had worse*, she'd said. She knew plenty about men like these.

'Are you really the bloke who started all this?' He glanced doubtfully at Trafford. 'Bert don't normally mix with important folk.'

'We've met, yes, but I'm not important. I'm just a journalist.'

'Bert said it was you who found the Butcher.' I had come to hate that word. 'But then you wrote bad things about Oswald Drake. Why did you change your tune, eh? Whose money did you take? Was it them women or did one of Gladstone's lackeys slip you a few quid? What did it take for you to betray your fellow man?'

Rosie blinked at him. 'We'll be going now, I think.'

He jutted his chin in my direction. 'This one hasn't answered my question.'

Rosie gazed around the Square, a light wind ruffling her sleeves. The traffic was near stationary, as ever. Nelson was standing on his column, looking out for a fleet that would never come. Ladies were pushing perambulators and gentlemen were strolling to their next appointment. The clamour on Whitehall had reduced to a dull, distant rumble.

'Not here, I don't think.'

She took my arm and steered me away. The bruise around her eye was starting to bloom; blue and a shade of amber.

I looked back once, and Trafford's cousin was still watching us. The others were heading back to the mob, which now seemed to me like a swarm of flies on rotten fruit. Is this what men do when they go to into battle, I wondered? Must they become insects in order to survive? I felt no comradeship with them, no common cause. I was a different kind of man entirely.

———

I suggested Rosie should come into the office for a little while to catch her breath and maybe get some ointment for her face.

'No, I want to go home to my children.' She smiled thinly. 'It's all I'm fit for, apparently. And I have to get to the market before it shuts.'

As we parted, she embraced me, right there on the steps, both of her arms around my neck.

'Propriety be damned,' she said, once we'd disengaged. 'I'm glad you're safe. I was worried when you got lost in that crowd. You're like a brother to me, you know that.'

'You don't have a brother.'

She put a hand to my cheek. 'I do now.'

I almost crawled up the steps and through the door. Harry was at his desk.

'You look like death,' he observed, without ceasing his typing. 'Three out of ten, and that's being generous.'

'I feel worse than that. There was a riot.'

'How exciting! Did you get an interview with the ringleader?'

I lowered my forehead to my desk. 'I think I may have *been* the ringleader. Possibly on both sides. My articles caused all this.'

'Sounds like fine work to me.' He continued pounding on the machine for a minute and then broke off. 'I've been meaning to ask you about Mrs Flowers.'

I closed my eyes, still face down on the desk. 'What about her?'

'Her likes and dislikes, that sort of thing. I'm taking her to Kew Gardens tomorrow evening, and I've realised I don't know her very well.'

'She likes … I don't know. She likes her pie shop and her children. She drinks coffee.'

He didn't reply until I looked up to meet his eye. 'Coffee? Is that all the insight you can offer? I mean, does she like to be wooed with flowers, compliments and so forth, or does she prefer a more forthright approach?'

'Forthright?'

He threw up his hands in exasperation, but I really didn't know what to say to him. I'd never seen Rosie in any kind of romantic circumstance. I would imagine she'd approach it much as she approached everything else: exactly as she chose.

Miss Chive was delivering typewritten pages to J. T. in his office. In common with the other senior men he refused to operate what he called 'the infernal instrument' himself, so five young ladies had been recruited to do all of their typewriting. Four of them were content to remain corralled in their paddock on the ground floor, but Miss Chive was apt to escape and make her deliveries personally.

She pointed me out to J. T., who approached my desk, brimming with intent.

'Where've you been?' he demanded.

'Surviving a riot. And I have a story, an exclusive. Agnes Munro has confessed to the murder of Oswald Drake.'

He deflated like a burst football.

'Good. Yes. Very good.' He squeezed my shoulder. 'Good work. Very good work.'

He'd been on the very brink of an explosion and was having difficulty adjusting his demeanour.

'Effusive praise indeed,' muttered Harry. 'And so eloquent.'

'Though I don't believe she's guilty,' I added.

J. T. raised his eyes to the heavens. 'You just said she confessed! Why do you have to make things difficult? Just write the bloody story.'

He was right, of course. I should just write the bloody story and move on to the next one. But I couldn't.

'She might be hanged for a murder she didn't do. Doesn't that bother you?'

He ran his fingers through his hair. He was, in his own way, a compassionate man, but he believed in printing news that the ordinary person in the street could comprehend. He had no time for what he called *complications*.

'Do you have a quote or a source who says she's not guilty? Have the police told you they're investigating someone else? Do you have someone else in mind as the real killer? Do you think they'll kill again? No? Nothing? Then write the bloody story. And show it to me when it's done. I want to see—'

At that moment, the window in J. T.'s office shattered, showering the room with shards of glass. We all leapt to our feet. Miss Chive screamed and fell to her knees, her hands covering her face, blood dripping between her fingers.

Harry was first to her side as she crouched on the floor.

'Miss Chive? Esme?'

She peeled back her hands from her face, and her skin was dotted with specks of glass like bright red stars. She was gasping, too shocked to feel the sting of it yet. Even her lips were bleeding.

'What the hell was that?' demanded J.T., his face white.

On the floor under the desk, among the debris, was half a brick. I picked it up.

'I'd guess that someone doesn't like my articles. They're sending us a warning.'

18

HARRY TOOK MISS CHIVE to a doctor on Harley Street. It would be an agonising task, removing those splinters of glass from her face, and she would carry the marks like a pox. I could only hope her sight would be spared.

I had no doubt who had hurled that brick; one or more of Trafford's cousins must have followed Rosie and me. Such hatred they had. And for what? I generally wrote articles about worm ecology and vegetable mould. I wasn't a threat to anyone. And yet Miss Chive had been injured and Sister Agnes was in prison.

Whatever I did, someone seemed to suffer for it.

The thought occurred to me that I should stand up and leave, run down the stairs and on to the street, breathing in the fetid fumes of London for the last time, pulling my hat low over my brow, shoving my hands into my pockets and gone, gone, gone. The rattle of the train, the new air, trees and rolling hills and finally, the smell of the sea. I hadn't seen it for years, yet when I closed my eyes, I could picture every detail; the spray on the pier and our names made of stones on the beach, Jane and me holding hands and paddling in the surf.

What a life I could have, with salt on my skin and sand between my toes. No more articles, no more damage to anyone.

But I couldn't do it. The truth needed to be told and Sister Agnes deserved justice.

In the end, I wrote two articles. The first was about the riot – the 'War of Whitehall' as I called it – containing vivid portrayals of wild-eyed vandals, strident suffragists and stalwart policemen. The second was about the confession of Agnes Munro, which I described in factual terms, going on to make a plea for leniency. She should not be hanged, I wrote, for the murder of a man such as Oswald Drake, who had taken advantage of young girls and was in debt to persons unknown and surely, I implied, disreputable. The courts should show mercy to a woman of the church with no history of villainy. I even managed to suggest some doubt as to her guilt, describing her confession as 'surprising', though I had no doubt J.T. would remove the adjective.

Once outside, I raised my collar and lowered my chin, and all the way home kept checking over my shoulder for anyone following. By the time I pushed open the pharmacy door I was damp with sweat, and not just from the warmth of the afternoon.

Alfie was counting his takings – a pleasing quantity of silver and notes – and Mrs Gower was keeping him company, perched on the stool. Of late, she had taken to watching him work, saying she wanted to learn how it was done in preparation for what had become known as 'the move'.

Alfie looked up. 'We've found new premises,' he announced gleefully. 'Not on Oxford Street, but almost as good, near Hanover Square. Double-fronted with space for two counters and the dentistry chair. Four rooms upstairs, so plenty of space. A bigger bedroom and a new mattress for you, Leo, and no extra rent!' He grinned amiably. 'I'm meeting the landlord next week.'

A bigger shop would provide more money and a better life for them, with the unspoken understanding that he and Mrs Gower would be married first. She wasn't the wife I would have chosen for Alfie, but she was a decent woman who made him happy, no matter what Constance believed.

'It's perfect,' she added. 'I went past it on the omnibus a few days ago and saw the sign.'

I sensed a slight unease from Alfie and wondered why. And then I thought about it: Mrs Gower went past on the omnibus? Didn't she have her own horse and carriage? Why was she taking the omnibus these days?

I tried to muster an appropriate level of enthusiasm. 'Congratulations.'

Alfie frowned. 'You look terrible.'

I ran my fingers across the counter, feeling the familiar contours of the wood. 'It's been a difficult day. Have you told Constance your happy news?'

'We will soon,' Alfie replied, with the air of a man contemplating the gallows.

The clanking of pots and pans coming from the back room told me that Constance herself was making dinner. Judging from the lack of any smoke or acrid stink, she was still in the initial stages. I smiled at that thought, though it brought me a pang of sadness too. Such a familiar routine Constance and I had. She complained that I knew nothing of science and was glum most of the time, and I chided her for her terrible cooking. She wasn't even *that* bad these days, but we knew of no other way to communicate. I could never tell her how fond of her I was, or how proud.

'What do you make of all the goings-on?' asked Mrs Gower. 'Isn't it terrible? A man hanged and rioting in the streets.'

I thought of Miss Chive, her face sparkling with glass and beads of blood.

'All we can say for certain is that Oswald Drake was murdered. No amount of anger and violence changes that. It just causes more anger and violence.'

Mrs Gower nodded vehemently. 'Quite right. The matter should be left to the police and the courts. These women, these suffragists, march around as if they're speaking for all of us. They jump on every chance to make a speech about this and that. I wish they'd stop it, I really do.'

Alfie filled two small tumblers with whisky. None for Mrs Gower as she had recently joined the temperance movement, though she was tolerant of her future husband's occasional indulgence, as long as he didn't end up like the 'sots and carousers', as she called them, who sang, puked and slept in the street.

'No politics,' Alfie said. 'It's early, but we can still celebrate.'

I took a sip and it was heavenly; exactly what I needed. Even so, my eyelids were starting to droop.

I staggered upstairs to attend to my sanitary cloth. My jacket and spare trousers had been relegated to the back of my chair, and my wardrobe was filled with dripping flannels. I was terrified of running out, so had purchased an entire drawerful of the things, along with spare undershorts and belts. The monthly curse was God's mockery of me, but I refused to be cowed.

Afterwards I lay on my bed unable to raise the energy to get up again, not even when Constance tapped on my door for dinner.

My last thoughts before I slept were of Sister Agnes, praying in her cell, listening to the scuffling rats and snores of the other inmates. Soon, she would be moved to the City Prison where, unless something redirected the current course of events, she would be hanged.

———

I awoke at nine o'clock in the morning after a twelve-hour sleep. Alfie called up the stairs that Mrs Flowers was here. I got dressed speedily and met her in the back room.

She had a determined set to her jaw. 'We're going to that convent,' she declared. 'We need to know why Sister Agnes lied about murdering that bastard, and we're not going to find out by lazing around all day.'

'I have to go to work.'

'This is work. And you're late anyway.'

There was no gainsaying her. I managed to parlay a cab ride, rather than having to walk, but regretted it when she complained most of the way that we were missing the lovely sunshine in order to be shaken in a wooden box like a pair of dice. Eventually, she withdrew into a brooding silence, breaking it only as we neared our destination.

'What's your Mr Whitford like, then?'

'Harry? He's a jovial chap, I'd say.'

'Is he a *good* man?'

I found that hard to answer. He was a man whose company I enjoyed, but did that make him *good*? I felt I ought to know, yet had never considered it before.

'He's a good reporter, when he can be bothered. He likes a drink.'

She looked at me sharply. 'You mean he's ill-tempered?'

I laughed at the thought. 'No, not at all. He gets quite affectionate and jolly after a few ales. He has a tendency to lead the singing.'

'Singing?'

'He likes a sing-song. He knows all the words to …' I faltered, realising that Harry probably wouldn't be singing that particular song – or any song – to Rosie. In truth, I didn't know what he would do, or what one was supposed to do, on a romantic assignation. I had only attempted such a thing once in my life, and the woman in question had not attended, though I held close to my heart the idea that she had wanted to.

I started again, trying to get to the heart of what I assumed she wanted to know. 'Harry is … perhaps not cut out to be a husband. At least, not yet.'

She turned to face me with a strange expression. For a moment, I thought she might take my hand affectionately in hers, but of course, that wasn't how we were.

'I'm not looking for a husband, Leo. Mother of God, I don't trust any man. I just want to know if I'll be safe with Mr Whitford for the evening, that's all.' She gave herself an irritated little shake. 'I mean, I don't trust any man but you.'

I was saved from having to reply by our arrival at Tooley Street. Rosie brushed her hands down her jacket and straightened her hat, which, I noticed, was her best one;

pale blue felt with silk flowers adorning the side. She lifted her chin as I knocked.

There was a sound of shuffling from within and a woman's voice. 'We're not available today.'

'I'm Leo Stanhope,' I said. 'I spoke with Mother Eugenie Doyle a few days ago.'

There was no reply.

Rosie leaned down with her mouth close to the lock. 'My name's Rosie Flowers.' The tiniest lilt of an Irish accent had crept into her voice, a legacy from her grand-parents. 'We just want to talk to someone.'

The voice came again. 'Are you the reporter?'

'I am,' I replied. 'But that's not why I'm here.'

'We spoke to Sister Agnes,' added Rosie. 'She needs our help. And yours.'

The lock turned and the door opened six inches, limited by a chain. A long face appeared at the crack. I recognised her as Sister Nora, the convent's second-in-command, who had seemed at odds with Mother Eugenie the last time I'd visited.

'I'm only interested in helping the convent,' I insisted. 'Please let us in.'

She nodded and undid the chain. As we entered, Rosie crossed herself and whipped off her hat, and then replaced it, unsure of the etiquette.

'Mother Eugenie is indisposed,' the Sister said, her hands clasped.

'May we speak with you then, Sister?' asked Rosie. 'I'm afraid Agnes has confessed to the murder.'

Sister Nora looked down at the stone floor for two or three seconds, gathered herself, and raised her face again. 'I'm very sorry to hear that. We shall pray for her.'

Again, something about her manner, her accent and her eyes seemed familiar. I was certain I hadn't met her prior to the last few days, but … she was like a song I'd heard before, but in a different key. A song I didn't like very much.

'We don't think she's guilty,' Rosie said firmly. 'Someone needs to speak to her and persuade her to change her mind. It would be best coming from one of you, don't you think?'

'Can you think of any reason why she'd confess?' I added, garnering an irritated look from Rosie, who hadn't had her question answered.

Sister Nora's eyes flicked from one of us to the other. 'I can think of one. Perhaps you'd better come with me.'

We followed her down the corridor to the end, past Sister Agnes's prayer room, where a door led to some steps down and a further corridor. Here, the walls were white plastered rather than bare limestone, and I could hear the sound of cheerful voices, quite unlike the oppressive silence of the older section. Sister Nora stopped by one of the doors, knocked and entered without waiting for a response.

There were two women inside, or rather two girls, in rough clothes, neither of them more than fifteen years old. Their laughter died on their lips and they sat up straight. Each of them had a baby in her arms.

One of the girls bobbed her head. 'Sister.'

She was rosy-cheeked and might have been called pretty if she weren't scarred across her forehead and down to her mouth, a steep-sided trench through her skin. I couldn't avoid staring at it, and the girl put her hand to her face, pulling strands of hair from her bonnet to cover it up. I tried to imagine how such a disfigurement might have occurred and could only think of one way; no slip of a kitchen knife or accidental fall could have made that long, smooth cut. Someone had carved her deliberately.

Her friend kept her eyes down, not out of innate politeness or shyness, I deemed. She had been quite chatty as we came in. It was our presence that terrified her.

Her baby was whimpering, and she shushed it gently.

'He needs changing,' observed Sister Nora. 'Best do it right away. He's not going to stink any less for waiting.'

The girl gathered up her child and shot out of the room.

Sister Nora turned to us, her expression grave. 'We get plenty like these. They've got no home, so they end up selling themselves or getting defiled in the street. We look after them here, for a little while.'

Rosie crouched down beside the girl with the scar. 'May I look?'

She removed the shawl from around the baby's face. The infant seemed well enough fed, though there was a listlessness to him. His eyes didn't follow hers.

'He was born here,' said Sister Nora. 'I delivered him myself. They'll have to leave in a few days when new girls arrive, needing the space. They keep coming. It never stops.'

'Did Agnes work with these girls too?' I asked.

Sister Nora's face hardened. 'Not generally. She preferred solitude. But one girl kept coming back. We saw her four times in total, each time pregnant. She never had the older children with her.'

'I see. And Agnes was fond of her?'

'She was. Too fond, some might say. They spent hours together and even slept in the prayer room.' She glanced at my expression and pursed her lips. 'Nothing like *that*, Mr

Stanhope. We're not innocents here. We comprehend the dangers of our mission. Agnes was like a mother to her, trying to persuade her not to return.'

'Return where?'

'To Oswald Drake, of course. He was the father of the babies.' She clenched her jaw, trying to maintain her serenity. 'Probably, he dashed them against a wall or threw them in the river.'

Rosie, now holding the young woman's baby, drew him closer. 'Is that what Sister Agnes believes?'

'I don't know. She was very upset when the girl died. Very angry. And when Agnes gets angry, she's … she finds it hard to control herself.'

I thought back to what Elspeth Drake had told me about her friend who'd been with her when she first met Drake.

'Was the girl's name Peggy?'

Sister Nora nodded. 'Yes. She was barely alive when they brought her in the last time. Four or five months' pregnant, but already comatose. Agnes stayed by her bed for days, but the poor thing never woke up. She wasn't even seventeen.'

Rosie sighed deeply, looking down at the infant in her arms. 'It's so unfair. These little mites. What's his name?'

'I call him Joe,' the girl with the scar replied. 'But you can call him whatever you want.'

'What do you mean?'

Rosie went to hand the baby back, but the girl pushed him away.

'It's all right, ma'am. He'll be safe with you.'

Rosie looked at Sister Nora and back again at the girl. 'With me? But he's *your* baby.'

The girl shrank into her chair, hugging herself. 'He can be yours now though, can't he? He's no trouble, honest. He sleeps well and hardly cries ever.'

Rosie stared down at the little bundle, holding him away from herself as though any more intimate contact might create a bond that she would find hard to break.

'No, I can't possibly. I'm sorry. I have three of my own and no husband.' She threw me a look. 'I can't take another.'

She made another attempt to return baby Joe to his mother, but the girl covered her face with her hands. 'I thought you wanted 'im. I thought that was why you was here.'

Rosie glared at Sister Nora. 'No, not at all.'

Sister Nora folded her arms. 'People need to understand what we do here. Especially those who work for the press. Agnes Munro has put us in a perilous position.'

She exhaled deeply and held out her hands for baby Joe. His eyes were open, but he made no objection to being passed around in this way. She thrust him towards his mother, who had little option but to take him, rocking forwards and backwards, looking as though she might weep or drop him on to the floor.

I could hardly imagine their future. The girl would leave the convent in a few days and probably be sold on the street, and baby Joe would be dropped from a bridge or left in an alley. I couldn't face the thought, and looking at Rosie, I could see that she couldn't either. If we stayed, I feared she might weaken and actually take the child. Or I might.

Sister Nora led us back into the corridor, and as we reached the front door, we heard a sound above us. Mother Eugenie was coming down the stairs.

'Mr Stanhope! I didn't know you were here.' She looked pointedly at her younger colleague. 'I wasn't informed.'

Sister Nora inclined her head. 'I was showing them some of the work we do.'

Again, I sensed the tension between the two women. Neither were fools, nor free of compassion, but the horrors of their mission had led the Superior towards gentleness and benevolence, whereas Sister Nora, three decades her junior and perhaps not yet adapted to the contrariness of life, seemed to hold to a more puritanical view.

Rosie introduced herself to Mother Eugenie with uncharacteristic deference, and the four of us stood awkwardly, closeted by the silence.

'Sister Nora,' I began. 'You said before that you knew of one reason why Agnes would plead guilty to murdering Oswald Drake. What was it?'

She opened her mouth to reply, but Mother Eugenie interrupted her. 'We mustn't gossip. We don't know anything for certain. And besides, it's a matter for the convent.'

'Not any more,' I said, as gently as I could. 'It's a matter for the courts now. Sister Agnes will be sent to the City Prison to await trial.'

Mother Eugenie drew in her breath sharply, which I took to mean she knew the place. The City Prison was the punishment mothers threatened their children with to scare them into silence. I'd lived in its neighbourhood for a short while, and locally it was known as the Camden Castle in honour of its towering battlements and sheer walls. I'd seen those great gates open and inmates come tottering out at the end of their sentence, cradling their few possessions in their arms, mustard-nailed and toothless, their backs twisted and bent like yew trees. Most of them ended up as beggars in the shadows of the walls that had once held them.

Sister Nora met the eye of her Superior. 'We've hidden things for too long.'

Without either of them moving a muscle, a battle was fought between them. After a few seconds, Mother Eugenie lowered her eyes and nodded.

Sister Nora pulled back her shoulders and lifted her chin. 'It's quite simple. While Peggy was lying insensate, Agnes smothered her. That was how the girl died.'

'Mother of God,' exclaimed Rosie, putting her hand to her mouth.

I stared at the Sister. 'You mean … you mean she committed a murder. And you, all of you, covered it up?'

Mother Eugenie clutched her hands together, close to tears. 'It's not what you think. The girl would have died anyway, and in a far more horrible fashion. Starvation or infection, which ever took her first. The babe was already dead inside her. What Agnes did was a simple act of mercy. There was no crime, not as you or I would understand it.'

Sister Nora pursed her lips. 'Whether that's true or not, Agnes felt the weight of it as a sin. She started behaving strangely after it happened. She became more reverent, but also more detached from the rest of us.'

I was trying to imagine the pity and rage that would lead a person to do such a thing, and how it might affect them afterwards.

'Was that when she took up wrestling?'

Sister Nora took a moment to reply, gripping her fingers tightly together before composing herself. Her severity was like a glaze, impermeable and rigid, but desperately thin. One crack and it would fracture completely.

'Looking back, I can see that she blamed Oswald Drake for what she'd been driven to do. Of course, I didn't know it at the time.' She glanced at Mother Eugenie, not for permission, but as an indictment. 'Had it been drawn to my attention I would've put a stop to it.'

'So, you're saying—'

'She confessed to the murder because she thinks she deserves to be punished. She did kill someone. Just not Oswald Drake.'

19

Rosie and I left the convent in silence and waited under a tree for a raincloud to pass over. Rosie was calm for the most part but occasionally overspilling like a pot of boiling potatoes.

'That Sister Nora was hoping my soft heart would take pity on the wee thing. But how can I? I've three kids of my own and a shop to run.'

'Quite true.'

'I can't go adopting a baby just because he's in need of a mother.'

I was scarcely listening, wrapped up in my own thoughts.

'You're quite right, it has nothing to do with you. You should forget about the whole thing.'

She shot me a look. 'You really are a man sometimes, aren't you?'

I didn't reply, partly because I had no idea what she meant by *sometimes*, but mostly because I was turning over this new information in my mind. Sister Agnes had confessed to a murder because she'd smothered a girl who would otherwise have wasted away to nothing in the grip of a long, dark sleep. It was mercy, not murder. Why was she punishing herself?

The entire situation was frustrating. I felt as though I was missing something obvious. 'If Sister Agnes confessed to murdering Drake because she was guilt-ridden, why did she initially claim innocence?'

'Something must have changed.'

'Yes, exactly. But what?'

Rosie put out a hand and looked up at the sky. 'The rain's stopped. Come on.'

'Where are we going?'

She rolled her eyes so hard I thought they would fall out of her head. 'The prison, of course. We need to answer your question, and only Sister Agnes Munro can do that.'

We were about to leave when a figure wrapped in a cloak appeared from around the side of the convent. Whoever it was must have exited through the back door and seemed to be in a hurry. She kept her hood raised and was staying close to the walls, cutting the corner over the grass and heading east along Tooley Street, away from London Bridge.

I nodded towards the figure. 'Who's that?'

Rosie squinted through her spectacles. 'It looked like Sister Nora. You should get Alfie to check your eyesight, you really should.' She sniffed and set off in the same direction. 'I want to give her a piece of my mind. She's no right to hand a person a child as if—'

'Rosie!' I ran to catch up. 'This is the wrong way to get to the prison. We have to get over the river. There's no bridge this way.'

Rosie turned to me, her eyes blazing. 'Do you not think it's a mite suspicious, her creeping out of the place like this? Do you not want to know why?'

I held up my hands. 'All right. We can follow her for a little while to see where she's going. But please, let's not confront her.'

We'd only been walking for five minutes, perhaps even less, when Sister Nora took a left turn towards the river. The wharves huddled in front of us as the street dropped down, so we were almost at eye level with the cranes, poised like herons at the shoreside. Beyond that, the Thames was obscured by a white, sanctifying fog. I was scarcely able to spot her, though I could hear the click-clack of her shoes echoing off the walls and arches. And then we were almost upon her. She half turned at the sound of our footsteps and scurried onwards, her face lowered.

As we plunged into the stink of the quays, the hubbub grew louder, and the criss-crossing gangways over our heads boomed with boots and wheels, though I couldn't see a soul upon them. I found myself slowing, unnerved by the hidden alleys and the hollow thump of wooden trap-doors under our shoes.

'Quickly!' Rosie called back over her shoulder.

As we neared the river, we reached a curious, circular building, perhaps fifteen feet in diameter and less than that in height, as if someone had intended to install a vast tower but had given up when the project had hardly begun. On one side of it, a door was propped open. When I looked inside, Rosie was already descending a spiral staircase into the ground.

'Rosie!'

Her voice echoed back to me. 'Come on!'

I followed her down, round and round, my feet resounding on the steps. Someone came up from below, an ancient fellow with an armful of empty sacks, and I had to stop to let him pass, taking the inner side of the spiral in deference to his age. He nodded his thanks, puffing with exertion. My hands were shaking so hard I could barely grip the rail.

At the bottom, a hundred feet or more below the pavement, the stairs ended in a room furnished with chairs, tables and lamps like a parlour. It was utterly surreal, and yet scarcely warranted my notice. All of my attention was taken up by a circular hole in one wall that simply disappeared into dimness. I had lost all sense of direction, but surely there was no other possible explanation: it was a tunnel under the river.

Rosie turned to me, her face bright. 'I've heard about this.' The glint of amusement in her eyes told me that she was enjoying my discomfort, just a little. 'Sister Nora went this way, so we have to follow. Come on, it's an adventure.'

A young fellow was reading a magazine in a wooden kiosk. He held out his hand without looking up and I paid him a penny for each of us.

There wasn't enough width to walk two abreast, so I trailed Rosie in silence, the gentle curve of the tunnel gradually eclipsing the moonish light behind me.

I closed my eyes, running my hand along the dank circumference of the tunnel, feeling the rust under my fingers and the freezing water dripping into my sleeve, and listening to the toll of my shoes and the hissing lamps that marked our progress. The sound was strange, plangent and yet muffled, as if I had ducked under my bathwater as a child, watching my hair dance like riverweed and hearing the clank and echo of my limbs against the metal sides. I could hear footsteps too, some keeping pace, others growing louder until they were upon me; a seaman with a box on his back, a child with his dog, a fellow eating battered fish from a bag. Each time, I stood aside and waited for them to pass, remaining still until they were nothing but a faint ringing in the distance.

The further I walked, the more my guilt crowded in on me.

In all my life I'd never done anything so difficult to forgive. I had abandoned my mother to her loveless marriage, although I'd promised faithfully not to. I had allowed two people to hang for crimes they didn't commit, though they'd committed others. I had exhumed the dead body of a friend and left it under the stars for someone else to find. I had become so absorbed in my own pain that when Jacob's little boy died, I neglected my friend in the hour of his grief.

And yet, through all these sins, I hadn't caused an innocent person's death. Not until now.

I had accused Agnes Munro of murder and she would likely be hanged.

Just the day before, I'd contemplated leaving, going to a new life by the seaside where no one would be hurt by my actions. But that wasn't enough. If I cared for justice at all, I should lie down in the darkest part of the tunnel, curl up against the wall and remain there. Better, I should go to Westminster Bridge, climb on to the balustrade, reach out to the horizon and just step off.

I shook myself. *Melodramatic idiot.* I wasn't the flawed hero of some penny blood novel, romantically perishing in the depths. What good would that do anyone? Punishing myself wasn't important; at least not yet. I should seek justice for Sister Agnes, even if she didn't want it.

I felt a cooler breeze on my face and opened my eyes. I was at the end, where the tunnel opened into another room, the twin of the one at the entrance. Rosie was waiting for me with an impatient expression.

'Where have you been?' she hissed. 'Quickly. We need to follow her.'

As we ascended the spiral staircase, the air became fresher and there was a glow of natural light. We came out on the north bank of the Thames, under the shadow of the Tower of London walls. I looked back at the river, iron black beneath the mist, and was hardly able to believe we'd passed beneath it.

'That must've been the route Sister Agnes took as well,' I said, basking in the daylight. 'It explains why she went to the Mincing Lane post office to send the telegram. Coming this way, it's the nearest one.'

At the top of the hill, by the north-west corner of the Tower, the road levelled out. There, a great works was underway behind some fencing, hurling dust and filth into the air. As we got closer, we could hear men's voices and the clanging of pickaxes on rocks.

We spotted Sister Nora in a queue, squeezing into a narrow gap between the diggings. We joined the line, a dozen or so people behind, passing a sign saying 'Metropolitan Railway Extension'.

Underneath it, someone had scrawled: 'Thy money perish with thee'.

The hollow sound of our shoes on the planks told me I wasn't walking on a pathway, but a bridge. Through a gap in the fence, I could see scores of navvies lugging barrows and shovelling dirt on to carts, carving a vast trench out of the earth beneath us, thirty or more feet wide. A mechanical crane was lowering a concrete buttress the size of an altar into position.

I was glad to reach the other side and feel firm ground under my feet. A patch of grass had somehow survived; half of an oval, sliced off by the works, bordered by a road congested with carriages and carts.

Sister Nora glanced hastily over her shoulder and sat down neatly on a bench.

Rosie and I crossed the road behind her and stood together under a tree, watching the back of her head.

'She's waiting for someone,' I whispered, and Rosie rolled her eyes.

After ten minutes, a man appeared from the north side of the green, heading directly for the bench. Whereas Sister Nora had been as furtive as a mole, he seemed not to have a care in the world. As he drew closer, I could see he was wearing a clergyman's collar.

'My goodness,' I said to Rosie. 'It's Iain Sutherland.'

The deacon sat next to Sister Nora and for a while neither of them spoke. He seemed quite content to take in the air and watch a couple of maids pushing perambulators along the path. Rosie and I edged closer, until we were no more than twenty feet behind them.

Eventually, Sister Nora sighed and folded her arms. 'Must you act as though we have the same freedoms as ordinary people? Do you care nothing for my station or your own?'

He shrugged. 'I'm not sure what either of those are worth at the moment.'

She didn't smile. 'Mine is worth plenty. I've done nothing wrong.'

'You're here, aren't you?'

They fell into another sullen silence, and I nudged Rosie: 'Can they be lovers?'

It was a big enough secret to motivate a murder. But Rosie shook her head.

'No,' she whispered. 'Can't you tell? With lovers, there's always something indefinable, a connection in the eyes, in the hands, the way their words overlap, even when they argue. There's none of that here.'

'Then what?'

She thought for a moment and then smiled as she reached a conclusion. 'Of course, they're brother and sister. She must be Nora *Sutherland*. We never thought to ask her full name, did we?'

Iain Sutherland stood up, seeming agitated, shoving his hands boyishly into his pockets. He was the younger sibling, if I was any judge.

'Why should I?' he protested, in reply to a question I hadn't been able to hear. 'You know what would happen if the truth came out. I'd be booted out of the church. Perhaps worse.'

Sister Nora set her shoulders. 'She'll be hanged, Iain.'

'Rather her than me.'

She stared at him with an expression only a sister can muster. I knew that look only too well. She was ashamed of what he'd become.

'Does your faith mean so little that you'll withhold the truth?'

He pulled a face. 'My faith was Father's idea, not mine.'

It was her turn to stand up. 'Tell the truth or I will,' she declared, and strode back the way she'd come, leaving her brother standing on his own like a lost child.

20

WE TOOK THE METROPOLITAN Railway at Aldgate. I wanted to talk to Rosie about Nora and Iain Sutherland, and what he might be hiding, but she shook her head and kept a firm hold of her seat, as anxious as Jonah waiting for the whale to cough him up. When the train burst on to the platform at Bishopsgate, the first station on the line, she gasped and grabbed my arm.

We all harbour fears of something.

We exited at King's Cross and headed northwards through the slums and cheerless dollyhouses, where women lacking most of their teeth and all the lacing on their upper garments hung out of windows and called down to us. Rosie pointedly ignored them.

'It's quite common for a brother and sister both to go into the church,' I said. 'Children of the clergy, most likely.'

Sutherland's fate might have been my own, if I'd been born into a man's body. My father believed the only worthwhile vocations were the church or the army, and I could never have tolerated all that marching.

Rosie was walking at speed. 'What secret is he keeping, do you suppose?'

She clearly didn't like the idea that a Catholic deacon, a man in training to become a priest, might lie to save himself. And yet he'd as good as admitted it.

'Something about Agnes Munro,' I said. 'Something that might see her set free.'

After that we continued in silence, eyes straight ahead, though we couldn't help but catch glimpses of the alleys and doorways: dull-eyed fellows with restless fingers; mothers and children clutching each other in the cold; a young girl hugging a three-legged goat.

Having previously lived in Camden, I had known what to expect, but I thought Rosie might be shocked. She was not.

'See that clock tower,' she said eventually, pointing. 'That's where the market is. Albert and I go there for our meat. Or we did before he got sick.'

The market was closed on Saturdays so no one was crowding the lanes that led to it, but we could easily see the route they usually took by the piles of cow shit, split barrow wheels, screwed up paper bags and, most of all, sparkling trails of bottle glass.

We turned right at the main road, and not long afterwards, the City Prison loomed up in front of us.

'Are you all right, Leo?'

'Of course.'

In truth, I was experiencing a peculiar sensation. I didn't consider myself to be a criminal, and yet, in the eyes of the law, I was one. Specifically, I was a fraud. I had gained my position at the *Daily Chronicle* and my lodging with Alfie as a man, which, as my friend Peregrine had informed me, would likely result in my incarceration, if I was ever caught.

I missed Peregrine considerably. According to the last postcard I'd received from him, his theatrical tour had now progressed to Morecambe and would remain there for the summer, but I dearly wished he was at home. I wanted to ask him whether this prison was the kind of place to which I would be consigned. I had a black vision of myself in a dress and mob cap, mending uniforms and picking oakum out of ropes with the women. Worse still, they might try to cure me using chemicals and electricity and holes drilled into my head. I was terrified of them trying, and even more so that they might succeed, after a fashion. What would be left of me then? A facsimile of a woman, skin pulled over bone with no mind or soul within.

A cold shiver ran through me and I wished I'd worn my coat. It was a masculine thing, that coat, with broad shoulders, thick lapels and a boxy shape, as though I had donned a coal scuttle. No one would think me other than a man in that coat.

Rosie didn't wait for me but crossed over the street towards the prison gatehouse. Whoever had designed the monstrous building had modelled it, as far as I could tell, on the kind of toy castle my brother had played with as a child, with narrow windows for his tin bowmen to shoot through, and tall battlements from which imaginary oil could be flung.

We passed between the lamps guarding the entrance and I followed Rosie to the front door, half expecting it to lower as a drawbridge on two reels of string.

Before she could knock, a guard in uniform sprang from his hut and straightened his cap. He was holding a clipboard.

'Do you have a 'pointment?'

He was an earnest fellow in his fifties with a face made all of vertical lines running down in parallel from his eyes and mouth.

'No. I'm from the *Chronicle*. I need to talk to one of your prisoners. I have reason to believe she's innocent.'

'Bit late for that.'

'She hasn't yet been convicted.'

He scratched his head, lifting his ill-fitting cap. 'She wouldn't be here if she wasn't convicted.'

'She's confessed,' I conceded, earning a loud tut from Rosie. 'But that doesn't mean she did it.'

Even to my ears, that sounded feeble. I hadn't considered that prisons didn't commonly allow visitors to speak to their inmates. I pressed the heel of my hand against the sore point on my chest where Coffey's boot had landed, feeling the flood of pain spread through me like lye through a sponge.

I shouldn't have come here. I'd been blinded by my own righteousness, or perhaps, more accurately, by my impatience for redemption. Finding my culpability indigestible, I'd sought to retch it up at the earliest opportunity.

'Sorry, mate.' He tucked his clipboard under his arm and indicated the street. 'No 'pointment, no entry.'

We walked back to the pavement just as a flat, atonal bell in the distance told us it was four o'clock.

Rosie stamped her foot irritably. 'I never thought … damn. What a waste of time. I may as well go home. Mr Whitford said he'd collect me at six-thirty.'

'Oh, is that today?'

She nodded, looking distractedly back the way we'd come. 'It is, though now I wish it wasn't. I've better things to do than swan around Kew Gardens with Mr Whitford.'

'Then why did you agree to go?'

'I don't know.' She drew in a long breath and lowered her chin so that, from where I was standing, her face was obscured by the brim of her bonnet. 'It's all right when you and I are out gallivanting and solving crimes, Leo, but most of the time I'm at home. And Alice is off to Hastings, so … it'll just be me and the kids. I know I'm being silly, but … I don't want to be lonely.'

I had never thought of her as being lonely. How could she be, when she harboured no secret that would for ever put a curtain between her and the rest of the world? And yet, she seemed so glum that I had the desperate urge to cheer her up. She'd heard all my jokes and was, inexplicably, impervious to my coin trick, so I had to settle for patting her on the shoulder.

At that moment, a cab drew up and, to my surprise, Mother Eugenie climbed out. She had changed her clothing; swapping the simple, greying habit she'd been wearing for a stark black and white one, creaseless and perfect, with a shiny cross on a chain around her neck.

'I thought you might be here too,' she said.

I noticed she didn't pay the driver. Perhaps religious Sisters got free travel around London, much like actresses.

'They won't let us in.'

She gathered herself. 'We'll see about that.'

Barely taller than Rosie, she could nevertheless muster a regal bearing. She glided up to the entrance and waited for the guard to come to her. He hesitated and swiped off his cap.

'Do you have a 'pointment, ma'am?'

'No, and neither do I need one. I am the Mother Superior at the Convent of Mercy and one of my Sisters is locked up in this dreadful place. I will see her immediately.'

To his credit, he did not wilt. Many a man would have.

'It don't work that way.'

She surveyed him, her lips pressed hard together. 'Were you by any chance in the army before your current employment?'

'I was, ma'am. Sixteenth Regiment.'

'Well then. When I was in the Crimea, I met a good many men like you. I salved their burns, changed their bandages and held their hands as they died. I prayed over them while bullets flew over our heads. I didn't do all that so I could stand out here in the cold while one of my own is in there. I will enter this place.' She made a shooing motion with her hands. 'Fetch whoever you need to get permission from so we can all get on with it.'

When the poor fellow had gone, Mother Eugenie turned to Rosie and me. 'And what's your plan?'

I smiled as winningly as I could, though Rosie had once told me the expression resembled a crazed Labrador. 'I want to write about the miscarriage of justice. If Sister Agnes is willing to tell the truth, I'll put it in the newspaper.'

'Will you know the truth when you hear it?'

'I hope so.'

Before long, a woman appeared at the door. She was mature, sturdy in the foundations and broad in the belly, with a high, crenellated forehead.

'I'm Mrs Jackman,' she announced. 'I'm in charge of the women's wing. Follow me.'

As the door shut behind us, we were thrown into darkness before emerging into a courtyard on the other side. Ahead, another building rose up, even larger than the gatehouse, stretching its vulturous wings on either side, four storeys high, brutal and impregnable.

I clasped my fingers together and kept walking, feeling my heart pounding in my chest.

Mrs Jackman swept a hand across the buildings. 'Boys on the left, mostly from the gangs. Girls and women on the right. Men in the blocks behind.'

Through the windows, dim faces were watching us. Hands reached out between the bars, not in some painful desperation but simply, it seemed to me, to feel the wind.

'Don't speak to anyone,' Mrs Jackman instructed as we reached the main doorway.

'What if they speak to us?' asked Rosie.

'They won't. They know better.'

We followed her through a further heavy door and, as it clanged shut, I could feel my fingers prickling. Ahead of us was a long nave, the upper storeys accessible via stairs and galleries with nets strung between them. The arched ceiling was half lit by grubby skylights, lending the place an infernal air, not helped by the knowledge that it was crammed with prisoners, out of sight in the cells on either side, their soft feet shuffling on the floors and their fingers pressing needles through cloth. The only voice we could hear was a keening squeal from one of the upper cells which I took at first for a buzzard, until it sank and growled and fell to coughing. Rosie and I exchanged a glance.

'I'm letting you see Miss Munro because she hasn't been tried yet,' said Mrs Jackman. 'Also, because …' she trailed off.

'Because I'm a woman religious,' said Mother Eugenie, finishing her sentence.

Mrs Jackman nodded, though I was almost certain that hadn't been what she was going to say.

The cell doors were heavy iron, with a barred window on each one. Most of them were empty, their doors open, sacking and chaff strewn on the ground. A few were shut, the inmates lying on their cot or, in one case, standing at the bars, observing me and sucking in air through her teeth. Mrs Jackman shot the woman a look, and she pushed away into darkness.

At the next cell, Mrs Jackman fumbled with her keys and threw open the door, revealing Sister Agnes kneeling on the ground.

I was struck by how little had changed. Another small room, another bible on the shelf, another cross hung on the wall. She smiled, indicating to Mother Eugenie and Rosie that they should sit on the bed beside her, which they did, resembling two small prayer books either side of a hefty concordance.

The warden turned to leave, and I followed her out. 'Excuse me, Mrs Jackman. Agnes seems to have been given everything she needs. The books and cross and so forth.'

She narrowed her eyes, unsure if I was complimenting her.

'So?'

'I was wondering why. It seems like a lot of trouble for one prisoner on her first day. Have you done it because of what she is?'

I only had half of her attention. The other half was hearing, feeling, smelling this place like a gamekeeper attuned to his land. Such a strange position to hold, I thought, guarding all these women. How they must hate her. When she went home to her family in the evening or spent a carefree Sunday picnicking with friends, did they ask her whom she had punished that week?

'We have all kinds here,' she said. 'I treat them the same no matter who they were before.'

'Then why?'

She leaned towards me and spoke in a low tone. 'I read the newspapers. I know what she did. And from what I can see, the swine had it coming. We've all wished we could do the same.'

Upstairs, the thin cry had started up again, sounding even more inhuman, a product of madness or agony. No one seemed to be attending to the woman or comforting her. I supposed they had got used to the noise, an accompaniment to their daily lives.

I waited for the three women in the cell to finish praying. I had no objection to others talking to God if it made them happy, but I could have told them He wouldn't be answering. They might as well be talking to one of the jackdaws presently defiling the skylights.

When Mother Eugenie had said her amen, I came straight to the point.

'Why did you change your mind?' I asked Agnes. 'Why did you claim you were guilty after so vehemently protesting your innocence?'

Mother Eugenie took the hand of her subordinate. 'Is it because of that girl? The one you … the one who died?'

Sister Agnes looked nonplussed. 'Do you mean Peggy?'

It was Rosie who answered. 'Sister Nora said you took pity on the girl.'

'She was piteous. Cruelly used by that …' She stopped herself before she used an unwomanly epithet. 'That man Drake. Of course I took pity.'

Rosie looked at me and then back at Sister Agnes. 'Sister Nora said the girl was due to die a horrible death. She said you chose to end her suffering. An act of mercy.'

Sister Agnes stood and began pacing up and down the little cell. 'That's not true. I prayed for the Lord to take Peggy, but He wouldn't.' She looked up at the cross with a fleeting expression of anger. 'I stayed by her bedside, waiting as her breath slowed and slowed. On the fifth day she stirred, and I thought she was going to wake. I should've taken her life then. She was far too weak to birth a child already dead, and I had no doubt she wouldn't survive. But I couldn't do it. I was a coward.' Her tears were falling on to the flagstones, scuffed into damp smears by her slippers. 'On the sixth day, she tried to scream, but couldn't raise her voice loud enough to be heard by anyone outside the room. Her throat was parched. An hour later, she died, but not at my hand. The Lord finally took her.' She slammed her fist into her other hand, shuddering with the pain. 'But it was Oswald Drake who was responsible, as certainly as if he'd put a knife into her heart. He was the one who deserved to die, not Peggy.'

Mother Eugenie gasped, but I'd heard such abstractions before and knew not to trust them. 'When you first went to the penny gaff, was it with the intention of killing him?'

Sister Agnes sighed. 'I watched him on the stage, preening and boasting. At the end of the evening, he invited members of the audience to come up and have a go in the ring. I'd spent my childhood fighting my brothers, so I accepted. I didn't think they'd allow me to take part as I am, so I fibbed a bit. Irina was my mother's name. She was Hungarian, from Szeged.' She glanced in Mother Eugenie's direction. 'I normally value the truth, of course. But Mr Drake was … undeserving. When I won, he invited me to come back the following Tuesday. One week became two and then three. I even enjoyed it.' The corners of her mouth pulled back a fraction. 'Perhaps I was never suited to the convent.'

Rosie nodded and took the Sister's hand. 'I understand. You wanted him dead, but to actually kill him? That's a difficult decision to take.'

Sister Agnes frowned at Rosie as if rethinking her initial assessment. 'I would hope so. Murder would be a terrible burden to bear.'

I leaned forward. 'If you didn't kill Drake, then why did you change your mind and tell the police you did? Why did you confess?'

She sat down, her elbows on her knees, and closed her eyes.

'Didn't you hear it?'

'Hear what?'

'The singing. Those women outside my cell, they were singing. They sounded like angels, wouldn't you say? It was the beginning.'

Her face was lit up like a painting of the Madonna.

'The beginning of what?'

She opened her eyes and they were shining with tears, a product of joy now, rather than misery. 'Don't you understand? Men like Oswald Drake think they can do anything, hurt anyone, and get away with it. But those women marched into the street and stood up for their rights. They stood up for me. They were a little flame that could become a blaze and then a conflagration.'

I tried not to wince at the thought. 'And you were the … the spark for that conflagration, is that what you mean?'

'Of course. And if I claim my innocence now, that flame will go out. It will be a simple legal matter and the trial will be over in no time. I'll be a woman who claimed innocence but was found guilty, and Mr Drake's crimes will be ignored. The newspapers will move on and everyone will forget.'

She was right, of course. J.T. would put her execution on page four and never think of her again.

'What if you're found innocent? It is possible.'

'I know. And then the police will be accused of incompetence and, again, everyone will forget about Mr Drake.' She smiled with genuine warmth, even in this place. 'But if I say I'm guilty and I killed him because he *deserved* to die, then I become a quandary, don't I? People will have opinions. Questions will be asked. I will be remembered as a symbol of freedom from men like him and the singing will continue for ever.'

Mother Eugenie, who'd been listening to all of this with her mouth hanging open, shook her head vigorously. 'You can't mean you intend to become a *martyr*, my dear.'

Sister Agnes lowered her face. 'It's why all of this happened. I finally understand God's purpose for me.'

I couldn't fathom what I was hearing. This woman, this powerful, fearsome woman, was claiming that God wished her to be hanged. My dislike of Him burned newly hot.

'But I put you in this position. It was my article that—'

She waved aside my protestation. 'It's not your fault, Mr Stanhope, if that's what concerns you. I whole-heartedly absolve you of any blame.'

'You cannot.'

'Because I'm a woman?'

I steadied myself to keep from spinning on the spot.

'Because I *am* to blame.' *For this and so many other things.*

She gave me a gentle nod. 'You don't understand. Without you, this wouldn't have been possible. I should thank you. You were His instrument, as unlikely as that may seem.'

Rosie, having said little so far, stirred. 'I don't know much about these things,' she began. 'I'm just a pie maker. But I do know that sometimes I have an idea about a filling and I'm certain it'll be delicious. I mix it up and bake it. But when I eat the pie, it tastes terrible. The ingredients don't go together at all. You can't always be sure.' She took Sister Agnes's hand again. 'Is it possible that you've misunderstood what the Lord wants?'

I didn't think anyone could possibly be swayed by an anecdote about baking, especially as it was clearly nonsense; Rosie had never cooked a foul-tasting pie in her life. But Sister Agnes seemed oddly moved.

'Thank you,' she said. 'But I am certain.'

I tried to steer the conversation towards more rational ground. 'Surely you can do more good for womankind out there than locked up in here.'

'Others will do that work; the good Mother here and all the Sisters of the convent. Only I can do this, and I intend to see it through to the end.' She bowed her head. 'You should leave me now. I wish to pray.'

———

Outside on the pavement, we bade farewell to Mother Eugenie. Her face was the colour of chalk.

'Our faith is built on the bones of martyrs, and yet when one presents herself in the here and now, it's unexpected. I can't see how this will end well, and yet I pray it will. Goodbye, Mrs Flowers. Mr Stanhope.'

She bit her lip, not able to continue without weeping.

Rosie put her hand on the old woman's shoulder. 'It's different when it's someone you know.'

We watched Mother Eugenie go, a small black shape among the other pedestrians, who parted either side of her and then came together again, obscuring her from view.

Rosie was shivering. 'The police will stop looking now, you know that,' she said, more to herself than me. 'They'll rush Sister Agnes into court as fast as they can and call it a victory. We have to find out who really killed Drake before they hang an innocent woman.'

She was still talking as we walked south towards the city, maintaining a brisk pace. She was going to be late for Harry. I replied with 'yes' and 'I agree' at what seemed like appropriate moments, but I wasn't really listening.

A plan was slowly taking shape in my head.

I almost told her what it was. I wanted to, but ... she would try to stop me and, when I wouldn't be dissuaded, she would insist on coming too. She was loyal and brave and foolish. I couldn't put her in that much danger. Better she went out with Harry for the evening and returned to her children and never knew what I had done.

21

AT TEN O'CLOCK THAT evening, I arrived at the penny gaff. It was heaving with people and the noise could be heard from a hundred yards away. Outside, the Othello sign had been painted over, and was now reading:

Wrestling Every Night
The finest sporting contests
brought to you by new proprietor
Mr Nicholas Coffey
MEN ONLY

I couldn't imagine how he'd come to take the place over. By rights, it should have gone to Reggie, which in practice meant to his mother, Elspeth.

I peeked through a gap in the advertisements littering the window, and the place was packed. Two men were wrestling in the ring, locked together like battling stags. They went to ground and one of them forced the other into a neck lock, only releasing him when the poor fellow beat his palm on the floor.

Coffey bounced on to the stage and held up the winner's arm. He was quite a sight. His old clothes had been colourful, but they were of the type a working man might afford, fraying at the hems and scuffed around the pockets. No longer. Now, his violet jacket was spotless, one sleeve sewn shut at the end, and his trousers were black, not in the normal way trousers are black, meaning somewhat grey at the knees and hems, but coal-tar black, with creases so fine they dropped vertically like a plumb, only breaking as they reached the laces of his shiny leather shoes.

I couldn't bear to watch him, so I sat on the pavement with my back to the gaff, waiting for my eyes to adjust to the dark again.

Children were gathering, though I had to be sharp-sighted to spot them. They were crouching behind the wall, peeking around corners and huddling together in dim doorways, their eyes glinting in the reflection from the window. I hoped Coffey would continue Drake's habit of allowing them to sleep on the floor at night. My plan depended on it.

I had long since made the decision that I would never again wear a dress – not for any reason. But that didn't mean I couldn't disguise myself in other ways.

I took off my coat, rolled it up and thrust it into the drawstring bag I'd brought with me.

After our last trip to the park, when we'd been caught in a downpour, I had bought Aiden and Ciara both a complete change of clothes that I kept in my room. Aiden's were considerably small on me, of course, but that suited my needs perfectly. Thus, Leo Stanhope, upstanding gentleman and diligent reporter, was replaced by an urchin of perhaps fourteen or fifteen years, newly sprouted, with wrists and ankles extending pinkly from his jacket and trousers. His face was grubby around the cheeks and chin, and his hair, though more neatly cut than one might expect, was greasy, almost as though someone had combed grease through it.

The first time I had looked this way was a decade and a half previously when I'd tried on my brother's clothes, striding down the hill towards the park with a spring in my step.

And the last time I had looked this way, my name had been Tom Cobb.

I strode up the road and back again, practising the swagger I'd adopted back then, before I became a gentleman. There was something in the heels, some elevation with each step, and a swing in the shoulders that didn't care if passers-by had to skip out of my way.

I felt in my jacket pocket and pulled out the syringe I'd taken from Jacob. It was a lovely thing, worth half a crown at least, made of brass with two finger-holes in the plunger and a fine needle. Back at the pharmacy, I'd dissolved some morphine crystals in alcohol and dripped them into the barrel.

The door to the penny gaff burst open and a dozen men came pouring out, many with the sour expressions of punters who'd won fewer bets than they'd lost. One of them, drunk and not looking where he was going, barged into me.

'Oy! Get out of the bloody way!'

I pressed against the window, the drawstring bag gripped tightly in my hand, and he stumbled onwards, swigging his bottle of ale.

The children clustered closer, skinny as minks, watching for anyone who might approach, whether that was prey or predator. When the lamps inside the gaff were lit again, they formed an uneven line along the pavement.

Unwittingly, I'd taken the frontmost position, though not for long. A heavyset lad of about my height barged in front of me, elbowing me into the street, and the line immediately closed up, affording me no gap to step into. I walked sheepishly to the back, passing all the other children, a dozen or more, each of whom gave me a look of pure derision.

The final few kids were the littlest ones. I felt giant and ridiculous standing behind them but couldn't bring myself to heave them out of the way.

The door opened and Mr Coffey emerged, standing in the exact spot where Mr Drake had handed out farthings just ten days before.

'All right then,' the dandy called out, jingling coins in his pocket. 'I'll give you the same deal you had before. But if anyone steps out of line, I'll have 'em thrashed.'

The lad at the front, with a dark complexion and deep-set eyes, took his coin and ducked his head to enter the gaff. Coffey put a restraining hand on his arm.

'You should be a wrestler, sonny. You're getting big enough. We should see what you're made of.'

Six further lads got their farthings before the first girl reached the door. I recognised her from the last time, when she'd given Drake a sarcastic curtsy. She was moon-faced and about Constance's age, on the brink of womanhood but still a foot shorter than me. Coffey took her chin in his hand.

'What's your name, darlin'?'

'Maria, sir.'

I felt a flush within my veins, bursting into my fingers and toes, stinging my lips and rushing in my ears. I almost leapt forward to pull her away, but Coffey let go and she passed inside. None of the remaining children was stopped until I reached the doorway and put out my hand for a farthing, keeping my face lowered.

Coffey narrowed his eyes. 'Why ain't you near the front?' he demanded. 'A lad your age should take his right place.'

I allowed my voice to quaver boyishly. 'Plenty to go round, I reckon, from a generous gentleman such as yourself.'

Coffey laughed and patted me firmly on the shoulder, making me wince. 'You'll get nowhere like that. If I'd taken that attitude, I wouldn't be standing here with my own establishment, would I?'

My own establishment – I wondered what tortuous path of events had made such a thing possible. I couldn't risk meeting his eye, but I could guess his expression, like a man who'd pocketed a pound note he'd seen another man drop in the street.

Inside, the room stank of smoke and alcohol, but it was warm and dry. Without waiting to be asked, the children spread out. Most seemed to have a favoured spot where they placed their bag or blanket. They wandered around, picking up rubbish from the floor, betting chits and broken glass, and dropping it into a crate. When they found a crust of bread or a morsel of meat, they stuffed it into their mouths, and every bottle was checked for dregs. Even a few drips was a prize. The larger boys searched the most fertile spots, along the window ledges and under the tables where the bookmakers did their business. I followed the lead of the smaller children and scoured the centre of the room and the edges of the stage.

Once the whole place was clear of detritus, one of the younger girls fetched a broom and began sweeping while the rest of them lay down. Some were asleep within seconds.

I sat on the floor with my back against the wall.

The girl next to me opened one eye. 'You're new, ain't you?'

It was Maria, the girl Coffey had stopped. She was sprawled on the hard floor, still in her boots, if they could be so described, comprising more hole than leather.

From memory, boys of fifteen treated girls of thirteen with little respect, and yet I couldn't summon up the necessary disdain. I didn't have it within me.

'Yeah, first time.' I was trying to mimic her plain vowels and consonants flung out like little darts. 'I'm in Soho most days.'

'Snob,' she mumbled, and closed her eye again.

Apparently, my attempt at an East End accent had not been convincing.

I indicated the low door through to the back of the gaff. 'Is that locked?'

She nodded without looking. 'Someone'll come in soon.'

I climbed to my feet, trying to appear more limber than I felt, and approached the girl who was still doggedly sweeping. She was no more than eight or nine, but she was diligent, doing each floorboard in turn and making neat little piles of dust.

I took hold of the broom.

'Shall I take over? Give you a rest.'

But she had her task and wouldn't give it up. She pouted her lips and held on tight to the handle.

'Why don't you let me have it?' I insisted. 'I'll do the work for you.'

I hadn't intended to sound threatening, but I needed that broom. It was my ticket to the rear of the gaff and the hut where the wrestlers got changed.

The little girl pulled on the broom as hard as she could, forcing me to let go. She flew backwards, still holding on to the broom, and landed on her behind in one of her piles of dust.

I dived forward to check she was unhurt, but she squirmed away, glowering at me. The largest of the lads – the one Coffey had suggested should become a wrestler – jumped to his feet. He was my height, but much broader, almost a man.

'What did you do?' he demanded, his face flushing.

'Nothing.'

'He's a snob from Soho,' offered Maria, unhelpfully.

The lad approached me with hostile intent, his fists clenching and unclenching. No one else moved. I was determined not to take a step backwards. Any sign of weakness and he would be on me.

I kept my hands at my sides and my voice steady. 'I don't want to fight you.'

He grabbed my lapel at chest level, something I had good reason to dislike. I chopped his hand away, but he made another grab for my jacket. I twisted and ducked under his swinging fist, but he whirled round, nimble on his feet, and pulled a jack-knife from his pocket.

I held up my hands. 'No need for any of this. I just want a place to sleep.'

He opened up the blade. 'You got no business here.'

Everyone was awake and watching now, but none looked as though they were about to help, on either side.

The lad took off his cap and switched the knife to his right hand. He had the advantage in strength and reach, and that made him dangerous, but he also had a temper. I could use that. It was the only chance I had.

I smiled.

'What are you grinning at?' he demanded.

'Oh, just a thing in my head. Kind of a joke. I'm thinking you wouldn't get it.'

'What joke?'

I laughed again, waving my amusement casually away. 'It doesn't matter. You wouldn't understand.'

'Tell me what you think is so bloody *funny*.' He spat out the last word.

'Oh, all right. I was just thinking how silly you'd look in a petticoat and bonnet.'

Baiting did the trick. The boy lunged forward, all his weight on his front foot. I stepped sideways and punched him, aiming for his right kidney and finding instead his lowest rib, the twelfth. He hunched over, wheezing, so I hit him in the face with the heel of my hand, not wanting to risk breaking my fingers with another punch. He crumpled, dropping on to all fours, still holding the knife.

I was about to bring my boot down on his fingers when he rolled and kicked out twice. I dodged the first but the second caught my knee and I went down on to my back.

He was on me like a fox on a rabbit. I flailed, twisting from side to side and banging the ground like a wrestler signalling his surrender, but nothing would dislodge him.

One of his hands was gripping the knife, blade upwards. I needed both of my hands to stop him slashing at me, so my throat was exposed, and his other hand was squeezing it. I could feel my breaths getting shorter and more painful as his fingers dug in. I tried to wriggle free, but his grasp was like a vice. I looked up at him and his lips were pulled back into a grimace that seemed like a smile.

His would be the last face I would ever see. All the fear, fire and chloral, the rope and the black water, all of that, and I would end up being killed by a boy whose name I didn't know, with whom I had no argument, for no other reason than because he didn't like the look of me and I'd accidentally caused a little girl to fall on to her behind.

Something scratched at me, some memory I was sure was important, if only I could bring it to mind.

I let go of his wrist with my left hand and he tugged the knife free, spinning it once so the blade was pointing down. He seemed to be calculating where to stab first.

His hold on my throat was tight, but he was more intent on stabbing than throttling me, and I was able to force a thin rasp of air into my lungs.

I fumbled at my pocket and found what I was looking for. I almost dropped it but managed to turn it in my hand and get a tight grip.

It was the most satisfying thump. I buried the syringe needle into the meat of his thigh and depressed the plunger, releasing a third of an ounce of morphine into him.

I hadn't mixed the stuff with the intention of using it. I'd wanted it to be easily detectable by the police, so it was a fiercely strong concentration.

The lad stared down at his leg, muttered something I didn't understand and raised the knife again. But his heart was no longer in the battle. His face changed from bare-teethed fury to confusion as the rush of morphine suffused his bloodstream, slowing his mind and numbing his senses. I pulled the syringe out of his leg and shoved him off me.

Breathing hard, I climbed to my feet. Some of the children were also standing, exchanging nervous looks. I had no idea what they might do, but at that moment, the back door opened, and Bert Trafford reversed through it, whistling and pulling a trolley.

I dashed forward to hold the door for him, hiding my face in the shadows. As the door swung shut, I poked my shoe into the gap, preventing it from closing completely.

'Thanks,' he muttered, without really looking.

He wrapped his arms around the crate, hoisted it on to the trolley and placed the broom carefully on top. His eyes scanned the room.

'Mr Coffey told me one of you might make a decent wrestler,' he said. 'We should have a try-out. Which of you is it?'

Everyone's eyes turned to the lad. He had crawled to the edge of the room and was curled up there, unmoving but for a twitching in his face and hands.

Trafford squinted and went over to him, crouching down. He picked up the knife and felt the blade.

'What happened to 'im?'

All eyes probably swivelled towards me, but I was already on my way, flitting through the back door and into the yard between the gaff and the shiplap hut. I had only seconds to find a hiding place. I squeezed between the hut and the high wall that ran alongside the street, cobwebs tickling my face.

I couldn't see the door to the gaff, but I heard it open, footsteps on the stones and the squeak of trolley wheels; Trafford again, hunting for the boy who'd won a scrap and immediately scarpered.

I tried to hold my breath but had to gasp in air, so hard was my heart pounding in my chest. I was certain he would hear me.

The door to the hut opened as well, bathing the yard in a thin light. A man's shadow was cast grey against the back wall of the gaff, his hat at a jaunty angle like a puppet.

'Any problems?' asked Coffey.

'No, sir,' I heard Trafford say. 'There was some quarrelling among the boys, but that's no bad thing.'

'And the girls?'

'Quiet as mice.'

'Good.' Coffey's shoes shuffled pensively in the gravel. 'You're a loyal man, Bert, and I appreciate that. You'll go far if you stick by my side. I'm the new Oswald, and you're the new me, in a manner of speaking.'

'Yes, Mr Coffey. I'm very grateful for the chance, sir.'

'You should get off home, Bert. Your missus'll be wondering where you've got to.'

'Yes, thank you, Mr Coffey. She was soaking some barley as I left, and I fancy there'll be some soup waiting for me.'

The gaff door opened, and the two men left. I was alone in the yard.

The clear sky meant a cold evening, and I could see my breath in the thin light. I wrapped my jacket more tightly around myself. Where was my coat?

I realised I'd left it inside the gaff, still in the drawstring bag. I couldn't go back for it, not after what had happened. There was nothing to be done. One of the kids would doubtless find it and be warmer through the winter than they otherwise would've been.

I waited.

I knew I ought to go home. The wall was taller than I was, but I could use the crate as a stepping stool; over and gone in a minute, and no one any the wiser. But then what?

Agnes Munro would hang.

I crept out of my hiding place and wiped the cobwebs from my face. Very softly, I put my ear to the door of the hut. I couldn't hear a sound from within, only the distant rumbling of a coal train heading into the city. I turned the handle and slipped inside, my heart now beating so strongly I thought it would leap out through my mouth.

The hut was as I remembered it, with curtains hanging from the ceiling, dividing the space into makeshift rooms. On my left was where Trafford had been stitched, and on my right was where Irina Vostek had changed her clothes. Ahead was a further area, the glimmering candlelight making strange patterns on the drapes.

I carefully pushed aside the left-hand curtain, revealing two wooden chairs, a table with a basin of water and a dresser containing the case of catgut and needles.

The back wall had been decorated with pencil sketches on sheets of paper. None were terribly good, but I recognised Coffey from his empty sleeve and opera hat, and Irina Vostek from her burlesque features and breasts even more gigantic than in reality. Another was of a girl with a gaunt face, spindle-thin arms and voluminous, pregnant belly. My first thought was Elspeth, but the hair was wrong; thin and straight where hers was curly. No, this must be Peggy. Her expression could have been a smile, but the picture wasn't well enough drawn to be certain. The other drawings were of various wrestlers who all looked much the same, and at the top there was a single, empty nail.

I froze as the door opened again.

Two people came in, a man and a woman, passing by me so close I could have put my hand against the curtain and touched them. I could feel myself shaking, my skin prickling as though spiders were crawling over me. I eased back against the wall of the hut, trying not to allow the smallest squeak to escape from the floorboards.

There was the sound of someone clearing the table, groaning as he straightened up. Coffey, I was sure of it. The woman remained standing. I could make out her silhouette against the curtain.

The chair creaked.

'You seem very comfortable,' said the woman, not meaning it politely. I recognised her voice. It was Elspeth Drake.

A drink was poured, and the stopper replaced in the bottle. Coffey took a gulp and set his glass on the table. I could imagine him sitting back and surveying her.

'Don't be like that, Elsie.'

'By rights, this business is Reggie's, which means it's mine. If there's any chance of making a profit, it should come to me. You've no right to start running it again.'

'That's the thing though, ain't it? Oswald had debts. You know he did. And you know who the creditor is. You know *very* well.' I could tell from his tone he was sneering at her, making some point that she clearly understood. 'That money's owed, and it seems I'm the one best placed to repay it.'

She turned her back on him. 'So, you can be the big man, do you mean, now Oswald's gone? Didn't think you was the envious type.'

'I ain't. My eyes have been opened, that's all. If a man like Oswald can be snuffed out by some Hungarian bitch, then what's life about, eh? We've got to look out for ourselves.'

She was breathing hard, trying to contain her fury. 'Look, Nick, I understand that a woman can't manage the gaff on her own. But I should be an equal partner.'

He downed his drink, and I heard the sound of the stopper being pulled out of the bottle again and a new measure being poured.

'Partner?'

'A business arrangement. You referee the bouts and gee up the punters, and I'll do the books. We'll share any profits, once the debt's down to nothing. It's more than fair.'

He sniffed. I couldn't see his expression, but I had the strong feeling he wasn't taking her seriously. She was persuasive and determined, but also young and female.

''Course, there's another solution, Elsie. One I've been considering for a while, and I hope you'll find amenable.'

'And what would that be?'

I could tell from the timbre of her voice that she already knew the answer.

'Obvious, ain't it? Marry me. We'll run the gaff together.'

I could see the shadow of her hands fidgeting like starlings as she tried to find the right response.

'I'm recently widowed.'

He clicked his tongue. 'It's the modern age. A new world. Six months is enough these days. Not long for us to wait. A pretty thing like you can't be expected to stay on the shelf.' I could tell he was attempting charm. 'You'll get dusty.'

She turned to face him. 'Why don't we be business partners first, as I've suggested. And then, in six months, we'll see about a marriage.'

He whistled through his teeth. 'How do I know you'll go through with it? No, I've been put in charge now, as you well know. And you ain't winkling me out.'

She exhaled deeply. 'I must get back. Mrs George is expecting me, and I don't want Reggie keeping her awake. Please consider my offer of a business arrangement.'

He stood up and I feared the worst, but his voice changed to a more plaintive tone. 'I'll make a good husband, Elsie. It won't be like with Oswald. I'll look after you.'

'I have to go.'

She turned, and he followed her to the door. I heard it open and close, and the sound of their voices diminishing. He was still pleading with her in the yard.

I felt a brief alarm that the key would be turned in the lock and I'd be trapped in the hut until morning, but I heard no such sound, or any sound save the flickering of the candle flame in the draught.

I crept around the curtain to where Coffey had been sitting. There was a mattress, two ragged armchairs with straw bursting through their arms, a knitted scarf on the floor, a table and a lidded wooden box with the candlestick set upon it. The candle was still lit.

I hastily removed it, taking all possible care not to extinguish the flame – my matches were in my coat – and opened the box. Instantly, I reeled back. It contained Coffey's old clothes, stinking of sweat, beer and camphor. I sorted through them, shuddering at the stench, finding three bottles of Lacey's Liniment and a pouch containing a razor and brush.

No syringe. Coffey must have disposed of it, knowing it would incriminate him.

Never mind. That problem could be solved.

I fished into my pocket and withdrew Jacob's syringe. It was empty of morphine now, but would still lead the police to the only logical conclusion: Coffey had murdered Oswald Drake to steal his wife and his business.

I tucked it closely into Coffey's jacket, put the jacket back into the box and closed the lid.

That syringe would set Agnes Munro free.

I crept back towards the door of the hut just as it started to open again.

22

I DIVED BACK INTO the left-hand room, willing the curtain not to flap in my wake. More boots on the wooden floor and a grunt of effort.

'Stop that,' Coffey instructed. 'Do as I tell you.'

'Let go, please. You're hurting me.'

It was a female voice, but not Elspeth's – younger. I peeked around the curtain, and Coffey had his arm around a girl, the waif Maria, the one who'd called me a snob. He was pulling her towards the back of the hut.

'Why are you making this so bloody difficult?' He sounded angry, frustrated. 'Why can't any of you just do as you're told?'

I ducked back out of sight, listening to the noises: muttering and a bump as a person was pushed on to something soft and a slap as she tried to get up.

'Please, don't,' she begged. 'Let me go.'

I clenched my jaw, recognising the desperation in her voice. I'd heard it before, out of my own mouth.

I could not permit it. I didn't possess the expedient mind that would use this brutality to cover my exit. Instead, I was consumed by other thoughts or, more specifically, a dark gap where those thoughts once lived, leaving only the taste of salt in my mouth and lamplight slanting across an attic ceiling.

I picked up the metal case containing sutures and needles, pulled back the curtain in one sweep and hammered the case down on Coffey's head.

He had been standing over the girl, shirtless and hatless, and he fell to his knees with a cry, putting out his hand for support. I raised the case to crash it down again, but he was quick. My God, he was like a snake. He twisted and reared up, and I only just managed to get in another blow, knocking him to the ground. Blood was soaking into his hair.

Maria was pressed against the wall of the hut, her mouth open and her fist clutching the bodice of her rag dress. I grabbed her hand, but she snatched it away.

'What the hell are you doing?'

'Rescuing you.'

She did up her buttons and glowered at me.

'You're a bloody lunatic is what you are. Is he dead?'

I crouched down and held the man's wrist. There was a pulse, strong and regular.

'He's alive. We have to go.'

'Wait.'

She picked up Coffey's jacket.

'You're not going to rob him?'

'Why not?'

She emptied a handful of farthings and two half-crowns from his pockets, and tucked them into her shoe. Then she stooped to open his box of clothes as well, but I stopped her.

'Leave that. I don't want it disturbed.'

'Suit yourself.'

Coffey groaned and the muscles in his shoulders started to move.

Maria dashed for the door and I followed her. By the time I reached the yard she was already sitting on top of the wall. She glanced down at me once and dropped out of sight to the pavement. I climbed up on to the crate and looked over, but she'd already disappeared.

———

I had to walk home. No cab would carry me, dressed as I was, so I didn't reach Little Pulteney Street until it was almost dawn. My key was in my coat and my coat was still back at the gaff, so I had no choice but to lie down in the shelter of the back wall of the house, shivering and sore, knowing for certain that I wouldn't sleep and yet falling asleep almost instantly. I awoke to the crash of Constance's pan on the stove, having had perhaps two hours of sleep.

I tapped on the window and she started, putting her hand to her chest. Huffam leapt up in a frenzy of barking.

'My goodness,' she exclaimed, shushing the dog and frowning at my peculiar clothing. 'I didn't realise it was you. What on earth have you been doing?'

'An investigation for the newspaper. I used a disguise.'

She continued to stare as she unlocked the door. 'It's most convincing. I took you for a beggar. Or worse, a thief. You'd pass for a person ten years younger than you are.' She pointed at my left cheek, the unburned one. 'Many's the lady who'd kill for a complexion like yours.'

'I'm very tired.'

She put her hands on her hips, forgetting her pan on the stove, which was starting to smoke.

'What are you investigating? Is it a scandal?'

She seemed excited by the prospect and was crestfallen when I shook my head and yawned. I was swaying with tiredness.

'Mr Stanhope! I meant to tell you, speaking of scandals, I've discovered more about Mrs Gower.'

'You should leave well alone, Constance.'

She leaned in towards me. 'Her first husband died without a penny to his name. And yet she leads a wealthy life. Why do you suppose that is?'

I yawned again. 'I don't think she's all that wealthy. She doesn't seem to have a horse and carriage these days.'

'Exactly.' Constance narrowed her eyes. 'She's spent her money and is hunting for her next victim. I was reading about a creature in Sierra Leone called a praying mantis. Have you heard of it? Apparently, the female eats the male after …' she dropped her voice, 'after *mating*.'

Even in my exhausted state I could see what she was driving at. 'And you believe Mrs Gower to be the human equivalent of a cannibal insect, do you?'

'Exactly.' She nodded triumphantly as if the two of us had reached the same conclusion. 'She's been tricking men into marrying her and then taking their money.'

Fascinating though her theories were, I was still wearing Aiden's clothes and didn't want to bump into Alfie so dressed. He might have had a less inquisitive nature than Constance, but his sense of propriety was much greater.

'I don't think that's how the finances of marriage work. She's not a praying mantis, Constance.'

I stumbled up the stairs to my room, where I washed my face, took off my clothes and fell into bed. The warmth and softness of my own sheet and blanket made me want to weep with relief.

I thought of Constance and Elspeth – just a few years apart and yet so utterly different. Constance was where she belonged, with a father who loved her and a home she could call her own, whereas Elspeth had nothing. She couldn't even take ownership of a business that was rightfully hers.

Drake and Coffey were to blame. It was as well that one had killed the other. I was glad to have created the circumstance for the crime to be uncovered. Tomorrow, I would write an article accusing Coffey of the murder and by Monday morning, the police would be knocking on his door.

Finally, I had done the right thing.

———

I awoke to the sound of Alfie's dentistry drill, which was unexpected as it was a Sunday. He looked up from his patient as I came into the pharmacy.

'Mrs Flowers was here earlier,' he said. 'I told her you were still asleep. She said she'd meet you at the Marble Arch corner of Hyde Park at two o'clock unless – and I'm quoting her directly – unless you're planning to waste the entire day.'

The woman in the chair flapped a feeble hand, and Alfie leaned back into his work. The foot pedal squeaked, and the drill in his hand growled and buzzed as it ground against the enamel of her teeth.

Mrs Gower was in the back room, dressed for church. I made us both a cup of tea and sat with her, our tranquillity spoiled by an occasional yelp of pain from the other room.

'Why is Alfie working today?' I asked.

'We were on our way back when we saw that poor woman,' said Mrs Gower. 'She'd had two of her teeth broken, poor thing. She and her friends were set upon by a group of men. And on the Sabbath as well. I don't know what the world's coming to. Why can't people be decent?'

She took a sip of her tea, her hand shaking, and I noticed she had a smear of blood on her sleeve. I guessed she'd been the one to find the woman.

'It was kind of you to look after her.'

'Someone had to, Mr Stanhope.'

Constance came in, casting a glance at Mrs Gower, aware that we had stopped talking. She silently fetched a block of cheese and cut a slice from it, alternately feeding herself and Huffam, making him stand on his hind legs to receive each mouthful. I was glad to see the little fellow in better spirits after his infection, though he was still sporting the gluey poultice she had fashioned for him. Mrs Gower pursed her lips and said nothing. She didn't approve of feeding a dog at the table, which was probably why Constance was doing it.

In the distance, the bells of St Anne's were ringing for two o'clock. I truly had slept for half the day. I would be late for Rosie.

I drained my tea – priorities must be maintained – and left the pharmacy just as Alfie was setting to work with his pliers.

The sun was out, and the streets were cheerful and gay, filled with bright awnings, elegant hats and even an occasional parasol. I didn't notice the strange atmosphere until I was crossing over New Bond Street and saw the first banner, artfully embroidered and hung from a frame held by two respectable-looking women. It read: *Society for Women's Suffrage, Kensington*.

As I neared Marble Arch, the pavement became more crowded and I could hardly move for the crush of women. Ahead of us, I could hear a cacophony of distant drums and instruments, and voices singing. The park had been transformed into a theatre of noise and colour, and everywhere there were placards and flags, many of them demanding the vote, some just displaying the name of a town: Colchester, Reading, Dulwich, Richmond, Feltham and Barking to name just a few, each raised above our heads like ships' sails on a restless sea.

I searched among the crowd for Rosie.

A woman with a bass drum came towards me, and I realised they were on the march. I stood aside as they proceeded out of the park towards Park Lane, led by the same Irish lady I'd seen previously, smiling broadly and swishing her arm in time. They followed her like a bride's train, eight abreast, talking and singing, holding their banners high. There were children too, running between their mothers or walking at their sides, some being pushed in perambulators or pulled along on trolleys. Any traffic trying to navigate the streets was stationary, and more than one horse had been decorated with flowers around its halter even as it stood waiting.

I felt the twinge of it; not a wish to be a woman, but a wish to fit wholly somewhere, to share the stitching of other people's lives, the casting on and casting off, the seaming and hemming and darting, all the pin pricks, scissor cuts and flatiron burns. They *belonged* and I did not. I had no place here or anywhere.

A few men were watching from the shade of the buildings, strung out along the pavement, wearing grey jackets and dour expressions. One of them beckoned a policeman over, and from the look of the exchange, importuned the constable towards some form of action, probably to clear the street. The policeman shook his head with the air of a fellow who was having to work on a Sunday and would prefer to get home with the minimum of fuss.

I wandered down through the throng, garnering hostile looks from some of the women, suspicious of a man who might've come looking for his wife.

'Leo!'

I spotted Rosie. She was walking with her three children; Samuel on her hip and the other two at her side. Her eldest, Robbie, was looking bored, his nose in a book, while her daughter, Lillian, was struggling to hold on to a placard in the sudden breeze. I took it from her. On it were painted the words *Free Sister Agnes*, surrounded by small handprints.

'Why are you here?' I asked Rosie.

'We're marching to Parliament. We want to speak to Mr Gladstone, if he'll listen.'

'I didn't think you were interested in all this. You said it doesn't put filling into pies, as I recall.'

'I know.' She looked glum for a moment and then met my eye. 'But it's not fair, is it? I would've thought you of all people would understand.'

I took a step away from her, shocked that she would make such casual reference to my physical incongruity.

'I don't see why.'

She laughed and indicated the marchers around her, their banners fluttering. 'Don't you see, Leo? You're partly responsible for all this. You and Sister Agnes. I thought you should see it. I thought it might make you less miserable.'

The crowd thickened as we reached the turn at the southern end of the park, where a statue of Achilles was staring up at the sky, a sword in his hand and a garland of pansies strung around his naked midsection.

Lillian tugged on the hem of my jacket and pointed at the placard. 'Can I have it back now?'

'We'll share it, all right?'

She nodded happily, and I allowed her to take the stick while I kept hold of the top. I didn't want her taking someone's eye out.

Rosie was smiling at me.

'What is it?' I asked her.

'Nothing at all.'

I didn't believe her, but doubted she would tell me, so I changed the subject.

'How was your evening with Harry?'

She looked downcast. 'Not very good. We didn't go to Kew Gardens. I was late getting home from the prison, and he said there wasn't time. We went to Cremorne Gardens instead. There was a funfair and it was noisy and ghastly. And then he … well, I had to say goodnight to him.'

I looked at her sharply. Harry fancied himself a ladies' man, but to hear him speak one would never have thought him unchivalrous. I had the impression they just wilted into his arms.

'Do you mean he was overly … forthright?'

She rolled her eyes. 'Only a little. Men only want two things from me and …' she glanced at her children and lowered her voice. 'And the other's my pie shop.'

I shuddered, picturing them in the gardens, him leaning forward, putting his arm around her waist, pulling her close, and her pushing him away, turning aside, trying to be polite. Is that how it was? Or worse, him steering her into a dark corner behind a tree and her resisting, staying near to the path, near to the people, praying they would keep her safe.

I should've known what would happen. I was uniquely well placed to know. I should've told Harry that I would suffer no ill-treatment of Rosie. Not ever.

'It's all right, Leo, I was quite safe. He was just … being a man, that's all.' She put Samuel down to walk for a while, watching with a gentle expression as he bounced along. 'The little ones are pleasant enough, but something goes wrong with them when they grow up.'

I had no answer to that, never having led the life of a little boy. I was still considering what punishment I should exact upon Harry Whitford.

Rosie took my arm. 'What I really need is a husband.'

'Didn't you just say—'

'Not a *real* one. Not any of *that*. Just someone who'll keep the rascals at bay, lend a hand when I need it and talk to me from time to time. Someone who won't pinch or punch me. Is that too much to ask?'

I grinned, joining in with her joke. 'Oh, I see, you mean a sham husband. A masquerade.'

'Exactly.'

'Aren't you forgetting the sanctity of marriage?'

She shrugged. 'I tried that, and it didn't work. Now I need something else.' She squeezed my arm. 'So, I was thinking that perhaps you and I should get married, Leo. Wouldn't that make everything simple?'

I didn't know if she was making fun of me. She didn't seem to be, but it was hard to tell.

'Married? You mean, to each other?'

She leaned in, her head almost touching my shoulder. 'Of course. If we were married, there'd be no more men harassing me, and we could go on adventures whenever we liked. It would be perfect.'

A woman walking near us gaped in disbelief, and I didn't blame her. The idea was preposterous. To be married as an act of theatre, a contrivance, sounded like ... well, everything Frederick Lampton opposed. On which basis, I supposed it must have some merit. But surely, she was jesting. She had three children. If I became their ... my goodness, their *father*, then I could never leave. She and I would watch them grow up as we became shorter and fatter and sprouted grey hair. I couldn't imagine ever being anywhere that I couldn't escape from.

She was still walking at my side, her face turned up to the sun.

I detached my arm from hers. 'I'm sorry, Rosie, but I can't go to Parliament with you. I have to go to my office to write an article about Nicholas Coffey. I'm certain he's the real killer. Tomorrow, the police will uncover evidence of it.'

'How do you know?'

'I just do. Take care of yourself, Rosie.'

The march continued southwards to Westminster and I strode west along Piccadilly. I looked back once, and Rosie and her daughter were holding their placard between them and chanting 'Free Agnes Munro' with gusto.

23

I HEADED STRAIGHT FOR the newspaper office, which I had never done on a Sunday before; articles on scientific discoveries were rarely so urgent.

The place was almost empty, with only a skeleton staff. I sat in the calm and quiet, my hands on the typewriter, and began. I was amazed at how the words flowed from my fingers to the keys without visiting my brain on the way. They seemed to write themselves.

I all but accused Coffey of the murder of Oswald Drake, citing his well-known affection for Elspeth, his appropriation of the penny gaff and his access to a syringe and morphine. I suggested that Drake had fought back, and in the struggle, the pinprick had been made unusually large, though it was likely made by a conventional needle. I called upon the police to take appropriate action and also to release Sister Agnes, who had been so unfairly dubbed the Butcher of Berner Street.

J.T. always said that there was no such thing as hypocrisy in the newspaper game.

By the time I got home, I was exhausted and tender, but still had to spend an hour standing at the bowl in my room washing my sanitary cloths.

Afterwards, I headed downstairs, hoping that Alfie might be persuaded to take some whisky. I was relishing the chance to waste the evening with him. But he was poring over a large piece of paper with Mrs Gower, each of them holding a pencil.

'What do you think?' he asked me.

The drawing depicted a plan view of the new shop, with twin counters angled to face the door and a number of rectangles denoting the dentistry chair and various cupboards, with labels such as 'Remedies', 'Products for Ladies' and 'Spectacles'. This last was an expansion for him, made possible by the larger floorplan and more populous location.

'You seem to have thought of everything,' I said.

He straightened up, a serious expression settling on his face. 'The thing is, Mrs Gower and I want to get things moving quickly. We're planning to get married in the next month or so.'

'A small ceremony,' added Mrs Gower. 'We hope you can come?'

'Of course. I would love to.'

I shook Alfie's hand, genuinely happy for him, but also wondering why it had to be so soon. I seemed to be filled to the brim with equal parts of gladness and misery.

I went into the back room and sat at the table, my favourite place in the world.

It wasn't long before my mind wandered back to Rosie's droll suggestion that we should get married. It might almost be worth it, I thought, just to see the look on my sister's face if she ever found out. She always acted as though the state of marriage was the pinnacle of human achievement, but I was certain my finding a wife was not what she had in mind. In fact, she would think me even more ungodly than before, responsible for another's damnation as well as my own.

But Rosie didn't think that way. She knew I was a man. Surely, she had been jesting.

On the shelf above Alfie's books, a microscope held pride of place. Its brass was polished to a glorious shine and its wooden plinth looked like new. Constance had bought it from a market stall in pieces and carried it home in a shoe-box. She had emptied it out on to the table, and she and Alfie had spent the following days cleaning each part and assembling the mechanism using screws as small as ants. When they'd finished, they discovered a lens was missing, so they scoured the shops every Saturday afternoon until finally Alfie presented her with the perfect one as a gift for Christmas. They fitted the final pieces together on Boxing Day, and since then had used it to examine all manner of things: water, salt, insects and their own fingernails. They were a family, bonded by love and time, with all the associated joys and irritations.

By comparison, I knew little of Rosie's children, understood nothing of making pies or running a business. In truth, I was entirely ignorant of her life beyond the adventures we'd shared, and she was ignorant of mine. She'd seen what I was underneath these clothes, but she'd never seen me dabbing the sores under my armpits or wringing out my sanitary cloths. We were the best of friends, yet virtual strangers.

I supposed marriage would change that, in time. Endless mundane minutes together, eating breakfast, polishing shoes, repairing gutters and saving pennies in a jar. The same conversations and the same complaints. It sounded awful, except ... except it wasn't, was it? Part of me yearned for exactly those things; leftovers for dinner, a familiar creak in the floorboards, a pillow shaped by my head.

But with Rosie?

Surely, she had been jesting.

The following morning, I arrived at the office and flipped through the newspaper for my article. I was gratified to see it had survived the subeditors' attentions almost intact, but was disappointed that it was on page five. Over the last few days I'd rather enjoyed having more prominence. I supposed the story wasn't salacious enough; 'man probably killed other man' didn't have the same appeal as the tale of a murderous, wrestling woman religious.

I'd barely finished reading it before J. T. approached me like a rat-catcher who'd finally found the nest.

'Any more on the nun? We need a lead article for tomorrow.'

I almost grinned. 'I believe they'll be arresting Nicholas Coffey very soon, and no one else knows it's going to happen. Just me. It'll be an exclusive.'

He looked surprised and ... was that a hint of pride? It was hard to tell. 'Good. In the meantime, you can finish that book review.'

As soon as he'd gone, Harry shuffled in, early by his standards. My guess was he'd been watching through the crack in the door until his father was off the scene. He sat down, making a play of organising his pens.

I cleared my throat to get his attention. 'How was your evening with Mrs Flowers?'

I spoke coldly, but he didn't seem to notice.

'Five out of ten. I won't be repeating it, if that's what you're wondering.'

'Why not?'

'It isn't cheap, something like that. I expected a bit more *gratitude*.'

'Gratitude? In what form?'

He drummed his fingers on the desk. 'Sometimes, two people simply aren't destined for each other.'

He cast a longing glance towards Miss Chive, who was filing papers in J. T.'s office. She sensed his gaze and turned in our direction before looking hastily away. Her cheeks and nose were speckled with marks where the glass had cut into her skin, and her forehead was wrapped in a bandage.

A hollowness opened up inside me. What had happened to her was my fault. They'd thrown that brick because of the articles I'd written.

'You should talk to Miss Chive,' I told Harry. 'She's suffering. Why don't you ask her if she'd like to go for a walk with you?'

He went back to arranging his pens, making the shape of a house on his desk. 'Maybe when ... you know.'

When she's healed, he meant. *When she's no longer visibly wounded. When she's presentable.*

The door banged open and Detective Ripley came in, eyeing the office with an air of a soldier caught in enemy territory.

J. T. hurried back over. 'Can we help you, Detective Sergeant?'

Ripley pointed at me. 'I've come to take Mr Stanhope to Scotland Yard.'

My plan was working. They must've arrested Coffey already.

J. T. raised himself to his full height. 'I should come too. I'm the Assistant Editor here.'

Ripley waved him away. 'Just Stanhope.'

I held up my notebook and pen. 'Don't worry, J. T., I'll get notes of everything. I'll be sure to make the deadline this time, I promise.'

This could be another top story.

————

A Black Maria was waiting on the street, and we climbed inside.

Ripley pulled the curtains closed so we were sitting in the half-dark, making me feel strangely as if we were sharing a coffin.

'I take it you've already been to the gaff today, Detective Sergeant.'

'I have. I spend more time in White-bloody-chapel than I do in my own patch, thanks to you.'

'Did you find anything significant? Incriminating, I mean?'

'I certainly did.'

He lit a cigarette, breathing it in deeply, closing his eyes and exhaling with a contented sigh. Only when he'd expelled all the smoke from his lungs did he offer me one as well. I took it and he struck a safety match, the flare illuminating the dust and mould in the carriage.

'Have you arrested someone?'

'Do you think we should?'

One of his eyes was half closed, making him seem somnolent, but I knew better.

'I think Nicholas Coffey killed Oswald Drake. If you've arrested him, I want an exclusive on the story. You owe me that.'

He gazed at me through the smoke. 'Do I?'

We pulled up at Scotland Yard, and I could hear the sound of hooves and wheels on the cobblestones. The carriage door opened, and the sudden light was blinding. I stepped out, shielding my eyes, and saw Pallett waiting for us. He tipped his helmet as we disembarked.

'This way, Mr Stanhope.'

'Have you arrested Coffey yet?'

'All in due course, sir.'

I felt a peculiar coldness in my stomach. The police should've been grateful for my help, offering to let me accompany them as they made the arrest. Perhaps a one-to-one interview with Coffey in his cell. Instead, they seemed secretive and formal, as though I wasn't a trusted man of the press, but a *suspect*.

I shot a look back towards the street, feeling the familiar urge to run.

Pallett put his hand on my shoulder. 'Come along, sir.'

He led the way into the rear entrance of the police head-quarters, along a smoky corridor, down some echoic stairs and into the bowels of the place. We passed a room full of secretaries, their fingers dancing on their typewriters, earmuffs tucked under their hats to block out the deafening racket.

I'd been in Ripley's office before and knew what to expect. The gas lamp overhead hissed and crackled and the waterpipes rang, as though somewhere far away, at the top of their long journey through every WC and sink in the building, someone was tapping on the porcelain. None of this bothered Ripley. I'd previously thought he'd been given this ghastly tank as some form of punishment, but he seemed to take joy in its plainness, in the sheen of condensation over the walls and furniture, in its remoteness from his colleagues occupying their airy, well-lit rooms upstairs.

I sat on the metal chair, facing him on the other side of the desk. Pallett remained standing by the door.

'Where's Nicholas Coffey?' I asked. 'Do you accept he's guilty now? What evidence did you find at the gaff?'

Ripley leaned back. 'No one knows where he is.'

'Then why am I here?'

He seemed to sense my discomfort. 'When did you last see him?'

I pretended to think back. 'Last Thursday in Whitehall Gardens.'

'And when did you last visit the penny gaff in Berner Street?'

All my senses were alert now, dragging my internal perspective back to its natural condition: *at all costs, hide the truth*.

'On the day after Drake was murdered. You and I were both there.'

'Not since then?'

'Why do you ask?'

Ripley popped his knuckles and turned to Pallett. 'Show him.'

Pallett reached into his bag and pulled out a black coat. He turned the label towards me. It read: *Leo Stanhope*.

My mind seemed to shrink back from my skull.

Ripley leaned forward. 'You said you last saw Coffey on Thursday in Whitehall. Did you lend him your coat?' He fished into the pocket and pulled something out. It was my door key. 'And invite him to your lodging?'

I clasped my fingers together on my lap and answered calmly, in the manner of an honest man explaining a simple truth.

'No, of course not. You already know I've been there before. I obviously left my coat behind by mistake.'

Ripley observed me, one eye half closed, and Pallett shifted his weight from foot to foot. I realised they knew more than they were telling me.

'See, Stanhope,' mumbled Ripley, his face contorted as if pained by my feeble attempt at deception. 'You and I saw each other on Friday at the police station before that little skirmish, and I'm certain you were wearing that coat at the time. So, you must've been at the gaff *after* that, to have left it there, mustn't you? Stands to reason. Which means you're lying to me.'

I could feel my heart beating. 'Are you certain it was the same coat? Do you normally take note of such things? And it makes no difference anyway. It's not a crime to lose your coat.'

'No, it isn't.' Ripley looked up at Pallett. 'Constable?'

'Sergeant.' Pallett corrected him.

The two men exchanged a slow look. Though opposites in temperament and physical design, they were the same rank now.

Ripley gave the merest nod. 'Sergeant. The newspaper, *please*.'

Pallett opened up a copy of the *Daily Chronicle*. 'Your article, Mr Stanhope. You clearly indicate here that you believe Mr Coffey is guilty of the murder of Oswald Drake.'

'Yes, that's correct. He is.'

'Yet previously, you accused Agnes Munro. Now you say she's been wrongfully imprisoned.'

Ripley shifted in his seat, uncomfortable that Pallett had started asking questions. 'A bit *fickle*, aren't you, Stanhope?'

I didn't reply.

Ripley took an age to light a cigarette. Even Pallett gave an audible sigh as the fifth match failed to spark. When he was finally able to inhale a lungful of smoke, the detective closed his eyes and breathed out slowly, allowing it to hang in the air between us.

'We searched through Coffey's possessions at the gaff, as your newspaper article demanded. The higher-ups ...' he pointed to the ceiling, where the pipes were gurgling with another gush of liquid. 'They like the general public to believe we leave no stone unturned. I didn't expect to find anything, not because Coffey's an honest man but because he's not a stupid one. For example, it would seem far-fetched that he'd leave incriminating evidence behind among his box of clothes. And yet, there it was, a syringe like the one used on Oswald Drake before he was murdered, with more than a whiff of morphine lingering about it.'

'Well then, Detective Sergeant, you should arrest Coffey, like I suggested.'

Ripley nodded. 'Believe me, I would like nothing more, if I could find him. I don't know what he's guilty of, but I'm quite certain it's something. Right now, I'm more concerned with you and your coat. See, a beggar boy gave it to us. Big lad he is and quite unpleasant. A life of crime ahead of him and probably behind him as well. On balance, we might as well hang him now and save ourselves a lot of trouble. But he was keen to show us your coat because he wanted very much to find the young fellow who'd left it behind. The two of 'em fought, I understand, and he lost, and so would like a rematch. Any thoughts on who that Cinderella might be?'

'No. Did he recognise him?'

'Strange you should ask. No, he didn't.'

'Well then. This has nothing to do with me.'

Ripley smiled congenially and I felt my stomach lurch.

'The thing is, Stanhope, we have him here in our custody. Why don't we introduce the two of you?'

Pallett left and came back with the lad, who was wearing a tatty jacket and a hangdog scowl. His cheekbone was bruised to a livid purple.

Ripley pointed his cigarette. 'What's your name, son?'

The lad's eyes swivelled from side to side, trying to work out whether he was in trouble. Finding no reason why he shouldn't admit the truth, he muttered: 'Lewis Hawkins.'

'Do you recognise anyone in this room?'

I straightened my bowler and jacket and adopted a severe countenance.

You're a grown man and a reporter with a newspaper. You have a room and respectable friends. You're nothing like the person he remembers.

Hawkins squinted at me, but there was no recognition in his eyes.

'No.'

Ripley looked disappointed.

'Tell us about the young man you met at the gaff, Master Hawkins.'

Hawkins opened his mouth, but no sound emerged. The detective sighed and poked the bruise on the lad's face, eliciting a yelp he seemed to find satisfying.

'Who beat you?'

Hawkins clenched his fists. 'Some bastard I don't know. It weren't fair. I would've won. He jabbed me in the leg with something.'

'Can you describe him?'

The lad squirmed, trying to free himself from Pallett's vast hand on his shoulder. 'He was my age. Funny-looking. Oily hair.'

Ripley pulled his face into a grimace. He'd clearly been hoping for something more damning. 'All right, *Sergeant*, boot this imbecile out.'

Pallett knocked on the door and a constable came in. I recognised him as the blond man who'd attempted to arrest Sister Agnes at the convent and been thrown against the dumb-iron of the carriage. It seemed like a lifetime ago. Clearly, he viewed Hawkins as a lesser threat, because he grabbed him by the collar and pulled him out of the room, kicking the door shut behind him.

I turned to the detective. 'You see? None of this has anything to do with me. I haven't committed any crime. You should be putting your attention to the murder of Mr Drake. Your job is to find Coffey, not sit in here wasting everyone's time.'

Ripley sighed. 'It's not me who's wasting time.' He waved a hand at Pallett. 'Bring in the other one.'

Pallett left again and returned with another constable, younger, with a fuzz of beard around his chin. Between them, moon-faced Maria was pulling and twisting, grubby as a stray dog, toes peeping through the ends of her shoes.

The young constable pulled up her arm, forcing her to stand straight. When she tried to scratch him with her other hand, he slapped her face hard enough to raise a red mark on her cheek.

Pallett released the girl from his subordinate's grip. 'Less of that, Eddie. There's no need.' It sounded like a suggestion, but the constable took it as an instruction and stood back, looking sheepish.

Ripley smiled at the girl, not unkindly. 'What do you have to tell us, young lady?'

She cast a brief, unimpressed glance around the room and folded her arms. I lowered my chin and pulled down the brim of my hat.

'Ten shillings,' she said.

Ripley blinked a couple of times and almost grinned. It was a rare thing to see in him, honest delight. So often, his expressions were deployed as tactics on the battlefield; a frown, a sniff, a raise of the eyebrows, all arrayed to unsettle

a suspect and elicit more information. But this girl genuinely amused him.

'What's your name, kid?'

'Annie Dowling.'

A lie. Or, I supposed, the name Maria might be the lie.
Or both of them. Or she was Maria and Annie, each at
different times, and a dozen other names besides. Or she
had no real name.

Ripley cracked his knuckles. 'What do you have to tell
me, Annie?'

'Ten shillings.'

'One.'

'Eight.'

Ripley paused for a heartbeat, a trace of that grin still
clinging to his face. He fished in his trouser pocket and
pulled out half a crown. In the gaslight, it cast a large
shadow on the wall, as if he was holding up the moon.

'This, and no more.'

She took the coin, gripping it tightly in her fist.

'All right then, I'll tell you.' She thumbed towards me.
'This one was at the gaff two nights ago. He came dressed as
one of us, but he weren't. He stabbed Lewis with a needle
and hit Mr Coffey on his head with a box.'

Ripley took a long, slow pull on his cigarette. 'I see.
And the needle used to stab that young man, did it look
anything like this?'

He fished into his jacket pocket and withdrew the
syringe.

The girl nodded. 'The very one.'

24

RIPLEY SEEMED SATISFIED. His mind was made up. 'You've been lying to me, Stanhope. I'm placing you under arrest for falsifying evidence. You went to the gaff and you placed the syringe among Mr Coffey's possessions to incriminate him. You'd have seen him go to the gallows for the sake of your silly newspaper article.' He shook his head, looking thoroughly miserable. 'Bloody newspapermen.'

'What about me?' demanded Maria-or-Annie, her fist in her apron pocket with the half-crown clutched firmly within it.

'You're a witness. You'll stay with us.'

'What? No, I won't.'

She made a dash for the door, but Pallett scooped her up and carried her out. I could hear her kicks and screams fading as they reached the end of the corridor.

Ripley's hand strayed towards his jacket pocket for another cigarette and then lowered again. 'My missus wants me to smoke less. She says she hates the smell of ash, but if she knew the shit I have to wade through …' He sighed and produced a notebook from his drawer. 'We may as well get the formalities done. Where do you claim you were on Saturday evening?'

I couldn't keep my voice steady. 'I don't remember.'

'You don't remember where you were two nights ago?' He rolled his eyes. 'All right, let's see if a night or two in a cell helps jog your memory. As I recall, you're not a man who takes well to confinement. Try not to piss all over yourself this time.'

I stood up. 'You have to believe me. Sister Agnes isn't guilty.'

Ripley shrugged, seeming more wretched than ever. 'Maybe she is, maybe she isn't. Either way, she won't be tried for killing Oswald Drake.'

'Truly? That's marvellous news. Why not?'

'Damn it, I'm having one whether my missus likes it or not.' He fished into his pocket for a cigarette and lit it with a match, first time. 'Your fault, Stanhope, as with so many things. You're the one who found the evidence that caused her to be arrested in the first place, and you're also the one who falsified evidence against Coffey. A syringe in both cases. So it's all equally tainted and no judge will allow it.'

I felt a swirl of emotions. My plot to incriminate Coffey had failed utterly, and yet, by some ridiculous chance, it had succeeded in freeing Sister Agnes. For a fleeting second, I wondered if God did, indeed, have a plan. That idea gained further credence when I remembered that I was now under arrest myself; He had a perverse sense of humour, did God.

'But Sister Agnes confessed,' I offered, cautiously.

Ripley looked gloomier than ever. 'Yes, but the head nun, Miss Doyle, says Agnes Munro is a lunatic. Soft in the head. Visions and all sorts. She'd probably confess to killing Lord Cavendish if we gave her the chance.' He spread out his hands, indicating the empty room. 'So, now I've got nothing, thanks to you.'

My elation was short-lived as I considered the consequences of Sister Agnes's new freedom. A lot of people still believed her to be guilty. A cold fear blew through me.

'Have you released her yet?'

'Soon. Maybe tomorrow. Paperwork takes time.'

'You can't do it. Not without another suspect in custody.'

Ripley closed his eyes and put his head in his hands. 'First you wanted her arrested because she was guilty, then you wanted her released because she was innocent, but she pleaded guilty. Now we're letting her out and you want her to stay locked up. Honestly, I wish to God I'd never met you, Stanhope.'

'You don't understand. What do you think that mob will do when they find out she's not going to be prosecuted? They'll lay siege to the convent. There'll be a war.'

'Not your concern, Stanhope.' He dropped the end of his cigarette on the ground, where it fizzed in the damp. 'You'll be in the cells tonight and in court tomorrow or the day after.'

———

They put me in the last cell in the row, the same one Sister Agnes had been in. There was a wind whistling through the high window and I could hear footsteps and the clatter of carriage wheels in the yards. Monday afternoon and everyone was busy. Only I was doing nothing, sitting and shivering on a scanty mattress, my hands covering my face.

At least I was alone, for now anyway. Not for long. Soon, I would have lots of company. Once I was discovered, word would go around the police station like a pox, and they would all come to prod and poke me. *Look at this freak. This abomination. It doesn't even know what it is.*

I lay back and watched the light from the high window creep across the ceiling.

I supposed Harry would write the article for the newspaper: *How We Were Fooled* or, more likely, *I Always Suspected*. I would be on the second page again.

My sister would gather up her shame and compress it into a dense, elemental hatred.

Jacob would waggle his beard and tell me that at least I was myself and damn all the rest of them – or at least, he would have, once upon a time. Now, I wasn't sure. He might decide that I deserved this fate, and never speak of me again.

Alfie's customers would gossip, and his business would vanish like April mist; no new shop on Hanover Square, no marriage to Mrs Gower. He and Constance would look back on every lie I had told and believe I had taken them for fools.

And Rosie ... ah, yes, Rosie. She wouldn't care a jot what anyone said.

Where was Rosie, anyway?

All afternoon, I paced my tiny cell. With my back to the wall at one end, it was step, step, step and a further half-step until my nose was touching one of the bars, then spin and do the same in reverse. I must have done it a hundred times, two hundred, sometimes starting with my left foot, sometimes my right, sometimes spinning clockwise and sometimes the other way. I tried it with my eyes shut and my hands behind my back, thinking at any moment I would trip. I tried it fast and I tried it so slowly I was hardly moving at all, my muscles tensed and aching. Anything rather than allow my brain to dwell on what I'd done.

Some time the next day Sister Agnes would be released. I could imagine the furious uproar. Those men I'd seen in Whitehall, men like Trafford's cousins, they wouldn't take this lightly. They would burn her out of the convent like a fox from its den.

And Ripley was right: it *was* my fault. My intervention had endangered her life and made Coffey seem *less* guilty. Whatever I touched, turned rotten.

I used the pail in the corner. My monthly blood was almost at an end, but still my cloth was blotched red in the centre and pink at the edges. I refolded and replaced it, wondering whether I should simply tell Ripley my secret and get it over with. I would soon be discovered anyway, when I was required to change my clothes or piss in front of other men.

Not yet, not yet.

Since I'd left home, I'd never actually *told* anyone. Not a soul. Those few that knew the truth had found it out for themselves. I never seemed able to find the right words.

Night fell and a copper brought in a prisoner, drunk and slurring, and tossed him into one of the other cells. I couldn't see him, which I considered a blessing. I heard him puke a number of times and afterwards snore like a bilge pump.

In the middle of the night, I was aware of the neighbouring cell door opening and closing, but I wasn't altogether certain what was real and what wasn't. I forgot about it until I heard the sound of someone moving around at dawn. I had no desire to introduce myself. Another drunk, most likely.

At seven in the morning, according to Big Ben, a portly constable came in with a tray. He handed bowls of foul-smelling soup to the other cells, and a glass of ale and a plate of bread and jam for me.

'Sergeant Pallett asked me to give you these,' he said curtly, making clear that providing such dainties wasn't his usual practice.

'I want to see Ripley.'

He didn't meet my eye. 'Detective Sergeant Ripley said to let you stew. He'll get here when he's ready.'

'Then please give a message to Sergeant Pallett on my behalf. Tell him I need to see Mrs Flowers. Will you do that?'

'What makes you think anyone'll come for you?' he sneered.

'Oy, where's *my* bread and jam?' demanded the person in the next-door cell. I recognised her voice. It was the moon-faced girl, Maria-or-Annie.

The copper sniffed. 'If you want nice food, you shouldn't go around biting people, should you?'

He left, and for a blessed minute there was silence.

'Are you going to eat that, Mr Soho?' she asked.

The better part of me remembered that she was a pauper child who'd suffered on the street her entire life. But the meaner part was still angry with her.

'My name's Stanhope. Who did you bite?'

'That big copper, Mallet.'

'Pallett. Why did you bite him?'

'We had a disagreement. He wanted me to stay in a cot upstairs and be quiet, and I preferred to go about my business.' She tapped her spoon on the brick wall between us. 'I'll forget all about your crimes in exchange for that breakfast.'

I didn't believe her for a second, but I wasn't hungry now. I pushed the plate between the bars and around the wall that separated our cells. A small, grubby hand reached out and took it.

'Don't you think you owe me some thanks?'

She cackled loudly. 'For this?'

'For saving you. If it hadn't been for me—'

'You lot are all the same, aren't you? You want gratitude for the littlest thing, but it's still you who gets jam and me who gets gruel.' She was speaking with her mouth full of my breakfast. 'And if we was in together right now, no doubt you'd have me on my back with your hand up my skirt.'

My irritation got the better of me. 'Not everyone's like Oswald Drake and Nicholas Coffey. Some people actually do mean well.'

She cackled again, slapping her palm against the wall. Eventually, her laughter drained to a trickle and then ran dry.

'Them bastards? I never thought of 'em as ...' she snorted again and gathered herself, 'as *meaning well*. It's the likes of you and that church bloke I was thinking of.'

'You mean the deacon, Sutherland?'

'Yes, him. He's the one who told us we should get ourselves to the gaff for a dry night, like he was doing us a favour. All God's children, he said.' She adopted a sing-song voice. 'Thou our guardian, thou our guide, stay close by every child's side. Ha! And what happens after that, eh? Mr Drake wants what he wants, and Mr Coffey likewise. We're expected to provide it.'

I sat against the wall with my back to her, trying to picture the scene; the local clergyman guiding stray kids to shelter in the warm, only for them to fall victim to the owner's lusts. But had Sutherland known what would happen to them?

An hour later, the main door opened again, and the portly copper came back, his keys jingling in his hand and his boots thudding on the stone floor.

'Are you going to let me out?' I asked him, standing up in anticipation.

'Not you.'

He unlocked Maria-or-Annie's cell.

'Sergeant Pallett says he hopes you've learned your lesson,' he told her. 'Now me, I'd send you off to Holloway for a stretch, but he's inclined to send you to Mrs Downes instead. She'll make sure you don't leave until all this is done.'

I'd met the woman. She ran what the police called the 'halfway house' for children. She had a severe countenance but would provide a warm dormitory and a decent meal. On balance, Maria-or-Annie was lucky.

On her way past, the girl winked at me through the bars as she hooked a tortoiseshell comb out of the constable's pocket.

'Wait!' I called after her. 'Did Sutherland know what Drake was doing to you and the others?'

She cackled again as the main door shut.

25

I SAT ON THE floor, wondering whether Sister Agnes was back at the convent yet.

Was she afraid?

My eyes filled with tears. When I blinked, I could feel the tiny rivulet of brine dripping down my cheek.

Where was Rosie? I wasn't sure she would come. No doubt she was cross with me for going to the penny gaff without her, seeing my actions as typically secretive. But I hadn't wanted to involve her in breaking the law. Better she was furious and safe than complicit and risking arrest. If the price of her freedom was our estrangement, I would pay it.

At lunchtime, the constable brought me another slice of bread and a glass of ale, shoving them disdainfully towards me.

'From the sergeant. His new stripes are making him soft.'

I waited for him to leave before setting upon them hungrily.

In the early afternoon, some time between two and three o'clock, the door clanged again. Ripley's uneven gait echoed down the corridor.

I remained seated on the floor. 'Have you released Sister Agnes?'

'Pallett's on his way there now.' He bit his lip pensively. 'Look, I'm sure she'll come to no harm with Pallett there. He's a big bloke.'

'He won't be enough. Why are you here?'

'Since you didn't remember where you were two nights ago, I went to your lodging and spoke to ...' He paged through his notebook. 'Yes, here we are. Alfred Smith, your landlord. He said you weren't at home on Saturday night.'

Poor Alfie. He had offered me a home and his friendship. While I had been recuperating from my burns, we spent almost every evening together, sipping whisky and talking, or simply enjoying the silence. He had instructed Constance not to badger me with questions, so instead, she'd furiously cleaned very instrument in the house, polished the floors and scrubbed the pans until they gleamed.

Ripley didn't care about anyone's good opinion, he only cared about facts. I envied him that. 'Mr Smith said you might have gone to see ... yes, here we are, Mr Jacob Kleiner. You sometimes stay overnight there, he said.'

I breathed out deeply. 'Sometimes.'

The detective tapped his notebook with his finger. 'I visited Mr Kleiner. He required a little persuading to talk to me, him being of the opinion that all policemen are in the pay of the Golden Lane gang and not to be trusted. But when he did finally cooperate, he said that you weren't with him either.'

'Why did you bother? You already think I'm guilty of something.'

'There's more to this than you're telling me, Stanhope. You have secrets and I want to know what they are. So, I paid a visit to Mrs Flowers, in whose company you're often to be found, more fool her, and she wasn't at home.'

My heart, which had briefly leapt, sank down again.

'Where was she?'

Ripley pursed his lips, as irritated as I'd ever seen him. 'Here, as it happens.'

I jumped up. 'Rosie's here? Well, why are you delaying? Send her in.'

He shook his head. 'I'm not your valet, Mr Stanhope. No visitors. You'll be seeing the magistrate tomorrow.'

Late in the afternoon, Rosie finally appeared, her face ashen.

'Oh, Leo. Have they treated you badly?' Her eyes slid down to the empty ale glass and plate of crumbs. 'I see not.'

'Why has Ripley let you see me?'

'We came to an arrangement.' She gave me a sheepish look. 'A free pie every day from now until mid-summer and a politic tongue in conversations with his wife.'

I laughed out loud, feeling wild and manic. The sound echoed off the walls.

'You are *brilliant*, Rosie. Thank you.'

She gave a little curtsy, and we spent a few seconds simply enjoying the moment. It couldn't last. The truth of my situation closed in over me like a fog.

'I've ruined everything, Rosie. They've let Sister Agnes go and she's in danger. And I'm in here, accused of placing false evidence to get Coffey convicted.'

She sucked on her teeth. 'Which you did, if I'm any judge. And Mr Ripley said you hit Coffey on the head with a box. Is that true?'

'Yes. He was trying to molest a young girl.'

'Oh. Well then.'

For a little while, neither of us spoke. I sat sulking on the mattress, and she stood with her hands on the bars so, from my perspective, she appeared to be the one in jail. Eventually, I met her eyes. They were wet and rimmed with red. I'd thought she'd be angry that I'd gone to the gaff without telling her, but more than anything, she seemed proud.

'Perhaps we really should do it,' she said eventually, with a tense little smile.

'Do what?'

'Marry. It would save so much trouble, don't you think? I've had enough of men.' She wrinkled her nose, realising what she'd said. 'You know what I mean. You'll have to pay rent, of course. And I don't intend … that is to say, we'll have a spare room soon, when Alice and Albert go.'

I thought her jest was in poor taste and gave her a sour look. 'I think my accommodation is arranged for the time being.'

She folded her arms, regaining some of her usual bearing. 'I intend nothing more than a convenient arrangement. No one to bother me and no awkward questions for you. Who'd doubt a married man?'

I was attempting to maintain my composure, but my mind was reeling. Given what was about to happen to me – humiliation and imprisonment – for her to propound this fantasy, this other life in which I could live freely as a man, wasn't funny. It was cruel. I didn't understand. No one on earth was less cruel than Rosie.

I put my head in my hands. 'Please, stop. It's too late.'

A glimmer of a smile crossed her face. 'Do you think I've done nothing while you've been feasting in here?'

I jumped to my feet. 'What have you found out?'

The door at the end of the room opened and I could hear footsteps.

Rosie stepped back. 'Here she comes now.'

Ripley led the way. A step behind him was Sister Nora, dressed in her usual garb of black tunic and scapular, her long face fringed by a veil, emphasising her frown.

She appraised me squarely. 'Mr Stanhope. I'm sorry to see your present situation.'

'Me too.'

Ripley glared at us both. 'This isn't how I prefer to do things. If she has pertinent information, she should be in my office telling me, not chatting with a prisoner in his cell.'

Rosie gave him a look which might almost be described as 'fond'. 'You agreed to our arrangement so we might as well get on with it.' She put her hand on the Sister's arm. 'Tell the detective and Mr Stanhope what you told me.'

Sister Nora straightened her back and cleared her throat. Despite being much younger, she was as formidable as Mother Eugenie, in her own way.

'My name is Sister Nora Sutherland and I'm at the Convent of Mercy on Tooley Street. Iain Sutherland is my brother.' She was speaking not to Ripley directly, but into thin air, as though confessing her sins to God. 'Oswald Drake persuaded my brother to invest in the wrestling club. He calls it the gaff. I don't know what convinced Iain to do it because he doesn't have a great deal of money, only what he inherited from our parents.'

Ripley raised his eyebrows. 'Is he allowed to make investments? Isn't he a vicar or something?'

She shook her head. 'A deacon. Not yet a priest. He's free to do with his money as he wishes, but his choice was … unwise. I advised him that Mr Drake wasn't to be trusted, but he wouldn't listen. It turned out that I was right.'

I sensed that, for her, rightness was enough to justify any action, even if it led to the arrest of her own brother.

'Drake accepted your brother's money,' stated Ripley, getting to the point. 'And, I assume, refused to repay him.'

Sister Nora nodded. 'As I predicted, yes. I don't know the details. My brother has a bad temper and the two men argued. It's unthinkable that Iain would've taken Mr Drake's life, but … I can't be certain.'

Her voice trailed away, and she wiped her eyes with her palms.

Ripley clapped his hands together. He seemed reinvigorated. 'Right. Excellent. I'll go and question him.'

I realised how much it had weighed on the detective, not being able to solve the case. He always appeared so laconic, it was easy to think he didn't care about anything. But he loathed the idea of criminals evading justice.

I caught his eye. 'Yes, arrest Sutherland and make sure everyone knows about it. We'll need him as proof that Sister Agnes is innocent to avoid a riot.'

Sister Nora looked anxiously from one of us to the other. 'When I left the convent, there were men outside and more arriving. Do you think we're in danger? We do nothing but help those in need. Why would anyone wish harm on us?'

'Why indeed.' I grabbed Ripley's sleeve through the bars. 'We have to hurry, Detective.'

He tugged his jacket out of my grasp. 'We? You're under arrest, Stanhope. You're not going anywhere.'

Rosie took a deep breath. 'Detective Sergeant Ripley, what you're accusing Mr Stanhope of having done happened two nights ago, is that right? Well, the answer is simple. He couldn't have done it because he was at my house with me. He's hasn't admitted as much to protect my good name. You can let him out now.'

'Rosie, no …' I couldn't bear to let her lie for me, not if the price was her reputation. She had tossed it away in a heartbeat for my sake; no hesitation, no equivocation.

Ripley cleared his throat, seeming as if he might spit on the floor, but swallowing instead. 'Let me get this straight. You're claiming Mr Stanhope was with you at eleven o'clock on Saturday evening. Just the two of you was it, *Mrs* Flowers?'

She pulled her mouth into a polite, flat smile. 'I'm a widow, as you well know.'

'I know the two of you stick together, which is why I checked that detail in anticipation of just such a claim on your part. Your lodger, Mrs Alice Brunswick, said Mr Stanhope *wasn't* with you. She said you came home alone at around ten o'clock and went straight to bed. It's my opinion—'

He wasn't able to continue. The door at the end of the room banged open and I heard a familiar growl. 'Bah! Let go of me! Do you think I can't walk on my own? When

I was your age, the dockers called me *medved*. The bear. That's how strong I was.'

A portly constable came into view and then came Jacob, leaning on his cane with, to my amazement, Lilya, holding tightly on to his arm.

I stood up and would have rushed to greet them had I been able. 'Jacob, Lilya, my goodness! What are you doing here?'

My delight in seeing them was tempered with concern. It was weeks since Jacob had left the house and Lilya almost never did, fearful of London's uneven cobblestones.

She caught my tone and waved it away. 'I was invited, so I came. Constable Pallett sent us a message, though he signed it *Sergeant* Pallett, I'm told. Anyway, yes, Sergeant Constable Pallett told us where you were. He said you needed help.' She felt for the bars. 'My poor boy, what have they done to you?'

It was Rosie who answered. 'Leo's been wrongly accused.'

Lilya nodded. 'Ah, Mrs Flowers, I'm pleased you're here. Always you come when he needs you. This is good. This is very good.'

She directed a sly grin in my general direction, which of course Rosie noticed.

Rosie gently took Lilya's hand. 'I'm sure he was at *your* house on Saturday night with you and your husband, wasn't he, Mrs Kleiner?'

Lilya nodded vigorously. 'Yes, that's right. We talked about the river, the most beautiful river. It flows like music, this way and that way.' She moved her hands in a sinuous motion. 'When this old fool, my husband, and I were young, we followed the music from Belgrade to Wien

– you would say *Vienna* – and all the way to Linz. We had only each other.'

She was describing the Saturday of the week before but was such a good liar I wondered whether she was genuinely mistaken. Ripley watched her acutely but, of course, her eyes could give nothing away; no shifty glances, no ersatz innocence.

The portly constable leaned forward and said something quietly to Ripley. They were standing close to the bars, so I could hear some of the words, though fortunately no one else could. They included: 'Can't be trusted' and 'Jew'.

Ripley narrowed his eyes at the man, staring at him for so long, the constable's face reddened.

The detective turned back to Lilya. 'Mrs Kleiner, are you absolutely certain Mr Stanhope was with you? It's just that …' He paused, biting his lower lip. 'You're blind, if I'm not mistaken.'

Her mouth twitched. 'You think another man could come to my house and pretend to be Leo, who is like my own son, to say the things he would say, to eat my bread and cheese as he would do, and I could not tell?'

Ripley studied her carefully, one eyelid half lowered. 'Your husband told me that Mr Stanhope wasn't with you.' He indicated Jacob, who was adjusting the nap of his trousers at the crotch. 'Why should I believe you over him?'

Lilya drew herself up. 'You should have asked *me*, not him. My husband is a fine man, a fine jeweller, but he's old. His mind was trusty once, like a flask. You filled it to the brim, and nothing ever came out.' She banged her hands together as if pushing a lid on to a jar. 'Now, it leaks and leaks until everything is gone.'

Ripley turned to Jacob, losing all remnants of patience. 'Is this true? Are you senile?'

'Of course, he isn't,' I protested. 'He's perfectly capable, aren't you Jacob?'

Jacob swallowed hard and brushed his hands down his jacket.

'It's true,' he said in a quiet voice, his chin trembling. 'I try to hold on to my thoughts, but they slip away. I can't reach them. They're gone. I see it in people's faces, when I forget or say the same thing twice. I can't bear it. Soon, I know, I will have no memories of anything.' He looked at Lilya, tears in his eyes. 'Or anyone.'

It was as great an act of friendship as any I could imagine.

Rosie folded her arms and glared at Ripley. 'So, Mr Stanhope has an alibi. You can't keep him in jail.'

'All right.' He held up both of his hands in surrender. 'Since you're all determined to save him from his just deserts – even Pallett from the sound of it – I'll let him out. At least for now. Not that I believe any of you.'

The portly constable unlocked my cell, giving the strong impression it was against his better judgement.

Ripley strode away in disgust and I had to shout after him. 'There's a lot of angry men out there, Detective. They'll become violent unless we can prove to them beyond doubt that Sister Agnes is innocent. You must arrest Sutherland and take him to the convent. I'll go with you. I know the priest at the church.'

He nodded without slowing his pace.

Sister Nora grabbed my sleeve. 'I have to go to the convent and warn them.'

Rosie glanced up at the high window. Dusk was already falling. 'I'll go with you. We have to keep the babies safe.'

Before I left, I embraced Jacob. He was initially shocked and tense, before returning the gesture, patting my back.

As we separated, I held his shoulders. 'Thank you.'

He sucked in air through his teeth. 'You're like another son to me. You know this. Now go and do whatever it is you have to do. Come and see me when it's all over. We can play chess.'

I hurried through the police station after Ripley. When I emerged into the chill air of the yard, the sliver of the moon was shining behind the clouds. I'd rarely felt so grateful to be seeing it.

Ripley was speaking urgently to the carriage sergeant. 'And find some men,' he instructed him. 'Send them to the convent on Tooley Street. Do you know it?'

'I do.' The sergeant scratched his head. 'I'll see who we have. Might be able to spare a couple.'

I made sure I caught his eye. 'You'll need more.'

I helped Sister Nora and Rosie into a brougham. 'Please just warn the Sisters and leave, Rosie. Take no risks. And thank you for trying to give me an alibi.'

She smiled and patted my hand. Her skin was comfortingly oven-hardened and warm. 'You'd do the same for me.'

Her tone indicated that I shouldn't pursue the topic, but she was right; I would do the same for her; no hesitation, no equivocation.

Her carriage pulled away. If I'd been prone to such things, I would have prayed for her.

As I turned back to Ripley, he grabbed my lapel. I tried to pull away, but he was far too strong. I was eye to eye with him, breathing in his foul breath. Both of his eyes were fully open and for once there was no cigarette in his mouth.

'Listen, Stanhope, I suppose you think you've got away with something, but you haven't. If you choose to plant evidence to send some sewer rat like Coffey to prison, I won't mourn. The city's best off without him. But you've put good people in harm's way today. They queued up to lie for you. Decent people, honest people. Mrs Flowers soiled her own good name just so you wouldn't have to pay for your crimes. You should think about what you've turned her into. I'd hate to see her land in more trouble because of you.' He bumped his fist gently against my chest. 'I'd hate it very much indeed.'

He turned away and I followed him into the waiting Black Maria, shivering as if a cold wind was blowing through the yard.

26

THE CARRIAGE PASSED MY office and Rosie's shop, the rumble of paving giving way to bone-shaking cobbles. As we headed east, the buildings became lower and greyer, and likewise the people. It was like watching a city decay before our eyes. Men stared at us, but when I looked back, their eyes slid away.

It took twenty minutes to reach the nondescript little church at Whitechapel and I counted every second. By now, I thought, Rosie would be at the convent.

'Wait here,' Ripley told the driver.

I wouldn't have thought the detective devout, but he straightened his jacket and bowler hat as we marched up to the door.

'You're here on sufferance,' he snarled at me. 'Keep your mouth shut.'

Once again, the elderly priest was the only person in the church. He was in his shirt sleeves, mopping the floor. When he saw us, he slowly climbed to his feet, his hands shaking.

'Do you remember me?' I asked, immediately disobeying Ripley's instruction. 'You were kind enough to give me

Mrs Drake's address. Can you tell us where Iain Sutherland is now?'

The old fellow wiped his brow and cast around for his jacket. He cleared his throat.

'Sutherland is just a deacon,' he croaked, 'though he sometimes forgets the fact. Anything you have to say, you should say to me first. I'm the senior man.'

'I'm a detective sergeant with the Metropolitan Police,' said Ripley. 'I've come to arrest him.'

The old man's demeanour brightened considerably. 'Oh, my word, that's terrible. What's he done?'

Ripley gazed despairingly up at the cross. 'Please, just tell us where he is.'

'He's with his niece in the cottage.' The old man indicated the little door in the right-hand transept. 'Through there.'

'His niece?'

I followed Ripley into the lane at the back of the church. The pavement was empty but for two boys playing with a wooden ball. Over the road, a lamp was lit in the front room of a terraced house.

The detective hammered the knocker. As we waited, I could feel my heart beating.

Sutherland opened the door wearing a green smoking jacket. 'What are you doing here?'

'Let us in,' said Ripley. 'I have questions for you.'

Sutherland glanced back over his shoulder. 'I'd prefer not,' he said. 'I'll answer all your questions right here, if you don't mind.'

A suspicion started to form in my head.

Ripley was watching him carefully. 'The priest told us your niece is visiting. Is that right?'

He swallowed. 'Yes.'

Behind him, a woman appeared, dressed all in black, with a lace collar and elaborately pinned mourning bonnet. She pulled back her veil, and my suspicion was proved correct: Elspeth Drake.

Ripley shoved his hands into his pockets. I could tell he was dying for a cigarette. 'Mrs Drake. You're not Mr Sutherland's niece.'

'Of course not.' Her young face was solemn. 'I'm relieved you're here. I'm as good as a prisoner. He won't let me out.'

Sutherland turned towards her, his neck reddening. 'That's a lie!'

Ripley chewed his lip, scowling at the deacon. 'It's illegal to keep someone against their will.'

Sutherland held out his hands in appeal. 'Officer, I promise you, she can leave any time she wishes.'

I knew from bitter experience that Elspeth could be untruthful and was adept at playing on men's sympathies. 'Mrs Drake, why did you come here in the first place? A new widow, alone.'

'He's a man of the church, Mr Stanhope.' She looked down at the floor. 'And he's been making demands.'

Ripley squared up to Sutherland. 'What kind of demands would a man of the church make on a young widow?'

Elspeth shook her head firmly. 'Nothing like *that*. I'm a respectable lady.' She produced a handkerchief and dabbed her eyes. 'Mr Sutherland loaned my husband the money for the gaff. Now Oswald's dead, he's demanding repayment from me, but I don't have a farthing to my name.' Her voice caught in her throat. 'He threatened me and … and my Reggie too. I begged him to let us go, but he said he'd hold Reggie until I came back with fifty quid.' She bit her lip. 'Where am I going to get fifty quid?'

'That's another lie,' bellowed Sutherland. 'You came here with the idiotic demand that I should install you as manager of the penny gaff instead of Nick Coffey. I declined, of course. I never threatened you.'

'I don't have anything.' She was almost weeping. 'How can I give you what I don't possess?'

'I've never asked you for a penny!'

'For the sake of clarity, Mr Sutherland,' said Ripley. 'Why did you loan money to Oswald Drake?'

The deacon breathed deeply. 'It was an investment. He claimed it would expand the business; chaps with boards on Piccadilly, some publicity in the newspapers, that sort of thing. We wanted to pull in wealthy punters from Westminster rather than the local hooligans and misers.'

'Of course,' I said. The parts were clicking into place. 'It was you who wrote that letter inviting me to the gaff on behalf of Mr Drake. The one that said there'd be a murder.'

Ripley nodded in agreement. 'A nice piece of misdirection that, to arrange a fake murder and then stage a real one.'

Sutherland shook his head furiously. 'Look, you've got it all wrong. Why would I kill Oswald? We were a partnership. We planned to start a tour soon, you know, in the northern towns. We had lots of ideas.'

'We were told that Drake stole your money and you were angry.'

Sutherland sighed. 'I'm not a rich man. It was all that I had, an inheritance from my father. Drake didn't invest it as we'd agreed. He wanted the high life for himself, a pleasant house in Cressy Place and lots of servants. Yes, of course I was angry with him, but I'm a Christian man. I didn't commit any crime.'

I spoke quietly to Ripley. 'You have no choice but to arrest him, Detective. He didn't previously mention that he was an investor in the business, and he admits he had a disagreement with Oswald Drake. Also, he claimed Mrs Drake was his niece and he imprisoned her against her will.' *If she was telling the truth about that.* 'At the very least, he's a suspect.'

Ripley raised his eyebrows. 'Not an hour ago, you were insisting Coffey was the killer.'

'I know. Perhaps they collaborated.'

In truth, I didn't particularly care whether Sutherland was guilty or not. I simply needed a new suspect to deflect the blame and fury away from Sister Agnes; anyone would do. Rosie was at the convent, and Mother Eugenie and all of them, and their patients, some with babies. None of them was safe.

In the distance, a clock was striking eight. If we left immediately and were lucky with traffic, we could be at the convent before eight-thirty.

Ripley rubbed his chin, as agonisingly unhurried as ever. 'Maybe. Thing is, I don't believe any of you.' He took hold of Sutherland's arm and beckoned to Elspeth. 'Until I get to the bottom of this, you're both coming with me.'

We headed south towards the river, but not fast enough for me. Every time the carriage slowed to negotiate a corner my fingers prickled with impatience. Opposite me, Sutherland was glowering, his hands cuffed in front of him, and beside me was Elspeth. She wasn't handcuffed, in deference to her baby, Reggie, who was lying peacefully in her arms. Opposite her, Ripley was smoking, apparently having forgotten his wife's admonition, occasionally thumping on the tarp and yelling at the driver to speed up.

We made it as far as the Aldgate pump before we halted. I looked out of the window, and ahead of us the traffic was stretched out in a long line, marked by carriage lanterns swinging in the wind.

'What's going on?' Ripley called up to the driver.

'It's the diggings for the underground railway,' the fellow called back. 'Everyone's stopped from here to the city. This is their plan. They want us delayed, so we have to use their railways instead, and pay 'em for the privilege. The slower we are, the happier they get.'

I was overbrimming with frustration. 'We don't have time for this. You're the police, can't you do something?'

Ripley rolled his eyes. 'Unless you want us to float over the river, we have to take the bridge like everyone else.'

Sutherland was frowning. 'But why are we going over the river at all? I thought you were taking me to the police headquarters.'

Ripley exchanged a glance with me. 'The release of our previous suspect might have caused a bit of resentment. We're taking you to her … place of work to help cool any tempers. Avoid any unnecessary fuss and bother.'

Sutherland took a moment to comprehend his meaning. 'You're talking about Sister Agnes, aren't you? Surely you didn't let her go?' He sat back in his seat, his eyes searching the floor of the carriage as if he might find answers there. 'We're going to the convent. You can't think … you can't mean that I should replace the Butcher of Berner Street? No, I won't do it.'

'They won't care about *you*,' I insisted. 'Sister Agnes has become … a symbol, I suppose. They're using her to whip up trouble. You're a gentleman, so you're in no danger, believe me.'

'I'm a Catholic! I'll get lynched.'

I almost felt sorry for him, but Ripley was as unyielding as a slab of granite. 'You're under arrest as a suspect in a murder. You'll do whatever I tell you to do, and right now I'm telling you to shut your mouth.'

Such was his authority that Sutherland subsided, though he kept grimacing as though being poked with a stick.

Elspeth, who'd been silent up to that point, stroking her baby's head, took a deep, uneven breath. 'I'm glad you've set Irina free. I never thought she was guilty of killing Oswald. Even though she lied about who she was and had that accent and everything, she was always kind to Reggie.' She started to sniffle and pulled out a lace handkerchief. 'My poor Oswald, murdered so cruelly for a debt he couldn't repay.'

Sutherland scowled at her, his face turning slowly purple.

Still, we weren't moving. I was shaking with exasperation.

And then I had an idea, though the very thought of it was loathsome. But there was no choice now.

'I know a way across the river without using the bridge. It's on foot. We have to hurry.'

Ripley hauled Sutherland out of the carriage and instructed the driver to take Elspeth to the police headquarters.

'No,' she insisted, holding Reggie close. 'I'm coming with you. I want to see justice done.'

'It's not safe, Mrs Drake.'

'I'll take my chances.'

We made a strange sight, the five of us, Sutherland with his hands cuffed, Ripley holding his arm, Elspeth carrying Reggie, and me in the lead, begging the others to walk more quickly. As we reached the end of the crooked street, it opened out to the half-oval park where Sutherland and Sister Nora had sat together. I considered mentioning to him that we'd seen them that day but decided against it. He might realise that his sister had given him away, and he was a man with a temper.

Our presence was causing a certain amount of commotion. Mothers and nannies gathered up their children and gentlemen examined us, their hands on their canes in case this was the sort of thing they ought to do something about.

I tugged Ripley's sleeve. 'This way, quickly.'

We squeezed through the gangway over the works and I almost ran down the hill alongside the Tower of London. Over the river I could see lights twinkling and wondered if one of them was on the spire of the convent chapel.

Then I saw it: an orange glow reflecting in the water. A fire had been lit.

I turned to the others. 'We have to hurry! Come on!'

We reached the circular structure at top of the stairway and Ripley stared at the dim hole. 'Down there? You must be joking.'

Sutherland's eyes were fixated on the distant blaze. 'You can't make me do this. I promise you I didn't kill anyone. I was at a church meeting when it happened. There are a dozen witnesses. You can ask them. Mrs Harrison was there and Mrs Lees and Jack Watt, the sexton. I can write you a list.'

Ripley narrowed his eyes at me. I could see the shadow of doubt growing in his mind.

'He and Coffey may have planned the murder together,' I said. 'More importantly, we need him to avert a riot.'

With a degree of reluctance, Ripley gave Sutherland a shove forward, but the deacon resisted, tugging his arm out of the detective's grasp. He was handcuffed, but he was younger and taller than the policeman.

Ripley stood his ground. 'Don't be silly, son.'

Sutherland swallowed. I was certain he would submit, but instead he leapt forward and punched Ripley in the face with both fists at once, like twin battering rams. Ripley staggered backwards clutching his nose, and Sutherland stamped down on his leg. I heard a crack and a roar of pain as Ripley fell.

Elspeth fled down the spiral steps, Reggie caterwauling all the way.

I blocked Sutherland's path, but he knocked me aside and ran after her, shouting: 'Stop, Elspeth! I just want to talk to you.'

Ripley tried to stand, but his knee gave way. 'Go back to the carriage and fetch help.'

I turned and peered into the hole. Sutherland's footsteps were getting fainter.

'Don't be stupid, Stanhope.' Ripley was speaking through teeth clenched in pain. 'You can't do this on your own.'

I plunged down the stairs into the gloom.

Round and round I went, descending into the earth. At the bottom, in the little lounge, the lad who took the pennies was scratching his head. Another, older fellow was with him, clearly affronted, gaping into the tunnel.

There was no time to explain or pay. I hurtled past them after Sutherland.

I couldn't see anyone, but I could hear Reggie's keening cries, accompanied by the drumming of my own footsteps. It was hard to tell how far ahead they were, and I was surprised when I reached them almost immediately, not two hundred yards from the entrance. Sutherland was facing away from me, silhouetted against the veiled lamplight. Elspeth was the other side of him, holding Reggie close. She was breathing heavily.

'Let us go, Iain.' Her voice was thin and weak. 'We've done nothing to you.'

He grabbed her by the arm. 'You have to tell the truth, Elspeth. They'll hang me, you know that.'

He turned when he heard me approaching. 'This has nothing to do with you, Stanhope. I just need her to be truthful, that's all. It was her who persuaded me to make the investment in the gaff in the first place. She told me it was a dead certainty, and it seemed so, until her husband started spending all my money on himself. Even then, she begged me to be patient. She used her … her womanly wiles on me. I'm ashamed of it now.'

Her eyes blazed. 'That's not true!'

He inhaled deeply, his face an agony of conflict and anger. 'She told me Drake would punish her if I didn't do as she asked. He was a violent man, a bully. She's knows I'm telling the truth.'

Elspeth wrenched her arm free and pulled something from her hair. Sutherland stepped back, but she swung at him, and in the gloom, I couldn't see what was in her hand. He went down, clutching his neck, blood pouring down his green jacket and on to the floor.

In Elspeth's hand was a six-inch hatpin, glinting in the dim light.

Sutherland was on his knees. He made a lunge for her, swiping the air as she jumped out of the way.

'Please, Elspeth,' he gasped. 'I'm begging you. You know I didn't kill Drake.'

She lifted the hatpin, pointed downwards.

'No!' I shouted. 'You've acted in self-defence and that's fair enough. But if you kill him now, it'll be murder.'

She raised and then lowered the hatpin, caught in indecision. Finally, she turned and ran, Reggie still clutched to her breast.

Sutherland sank down, sprawling against one of the ribs of the tunnel, bleeding from a wound at the base of his neck, his hands still locked together. He lifted his eyes to mine. 'I didn't kill anyone. You have to believe me.'

Unfortunately, I did.

I pressed my hand against his wound, staunching the blood. 'You realise Drake sent her to your bed? He used her to gain leverage over you.'

Sutherland closed his eyes. 'I acted like a buffoon.'

'Yes. And now you need a doctor. You're losing a lot of blood.'

He pushed himself to his feet and shrugged me away, staggering back the way we'd come. Footsteps were hurrying towards us; no doubt the lad who took the pennies. He arrived just as Sutherland fell to his knees. I heard shouts, but Sutherland was no use to me now. I couldn't carry him, and even if I could, a bleeding invalid wouldn't convince an angry mob to stand down. Without Ripley to lend force to the accusation, why would they believe me?

All my hopes of averting a riot had evaporated.

27

I REACHED THE TOP of the stair and ran up the hill, past the wharves to the junction with Tooley Street. There was no sign of Elspeth Drake.

I forced myself to sprint, my lungs aching and my heart thumping in my chest. As I grew closer to the convent, smoke bit at my throat and shadows from the flames danced against the buildings; a beast with a thousand arms. My calloused cheek seemed to tighten, stinging the soft skin of my neck and mouth. I pinched myself viciously under both armpits, digging my nails deep into my raw flesh until I almost puked.

The pavement outside the convent was crammed with men. Angry voices were shouting, and fire baskets had been set in a row. As I reached them, still thirty yards or more from the convent, a fellow climbed the steps and began hammering on the door.

It was Nicholas Coffey.

'You murdering whore!' he yelled, loud enough for all the crowd to hear. 'You killed the finest man in all of London!'

The door remained shut, and Coffey turned to face us, his arms outstretched as if to say: 'I tried my best'.

I began pushing through the throng, but my headway was agonisingly slow. One woman shoved me back and stood pointedly in front of me, elbows out like a doorman. The closer I got, the more tightly packed they became. I wouldn't be able to get inside the convent.

'Over here, Leo!' Harry was waving to me from the pavement, where a gaggle of journalists were huddling under a lamppost. He put his arm round me as I reached him. 'This is quite an event. Sister Butcher's inside and these fellows want her out. There's going to be a riot.'

I looked up at the top window of the convent. A silhouette appeared and I knew instantly it was Rosie, so familiar was the angle of her chin, the irritated fidgeting of her hands and the set of her jaw. Even though I couldn't make out the features of her face, I knew her expression exactly: eyes narrowed and lips pursed. If I'd been there, she would have scowled at me and muttered: 'It's a wonder these fools have nothing better to be doing.' I could hear the precise timbre of her voice.

'Rosie!'

I waved, but she didn't see me. Mine was one arm in a forest of arms, none more noticeable than any other, whipping and waving in a furious gale.

Around us, I could hear shouts. In the density of the mob, scuffles were breaking out.

Another figure appeared behind Rosie, taller and broader: Sister Agnes Munro.

I turned to Harry. 'I need to get inside the convent.'

He scoffed. 'No chance. Stay here where it's safe. You can help me describe the events for our readership.'

But I couldn't simply stand at the outskirts, scratching words into my notebook.

'I'm sorry, Harry. That's not enough for me. I have to take some action. I have to try to make things better.'

He shook his head. 'That's not our job, Leo.'

I looked up at the window again and Rosie was still there, now alone. I was almost certain she saw me. I pointed at the door and she rushed away.

I shoved through the crowd, not caring whose elbows obstructed me, even pushing a fellow to the ground in my impatience. As I got to the bottom of the steps, I almost bumped into Coffey coming the other way.

His eyes widened and he pointed at me. 'That's the bastard who tried to get me nicked for murder!'

I dodged past him and threw myself towards the closed door. Exactly at the moment I reached it, it opened, and I launched myself inside. It slammed shut behind me.

I'd been running so hard I skidded on the stone floor and fell in an undignified heap on my backside.

Rosie put her hands on her hips.

'You took your time,' she said.

———

I followed Rosie upstairs, hearing the rising clamour outside. There was chanting and drumming and the crashing of metal. From the window, the street looked like a battlefield.

In her room, Mother Eugenie was perching on a stool and reading her bible while Sister Nora sat in the sofa. They both looked up as we entered, their faces a contrast: the younger woman was a picture of anxiety, fidgeting and biting her nails, while the older was as serene as a lake in winter.

The clock was standing at half past nine.

'The crowd outside is growing,' I told them. 'You're not safe.'

Mother Eugenie pursed her lips. 'They'll go home soon, I'm sure. They're all roused up, but it'll ease just as quickly. They know the importance of the work we do here.'

I shook my head. 'I don't think they do. Where's Sister Agnes?'

'She retired to her prayer room.'

A young Sister came in with a tray of tea and set it down on the table. In the midst of such pandemonium, it was a surreally civilised act.

'They're pushing on the front door,' she said. 'But I think the lock will hold.'

She laid out the saucers and cups in a ring and placed the sugar bowl at the centre.

Sister Nora could contain herself no longer. 'What of my brother?'

She appeared close to tears and I had the urge to put my hand on her shoulder for comfort, but I so rarely touched anyone, I wasn't sure how. I leaned down and patted her on the forearm. The gesture was both earnestly meant and entirely futile.

'He injured a police officer and was himself injured. Both will recover, I think, but I imagine he'll be in some … legal peril. However, I don't think he was directly involved in Drake's death.'

'I see.' She hugged herself briefly. 'Thank you. I'll pray for him.'

I couldn't imagine what miracle she was expecting from the Almighty. Even stopping the lions from eating Daniel would be a paltry trick compared with dissuading Ripley from arresting Sutherland after what he'd done.

There was a knock at the door, hardly audible against the pounding from outside. A girl stood on the threshold and I recognised her as the mother of little Joe. She bobbed her head, fiddling with her hair to cover the scar that ran across her forehead and down her face.

'Pardon me,' she said. 'I don't mean to intrude. Me and the girls was wondering what we should do.'

With the door open, we could hear the sound of a baby crying downstairs.

Mother Eugenie attempted a comforting smile. 'Stay where you are. Those men won't dare try to get in.'

The girl nodded and was on the brink of leaving when Rosie looked up. 'Wait. Sister Nora, there's a back door out of here, isn't there? Will you show me?'

Mother Eugenie shook her head. 'No, we're all safer inside. When I was in the Crimea, we often—'

'Mrs Flowers is quite right,' I said. 'We can use the back door and sneak away before anyone notices.'

'And abandon the convent?' Mother Eugenie shook her head. 'I won't do it. Besides, we've got sickly and pregnant girls downstairs. They can't travel and we won't leave them.'

'Some of us can travel well enough,' said the girl with the scar. 'We want our babies to be safe.'

Rosie stood up and set her hat. 'Good. Let's gather them up. Everyone who can leave, should.'

Sister Nora led the way and we followed. I was glad to be doing something useful. There was nothing worse than waiting.

In the corridor, the din was louder. The mob outside was yelling: 'Justice for Oswald Drake! Justice for Oswald Drake!'

The girl with the scar shivered. 'Why don't we just give 'em what they want? They won't really do anything to Sister Agnes.'

Rosie's face was grim. 'Yes, they will.'

We hurried down the stairs to the hallway. The noise was deafening. Men were banging on the door with their fists and pulling on the handle. The iron ring on the inside was turning and clanking as if it had a life of its own. Demons were glaring in through the windows, contorted and vague in the wavering glass. They must have been clinging on to the ledge or sitting on each other's shoulders.

'They can see us,' said Rosie. 'We should turn out the lamps.'

We walked around the room, extinguishing them one by one. As each was snuffed out, the lobby grew darker and the scene outside more terrifying; faces grimacing and shouting, hands pressed flat against the windows, fingernails tapping, and behind it all, that orange glow.

As the final lamp went dark, the first window was smashed, scattering stained glass across the floor.

28

WE RUSHED ALONG THE darkened corridor past the windows and the faces. Behind me, I could hear the girl with the scar whispering the Lord's Prayer under her breath, over and over. Even if He's listening, I thought to myself, He won't help you. The next time a window breaks, the glass could tear the skin from your face, and He won't care a jot. Just ask Miss Chive.

We descended the steps to the lower part of the building, passing Sister Agnes's prayer room and a passageway off to the right. At the end was a door. I could hear voices singing a hymn. All but a couple were wavering and weak.

Sister Nora pointed towards it. 'The dormitory. Last room.'

As we entered, at least twenty faces looked up. Five were Sisters and the rest were young women, many lying in bed, some with babies. One or two were asleep.

I tried to look confident. 'Anyone who's fit to walk should follow me. Be quick.'

The crying baby was little Joe. The girl with the scar picked him up.

'Can you soothe him?' I asked. 'We have to be silent.'

She jiggled and joggled and stroked his head, but he wouldn't settle. Meanwhile, Rosie shooed some of the girls into what clothes they possessed: shoes, hats, coats and shawls for their shoulders. Two were heavily pregnant and three had infants in their arms. Another was as pale as a screech owl, with rings around her big brown eyes.

The rest were too weak to be moved. Sister Nora and the others pushed their chairs and beds together, and the invalids held each other's hands.

Eventually, we had a group of seven young women and three babies ready to leave, but still little Joe wailed.

'Leave him with me here,' Rosie said to the girl with the scar. 'You go. I'll take care of him. Come back for him later when you're safe.'

But the girl wouldn't let go of her child.

I sat on the bed next to her. 'There won't be another chance to escape. It's now or never.'

'I know,' she mumbled. 'But I can't leave without 'im. Not with all this.'

Sister Nora gave the girl an affirming nod. 'Good. We'll stay here together.' She smiled bravely at me. 'Someone has to, Mr Stanhope.'

Rosie herded the six remaining girls into the passageway. I pushed past them to the back door and put my ear to the wood. I couldn't tell if anyone was outside.

As gently as I could, I eased the bolt up and across, keeping my weight against the wood to avoid the slightest squeak. I turned the handle gingerly, but the door wouldn't open.

It was locked.

In the narrow passage, the girls were whispering to each other. The ghostly pale one was leaning against the wall, her breath wheezing in her chest.

Rosie's face was tense. I could tell what she was thinking: that these girls would sink into despair if we delayed too long. 'The key must be upstairs,' she said. 'I'll go back.'

Another crash of glass shook the corridor. The noise outside grew immediately louder.

'No.' I was trying to keep my voice from quavering. 'I'll go.'

'Why you?' she whispered.

'Because all this is my fault.'

'Leo—'

But I was already leaving, retracing my steps. I got as far as the stairs before I heard a voice behind me.

'Mr Stanhope?'

I spun round and there was Sister Agnes, standing in the corridor. She must have been in her prayer room and had come out when she heard the noise. She held something up.

'Do you need the key?'

I grabbed it from her and looked into her eyes. She seemed calm, as if unaware of what was happening.

'You should leave too.'

She turned back towards her prayer room without giving me an answer.

I ran back to Rosie. The girls were whispering among themselves, and I could tell we were losing them.

'You should go as well,' I told Rosie. 'See them to safety.'

I turned the key and pushed open the door. Cold air blew in. Outside, a little set of steps led to the back of the convent. There was no one in sight, though we could hear the crowd roaring at the front, just a few yards away.

But there was another sound too: drums beating and voices singing; women's voices.

The girls filed out and gathered on the steps.

'Quickly,' I instructed them. 'Stay quiet and don't go near anyone. Head east away from the mob. Don't get caught. Come back here in a day or two when it's safe.'

If the convent is still standing. How long would it be before these men started throwing lit torches inside?

I kept the door open for Rosie. This was her route home too, back to her children, back to where she belonged.

She hesitated and then shook her head. 'I'm staying with you,' she said, and pulled the door shut.

We hurried back along the passageway to Sister Agnes's prayer room. She was kneeling on the floor in front of her cross, head bowed. As Rosie closed the door behind us, the noise instantly dropped to a distant rumble, like furious thunder on the other side of the city.

Sister Agnes crossed herself and took a deep breath. 'Are they safe?'

'I think so,' said Rosie.

'Good.'

I had to ask her. 'I need to know the truth. Do you know who killed Oswald Drake?'

'The same question again? It seems you can't make up your mind.' She glanced at me sidelong and allowed herself a tiny smile. 'You're not very consistent, Mr Stanhope. About anything, I deem.'

My fears spat and popped like hot wax in water, though I kept my face calm. 'What are you talking about?'

'First, you thought I was guilty, then that I wasn't and now you think I know who is.' Again, that tiny smile, even as the crowd outside were screaming for her blood. 'But I have no right to lecture you on consistency, do I? I did pretend to be a wrestler, after all.'

My anxiety subsided. She didn't know what I was. As so often, my derangement was entirely of my own making.

'You *were* a wrestler,' I said. 'You didn't pretend. I saw you. You were very good.'

She inclined her head, her bruises shining in the candle-light. 'I was, wasn't I? When I was a little girl, I could always win against my brothers. Of course, they grew up and joined the army, and I was expected to learn embroidery. I can't tell you how disappointed I was when I found out. I should've known, but I was a dreamy child and the only daughter, so what can one expect? I settled for this life, eventually. But when I discovered Drake was running a wrestling hall, a small part of me was thrilled. Is that so wicked?' Slowly, she climbed to her feet. 'I've already told you that none of this is your fault.'

I felt my face colour, though no one could have noticed in the dimness. 'I beg to differ.'

She took my hand. 'You are forgiven, Mr Stanhope. Absolved completely. Don't let regret and remorse ruin you.'

'But what of you? Didn't you say that your part is to be convicted of the crime? You called it your *purpose*.'

She gave me a broad smile, one of genuine joy. I stared at her, thinking she'd been driven mad.

'Don't you see, Mr Stanhope? All of this has revealed the Lord's *true* purpose for me. It's what I've been waiting for all this time.'

'And what is it?'

'You'll know soon.' She gave herself a little shake. 'Where's Mother Eugenie?'

Rosie stirred. 'She's still upstairs.'

'Very well. We should go to her. She'll be worried.'

Rosie opened the door, and the noise hit us. Every window in the corridor had been broken, glass scattered across the floor. Faces were crowding at the window frames.

'It's her!' one of them screamed, pointing a finger. 'It's the Butcher!'

The shout was taken up by the others. A beardless lad lunged at me with his fist, screeching as the skin of his arm ripped on the jagged shards left in the frame. More hands reached for us and faces leered and spat. We crept along, pressed against the inside wall, inches from their grabbing fingers.

A cracking sound reverberated along the corridor behind us. A boy had been launched in through the broken window. He landed on his hands and knees in the corridor and cried out, blood pouring from his wrists.

He wasn't more than thirteen years old.

Agnes took a step towards him. 'You're hurt.'

He backed away down the corridor in the direction of the dormitory where the invalid girls and Sister Nora were hiding. His skin was ashen. He put a hand against the wall, leaving a red print behind.

Agnes pointed behind him. 'Go,' she said. 'The last door. They'll take care of you.'

Another man appeared at the window, wobbling on whatever was supporting him. He managed to get one knee up on the ledge, but Agnes gently pushed him backwards and released him. He disappeared from view.

'Come along. Quickly.'

She led the way, with Rosie and me running to keep up.

In the hallway, the oak door was still under attack, but rhythmically now; pull and release, pull and release, like a rower on his oar. Someone had got them organised. Mother Eugenie was standing at the top of the stairs, her hands over her mouth, as the wood creaked and groaned.

'Why are they doing this?'

At the edge of my hearing, almost too faint to detect, that sound again; a drum beating and women singing.

'The suffragists,' said Rosie, a hint of pride in her voice. 'Maybe they'll help us.'

Mother Eugenie shook her head. 'They'd do better to stay out of the way.'

I felt Rosie bristle beside me, but she refrained from arguing.

'We don't have much time,' I said. 'We need to get everyone down to the dormitory to protect the sick and the infants. There's no other option now.'

I was almost at the top of the stairs when I realised Sister Agnes wasn't with us. She was standing by the door, watching the twisting and tensing of the iron ring, on and off, on and off, as it was pulled and released on the other side. Her hand was on the bolt.

I ran towards her, but at the next release of the door, she slid back the bolt. On the next pull, the door flew open.

In the centre of the group, Coffey was grinning wildly.

She stood facing them. 'I am Agnes Munro,' she declared. 'I murdered Oswald Drake. I deserve to be punished.'

29

HANDS REACHED FOR HER. She chopped down on the first and bent back the fingers of the second, swivelling and delivering a round-house punch to a fellow who clawed at her clothing. But soon there were too many hands. They caught her wrists and groped for her ankles. One of them tugged her cross from her neck and she screamed with anger, managing to tear it from his grasp and clutch it to her chest.

But she couldn't fight them all.

She was lifted up, floundering and kicking, and raised above their heads like a trophy. A huge cheer went up.

Coffey led the way, waving his opera hat in the air.

I threw myself after her, trying to swim through the mob, but they were too many and too dense, closing in behind the leading group. They paraded in a great arc around Tooley Street, and, in the commotion, a fire basket was knocked over, sending coals pouring across the pavement and into the gutter. I shied away from it, feeling my skin boiling and contracting in the heat, and my hair scalding against my scalp.

'Come on!' shouted Rosie at my side.

I could still see Sister Agnes, lifted aloft by a dozen hands, and Coffey's hat capering in the glow of the flames.

'String her up!' one of them shouted, and then they all took up the call. 'String her up! String her up!'

Coffey led them to the wharf building and indicated that they should lower her to a standing position. Above their heads, a horizontal iron arm was attached at the second storey, and from its pulley, a rope was dangling. Coffey took the end in his hand and casually swung it from side to side.

'Anyone know how to tie a knot?'

The crowd surged forward.

'Stop,' I yelled. 'This is murder.'

Sister Agnes raised her eyes to meet mine. Her veil and scapular were missing, but she seemed at peace. Her mouth was moving, and I realised she was praying.

One of the men tied a noose in the rope and looped it over her head.

Coffey raised his hand and the mob quietened. 'This woman has just confessed to the murder of Oswald Drake, my best friend since we was nippers. But the authorities let her out, like they always do. They don't care about us. They live in their fine houses and drink their fine wine while we get murdered in our beds. There's no justice but what we make for ourselves.'

The mob roared their encouragement. I looked from face to face. Some were old and some younger, some blue-eyed and some brown, some well dressed and some untidy. They probably had families and positions, a regular pew at church. They weren't killers on any other day.

'Stop!' I yelled, furiously waving my arms. 'You can't do this!'

I tried to push in between them to reach Sister Agnes, though I had no idea what I would do if I succeeded. A hand took hold of my collar and I felt myself being dragged sideways. There was a cry and I jerked up my head.

Rosie, Rosie, Rosie.

I didn't care what they did to me as long as they didn't touch her.

I flinched as a punch landed, and then another, to my neck and stomach. But they lacked full force. The mob was getting in its own way, unable to muster proper leverage in the crush. I caught a glimpse of Rosie's skirts and heard her shout. Hands were on me, gripping my clothing, tugging at my hair. A lump of spit hit my cheek. Faces crowded in; broken teeth and wet mouths.

I felt myself stop. I took a breath. My mind cleared, all but a single thought.

That Tom Cobb, he was a violent boy.

I pushed my finger into the nearest face so hard that it went between his eyeball and his skull. He squealed and fell to the floor. The next one I kneed in the testicles and the next I elbowed in the mouth. His head snatched back and there was a cracking sound I hoped was his neck. The next got a punch in the throat and the one after a broken nose. He twisted as he fell, half tripping the man in front, who stepped backwards on to his fingers.

Rosie was ahead of me, stumbling, bent under the weight of hands pushing her down. She flailed her arms and made contact with a man's ribs. I charged forwards, barging two of them aside and dragging the rest away from her. She staggered upright, her face red and scratched, her eyes ferocious.

Another cheer went up.

We all turned.

Sister Agnes was being hauled upwards on the rope, thrashing and kicking, her hands clawing at the noose around her neck. She couldn't scream. Higher and higher she went, pulled by half a dozen men while Coffey yelled, 'Heave! Heave!' and swept his hat from side to side.

When she could be lifted no higher, everyone stopped, the whole street noiseless but for the squeaking of the pulley as she danced, slower and slower, convulsing, twitching and finally hanging still.

When all movement in her body had ceased, they let go. She plummeted to the ground, and the rope unravelled on top of her.

30

AGNES LAY BROKEN.

Coffey stared at the mob, his eyes swivelling. For two seconds, no one moved. And then, as if someone had blown a whistle, they fled, scattering in all directions like the rats they were.

Rosie dashed forward to Sister Agnes's shattered corpse, but I had someone else in mind.

Coffey's dandy jacket was easy to spot. He was running parallel to the river, keeping close to the walls of the buildings. I didn't pause to think, I sprinted after him, closing to within twenty yards before he heard my footsteps and glanced over his shoulder. I accelerated, my lungs burning, but he was quicker. Twenty yards became thirty as I passed his fancy hat, bouncing in the gutter. I was losing him.

A single streetlamp was working, and as he reached it, he turned to face me, his chest heaving.

'No more,' he gasped. 'It's over. Nothing you can do now, Stanhope.'

I was trying to catch my breath too. 'Why, though? Why did you lynch her?'

He frowned. 'Justice for Oswald. She was never getting punished by the authorities, was she? We had to take a stand.'

I shook my head and swallowed. 'It was *you* that killed Oswald Drake.'

'No.' He sank back against the streetlamp, his face flushed red. 'It was her, the nun. You heard her confess.'

'That was to stop you burning the convent. She sacrificed herself. I'm taking you to the police.'

He shook his head. 'No, you ain't.'

He started in the direction of the bridge but didn't make it further than a single step. I hardly saw the movement; a black shape emerging from the shadows and a flicker of metal. There was no sound. Coffey sank to his knees. The black shape raised an arm, her hatpin clasped in her hand, pointing downwards.

Elspeth Drake's eyes met mine. 'This time?' she asked.

I nodded, barely thinking.

She pulled Coffey's head back by the hair and drove the hatpin into his neck. Three more times the hatpin was raised and lowered, once more into his neck, once into his stomach and once into his groin as he fell backwards. The blood leaked out of his body and pooled in the gutter.

She straightened up.

We were alone.

'Don't worry,' she said. 'You're a fool, but you're not a wicked fool. I'm not going to kill you.'

She wiped the hatpin on Coffey's jacket and replaced it expertly into her hair. Throughout the entire killing, she'd been cradling baby Reggie in one arm.

I took a deep breath. 'It was you.'

She brushed a wisp of hair from Reggie's forehead. 'Not just me. Oswald caused a lot of people a lot of pain.'

'The children who sleep in the gaff.'

She angled her head in acknowledgement. 'Some of 'em. You have to remember, I was one of 'em once. You met Lewis, didn't you? He sometimes does a shift in the meat market. They inject the cows with morphine, you know, and—'

'With thick needles to go through their thick hides?'

She gave a little laugh. 'Probably. Quite fitting for Oswald; no one had a thicker hide than him. Young Maria stuck him with it to knock him out. I tied a knot in the rope and put it round his neck, and we all pulled him up. He was dead in three minutes.'

She started walking towards the bridge and I matched her pace for pace, just as if we were a family out for a stroll. I thumbed back to where Nicholas Coffey was lying crumpled on the cobbles.

'What about him?'

She gave a little shrug. 'I thought Nick would be different. I thought he'd help me out running the gaff, doing the bits a woman can't, and we'd pay back Mr Sutherland's money together. But he had ideas of his own. He wanted to follow in Oswald's footsteps and have all the things Oswald had. *All* the things.' She shot a glance at me. 'And he killed a nun, which is a sin in anyone's book. He deserved to die.'

I couldn't argue with her. Not about that, anyway.

'Elspeth, what do you imagine will happen to you now?'

She smiled. 'I've an uncle in Derby who breeds dogs the size of horses, and he's trained them to pull his house like a carriage. He and I will visit all the countries of the world without ever leaving his front room.'

I shook my head. 'Elspeth, this is serious. You've killed two people. Do you understand what that means? There'll be a trial. You're guilty of murder.'

She stopped and faced me. 'And did you try to stop me, Mr Stanhope? It's my recollection that you didn't.' Little Reggie stirred briefly and went back to sleep, sucking his thumb. 'Are you going to tell 'em what we did? Make my boy an orphan?'

'They lynched Agnes Munro for a crime *you* committed.'

I realised my throat was closing up and I could hardly get the words out. Tears were running down my face. *They lynched her.*

Elspeth looked at the ground. 'I'm sorry about that. We never guessed Irina wasn't what she claimed, or that she'd end up being arrested.' She threw me a quick glance. 'Though you had something to do with that as well, Mr Stanhope.'

We'd reached London Bridge and she climbed the steps slowly. All around us, people were hurrying along the pavement or sitting in stationary carriages. It must have been midnight or later, yet still the city was alive. Among all the bustle, I noticed children, scrawny and grey, skulking in the shadows, hands out for farthings, picking among the paper bags for scraps left behind by the seagulls.

Elspeth looked over the balustrade at the water glistening in the lamplight. 'I can't go to prison,' she said. 'I'll drown first. Me and Reggie together.'

I shook my head sorrowfully. 'You won't. It's not so easy to jump, Elspeth. Trust me, I know.'

She cocked her head to one side, realising I was speaking from experience. 'You're full of surprises, Mr Stanhope. But it doesn't make any difference.' She leaned backwards against the balustrade, clutching Reggie tightly. 'I won't be separated from 'im.'

She shifted her weight, so, if she chose, she could twist and throw herself over the side before I could reach her.

I put up my hands in surrender. 'Very well. You're right. Drake and Coffey deserved what they got. But you're free of them now. No more. I won't tell the police or write an article about you, but you must promise it's an end to the killing.'

She lifted her chin and stared back at me, fiery-eyed, and I could see how this girl, so slight and pale, could have survived a life on the street. I admired her. I wasn't sure I could have been so resilient.

'What about that Mr Lampton from Parliament?' she said, rolling her eyes. 'He might benefit from a new hatpin, don't you think? Men like him never seem to get what they deserve.'

She was right, of course. It rankled that he would never suffer the consequences of the movement he'd started. It was the way of power though, wasn't it? The troops are slaughtered in the field while the generals die in their own beds from old age.

'No. You must promise me, Elspeth.'

She smiled and turned away. 'Goodbye, Mr Stanhope.'

'Promise me,' I called after her.

She looked back once, her face catching the light before she covered it with her veil. 'All right. It's over.'

And with that, she was gone, lost among the crowds on the bridge.

Epilogue

We talked and talked, Rosie and me. We wept a good deal too, which wasn't very manly on my part, but I couldn't stop myself.

I went into my office on the day after the lynching and wrote a long piece for the newspaper, and then told J. T. I would be back in a fortnight and he could fire me if he objected. I received a message the following day to say he would expect me some time in June, with a postscript that my first task would be to finish my review of *Clever Things Said by Children*.

Otherwise, I spent my time with Rosie, talking and weeping, and with my other dear friends. I drank whisky with Alfie, and quizzed Constance on the names of the bones in the hands and feet, while Huffam dozed under her chair. I played chess with Jacob, charades with Lilya, and I flew our kite with Aiden and Ciara, who were delighted to teach Robbie and Lillian the finer points. Little Samuel spent his time leaping about the grass trying to catch the ribbon, while Rosie and I sat on a blanket with the picnic.

At the end of the fortnight, we were decided. We had talked enough and wept enough, and it was time.

Rosie refused to go to the same church in which she'd married Jack, so we walked through the summer sunshine to the Church of the Martyrs, near to the gaff. The old priest stood in the pulpit smiling benignly at his little congregation, and so we were wed.

Never again would anyone pester her with proposals or question my sex.

As the congregation stood, we kissed, the briefest of brushes, like two children playing at being grown-ups.

Alfie shook my hand at the door. 'We could've had a joint wedding if you'd waited a couple of weeks.' He beamed at the soon-to-be Mrs Smith.

We had discussed the idea, Rosie and me, but she hadn't wanted to taint their genuine romance with our expediency. I told her I wasn't sure their marriage was all that different from ours – the larger shop and better location suited them both – but she was having none of it.

Constance clasped my hand, one of the very few times we'd ever touched. There were tears on her cheeks. 'I wanted this for you very much,' she said, smiling damply at Rosie and me in turn.

'And your father? Have you accepted his choice of bride as well, or do you still think she's a cannibalistic insect?'

She let go of me and wiped her eyes. 'It turned out she sold her carriage to afford the deposit on the new shop.' She had the decency to look abashed at her previous suspicion. 'Father's hiding it, but he was terribly disappointed. He loved that carriage.'

'She spends her own money as she chooses.'

'I know.' Constance leaned in. 'That doesn't mean I have to *like* her, does it?'

Jacob and Lilya were standing on the path, along with Aiden and Ciara, and Robbie, Lillian and Samuel, holding hands. On the other side, Pallett was attending to his wife, Cecilia, who looked on the very brink of giving birth, and Harry Whitford, with whom I was back on good terms at Rosie's insistence. They all wished us well, patting me on the back, shaking my hand and calling Rosie 'Mrs Stanhope'.

I could have danced. I could have whirled around the graveyard with my arms outstretched, waiting for the wind to lift me from the ground, light as a mote of dust. I wanted the day to last for an eternity. Finally, finally, finally, I *belonged*.

But then, as so often happened, my thoughts turned to Agnes Munro. I tried not to picture her as I'd last seen her, a crumpled body on the ground, but as she'd been during that night in the convent, strong and brave. She had told me I was forgiven. I didn't care a jot about God's forgiveness, but to be truly forgiven by another person – that was a remarkable thing. I felt as though my life could begin anew.

I told myself she'd known exactly what she was doing. She had chosen death, and not in vain. The public had been shocked and appalled after reading my article, and hundreds of donations were already funding repairs to the convent. The suffragist movement had begun to grow. On their most recent march, Rosie told me, the whole of Trafalgar Square had been filled with women, singing and waving banners, chanting the name of Agnes Munro.

The politician Frederick Lampton had, by all accounts, fallen out of favour with Lord Salisbury, who'd decided it would be prudent to support the Married Women's Property Bill after all. It was set to pass later in the year;

wives would be able to keep their own possessions and be accountable for their own debts. Rosie had declared it the only basis on which she would consider another marriage, even a pretend one.

After the wedding, we walked back to Rosie's shop, side by side, occasionally smiling at each other for the sheer joy of it.

At the door, I pulled my new key from my pocket and turned it in the lock.

She went in first. 'Well, don't just stand there, husband, come in and be useful.' She waited two heartbeats and then grinned. 'Oh, and welcome home.'

Historical notes

THE MARRIED WOMEN'S PROPERTY Act of 1882 was a major step forward for women's rights in the UK. Prior to its introduction, wives were unable to own, buy or sell property, take out a loan or make a will without their husband's consent. Despite strong opposition from some Members of Parliament, the Bill eventually passed with a significant majority, giving wives an independent identity in the eyes of the law. Another thirty-six years were to pass before most women gained the right to vote, but the suffragists of the late nineteenth century, including Lydia Becker, Millicent Fawcett, Frances Power Cobbe and the incomparable Josephine Butler, fought tirelessly and heroically to pave the way for future generations.

The Tower Subway is a tunnel under the River Thames running between Tower Hill on the north side and Vine Street on the south. It was opened in 1870 with passenger lifts at each end and a cable-drawn carriage on rails for passengers, making it arguably the world's first underground railway tunnel. However, following a number of mechanical breakdowns, it was quickly converted to pedestrian use only, with a halfpenny toll. The Subway was closed to the public in 1894 following the completion of

Tower Bridge, which was quicker, pleasanter and free to cross. But the subway is still there, now used as a conduit for industrial cables. You can see a later-built entrance to it on Petty Wales, next to the Tower of London.

Penny gaffs were small halls and pub back-rooms where entertainments such as short plays, music hall acts, cock fighting, and occasional sporting events were put on for the paying public. Some of them even staged heavily bowd-lerised versions of Shakespeare's plays. They were quite numerous in the East End of London during the middle part of the nineteenth century but had all but died out by the turn of the twentieth.

The Convent of Mercy in Bermondsey was built in approximately 1838 and was destroyed by a V2 rocket in 1945. The Sisters moved to new premises and they're still there, doing good work in the community. None of the characters in this book are based in any way on real people, living or dead.

Tens of thousands of homeless children lived on the streets of Victorian London. Many were orphans, others had been cast out or sold by their parents. Having few options, the children often became beggars or prostitutes, turned to thieving or joined a criminal gang. During the second half of the nineteenth century, some efforts were made to house, feed and educate them, but relatively little was done to solve the causes of their poverty.

Acknowledgements

THERE ARE SIMPLY TOO many people to thank, and I'm bound to have left some out. For this, I apologise.

I am extraordinarily grateful to Carrie Plitt at Felicity Bryan Associates.

My huge thanks also to Chief Raven Alison Hennessey, Sara Helen Binney, Ella Harold, Amy Donegan, Lilidh Kendrick and everyone at Bloomsbury. Also, to Dr Paul Vlitos at the University of Surrey for his sage advice and patience.

Thanks also to everyone who helped with the research, including the Bar Convent in York, the V&A, the Geffrye Museum, the Museum of London, the British Library, Gladstone's Library, the Women's Library in the London School of Economics, the National Archives and lots of others. Also, the Beaumont Society, a charity doing important work supporting the transgender community and advising on transgender issues. You can find them at www.beaumontsociety.org.uk.

And finally, I'm for ever grateful to my wonderful family, Michelle, Seth and Caleb, who exercised remarkable tolerance as I wandered about the house muttering about suffragists and wrestling.

A Note on the Type

The text of this book is set in Bembo, which was first used in 1495 by the Venetian printer Aldus Manutius for Cardinal Bembo's De Aetna. The original types were cut for Manutius by Francesco Griffo. Bembo was one of the types used by Claude Garamond (1480–1561) as a model for his Romain de l'Université, and so it was a forerunner of what became the standard European type for the following two centuries. Its modern form follows the original types and was designed for Monotype in 1929.

Also available by Alex Reeve

The House on Half Moon Street
A Richard and Judy Book Club pick

When the body of a young woman is wheeled into the hospital where
Leo Stanhope works, his life is thrown into chaos. Maria, the woman he
loves, has been murdered and it is not long before the finger of suspicion
is turned on him, threatening to expose his lifelong secret.

For Leo Stanhope was born Charlotte, the daughter of a respectable
reverend. Knowing he was meant to be a man – despite the evidence of
his body – and unable to cope with living a lie any longer, he fled his
family home at just fifteen and has been living as Leo ever since: his secret
known to only a few trusted people.

Desperate to find Maria's killer and thrown into gaol, he stands to lose
not just his freedom, but ultimately his life.

'Enthralling, exciting, extraordinary and utterly convincing. Everything a
great book should be'
Sarah Hilary

'Wonderfully atmospheric, each page carries the whiff of sulphur
and gaslight'
Red

Order your copy:

By phone: +44 (0) 1256 302 699
By email: direct@macmillan.co.uk
Delivery is usually 3–5 working days.
Free postage and packaging for orders over £20.
Online: www.bloomsbury.com/bookshop
Prices and availability subject to change without notice.
https://www.bloomsbury.com/author/alex-reeve

https://www.bloomsbury.com/uk/
the-house-on-half-moon-street-9781408892718

The Anarchists' Club

It's been a year since Leo Stanhope lost the woman he loved, and came closing to losing his own life. Now, more than ever, he is determined to keep his head down and stay safe, without risking those he holds dear.

But Leo's hopes for peace and security are shattered when the police unexpectedly arrive at his lodgings: a woman has been found murdered at a club for anarchists, and Leo's address is in her purse. When Leo is taken to the club by the police, he is shocked to discover there a man from his past, a man who knows Leo's birth identity. And if Leo does not provide him with an alibi for the night of the woman's killing, he is going to share this information with the authorities.

If Leo's true identity is unmasked, he will be thrown into an asylum, but if he lies... will he be protecting a murderer?

'A gripping tale that twists like the dark back streets of Victorian London … Powerful and enthralling' Sam Blake, author of *No Turning Back* and *In Deep Water*

'Leo is a brilliant hero: clever and flawed, infuriating and at the same time someone I root for at every turn'
Stephanie Butland, author of *Lost for Words*

Order your copy:

By phone: +44 (0) 1256 302 699
By email: direct@macmillan.co.uk
Delivery is usually 3–5 working days.
Free postage and packaging for orders over £20.
Online: www.bloomsbury.com/bookshop
Prices and availability subject to change without notice.
https://www.bloomsbury.com/author/alex-reeve

https://www.bloomsbury.com/uk/the-anarchists-club-9781526604187